BLACK PYRAMID

Book one of The Ancient Breeds Series

A.D. Stewart

authorHOUSE®

AuthorHouse™ UK Ltd.
500 Avebury Boulevard
Central Milton Keynes, MK9 2BE
www.authorhouse.co.uk
Phone: 08001974150

First published by AuthorHouse   6/25/2010

ISBN: 978-1-4490-6132-6 (sc)

This book is printed on acid-free paper.

DEDICATION

To my loving husband, Michael. Without you, I wouldn't
be here today. I love you too much!

ACKNOWLEDGEMENTS

I would like to thank all my friends and family who have read and re-read copy after copy of my book or had to listen to my ramblings on a daily basis. You guys are the greatest! Becks, Beth aka my partner in crime, Bonnie, Candy aka Mom, Crystal, Colleen, Crystal D, David, Grant aka blue bear, Heather, Johanna, Kim, Laura, Leigh, Melinda, Melissa, Michael, Nikita, Pamela, Rachel, Raven, Ruthie aka Jojogun, Susie, Taz and Tina.

I would also like to thank Andrei Claude for his generosity in allowing me the use of his image for my book cover. If you would like to see more of Andrei and follow his career, the link is: http://www.andreiclaude.com/

And before I finish, there is one more person who I have to say thank you too. My graphic artist. Taz, without you my book would be faceless. Thank you for all the hard work and putting my ideas into a beautiful and stunning cover! You are the best friend a person could ever have! Hugs.

PROLOGUE
EGYPT 5091 BC

"I am trapped! No wretched SandWalker has the right to bind me to this prison!" Her frustrated words carried through the stale air in a drawn out hiss.

Her startling silver eyes, outlined in thick, black, kohl, swept over Pharaoh's chamber. A room built for the King's final resting place. Fools. Believing in an afterlife. She'd died and look where she was. Trapped on this miserable planet being hunted like a filthy human. Just because she had gotten bored and gone on a worldwide killing spree. As a Goddess, she deserved to be worshiped by all the pathetic breeds of her world. Including the humans.

Moving into the centre of the room, she felt a cold, pinprick of magic and dropped into a low crouch. Growling deep in her throat, she was spellbound. Magic sealed the only exit and there was no place to go, unless she blasted a hole in a wall. Not a good idea, as that would bring the whole building down on top of her. There was no way she was leaving this room without a fight.

Baring her teeth in determination and anger, she gave a breathless groan as she kicked her tanned legs up through the air, and dived backward across the room. Trying to avoid any dangerous spells embedded in the floor, she stumbled when a fire-globe exploded near the right side of her face. With super fast reflexes, her slender body spun in the opposite direction, and bounced a few times as she hit the sandy floor, causing a dust cloud to surface and linger.

The rough landing wrenched beads off her neck collar and dislodged her kilt, dragging it down below her hips.

The bronze, layered, discs made up intricate battle armour that covered her from navel to mid thigh, like snake skin. Designed to keep the wearer safe and right now, it was digging into her hipbone. Cursing, she quickly tugged it back into place. Relieved that the red bruises were hidden, she rested on the floor until she got her bearings. The last thing she wanted was to show how weak she really was.

Suddenly, the room filled with patronizing male laughter. Instantly she jumped to her feet, ready to fight. Her eyes narrowed in suspicion as an additional sphere tumbled around in midair.

A miniature fire sparked to life inside the tiny orb of clear glass. The bright flame inside refracted off the surface, casting an array of colors on the stone ceiling above her.

She froze at the distinctive *clank*. It was a subtle warning.

Her head fell forward, slamming her forehead into one slender kneecap as she dropped into an open leg split.

As a deafening BOOM echoed in her ears. The ball self-destructed, spraying a fine shower of charred black glass over her and the floor.

Having come across this spell before, she knew what to expect. Fire shot out forming a deadly ring around her body. The circle of fire rotated around her, daring her to try to escape. She flashed a knowing smile as the ring split, forming a second ring. This was different. Seemed Myaten had improved his little trick.

Taking a deep breath, she pulled her arms in close as the rings began to shrink. The spell was meant to restrict her movement and bound her in one place. Giving them time to catch up with her. Cheating bastards. But the image of blisters and peeling flesh was enough to maintain the timed flips, twirls and tiring somersaults.

She realized after a while that Myaten wasn't connected to the fire-spell and the energy within was expiring. And as the ring began to break up, she continued darting around, under and over them until the smallest ring vanished in a puff of smoke.

She didn't dare move a single muscle, as she waited in silence. When there were no further attacks made on her, she turned her head to the side and caught the image of a handsome face within the flickering yellow and orange flames. Her lips pulled back in a sneer before she opened her mouth and hissed in warning.

Give up Osiris! There is nowhere to run!

His disembodied voice drifted past her ears as he offered a second chance. His toying laughter and fiery smirking image fizzled out in a puff of bluish grey smoke.

She wanted to scream as she envisioned ripping his head clear off his delicious neck! However, giving into her anger and desire for revenge was meaningless. Like her, the hunters had excellent hearing and eyesight. If she had an inkling of escaping this day, she must keep her mouth shut and examine the room quietly for more traps.

She couldn't help but dwell on her close demise. If not for her fast reflexes, the fire spell would have been a painful reminder of what happens when you let your guard down. And she was weary from running and constantly looking over her shoulder. Never, in her long life, had she felt this deep seeded fear. Having the SandWalkers lurking in every corner eagerly waiting to capture her, was proof her reign was finally over.

Waving her hands around, her dry lips parted to chant the words of a spell, and then she stopped. On the verge of casting a trap, she caught a wave of strong, masculine magic in the air. Closing her eyes, she swallowed the cold fear of desperation that was welling up inside her. For the first time in her life, she was scared.

At the sound of slow deliberate footsteps, she dropped her arms and backed away from the approaching hunter. There was no time to complete the magic spell.

With arms stretched out wide to keep her balance, she lunged back in a blur of color until she hit the hard, stone, wall.

Ignoring the sting of heat trapped within the limestone bricks from the fire, she flipped around and launched her body up. Her eyes skimming the distance as her fingers and toes dug small holes into the stonewall, giving her the leverage to pause mid way up the wall like a scorpion; beautiful, but deadly.

Scampering across the ceiling, she swivelled around to watch and wait for them, upside down. Where there was one, there was more to follow. And she wasn't giving up so easily.

Hissing loudly like a viper, her red blood stained lips pulled back, showing off her elongated fangs. Her hair fell away from her almond kissed shoulders in long damp, black, rope like coils, gently swaying as she backed away from her aggressors. Her mind filled with extreme hatred as her body trembled with the indignity of being hunted like some prized animal trophy.

The darkness of the ceiling wasn't the perfect hiding place. Now wasn't the time to question her actions. It was time to formulate a final attack!

Siaak exited the Queen's chambers and stood inside the doorway of Pharaoh's final resting place. He kept his guard up as his eyes adjusted to the flickering light.

His nose twitched as he sniffed the air. The strong odour made his stomach lurch. She was here. There was no mistaking the smell of old blood. It was how her kind lived, by taking the blood of humans.

He took a step into the dark room and tilted his head back. Instinct alone, told him where she was. With a victory smile, he looked straight at her. Their eyes locked as he summoned the others with a single thought. They would surround her and this time she wasn't going to get away.

"Escape is beyond your grasp, we have bested you." Siaak spoke with an air of self-assurance, bordering arrogance.

That made her want to bite his tongue off and dig his eyes out with her nails as she watched him barricade the exit with his body. Dressed in a long flowing white cloak to shield his body from the sandstorms outside, she knew from previous encounters who this hunter was. Her hopes for escaping dropped even lower. "I shall take all of you with me!"

His jaw hardened. One had to keep his wits about him when tracking Gods and Goddesses. This one was the last and most powerful of them all.

"My brethren will be free once more, SandWalker. I will have the satisfaction of hunting you down. But first, I think a refreshing drink is most acceptable in honour of your death." A soft purring sound met his ears before she licked her lips in anticipation of drinking his blood. Nothing equalled the taste of a SandWalkers blood, it was clean and pure. If she could feed from him, her body and powers would be completely restored. All she needed to do was get close enough to sink her teeth into his skin.

With both hands, he reached up and lowered the white cowl from his head. He wanted her to see him, to look in the eyes of the *Omari-gahiji.* The Highborn-hunter who had dedicated his life to ending hers.

Dragging the cloak across his broad shoulders, he tossed it behind him and summoned his weapon to hand. White sparks shot off the end like miniature fireworks as he dug the metal rod into the limestone beneath his bare feet. Using the staff as a distraction, Siaak summoned three deadly barbed spears and ordered them to hover behind his back. "You know this would be easier if you came down." Siaak didn't bat an eyelash at her crude reply.

Make sure she doesn't piss on your head.

Shut up Myaten.

Siaak ignored the deep laugh inside his head as he spoke the trigger word. The spears launched from behind his back, aimed at Osiris's chest and head.

Osiris was not amused as she rolled across the ceiling dodging the sharp spears. Using up valuable magic to keep her position, she clamped her mouth shut at the racking pain down her lower back. The spear had cut her open. With a single spell, she closed the wound. Glaring at Siaak, she roared loudly. "Spears? Siaak you must try harder."

Bending down to the floor, knees tucked against his firm chest, Siaak gritted his teeth as he leapt into the air. He hovered for a second before he fell fast and hard. Without making a sound, Siaak landed on the balls of his feet with his forearms braced against the crown of his head.

His aim was dead perfect. The staff was now wedged between two glass tiles that made up a large diamond pattern on the floor between his feet. The limestone block beneath the tiles cracked as he pushed down on his staff with all his weight, making sure the metal rod was anchored deep in the floor.

"Insolent peasant! I will skin you alive!" She spat, "and then I shall bathe in your blood Siaak!"

"Is that supposed to make me sick or run away screaming in terror?"

The sound of clapping caused his lips to shift momentarily upward into a haughty smile. Siaak cast a quick glance across the room.

In a hidden doorway directly behind Osiris, emerged Myaten and Kiros, shoulder to shoulder, acting up like a pair of free-range idiots.

Myaten was giving the 'golf clap' where he lightly tapped one hand against the other while making a pompous face. Much like the one Osiris was wearing when she saw Kiros Moon walking in circles before rudely grabbing his crotch.

He was going to have to speak to Myaten. He was filling Kiros's head with nonsense from the future again. Shaking his head at their antics, Siaak used the 'thumbs up' signal Myaten had taught him.

At once, the comical duo flashed from the doorway and took up their positions. The combined sound of metal striking stone vibrated through the room, telling him they were ready.

When Sehkem appeared in the room with them, Siaak sent a silent message of thanks to Kiros. Kiros had promised the old man the right to aid them in the capture of Osiris. After all, they were running around in Sehkem's pyramid.

The tall, dark, skinned SandWeaver raised his hands and black sand filled the open doorway. He turned and bowed gracefully to each SandWalker before speaking. "The walls of my pyramid will stand as testament to an end of your vile rule BloodSeeker..."

Sehkem paused as he ran his hands in a caress around the

magical links that made up his necklace, his *shashaiti*. Before he carefully removed the silver *shashaiti*, his dark almond eyes roamed around Pharaoh's final resting place.

"My time in this life is almost complete. I appoint you *Omari* to reign as master of my pyramid." He held his arms out to Siaak. "May your heart and soul guide you in this life and the next..."

The metal links of the *shashaiti* collapsed into tiny piles of silver sand on his leathery, cupped palm. Sehkem lowered his face to his outstretched hand. Placing his thin dry lips near his palm, the old man took in a lung full of air and blew.

Siaak stood transfixed, as the tiny grains of sand flew across the room like twirling strands of silver lace caught up in a gentle wind. He relaxed his body, allowing the soft particles to gather against his skin before merging into the familiar thick metal chain housing Sehkem's silver Obelisk. Unable to refuse the honour bestowed upon him, Siaak bowed low and watched as the ancient SandWeaver faded from view.

Osiris shook her head in denial. This was unheard of. A SandWeaver would never part with its *shashaiti*. That alone made her act quickly. "You could be King among Kings, with women to satisfy your manly appetites." Her voice floated down to them, a siren song filling the room, to tease and tantalize them with dreams of treasure and power as she changed tactics.

"Oh no you don't!" Myaten shouted as he pulled the headphones free of his cell phone. Loud heavy metal music filled the tomb, blocking the soothing lyrics she used to force their compliance. If she succeeded in hypnotizing them, it would leave the SandWalkers powerless to defend themselves against further attacks. Osiris would be free to feed from them at her leisure, restoring her powers as well as any lost blood.

Osiris shrieked at the strange loud drumming that attacked her ears and made her temple throb. Slamming her hands over her ears, she stopped singing as she tried to block out the offensive noise.

Siaak didn't approve of Myaten's methods, but at least it worked. Ignoring the loud noise that Myaten called, music, he returned to his staff as Myaten and Kiros took up their places.

Heads bowed one by one as each man concentrated on controlling, weaving and maintaining his part of the spell that would transcend time. And save the world if luck was on their side.

The staves glowed softly as the spell merged with the metal, giving it structure while containing it within the room.

Three dark heads tilted back as three arms rose up into the air. Palms out, fingers spread wide. White-hot light erupted from the tips of each finger in the order of: Siaak, Myaten and Kiros. Moving in unison, like a well-oiled machine, each SandWalker knew instinctively what the other required without asking. A true testament to their bond as brothers in arms.

Myaten quickly began chanting the binding spell that would reinforce their staves to withstand the ravages of time itself. He flashed a lopsided smile as each staff pulsated faster and faster until all three staves were glowing like neon signs.

Kiros waited and spoke the words that fired three beams of energy up toward the ceiling, surrounding Osiris.

"Cowards, you dare attack a goddess with magic," she screeched at them. "I curse you with my last breath."

"Since you brought it up Osiris," Myaten shook his orange flavoured tic tacs at her, "here have the whole box. With breath like that, you need them more than I do." Myaten tossed the box up at her as he waved his hand in front of his mouth and blew. His breath was minty fresh, nothing like Osiris's dead rat breath. He scrunched his nose up at the mere thought of it. He dropped his hand from his face as he graced her with a cheeky smile. He loved making fun of her.

Osiris caught the small box and crushed it with one hand. She ignored Myaten's statement of wasting good candy as she advanced. With an ear-piercing scream, she threw her body at them, arms out, claws and teeth aimed for the kill. Her eyes grew big with surprise as the spell plucked her from the air. She had never experienced a spell of this magnitude and felt one of her hearts explode at the adrenaline pumping through her body.

She hit the limestone floor face first. The loud smack of her body on impact echoed around them. Blood gushed down her nose and chin as she moved her bloodied lips, trying to hurdle more insults at them. Her black hair hung in a wild mess around her face as she managed to lift her body from the floor. The palms of her hands and the tops of her knees scrapped the cold stone floor as she struggled to crawl, to push her body forward, desperate to reach one of the men surrounding her. She gradually dragged herself up so that she was balanced on her knees.

Oh how she longed for the day when she would rule the world again. She cracked a sly smirk as a vision clouded her sight! She saw a world full of people bowing at her feet. It was a small consolation, but she would have retribution!

Her evil smile of triumph fell from her face as she stared in horror at her captors. Losing her balance, she fell back. Her body slammed against the stone floor. She didn't feel a thing from the waist down. She was immortal! How could this be? Her mouth opened wide showing her fangs in a futile effort of defiance as she tried to combat the spell that was taking over her body.

She lost.

"I will return to reclaim what is rightfully mine…"

Siaak heard the echo of her voice inside his head. What had she seen in her last moments of life? Osiris was gifted with the 'sight.' If she had seen the rebirth of her kind, they were in deep shit! He had never known her to boast in jest before.

"Well, as they say in the future, that's all she wrote." Myaten wiped his hands together as he walked over to the goddess lying on the stone floor. He crouched down to look her full in the face. Her pupils fully dilated with fear, left her silver-rimmed eyes frozen in an unblinking wide-eyed stare.

He shook his head in mock pity before skimming his fingertips over her left arm. It was warm. The heat from her body would eventually fade over the coming centuries. He raised an appreciative eyebrow at that before he got back up to join his team.

"Did she mean what I think she meant?" asked Kiros as he adjusted his white, blood, splattered kilt.

Her last words forever imprinted in their minds. They weren't looking forward to doing battle again. Osiris had led them in a dance all around the world, leaving death and destruction in her wake. None of them wanted to think about the devastation she could cause in the future.

"I have to believe there is a possibility that she is lying, but I cannot take the chance. That means we now have to take precautions. Two of us will guard her tomb while the other watches and waits through the upcoming years." Siaak looked at each of them in turn.

Myaten was a candidate, he knew more about the future as he spent most of his time there. As for himself, he did not wish to spend his life in that lifestyle Myaten boasted about.

Kiros would be better suited as a guard. He could defend the pyramid against looters and tomb robbers. Trained as a royal guard, he was big in built and knew how to take down the enemy with one blow. And there was his magic if he needed that to aid him.

"We came to a unanimous vote," both men shook their heads and winked as Myaten voiced their opinion. "We think you're the right man, ah, SandWalker for the job."

Kiros grabbed Siaak's hand and clapped him on the shoulder. "When it's time to wake me, I want coffee and three boxes of KK's, assorted of course."

Siaak's confused expression fell on Myaten as Kiros made yummy circle motions with his right hand on his flat stomach.

"It's a long story." Myaten flashed a cheesy smile at his brother while wiggling his dark eyebrows up and down.

"With you Myaten, it is always a long story". Siaak gave a long heartfelt sigh that made his shoulders lift up and then sag. How was he going to manage being without them?

Pushing that aside he steadied himself as Myaten and Kiros handed him their clothes and weapons. Siaak helped wrap their bodies in thin strips of linen woven by the SandWeavers. This would keep both men safe from the ravages of time, sending them into a hibernation that would last for thousands of years.

Once he was finished with his tasks, he sealed the tomb with magic. Hoping that when he returned it would be to awaken his brothers to celebrate victory.

CHAPTER ONE

"Jonathon, I don't know what this says. I've never seen anything like it before. And in my honest opinion, it could be a warning of sorts. Jonathon, did you hear what I said?" Ambers frowned after her boss pushed past, a little too impatient, if you asked her.

She could see him standing a few feet ahead of her, a flashlight in one hand and a white handkerchief in the other.

The white beam bounced wall to wall, giving her a brief peak of the ancient artwork before moving further down the dark, dank, tomb. Colorful drawings depicting scenes of court life and family were all the usual murals decorating the inside of the Queen's chambers.

With her own flashlight, she could just make out a faded cartouche on the wall nearest her. A replica of the black wax seal Jonathon had decimated when he blasted the doors open yesterday.

Luckily, for her, he'd managed to take a crappy picture before carelessly destroying it! Unfortunately, the drawings inside the cartouche hadn't escaped the ravages of time. She could just make out two, Hieroglyphics but it wasn't enough to give her a name.

Like many tombs, there were hundreds of hieroglyphics just waiting to be deciphered. She couldn't wait to translate the amazing stories from the owner of this incredible tomb!

"Jonathon, am I talking to myself?" Ambers smacked the dirt from her blouse and coughed as dust particles rose up to her mouth and nose. Waving her hands across her face, she tried in vain to move it away from her eyes. Too late, they were watering like mad. Just as well, she had taken her contact lenses out. Pulling her sleeve up to blot the corners of each eye, she blinked against the grit that was irritating them. By the time she looked up, Jonathon was gone. For someone that desperately needed her experience in ancient languages and Egyptian history, he sure didn't seem interested in waiting around to hear what she had to say.

"Great! Yeah! Leave the Yankee behind! Just as well I left a bread crumb trail!" She turned and muttered under her breath, *"So someone can find my dead body!"*

"What was that Ambers?" He obviously hadn't heard a word of what she had been saying. He was too preoccupied with something he had seen on a nearby wall. He turned to face her and raised his flashlight aiming it straight at her face.

"Never mind," she bit her tongue at what she really wanted to say as she joined him. Shielding her eyes with her forearm, she swung her other hand up and shoved it over the end of his flashlight, capping off the bright light making her flesh glow pinkie white in the dark. "Do you mind? I'd like to see where I'm going. I don't want to fall head first into a pit full of rusty spikes that were left for tomb robbers. Not to mention, opening up a sealed room and letting lose some hideous monster that wants to eat your face. Or better still, it kidnaps you in order to sacrifice and appease its demon master."

"Let me guess, you were subjected to horror movies as a child?"

She stared at him with a 'duh' look on her face. "I love horror movies." She played with an imaginary curl as she crossed her eyes at him in fun.

"You think we'll find any flesh eating zombies in here Ambers? We are all going to die down here?" He threw his head back giving an evil exaggerated theatrical laugh before yanking his torch away from her tight grip. He looked straight at her with the light beneath his jaw, highlighting his cheek bones and adding dark circles under his eyes as he rolled them backwards, turning his features into that of a zombie. He even added a few moans while smacking his lips together.

"Now you're being stupid Jonathan!" She pushed past him and smirked at his audible, *'Bloody hell!'* as he dropped his torch and fell over something in the dark.

"You know there's a good reason for having that thing," she clicked a slightly smaller flash light on and aimed it at him, "and it's not directing traffic." She felt a sense of triumph as another string of English curse words filtered from behind her. Ignoring him, she let her eyes trail after the light, feasting on all she could see as she carefully picked her footings.

There was no conceivable way to guess the stability of the tombs within the pyramid without good strong light to allow them to see. Rubbing her forehead, she hated playing the waiting game. There were plenty of portable light units on the trucks outside, but until the pyramid was deemed safe, they would have to make do with flashlights.

The inspector Jonathon hired to survey the site was half way across the country. It was anybody's guess when he would turn up. Ambers had a feeling he wasn't keen on showing his face due to the mysterious and mystical appearance of the pyramid.

Many of the natives still believed in their ancient gods. Messing around in one of their sacred burial tombs was frowned upon. And to be perfectly honest, she wasn't shocked when Jonathon started receiving numerous death threats from local activist groups. The messages warned him, and everyone involved, that if they proceeded with breeching the tomb, the locals would not be held accountable for their actions.

Ambers wasn't sure if she believed they would go so far as to kill them, but then again, what did she know. Groups of activists had been known to show extreme aggression, killing down through the ages for nothing more than religious beliefs. She felt extreme anger when important men and women used higher benevolent beings or events as an excuse to kill in cold blood.

Jonathon had argued with her before entering the pyramid this morning. She was totally against racing the clock just so they could be a part of 'history'. Nothing warranted losing their lives as far as she was concerned. But Jonathon saw it differently, he accused her of being ignorant of the astounding importance and impact such a find would bring to the world.

Of course, I know the importance of such a find, what is it with men? Ambers thought to herself. She mumbled a few choice words under her breath at Jonathon's criticism as she walked through the Queen's chambers. Times like these made her thankful she was single. *If* he were her boyfriend, she'd kill him!

Coughing again, she rolled her eyes. Her old teacher's loud nasally voice echoed inside her head; *you must always follow safety protocol. Harmful bacteria still lingers inside ancient tombs and especially in the body's mummified remains.*

She stopped and shucked off her black Patagonia pack. Placing a slim silver flashlight between her teeth, she pulled the two sliders in opposite directions. Reaching inside, she took out a disposable mask, two pairs of powder free gloves, goggles and a brand new slim line Patagonia vest. She took the silver flashlight out of her mouth and balanced it on the floor before putting the mask on. It was easy enough with her hair up in a ponytail. It fit snug over her nose and mouth and was held in place with two narrow yellow elastic bands, one of which was above her ears and the other around her neck.

She tugged the opening of the black vest over her head and at once straightened the front panel. Sliding her hands down the front, she pulled it over her breasts making sure the side release buckles aligned with the back panel. With an audible click, she snapped the left side together before reaching around to snap the other side.

Ambers was more than satisfied with the vest. A dozen or so reflectors made into the fabric would make it easier to spot her in the dark, not to mention the endless storage room. There were at least twelve pockets, which came in handy. Some held her tools along with a small med kit, two days rations and twenty-four ounce thermal water bottle. She slipped her backpack on and fastened it around her waist with a quick release buckle then felt inside an unzipped compartment for a stick of gum.

As she walked, she snapped her white gloves on and separated another pair before balling them up and shoving each one into the pockets of her khaki shorts. She reached down, picked up her flash light and began humming softly to herself, wishing she had brought along her mp3 player. She carried on walking. Even with her soft rubber heeled boots, she could hear her footsteps as she moved around inside the ancient tomb.

She had always had a certain fascination for ancient cultures. As she looked around, her mind devised an endless list of questions. What was life like back then? How did people cope? What was medicine like and how did they learn to use it? As much as she desired knowledge, she couldn't envision herself living ten thousand years ago. No electricity was enough to put her fantasies aside as she stopped and took note of the walls and high ceiling.

She allowed herself to imagine it. The room filled with rich sunlight as servants worked on the tomb around her. White robed priests, partaking in rituals as old as the sand, sun and sky supervised their God's final resting place. As Ambers turned around the active scene created by her mind faded into darkness. Her breathing sounded loud to her ears. A creepy feeling of being watched filtered into her subconscious until she found an exit from the Queen's chambers.

The doorway itself was filled in with some kind of black cement. How odd. Reaching inside her pack, she pulled out a hand size pick and chiselled away at the surface. Once there was a big, enough hole to see through, Ambers shone the flashlight through. "Pharaoh's chamber," she whispered. Without thinking, she bit down on the flashlight, holding it with her teeth and lips as she dug her hands into the sandy wall. Shock and excitement made her shovel faster until the doorway was clear.

She turned to look back. *Should I go through?* It wasn't everyday you were asked to investigate a new pyramid. Squaring her shoulders the feelings of guilt evaporated as quickly as it came. She took one more look over her shoulder and stepped inside. Jonathon's strong English voice became muffled as she passed through the doorway leading into the King's chamber.

She came to a standstill at the sight before her. Pulling her goggles off her face, she just stood there with her mouth wide open. The beam of the flashlight reflected off something metallic. She squinted in the dark trying to see what it was. A staff or pole, she wasn't sure. As she moved in a tight circle around the room the white beam passed off two more. She had to record this.

She slid the slim silver flashlight into the Velcro holder on the right shoulder strap freeing her hands to work the camera. She unzipped the large pocket at the base of her vest and took it out. Thumbing the screen open, she pulled the lens cap off and tapped the power button on. Her skin turned blue as the camera powered up flashing a full battery followed by the menu screen. Holding it up to eye level, she hit record and swept the room with a precise slow back and forth motion.

The camera light lit up the room making it easier to see what she was taping. There was a statue of a beautiful woman dead centre of the three poles. The pose was a bit eerie, but Ambers dismissed it and carried on taping the murals and hieroglyphics. Only when she looked closer, she noticed the hieroglyphics were different.

Walking slowly backward, she managed to keep the camera steady as she zoomed in and out making sure; she got the whole wall before she turned to the next one.

'Shit!' she tripped, almost losing her grip on the recorder. Something had brushed past her back.

"Damn it, Jonathon! You scared the shit out of me!" She whirled around and dropped the camera. It hit the floor with a clatter. Her heart hammering away as she looked wildly around the room. Her ponytail swung back and forth as her head jerked around to check the dark eerie room. Tilting her shoulder back, she turned in a tight circle. There were no hiding places.

No one was there.

There had to be someone in the room with her, she felt it.

Shaking her head, she crouched down to reclaim her camera. With searching fingers, she felt it again. The hair on the back of her neck stood up. The sensation of eyes watching her made her blood run cold. She could feel beads of sweat running down the dip of her lower back as well as behind her knees as she tried to stay still. Closing her mouth, she took in a deep shaky breath through her nose. She ignored the sound of heavy breathing and blamed it on Jonathon. All that talk of creepy monster zombies and she was cowering in the dark. What if she was sensing something real? Was it evil? Perhaps she had angered the spirits within.

"There's no one here, just my over active imagination hard at work." She voiced out loud trying to calm her nerves.

"Who are you talking to Ambers?"

"I was talking to myself." Ambers closed her eyes in relief at hearing Jonathon's voice. She almost flung herself at him as he entered the door behind her.

He looked around the room once before he shone his torch at her. "You okay?"

"Yes, just peachy." She took the empty space to his right and packed her camera up. Their combined light reflected off the walls in tones of warm browns and yellows. Showing her the room was empty except for her and Jonathon. Ambers wanted to hide her face. She felt a presence in the room with them. Unable to explain it, Ambers felt drawn to the metal poles but stayed put, refusing to make herself look completely stupid in front of Jonathon.

At her look of panic, Jonathon quickly raked his eyes around the room. He didn't see anything menacing, just three six foot metal rods and a statue in an otherwise empty room. He moved to the centre of the room and ran his hands over the statue. It was icy cold. Extreme pain marred her face; who ever sculpted it must have had a fascination for the morbid.

Looking at Ambers, he shook his head as he cupped the nape of his neck. If she were scared, he would respect her feelings instead of chiding her belief in legends. He knew it was an American thing and if he said anything, she'd bite his head off.

"Come, we can return later. You need something to eat. A nice cup of tea and a sit down will do you the world of good." He flashed a reassuring smile as he held his arm out for her to lead the way.

She seemed unsure at first.

He kept his smile in place as he stepped in behind her. "Come luv, let's get you sorted. It will be here in the morning. If luck is on our side, the inspector will give us permission to excavate and we can have the lights in place."

He ushered her through the doorway leading back through the Queen's chamber and out into the descending passage. There was only one other pyramid that had two passages and that was Giza. It too contained an ascending and descending passage.

As he passed through the doorway, he felt a cold tingling sensation run down his neck. The kind you get when someone is standing behind you, reaching a hand out to grab hold of you. He shuddered and shook his head in denial but quickly hurried to catch up with Ambers.

Standing atop the golden cap of the black pyramid, his body defied the force of winds that pulled at his clothing and hair, threatening to knock him from his perch. Clenching his hands into fists, he lowered himself into an attacking crouch.

Long dark strands of hair hung over his glittering eyes as he stared into the distance.

He knew the moment Osiris's prison was breeched. He felt it like a punch to his stomach.

He knew this day would come. The nights he'd spent laying awake wondering if tomorrow was the day Osiris would return. Now he was faced with his worst nightmare. He only had a small window of opportunity to hide his brothers and keep the intruders from finding his prisoner.

Adjusting his vision in the same manner as binoculars, he spotted two people exiting the pyramid down below. He watched with keen interest as the female pushed the male away. Tilting his head to one side, he witnessed them arguing while making their way to the trucks that formed a long snake-like trail. He willed their voices to him on the winds that gathered around him.

"I felt something, Jonathon, so don't patronize me. Something was in there and it's up to us to find out what it is."

"Look, I stand firm with your decisions Ambers, but you Americans believe in fantasy, ghosts walking the earth, shit like that."

"Kiss my ass Jonathon! That was no ghost!"

"Perhaps not, but I'm positive whatever you think you felt, can be explained with modern science."

"I'm going back in there, lights or no lights. You can do what you want, but that room is mine!"

Siaak frowned at her words. Rising up to his full height, he jumped into the air and landed on the metal inlays that made up the edges of his pyramid. Arms out by his sides, knees bent, he rode down the side of it, leaving a trail of tiny sparks from his steel-heeled boots. His hair trailed out behind him like black ribbons as gravity increased his decent. Seconds before he hit the bottom, he pushed off with his feet flipping his body forward into a somersault. His boots had barely touched the sandy ground when he started off in a steady run.

He directed the wind like a giant hand wiping away all traces of his footsteps as he stalked his prey. Stretching his arms out wide, he chanted a spell making his presence undetected. He was a lone warrior in a world full of violence. The one lesson he'd learned early in life was to never trust a human, to never allow the humans to know of his existence.

Once he was done, no one would ever remember the pyramid.

He had kept it secret for over eight thousand years. There had been a few close calls in the early seventies. Technology had become his worst enemy, satellites especially. He had tried to eradicate space exploration on more than one occasion, but it never stopped the warring power-hungry countries from racing to gain control of the universe. In the end, he gave up and used the human's technology for his own purposes. That, combined with his magic, gave him the ability to keep this pyramid and a few others camouflaged, until now.

Once he was inside, he moved swiftly through the hidden chambers that made up the prison of the famous god of Egyptian history. Although 'he' was in fact a 'she', Siaak had changed all records containing proof of Osiris as ruler of the BloodSeekers. It was the only way to keep the humans safe. He knew the moment the truth was found, scientists from all around the world would gather and attempt to bring her race back and for what purpose?

Knowledge would be their lame excuse. Early extinction would be Osiris's. The humans could be so naïve at times.

Their own demise was a fascination for them, in itself. It had been clearly documented in several high budget movies. At least he was safe in the knowledge that she was still contained within the pyramid, guarded by his brothers.

Myaten and Kiros were all that was left of his *chibale,* his kinsmen. *Bomanis,* meaning warriors in his language, trained to fight the BloodSeekers, a task that had taken the lives of thousands of men and women.

Filled with renewed anger he picked up speed as he reached the long narrow corridor that separated him from his goal.

Ambers ate her sandwich with gusto. She was starving! She had to be, in order to eat it. Something about butter with tuna and cucumber made her yearn for a nice juicy hamburger with fries. As she nibbled on the crusts, her eyes swept over the sandy horizon.

Egypt is, by far, one of the few mysteries left in the world to explore. It leads one to believe in romance and hunger for the knowledge of the mysterious civilization. She looked up at the clear blue sky. And felt drawn to the unusual colored pyramid that was unlike any of its neighbours. Its lustrous cap, a crown of sparkling gold, reflected the sunlight across the sky like a beacon. So far, it was the only pyramid in existence to have one intact. The normal sandy brown of the Giza pyramid was lost on the black pyramid that stood out against all the others.

Her eyes kept flickering back to the entrance of the towering pyramid. She felt the thrill of finding it. The pyramid was already becoming a worldwide phenomenon. It would bring hundreds of thousands of tourists here to photograph it and say they had witnessed a part of history.

To her, it was an enigma that held an infinite amount of questions. She desperately wanted to be the one that uncovered its secrets. How had it gone undetected for so long? Especially when it wasn't more than a hundred feet from the Giza pyramid.

Scratching her neck, she sat on a giant crate watching the chaotic scene unfold in front of her. Several drivers began removing black tarps off the massive trucks while shouting instructions to the hired help as the unloading process began. Crates packed full of food, clothing, medicines, boxes of filtered water, lights, camping gear, and tools, had been bought and paid for by Jonathon. His family was one of the oldest in England and the richest. She really owed him a hell of a lot. If not for him, she would still be in a boring classroom filled with indecisive teenagers, waiting for an adventure to fall in their laps.

Using a wet wipe, she quickly cleaned her hands and face. She jumped off the crate and walked purposefully across the sand. She was too impatient to wait for the lights to be hooked up. Checking the batteries in her camera, she flipped the screen open and pressed record as she entered the doorway. What Jonathon didn't know wouldn't kill him.

Siaak touched each silver staff with a flick of his index finger. With that single action, he recharged the binding spell that kept Osiris imprisoned. He didn't have time to inspect the outside walls of the pyramid now. That could be done after he scared off the humans.

He froze at the sound of someone approaching.

Quickly, without making a sound, he took his place by the third staff. As soon as his long fingers curled around the smooth cold metal, he vanished from sight. He could keep the illusion of an empty room for as long as he desired. Unfortunately, he didn't find the idea of being there permanently appealing in any form or fashion.

"Helloooooo," her voice boomed inside the room, bouncing off the four walls.

Siaak kept his body still as the female moved around the room. He used his powers to observe her. The ability to leave his body gave him the mobility he needed to be in two places at once. Like earlier, he could follow the humans unnoticed and still hide his brothers from view.

Ambers clung to her camera by its leather strap. The last thing she needed was to break it. Given her luck recently, she wasn't going to tempt fate. It had taken her a week to decide on a new digital camcorder. Then it hit her. She had forgotten to bring along her laptop, not that it was much good out here anyway. The sand would get inside and create all kinds of technical problems or send it to an early grave. Perhaps, Jonathon would lend her his Net book so she could upload the video files afterwards, to help reconstruct the rooms for cataloguing later, when they returned to England. With that, part settled in her mind, she began to focus on the room she was in.

She could only guess its size with the small light she was using to see. To her, it looked about eighteen ft. in length and eleven ft. in width. Shrugging her shoulders, it didn't really matter to her how big the room was. She wanted to find the treasures within, to decipher the hieroglyphics on the walls and learn who built *this* pyramid.

She did a clean sweep of the room. A chill went down her spine making her belly tingle. She made herself ignore the sensation of being watched again by talking aloud. "My name is Melissa Ambers, I'm an explorer like so many before me and my intentions aren't meant to offend the gods buried within this tomb. To be honest, I'm only interested in learning how the people of long ago lived life. Well that was stupid. Thank god, Jonathon wasn't here to ask for an encore." Her voice dripped with sarcasm as she imagined Jonathon's smart-ass comments about all Americans. "Maybe he's right. We do put a lot of faith in the spiritual plane," she mumbled under her breath.

She slammed the screen down and slipped the strap over her head to secure it on her shoulder. As she walked around the room for the third time, she found herself standing near one of the metal rods again. Reaching out with both hands, her fingertips near a pole, licking her lips she paused to rub her thumbs against her fingers, 'I can do this…' Her fingers curled around to meet her thumbs as her palms rested against the cold metal. She stood there with a puzzled look on her face and released the pole with a frustrating curse.

Siaak took in her scent. She smelt of lemon and sunscreen. It was an unusual combination. He watched her shoulders droop as she glared at the staff he was holding. His fingers began to uncurl as he shifted his weight off the solid metal pole, ready to strike out. He heard footsteps and stopped as a man entered the room.

"What did you expect? A dazzling light show or where you waiting for the doors to seal you in and hope that I'd come along to rescue you in the nick of time?"

Her head dropped for a mere second before she twirled around to face him. "Nope, I thought you might charge to my rescue as a giant ball of rock tumbles down ready to mash you flat," her voice full of rancour as she glared at him on passing.

Jonathon didn't know what to say to her. Nine times out

of ten, when he opened his mouth, he wished he hadn't. "I left my whip and fedora at home," he teased as he followed her into another chamber.

"So, you're an Indiana Jones fan?" She graced him with a questioning stare that made her eyes wide as she stood there with her hands on her hips.

"Not really, but then everybody knows about the fictional character. Although, I have met Harrison Ford a time or two. He's a nice chap, funny," he paused and pointed a finger in the air.

That figures, she thought. The rich always mix with the celebrities.

"Did you know he's also a carpenter?"

"Yes."

"So *you are* a fan I take it?"

"Yes, I have his face plastered all over my bedroom wall. I stalk him on a regular basis and have a shrine in my house." She rolled her eyes; in truth as a teenager, she had a small crush on him, but who didn't back then? Now she just had a very large fish tank above her bed and one stripy fish in particular called, Indy.

"I didn't peg you as a Harrison Ford fan. Perhaps I should have donned a whip and fedora for you luv?"

His American accent sucked as far as she was concerned. Ambers flashed him a sickly sweet smile that faded as she spotted a few trinkets buried with furniture and hand woven baskets.

"Hey, do you happen to know who's buried here?" She loved putting him on the spot. After all, he was British. They had been known to collect a few artefacts, especially the Rosetta stone, a permanent addition to the British Museum since eighteen hundred and one.

"No, I don't, as a matter of fact. I've had as much time in here as you. And as I recall, both times have been spent in idle chit chat."

She shrugged her shoulders making the camera sway back and forth. "Well you carry on. I've got more looking around to do in Pharaoh's chamber."

"Don't forget to take a portable spot light with you. You'll be able to see more…," he advised as he watched her.

Ambers grabbed a battery operated light and hummed to herself as she back tracked her steps. Snapping a plastic bottle open, she crouched down and scoped up a sample of sand before securing the lid in place. This being her first trip to Egypt, she couldn't resist taking a memento back home. Quickly putting it away inside her vest, she looked up with a sweep of her lashes to view his rear as he bent over to pick something off the floor while standing in the doorway. She resisted the urge to kick him as she walked around to see what he was looking at.

"Here," he passed it over and went back to work on the room adjacent to hers.

Ambers turned the piece of metal over in her hands. It looked like a pendant in the shape of an Obelisk. Dismissing the piece of jewellery, she placed it in a plastic baggie, sealed it shut and labelled it 'artefact?' before it joined the collection of unusual items in her vest. She was beginning to feel like Lara Croft. All she needed was a pair of guns strapped to her thighs and the English accent. Shaking her head, the images of her flipping and jumping around the room made her feel depressed and out of shape, she decided to get some real work done.

After a few hours of cataloguing statues, furniture and pottery, she was beginning to feel the workout from the constant bending and stretching as she sifted through the sandy floor. Bracing her lower back, she flinched at the aching muscles. She decided to take a break and sat down. Looking at the walls around her, she let her mind wander back in time again.

Smiling, she imagined the people carrying all the artefacts she had found inside this room. It would be nice to meet one of them, a King perhaps. Slapping her hands on her thighs, she huffed at herself. Why, all of a sudden, was she daydreaming so much? Perhaps she was tired from the heat and the previous flight from England.

She reached into the side pocket of her backpack and pulled out her water bottle. "Yuck," warm water, not very refreshing she thought as she held the water bottle up and read the label on the back. "Holds hot or cold liquid, for those long treks around the world." More like, "enjoy your beverage at room temperature, if it's not evaporated in the heat!" At least the water wet her mouth a little. With a shake of her head, she capped the silver thermos and put it back in her pack before she carried on with her cataloguing.

Siaak had always been labelled the patient one. The two intruders were beginning to irk him a bit, pushing his reserve to its limits. As his ghost self wandered secretly, it was becoming apparent that they were the only ones inside the tomb. He needed to act soon otherwise more would come. He resisted the urge to cough and clear his throat before he began.

Go back while you still can.

Ambers stiffened. The feeling of being watched returned with a vengeance. This time, it filled her with images that made her fall to her knees and cry out for help.

Death surrounded her in the form of lifeless piles of rotting human remains. Skeletons, sprinkled with cobwebs as larger than life spiders crept through empty eye sockets made her shiver. She hated spiders with a passion. No matter the size, a dead spider was a good spider as far as she was concerned.

She managed to climb to her feet and stepped back as her eyes drift over some of the skeletons. Some had died in agonizing pain; she could see it in the way their gaping mouths showed their dying screams. As she turned around, more bodies appeared. The dead surrounded her. Was this real? Had she angered one of the gods? No that was just stupid. She felt like closing her eyes and banging her feet together while muttering there's no place like home.

She almost jumped out of her skin as blood-curdling screams filled her head. There were pleas for help in English before her ear drums were blasted in several different languages. She could only assume the hysterical voices were begging for their lives.

Her eyes began to water against the sudden pressure inside her skull. Her breathing turned short and raspy as she saw countless scampering beetles. Each step she took made her lips curl up in revulsion. The sound of crunching shells signalled the turbulent roller coaster in her stomach. Her palm cupped her mouth, hoping she didn't lose her sandwich.

Jonathon's heart raced at her screams. He dropped a decorative pot and swore as it shattered into a thousand pieces. He ran full throttle, the beam from his torch bouncing up and down with his movements. He skidded to a halt making a dust cloud rise up from the floor. When the dust settled, he stood there staring at Ambers and wondering what in the world was wrong. He envisioned snakes or scorpions, but the tomb had been sealed until they had broken in, so no wild life should have managed to sneak inside.

Ambers ran around the room in small circles. Her legs pumping as her arms flapped about and a long 'eeuw' seemed to go on forever as she continued to dance around.

"GET THEM OFF!" she shouted.

Jonathon continued to look confused until he heard the unmistakable scrambling sound of beetles. "Where did they come from?" He shouted above her loud sounds of disgust.

"How the hell should I know? I didn't stop to ask," she retorted in a high-pitched voice.

Jonathon grabbed hold of her and yanked her close. He hadn't seen anything like it before in his entire life. Of course there were Scarab beetles, but not in the hundreds that zig zagged along the walls as well as the ceiling and floor like the movies depicted.

She slapped his arm and shrieked at the feel of them in her hair. "Jonathon, get them off me!"

"There's nothing in your hair!" he shouted back in a firm tone. He shivered as he imagined them crawling down his naked back. He pushed the vivid images out of his mind. He had to get Ambers under control before she hurt herself. Then he *saw* snakes and spiders dropping from holes in the ceiling. "Oh fuck!" Jonathon covered her with his body, trying to shield her from them. She hadn't noticed the hissing cobras, but then again, she was screaming at the top of her lungs. If she saw the spiders, he would have to carry her out. She was a total arachnophobe. "Now we could use that ball of yours," he shouted trying to make light of the situation.

'I said leave this place or die!'

When a disembodied voice boomed inside the room, his eyes went wide as saucers. He couldn't believe for one insane minute that he was standing inside an ancient pyramid that had been hidden until now being overrun by carnivorous beetles. He had hoped that he and Ambers would make an astounding find. To be the next Howard Carter would put him in line for the most prestigious job ever, Head of antiquities at the British Museum.

"Did you hear that?" his voice mirrored the look of surprise on his face.

"Yes." The word barely left her mouth before he yanked on her arm pulling her from the room that seemed to be moving all around them.

Ambers ran as fast as space allowed, the descending passage was hard enough to manage walking, impossible at an all out run. However, she didn't care, her ass was making tracks, she wanted out!

Jonathon could just make out her stooped figure. Each time his light hit her vest, the reflectors stood out like a beacon in the dark. He thanked god she had the good sense to wear it. Most archaeologists, him included, never wore them.

Leave and never return or you shall die a horrible death!

"We're going!" Their admission was swallowed up in the trembling tunnel that surrounded them.

"Who in the bloody blue blazes did you piss off?"

"I didn't do anything," Ambers shouted over the roar of falling rocks and ceiling debris.

"Well, the Vincent Price wanna be doesn't think so," he covered his head with his forearms as another tremor hit putting them off balance. He fell to his knees and quickly recovered as he pushed off the floor with his hands.

"You think so, he sounded more like Jack Palance to me," Ambers shot back.

"Could we possibly move a little bit faster, we can discuss voice-overs later?"

Ambers swore in an unladylike fashion, "Fuck you!" When he started laughing at her, she growled. "Kiss my ass; I'm going as fast as I can Jonathon!

Siaak flung his head back letting his jaw move up and down like a mechanical vice grip. His evil laughing echoed through the ancient structure as he continued with the charade of 'The Cursed Tomb.' The woman pleading to the gods made it too hard to resist. Projecting his voice and adding in the special effects was priceless. Myaten and Kiros would have loved it. He was quite satisfied with his handy work as he witnessed the intruders fleeing for their lives down the winding passages. Laughing his ass off, he continued to watch the impression of the tomb spitting them out like leftover meat.

Once he was sure they weren't returning, Siaak released his staff and stepped from the protective spell placed on the rods.

He knew when the pyramid went public that there was nothing he could do. If he placed another spell over it, there would be more snooping humans and a hell of a lot of questions. Therefore, he'd left it as it was.

For once in his life, he wished he could travel back in time, to fix his current problem. He would have broken the golden rule just like that. No altering the past time line. Period. He snapped his fingers as he stood there thinking of his next move. He was a fool if he let them leave with evidence of the inner prison. No evidence could be released to the public of what was really inside. It would cause wide spread pandemonium. People from all over the world would be lining up to see the metal and stone pyramid that appeared from out of nowhere. Sure, they thought Osiris was a harmless statue. Slamming his hands on his hips, he tipped his head back on his shoulders and glared up at the ceiling.

He had no choice in the matter. He'd have to go and kill them. Damn, he hated his job.

He made his way through the fifteen inner rooms in Osiris's eternal dwelling. As he walked, he made impatient hand gestures. Another bad habit he'd picked up. It never ceased to amaze him how the humans loved to make up stories about the ancient Egyptians. If they knew the real reason of the pyramids, the evil that lurked within them, their blood would run cold.

Siaak passed his broad hand across a symbol of a falcon in the wall. The mechanism clicked followed by the loud grinding sound of stone against sand. The walls of the rooms inside began to alter like a Rubik's cube. Hopefully, it would confuse anyone that might enter again later. An image of the man and woman snooping around made him snap his teeth together.

He pushed them out of his mind as he quickly found his way back to the Queen's chamber where only two doors allowed access to and from it. The main ascending passage would now lead them in a circle unless they could walk through walls or find the secret entrance. He seriously doubted the latter.

The thought of Osiris being free made his frown deepen as he carried out his diagnostics check. The pyramid needed continual maintenance from the destructive sand storms and extreme hot and cold temperatures. He was in the middle of repairing one of the larger base sandstone blocks when he muttered under his breath, 'video camera.'

How had he forgotten that?

Standing up, he raked his fingers through his hair and mouthed an oath in his native language. Now he was pissed. He had no option but to go after the woman. Slamming his fist down, he made the crack extend all the way through the grade A block.

"Great Siaak!"

He had developed a habit of talking to himself when he was alone. Who could blame him; he'd become what the humans referred to as a hermit. Travelling around the world kept his mind busy. He was always one-step away from home if he suddenly felt home sick. In fact, he was in the middle of rock climbing in the mountains of Tibet when the alert went off.

He wore a *shashaiti*. The infinite power source within it allowed him to teleport from one Obelisk to another. There were hundreds of the four-sided pillars spaced far enough apart to 'jump' from one place to the next. Most of these were invisible to the populace that littered the entire planet.

The ones that could be seen were rare. Seven in Egypt, thirteen in Rome and another ten spread out over the rest of the world. The Obelisks that lay scattered in ruins, was down to the destructive storms and wars down through the centuries.

Pushing the humans from his mind, he focused on replacing the entire block. Using his magic to take the immense weight of the countless layers above him, he pulled the damaged block out and pushed in a new one.

Once he was finished, he teleported.

When Ambers and Jonathon got back to the hotel two hours later, the manager insisted their injuries be treated. Luckily, a member of staff knew first aid. Even after the first aid, half of her body was still throbbing all over.

When she managed to catch up with Jonathon, she flashed

him a weak smile and tensed up when she saw the tall stool. "I think I need a mounting block. I don't see how you can sit down, my ass hurts." She was rewarded with a chuckle from the bar tender.

Jonathon glanced up and stared at him. "I told you to go and lay down." Jonathon never found her jokes funny and didn't bother to look at her as he went back to writing his report.

Ambers puckered her lips and closed her eyes as she raised one leg and stretched it over the side of the metal frame. The thin red-foamed cushion didn't look very comforting, but she didn't plan on staying long either. An audible sigh gained her another stern look from Jonathon.

"You need a bath and bed Ambers. We are up early tomorrow. I had a text from the Inspector. He's going to meet us at nine am." He glanced at his watch and clicked his tongue. "It's gone midnight now." When she didn't answer he looked up from his work to find her face down on the counter. Jonathon shook his head in wonder until her body began to slide sideways. His arm flew out and caught her before she fell off. When she was seated and upright, he cut her a disgusted look. "Go to bed before you fall on your face."

"Thanks," her voice slurred. She rubbed her tired eyes as she stepped down off the stool. She left him sitting at the bar absent-mindedly stirring his drink as he worked on his report. She knew that's where he'd stay until it was completed before dragging himself to bed, if he bothered to go to sleep.

She stopped at the front desk to collect her key card to her room and ask the receptionist for a wakeup call. She stumbled into the elevator, too tired to notice the appreciative looks from a tall man dressed in a tuxedo. He winked at her as she stepped from the elevator.

She found herself in a long white hallway. A navy blue

carpet beckoned her out of her shoes. She bent down and removed her sneakers, not bothering to untie them. Squishing her nose up at the amount of sand in them, she had already emptied them three times since their escape from the tomb of hell. What was it, magic sand? *I'm not going to think about it*, she promised herself.

Brushing her hair out of her face, Ambers glanced from her card to the shiny numbers on the doors. "Twenty-four," she looked to her right. The numbers were going up. Turning left, she cursed Jonathon for moving her to this hotel. What's so wrong with the one she had chosen? His excuse was like most men. *"Ambers, love; it's not a safe place for a young unattached woman. You know it makes sense..."* She hated it when he called her 'love'. It sounded patronizing when he did it and that bugged the shit out of her. Turing left she managed to stumble down the long corridor before spotting her room.

She slid the card and turned the handle. With a hard shove, she pushed the door open and felt a burst of cold air as she stepped inside. The door snickered shut behind her and she automatically locked it before dumping her Keds on the floor.

Her eyes took in the lush bed with its fluffy pillows as she surveyed her room for the first time. She knew the minute she lay down she'd pass out.

So she threw her travel case open and pulled out her small overnight bag. It held all her personal effects. Not bothering with her nightly ritual of lotions and facial mask, she stepped into the shower stall with her shampoo and body wash.

Hot water cascaded down her tired body as she felt her eyes closing. Jerking awake, she hissed and drew her breath in as the hot water hit the nasty cuts on her legs. Cursing up a storm, she lathered up and vigorously scrubbed her body free of sand and sweat.

Tackling her hair, she inadvertently shivered at the image of beetles crawling around in her hair. Poking her tongue out, she shut the water off and shoved the shower curtain open before she climbed out. "Damn bugs, yuck!"

She patted herself dry as she walked out of the bathroom naked. The air conditioning felt good after a hot shower. Yawning she hurried around the room switching all the lights off. She slept better in total darkness and in the nude.

Standing next to her bed, she untied the towel around her head and gave her damp hair a furious rub before dropping the towel on the floor. Reaching up, she stretched and yawned again before crawling into bed. It felt so good to be lying down with the smell of clean sheets being the last thing she remembered before falling into a deep sleep.

He was more than pissed off, he was furious. It had taken him over an hour to track the American woman from her original hotel to this one. He'd hopped from one Obelisk to another and walked the rest of the way. Now he stood outside the new hotel that over looked the Nile. The moonlight glittering across the surface like millions of diamonds as the cool breeze stirred up ripples here and there. He was glad it hadn't changed much over the years since his birth.

Shifting his weight from one foot to the other, he stood staring up at the tall building. His ghost self had followed her up to her room and was hovering over her balcony. Like a beacon, it flickered to gain Siaak's attention. He smiled and was about to make a move toward the main entrance, until he heard the sound of footsteps.

A security guard exited the hotel.

Siaak caught a flash of light as the guard lit up and stood on the corner smoking a cigarette. Siaak quickly stepped back allowing the shadows to cover him as he waited for the guard to smoke.

He kept his eyes on her window the whole time. Would she have someone with her? He hoped not. Last thing he wanted was to have to kill an innocent bystander.

He saw her lights blink off as the guard strolled over the fake lawn towards the opposite side of the building, obviously checking out the parked cars of the guests in the hotel. The guard's torch guided his way, as there wasn't much in the way of lighting in the parking area. When the guard disappeared behind the rows of automobiles, he made his move.

He carefully inspected the area, and then looked around a second time, hoping there weren't any guests lurking in the area as he commanded his body to fly straight up through the air. The last thing he wanted was his picture plastered on the front page of every newspaper in the morning.

The toes of his boots connected with the overlapping metal rim with a dull thud. He bounced once as he took in the steel frame holding the balcony in place. He hoped it took his weight. He groaned with relief when nothing fell off the man made balcony.

His fingers curled around the smooth railing and swung his legs over the polished bar, allowing his body to follow. He let go of the railing to drop down on the opposite side. And he noticed straight away that most of the balcony was made of glass and steel. There wasn't a single bolt he could loosen and cause her to fall to her death. Scrunching his nose up at the idea, he wondered what made him think of that. It was probably too many episodes of Murder, She Wrote. He needed to give up the murder mysteries.

He glanced over his shoulder with a jerk of his head. He paused to listen.

Nothing.

Relieved at the lack of an alarm; he was breaking into her room with the intent to steal private property. He was quite glad he could get on with his reconnaissance mission. This was *not* what he really liked doing at one in the morning.

Directing his ghost self to enter her room again, Siaak made sure she was alone. He caught the outline of a person in bed. Fantastic, she was alone. He summoned his ghost self back into his body and waited a few minutes for his eyes to settle from double vision. He hated that more than anything. It was nice having the ability to spy on others undetected, but the after effects were a pain in the ass.

Once his vision cleared, Siaak balanced the tips of each finger on the sliding glass door. He loathed locks. They could be tricky and most were connected to silent alarms. His brow creased up as his fingers walked up the glass, stopping above the locking mechanism. One eyebrow rose in question as he willed the lock to turn. He gave a cocky grin as the handle turned. He opened the door, slid through the small gap and shut it quietly behind him.

Blinking to focus his eyes in the dark room, he spotted her bag on the floor by the counter. Figuring the camera might be in there, he 'blinked' across the room to keep from making any noise. It was similar to 'jumping' only he used it for short distances, like now.

When he picked it up, he noticed straight away it was too light to have a camera in it. But decided to look anyway. He was right, just a cell phone, empty gum wrappers and a wallet. Spying her passport, he took note of her full name. Miss Melissa Carrie Ambers. And her picture before placing the wallet and purse back where he found it.

Now where would she keep her camera? He imagined a safe as he turned to look around the room. He noted the size of her suite. It was your standard size room, double bed, bathroom and a sitting area. A bit small for his liking but then again, he was used to living in ancient temples.

Dropping to his belly, Siaak scanned the dark area under the woman's bed. There were two brown leather suitcases side by side. Sliding the cases toward him, he opened both. His victory was cut short. No camera. Where the hell was it? He pushed the cases back under the bed as he tried to think. If it wasn't with her then it must be with the man she was with earlier.

He stood up and shoved his arms in the air in a futile gesture of impatience seconds before he felt a blinding pain at the back of his skull. He stumbled forward and whirled around as the lights blinked on. He growled in warning, showing a hint of fangs as he lunged back avoiding the huge statue being swung towards his head.

He grabbed the offending weapon with one hand and yanked it free from his attacker who ran off. His lips curled in anger as he squeezed it between his hands. A loud bang filled the room as the granite statue shattered into dust leaving it piled on the floor by his feet.

"What the hell?" Her exclamation gave away her position. He locked onto it before she had time to grab something else to cave his head in.

"I want your camera," his fingers tightened around her upper arm as she tried to unbalance him by bringing her right knee up to his crotch. He raised an appreciative eyebrow at her quick moves. It had been a long time since he'd fought a woman.

His free hand grabbed hold of her offending leg by the ankle as he swept the other one off the floor. The look of shock, quickly followed by anger made him laugh as he slam-dunked her body on the carpet.

"Give me the camera," he moved his head closer; he wanted her to know he meant business. His eyes glittering dangerously as his mouth opened wide showing her his razor sharp teeth.

"How did you get in my room?" Ambers demanded as she caught sight of his eyes and his teeth. *"Oh please, those aren't real. Give me a break"*, was all the warning she gave him. Her head shot forward hammering into his. The force of the blow propelled them in opposite directions. A flash of blue light caused her to flinch when their heads connected. She focused on getting away rather than the pulsating pain along her forehead.

Her heart pounding like a jackhammer, she managed to roll to her feet and run like hell toward the door. All she had to do was get out of her room and call for help! As her hands grasped the door handle, she smiled in relief as she pushed down, nothing happened. It was locked! The smile slipped from her face, her eyes scanned the door in a wild desperation while her fingers clawed at the lock. The light remained red even though she had unlocked it manually.

"Are you trying to get yourself killed?" He didn't hide the irritation creeping into his voice as he stared at her while rubbing his forehead. Damn that hurt. He threw his arm out and yanked her back. His eyes bore holes into hers as he looked at her beneath dark strands of hair. She wasn't going to get away that easily. His magic would keep the door shut giving him time to catch up.

Ambers eyes went wide as she felt his strong arm around her waist. She had visions of him raping her and dumping her body in the Nile. Next thing she knew, she was on the floor.

He held both her arms held above her head as he loomed over her with an annoying, coy smile on his handsome face.

"You won't get away with stealing my things!" she shouted as she bucked to get him off her.

Siaak rolled his eyes in a sarcastic way, she stole from him first. Evidently, she didn't see it that way. "Well, actually, it is not considered stealing if you give the camera to Me." He said, stated the obvious.

"Why would I give you anything?"

He looked down at her and was about to answer when his mind veered off track. Here he was, in a room with a naked woman lying beneath him. She smelled divine. *"I must be slacking,"* he muttered under his breath.

Kill her. Now! Stay decided, he thought.

The muscles in his back rippled as he spread his arms out and struck with the speed of a cobra. The moment he felt her warm skin against his mouth, his lips parted and his tongue swept across the vein leading up along her neck.

Ambers cursed as his lips brushed across the soft skin of her neck. She felt his teeth and tongue and immediately held her breath in anticipation. How could she find a thief attractive? The answer lay in the hard muscle that mashed her breasts flat and the heat that scorched her thigh where his crotch rubbed every time he moved his pelvis. Then to her amazement he stopped, all she could feel was the hammering of their hearts.

His head flew back so fast he almost believed someone had grabbed him by the hair. He blinked repeatedly trying to clear his sight, as everything turned cloudy before a piercing white light stabbed his eyes.

Still trying to figure out what the hell was going on; it took Siaak a few seconds to realize his surroundings had altered.

He was stunned.

And he was definitely *not* a 'seer'. Normally it was a female from a long line of 'old blood' that could glimpse the future, or an event of a person's life.

So, why him?

This vision made his fangs retract involuntarily before he could mark her skin.

He didn't dare move another inch. The real life sensation of him buried deep inside her as her hands caressed his body made him painfully hard.

Siaak was more than stunned now, he was dumbstruck. But what caught and held his attention in this altered reality the most? The unusual mark on her right hip.

When he felt the vision shift, he came crashing back to the present. Shaking his head, he noticed his hand wasn't above her head holding her arms down. Inadvertently he'd rolled his fingertips across the area where the mark should be. He noted the catch in her breath and the goose bumps across her skin in response of his mild caress. It was good to know he hadn't lost his touch.

"What are you doing?" How she managed to keep her voice steady, she didn't know.

"I was searching for your camera but now I think I found something far more important." His voice turned husky as he spoke into her ear. The words had barely left his mouth when she bit him.

Ambers wasn't about to let some strange man touch her even though her body was whimpering in denial. He may have the voice and body of a god, but it wasn't going to get him to third base.

Siaak saw red at the feel of her teeth sinking into the flesh of his forearm. He pulled his arm back ready to strike when he saw fear mixed with anger in her brown eyes. Every fibre in his body told him to strike, end it here, but if his vision was true along with the mark, she was much more than a quick romp on the floor.

"I am going to let you up, but I warn you now; open that pretty mouth of yours and scream, I will shut it permanently." He straddled her body as he sat up, allowing her to feel his erection, proof of his desire for her. He lowered his face to hers once more, "And no more biting my arm or any other place." He graced her chin with a bold lick of his tongue, "Or I might have to bite you back."

CHAPTER TWO

Ambers cut him a dirty look that said, not on your life. When he shifted his weight to his knees, he winked at her and blinked out of sight.

She rose up slowly, her shaking arms held her bare back off the floor. The little voice inside her head told her he was behind her. The hair on the nape of her neck stood up along with the feeling of cold dread sprinkled down her spine, making her shiver. Looking over her shoulder, she flinched half expecting him to kick her for biting him. Instead, he put her off guard by offering his hand. She wondered if her tired mind was refusing to allow her to wake up from what was obviously a good fantasy. She really needed to have sex more often.

Refusing his offered hand, she jumped to the balls of her feet. Feeling confused as well as aroused, she crossed one arm over her chest and tried to cover herself with her other hand, like it really mattered. He had pretty much felt all of her in one go. "Um, do you mind turning around so I can cover myself?" She asked while twirling her index finger around at him. She was feeling more than a little pissed at him for standing there staring at her.

Siaak shoved his hands in his pockets as he turned his back to her and scanned the room. He spotted a towel on the floor by her bed and took his sweet time picking it up. He threw it at her and looked away. A mischievous glint entered his eyes; he had enjoyed it, even if only for a little while.

Ambers grabbed the white towel from her feet and quickly wound it around her chest in an angry jerk; tying a knot above her breasts before turning back to face him. She didn't trust him. Then who trusts a man that breaks into your room in the middle of the night demanding your personal effects and then rubs himself all over you like a tomcat? If he thought for one moment that she was a push over, he had another thing coming. First, chance she got, she was going to scream her head off or at least make a phone call to the police.

"So tell me," she walked to her purse and grabbed a hairclip. Holding it between her teeth, she twisted her hair up and clipped it in place as she walked past him into the bathroom. "Why do you want my camera in the first place? You won't get much for a second hand camera." She paused, "Why me? Better still, how did you find me?"

He cocked his head to the side as he ran his tongue over his teeth making his upper lip move in a gesture of irritation. She thought he had picked her out amongst the tourists as a way of earning some quick cash. He was utterly insulted and opened his mouth to put her in her place, then closed it. Why was he even thinking about explaining it to her? It was simple. She had damaging evidence about the inside of the Pyramid. The last thing he wanted was more archaeologists digging around and poking their noses where it wasn't wanted. He knew there was a science team still exploring Giza, trying to unravel its secrets. God forbid, they learned that it too contained a BloodSeeker.

She noted how he seemed to be holding himself back. Was he going to attack her again? Her eyes snapped in the direction of the bathroom. There was nowhere for her to hide. Something told her that if she locked the door, he'd only kick it down. Next time she stayed in a hotel it would be on the ground floor, at least then she could jump out a window and run for her life.

"Keep the door open." He ordered when he saw her looking at the only place she could hide from him.

That did it; she wasn't going to dress in front of him. She marched over to him waving her finger in his face, "So you're a pervert as well as a thief?"

"No," he didn't care what she thought of him. He let his eyes roam over her body before he spoke again. "If I want sex from a woman, I get it. I have no need to lower myself to such tactics. I can contain my lustful thoughts without sneaking little peeks through your keyhole." He licked his lips on purpose to toy with her.

She glared back at him as she walked to her suitcase. She grabbed some clothes and huffed as she disappeared into the bathroom. As she got dressed, she shouted out to him, "Are you going to tell me why you got a hard on about my damn camera and how come you picked me or what?"

It didn't matter if he told her the truth; she was going to die, after he found out what his vision meant. Closing his eyes, he rolled his shoulders back and shoved his hands deeper in his pockets. He stared at the double doors as he crossed the small living area. "You would never believe me if I told you."

"Probably not," she said as she exited the bathroom trying to fasten a slender belt around her waist. "But try me anyway."

"A powerful tracking spell." What he didn't tell her was how he had found her. The scent of her was all over the place. It didn't take much to track anyone once you had a sample of their blood. He shifted his weight on one leg as he turned to face her.

She didn't like his eyes. Dangerous and unsettling, they made her feel uncomfortable. As if, he was looking straight into her mind, searching for information. Without thinking, she made a cross with her index fingers and aimed them at him while hissing.

Siaak threw his head back and roared with uncontrollable laughter. He had to give her credit, she was funny. Damn shame she was the enemy. "You are the first person to succeed in breeching Osiris's tomb since its creation and instead of killing you outright like a good little warrior; I am standing here laughing like a drunken lunatic."

Ambers dropped her arms and blinked in confusion. "That's not possible? Osiris is a myth, he's not real."

Siaak shook his head no, all traces of amusement gone as he came to stand in front of her. "No he is not real. She happens to be as real as you and I and she damn near came close to ruling the entire ancient world." His voiced drifted off as Ambers's eyes glazed over. He clicked his fingers as he waved his other hand close to her face, "Did you hear what I said?"

The archaeologist inside took over; she left him standing there as she reached under the table and dragged two old brown leather suitcases over to him. Damn, how had he missed those? He watched her unzip them and to his utter amazement, she took out what looked like an entire library on Egypt.

"What did I miss?" she asked in earnest, more to herself as she tucked tendrils of hair behind her ears.

"A computer by the looks of things, you know most of that is stored online, somewhere."

She paused long enough to give him the evil eye before she opened a large volume, its pages made of fine paper, almost translucent like the kind you would find in a bible. Her great great great grandfather had uncovered it in a cave near Luxor back in the early eighteen hundreds. On her graduation day, her father had given it to her, hoping that she might be able to make some sense out of the writing. She grunted as she heaved it from the pile.

He squatted down to her level, curious to see what she had found. Anything that was more serious than him killing her deserved his full attention. "Can you actually read that?" he asked.

She shook her head no, refusing to allow him to see the frustration in her eyes. "Most of them I can read," She sat the heavy book on the floor, "but this one isn't like any written language I know of." She stole a quick peek at him from under her arm. He didn't seem the scholarly type to her. "Why?" she asked.

He didn't answer her as his eyes scrolled down the pages of his Lor'ship's neat handwriting. The book had been written mainly to document their enemy. Roris was always recording their history; wars among other Breeds, battles lost and won, treaties gaining freedom among the great races, until Osiris came and destroyed it all. She was the beginning of the BloodSeekers. She created armies that swooped down like a plague, killing for pleasure or food, sometimes both. He would never allow anyone to find out what was in that book. He would give up his life to preserve the human race.

"So what does it say?" She knew when someone was faking it and he was definitely reading what was written on the pages. He didn't realize his mouth was moving as he read. It was a habit some people had when reading to themselves.

She handed him the book while showering him with a sour look. "Well Einstein, what's it about?"

"Need to know basis and you definitely do not come under that category." He closed it with a loud thud. The lettering on the front was badly faded now but he knew what it said and he wasn't going to tell her that either.

She held her anger in check at his blatant heavy handiness with the ancient book. "So, what's your answer?"

He liked her boldness but he wasn't telling her anything. "I think you are nosey and some mysteries are best left alone." He held the book between his hands; his eyes dared her to take it from him. He was actually hoping she would try.

"Okay mister, who are you really? Were you sent to spy on Jonathon and me? If you are, we found the entrance to the Black Pyramid first…" She hung her head for a few seconds before she snapped her fingers. "That's why you want my camera…"

"Siaak– and that is part of it," he supplied her with his real name and stopped before he told her the truth.

She paused at his name. She hadn't heard of a Professor Siaak and it didn't match up with any of the other well known archaeologists. "First name or last?"

"Just Siaak." His abrupt manner left her wanting to call him a few other names but she figured that probably wasn't the best idea. He had already shown he was stronger than she was.

"I've never heard of you before." Perhaps he was a newbie. No, she thought to herself. If she couldn't read it, then there was no logical reason for him to be able to.

"Well you have now, so can we dispense with the pleasantries and get back to the business at hand?"

"Whatever! Are you going to explain how you can read this?"

He shook his head no.

"But you admit to having the knowledge to read it?"

He cracked a smile at her. She didn't know when to give up. If he ever needed someone to question the sanity out of his enemies, he knew whom to ask.

She swore in a manner that made him raise his eyebrows in distaste.

"Fine, I know the answer even if you won't admit to it.' She turned her back to him. It was the last thing her father had given her before she stopped speaking to him. Damn, she hated to part with it, but she knew she couldn't fight him for it. No self-defence classes would ever make her a match for him. *Gods, why did he have to take that book? Because he knows more than you do.* That stung her pride. *I've got to pull myself together.* The last thing she wanted was to show weakness in front of a complete stranger. By the time she carefully packed all her books back in the cases, she had managed to get a grip on her anger.

"So you've stolen my book, now what?" She sat back on her knees and stared up at him. "Happy now," she shot back with a sarcastic bite to her voice.

"It was never your book. It belongs to me. I am only reclaiming it. So now who is the thief, huh?" his voice had a chill to it. It made the hair on her arms stand up again.

She pressed her fingertips to her temples. That didn't make sense. How could the book belong to him? "Look, if you don't want to admit knowing how to read the language written in my– um 'your' book its fine by me, but honestly come on. You can't tell me you are the original owner of it. I mean how stupid do you think I am?"

He shook his head no, as he took a firm grip on her elbow. He helped her off the floor while steering her towards the door. "That happens to be the major problem with you. You are too intelligent for your own good. Now, I need your camera and then I shall decide what my plans are for you."

"Gee, you're such a gentleman.' She grabbed her sneakers and card key as she flung the door wide open, hoping that someone might hear and come to her rescue.

"No tricks Melissa."

"Don't call me by my first name, I hate it! Let me guess, you found that out by magic too?"

"No, it's on your passport and I happen to like it. It suits you." At her grunt of displeasure, he held the door for her and let it close without a sound.

"If it floats your boat, tickles your pickle…"

He never did understand those stupid sayings and ignored them as he led her into the hallway. "Jonathon Strathmore." He said as he pointed to the tall white door with its shiny twenty-three before gracing her with a smug look.

"How did you know?" She asked then shook her head no, "Never mind I don't want to know, Mr. Stalking pervert."

He chose not to bite at her insulting nickname and carried on. "I saw you both at the Black Pyramid. He is attracted to you, is it not obvious?"

She shook her head again, "No, he's just a friend and it's none of your business Einstein! And that proves you've been stalking me!"

"Okay," he looked her full in the face, "I admit I have followed you, but not in the way you are suggesting. Now, your man seems anxious to keep you under supervision. That explains why you changed accommodations." Siaak pushed her against the door. "He is in bed now. He longs for your touch and something tells me he masturbates knowing you are in the room next to his. I am surprised you have kept him at bay for so long."

"You're one sick son of a bitch!"

"No. I happen to be stating a fact about how the man feels about you. I meet an attractive woman like you; I tell her my intentions. It is as simple as that."

"Well you certainly don't say it with flowers." She raked him over with a disgusted look.

"I find it easy to tell a woman I want to lick her from head to toe before sinking my teeth into her luscious body while I fuck her long and hard." The color of his eyes reminded her of brown sugar. When he moved them, they seemed to sparkle like light reflecting off crystal. She found herself staring and squeezed her eyelids shut as she jerked her head away.

The image his words projected flooded her with lust. Her cheeks felt like they were on fire as his eyes bore holes into hers. *Hot Pervert,* she thought.

"You like that idea?" He leaned closer, his breath hot on her cheek. "Perhaps if you give me what I want, then I might be persuaded to give you what you want."

The cold surface of the door rubbed against her cheek and arms as she tried to inch her body away from the heat of his. "I thought you were going to kill me?" She kept her voice neutral as she swept her eyes under dark lashes up at him. She felt chilled to the bone even though every molecule in her body was melting under that unblinking hot stare of his.

He took in the scent of her sex as his eyes roamed over her face. Such a pretty face too. Large brown eyes that mirror her distaste. And that mouth of hers, delicious in spite of wishing she's stop talking for one second. "I never said how I would kill you." He gave her a roguish look, full of promise as he stepped back to give her a little breathing room.

"What better way to die than on the wings of a deep satisfying orgasm."

"Why do I get the impression you do phone sex?" she snapped.

He cut her a look that made her catch her breath. "Knock the door, ask for your camera," his voice low and menacing. He was done playing games with her.

She shivered at his short order. "At least tell me what the deal is with my camera," she barked back as she knocked loud enough to wake the dead.

"It has evidence of the pyramid that would be best kept secret. Now get ready, he is coming," he whispered into the air above her head.

She turned to ask him how he could possibly know that. Their eyes met as the door opened and Jonathan yawned while scratching his head. "Ambers?" his voice filled with genuine surprise as he glanced at his watch before lifting his wrist closer. He couldn't see without his glasses. She had tried to convince him to switch to contact lenses like those that she had, but he refused. He was a cry-baby when it came to putting eye drops in much less contact lenses.

"Sorry, it's late," she began to apologise for waking him.

"Who's the bloke?" his manner changed so abruptly that Ambers was taken back. She was almost positive her would-be killer was grinning like a fool. She resisted the impulse to Stooge slap them both before she kicked each of them in the groin.

"Pardon Melissa's manners, I am an old friend. She asked me to join her here in Cairo," he flashed a charming smile that lit up his eyes and Melissa noticed his fangs had disappeared too. How freaky! "I came as quickly as I could when she offered me the once in a life time chance to examine the video footage from the Black Pyramid." Siaak offered a business card and winked at Melissa as her mouth fell open at his deliberate use of magic in front of everyone.

Jonathon took the card, his blue eyes full of suspicion as he held the card close to his eyes. He had known Ambers for a long time and not once had she allowed him or anyone else to call her by her first name. Perhaps he was telling the truth and they were just friends, but his gut told him there was something more to this than meets the eye. His jaw ticked at the mere thought of them being lovers as he handed the card back. Jonathon mouthed a stern good night to them and moved to shut the door.

Siaak put his foot in the way of the door, "We need the camera, Jonathon."

"Oh yes, of course, hold on, I'll only be a moment."

"I told you, he has the hots for you."

"Yeah, he wanted to tear you limb from limb." She frowned as she remembered his lame introduction. "An old friend? Couldn't you have been a little more creative? Oh, I forgot, you only specialize in stealing things from naked defenceless women."

"I could tell him I just took you on the floor, made you scream the way he wants too."

Her arm shot forward, the flat part of her fist connecting with his palm as he blocked her punch. His other hand encircled her wrist, holding her arm firmly in place as she tried to pull it back. He growled a warning and dropped her wrist as Jonathon pulled the door open and held the camera out.

"Thank you so much." Melissa reached to take the strap from his fingers as he it let go. She managed to catch it before it hit the floor.

"Let me know what you find, I've made a few phone calls. M&E are leaving on the next available flight. So try to be up early." With that, he eyeballed Siaak before he slammed the door shut in their faces.

Siaak rammed his fist against the wall making a thud sound and muttering something she couldn't understand. When he was done hammering the wall, he wiped his mouth with his hand and looked at her. "Great, more witnesses! I liked my job better when people thought the world was flat. Now they hop a plane and I have a whole bus load of them to deal with in less than twenty-four hours."

"It's just Mark and Elizabeth. They're pyramid junkies and I trust them." She announced as if he really cared to know her personal feelings about two complete strangers he had no plans on meeting. Ever!

"Well, I have no reason to trust people, especially you." He flicked his index finger across her chin.

"How can you honestly say that about me? You won't find me creeping around your bedroom in the middle of the night, searching through your private belongings, taking you hostage or insulting you *and* your friends while talking of murderous sex."

His head turned giving her a quick glimpse of fangs as he smiled. "If you change your mind, let me know." He paused as he tugged the camera strap from her fingers and placed it in a black satchel with his book. Funny, she hadn't noticed a bag on him earlier. That was very weird.

"So what now? Are you going to whisk me off to your underground cave and pound me into oblivion in order to get your rocks off?"

"Pound?" His eyebrows drew together in mock confusion. "Underground cave huh?" He didn't give her time to answer before he started. "I believe you need a demonstration. You obviously 'did not' take in what I said back in your room." He snorted with disgust at her snide comment as he wheeled her around and guided her over to the elevator.

"I think you really misunderstood me, Melissa."

"There's no way I got that wrong."

"Got what wrong Melissa?" His face stayed neutral as he egged her on.

She felt like pulling her hair out by the roots. She wasn't going to let him get the upper hand.

"Forget it."

"Oh come, come, no sharp rebukes. That would be like skipping foreplay before sex. Please refrain from letting me down; it is the only fun I get these days."

"You're not right in the head." She said as they entered the elevator.

Jonathon swarmed through his private rooms, trashing everything in sight. "He's an old friend, my arse! Bollocks'! He obviously thinks I've got 'cunt' written on my forehead!" He shouted until his throat was so sore he could barely speak.

He flopped down on the sofa and kicked the coffee table over. The sound of smashing glass was a small comfort. Pursing his lips together, he mused over the meeting tomorrow. He reached down the side of the couch and pulled out the memory card for her camera. Damn, he forgot to put it back. Oh well.

Jonathon traced the thin plastic card before snapping it in two. Then made a face of complete horror, "Oops, oh dear." He spoke through his hand before he threw his head back and chuckled.

Standing he reached over the broken coffee table and found his mobile among the shards of glass. After giving it a good shake to remove any glass, he slid the face up and pressed two, it rung twice.

"What do you want?"

"I have a job for you."

"Okay. Now you have the book, the camera and me. So what's the game plan? Oh, I know! Silly me," she tapped her cheeks in a thoughtless manner. "Gee, how could I forget, I die." Melissa's sarcasm was lost on Siaak.

The elevator doors split open and he pushed her out.

"Hey, watch the hands," she jerked her shirt out of his grasp and side stepped his other arm that seemed to find its way around her waist at any given time.

"If you value your friends' life, I advise you keep that smart ass mouth shut." He lowered his head to her ear, his warm breath sent shivers down her spine. Her eyelids closed briefly at the sudden spark of liquid heat rushing through her body as his lips brushed against her earlobe. "And place your arm around my waist. If anyone sees us together, I want them to see a couple in love."

"It's after midnight for Christ's sake. Who in their right mind, except you, would be out walking for recreation purposes? Most normal people are sleeping, like I *was*." She gritted her teeth together praying someone might spot him or her before reaching the exit. Where was a security guard when you needed one? Not that it mattered. Something told her that her new friend would tear through them like tissue paper.

His tongue flicked out as he nipped the tender flesh and was awarded with a breathless 'fuck you'. He knew she was attracted to him and it made her angry to feel so out of control around him. She didn't have a clue that her body, regardless of what she thought about him, was secreting sexual pheromones around him.

Most humans, women in particular give off a scent when they are ready to mate. Her subtle musky scent was the beginning. When she reached her full cycle, he'd find it damn hard to resist the impulse to take her to bed.

He licked his lips at her taste and immediately knew that was a mistake, as he wanted to kiss her. Instantly, an image of her mouth flickered through his head. He fought it back. And before she had a chance to argue, he'd wrapped his arm around her waist and slipped his hand in her back pocket. He liked her ass too, nice and firm. "That mouth of yours is going to get you into trouble?" He nodded solemnly. "You know, I wonder what it would take to turn that bark of yours into a purr."

"In your dreams, buddy boy," she snapped back, a bit too quick.

He wanted to laugh at her. She didn't know how close to the mark she was with that one. Melissa certainly had him by the balls. He didn't know anything about her. And he definitely had no idea why they were together in the future. Obviously, they were lovers in his vision. When? He couldn't say. And by the look on her face right now, it wasn't going to be anytime soon.

They made it to the front lobby without any out bursts from her. Which Siaak felt was a gift from the gods. He half expected her to bolt screaming at the top of her lungs, but obviously she cared about that dick more than he though.

The moment he detected the night vision security cameras he allowed his body temperature to drop so the device would only pick up Melissa's heat signature. To anyone viewing the tapes, it looked perfectly innocent.

He allowed Melissa the courtesy to exit the building first, but kept his eyes on her at all times. She shivered at the change in temperature as they walked down the wide deserted road. "It's freezing out here." She rubbed her arms against the cold. She quickly scanned the parking lot off to the right of the building hoping that someone might see them.

"Which one is yours?" she asked walking faster hoping it was parked near the front so she didn't have to walk much further.

"None of them, I never drive."

Her mouth dropped open. "You're kidding?"

He gave her a look that meant he was anything but a joking kind of person.

"Okay, so how did you get here then? Oh let me guess, you flew like superman or better yet," she cupped her mouth in fake excitement, "you don't drive cause you've got a magic convertible sports carpet." Her mouth twisted up at one corner as she waited for his outrageous explanation.

"Magic," he answered, straight to the point; she didn't need to know the mechanics behind it.

She closed her eyes and smacked her forehead. "But of course, it slipped my mind. I never got around to getting my magic degree."

"You take great pleasure in pissing me off, Melissa."

"What can I say; you bring out the worst in me." She batted her eyelashes at him.

Siaak felt like breaking her neck. She was shredding his nerves to hell and the idea of killing her was becoming more attractive by the minute regardless of his vision.

"What's with the fangs anyway? You a vampire wanna-be or something?" She winced as his grip tightened on her forearm. And before she could say anything, Siaak stopped walking and, in a sling shot, she found herself tugged around his body to face him.

"I am NOT a vampire. You would not understand what I am."

Her eyebrows rose up in surrender followed by her arms when he let go of them. "Okay. The fangs are an issue for you, no problem, I totally understand. You know there are some really good dentists out there, fix you right up."

"Stop talking about my teeth. How would you like it if I picked out something about your person and made jokes about it?"

"Hey you wouldn't be the first man and you won't be the last, so, fire away!" She stood on the sidewalk waiting for his insults. When he didn't open his mouth, she almost sighed with relief. The last thing she really wanted was put-downs from him.

"So where are you taking me? Obviously not a cave, so I'm thinking hut, caravan, tent perhaps?"

He didn't answer.

"Okay, so you're ignoring me, great! Men do that one too!" She looked across at him and noticed he was holding a long silver object in his hand. Was it a weapon? How long had he been holding it in his hand? Better yet, where had he been keeping it? Her heart skipped a beat. Maybe he wasn't joking when he said he was going to kill her.

"Oh shit, look, I think your fangs are neat," her hands started shaking as she put them out in front of her. "You don't have to kill me, honest. Nobody takes my opinions seriously…I'll just be quiet, see." She closed her mouth and nodded really fast.

"Has anyone ever told you that you are nuts, lady?" He asked as he pulled her hard against his body.

She nodded again but slower this time as she realised he wasn't attacking her.

He muttered something under his breath before he looked

down at her. Their eyes locked as he teleported them miles away.

She screamed as darkness surrounded her. *Where am I? What have you done Siaak?* All she could feel was cold and then heat as he shifted his body and pulled her even closer.

Relax, I have you.

The realisation of falling hit her and she screamed louder. *I'm going to die!* She fought back with every ounce of strength she possessed. Trying to push his hands away to gain her freedom. She didn't take in the reality that he'd spoken with telepathy while struggling in his arms. Realising her attempts at freedom weren't working, she brought her knee up and rammed it between his legs.

She screamed bloody murder as her body plummeted, spinning around and around. Straining to see in the inky darkness, her inner voice went into a charade of name-calling as she desperately searched for something to anchor herself too.

When she was sure she was going to die, her head lurched forward slamming into something hard. She began to struggle again until she realized it was him again.

Instantly his arms wrapped around her like steel bands. The free falling sensation changed to a slow descent. *"Never do that again!"*

She knew he was angry with her as he barked out the command. What did he expect? He scared the shit out of her!

"You can open your eyes." His voice sounded almost tender until he yanked both of her arms from around his neck. "And you can let go of me while you are at it."

Melissa opened one eye and then the other. "What did you just do?"

"Teleportation," his voice filled with rancour at her brainless question.

"This can't be real. I'm still asleep in my bed." She pointed at his feet. "You are a figment of my imagination and when I wake up..."

He swept his arms out wide and rubbed his forehead with his middle finger, wondering if she had lost her marbles.

"You'll be gone. You know what?" She didn't give him a chance to answer as she went into another rant. "I bet I've seen you on TV, one of those exercise commercial, pumping weights." She shoved her sleeve up to her shoulder and pressed her fist into her forearm, showing off her muscles.

"No Melissa. I am real and you need to accept that nothing in our world is what it seems."

Then it dawned on her. "You dropped me," she accused as she tried to steady her body, which was shaking so bad she could hardly talk.

"Yes, after you kicked me in the balls, which I might add, is not very friendly. And you are lucky I caught you. Next time, stay still, or you may find your nine lives are up."

She stared up at him, her mouth open. "Next time… I don't think so buddy!"

He reached up and touched her back. "You are suffering from shock, it will pass."

"You'd be in shock too if you were snatched from one place into another. It's not like I do that on a normal basis." She eyeballed him and nodded with disbelief before she set off with the questions again. "Where are we?"

"The desert," he said as he dropped his hand from her back.

"Where is the light coming from?" She noticed that everywhere he moved a light seemed to follow him. She had an image of god holding a flashlight over his head.

"Me."

"How," she asked, looking him over, not sure what to expect now after that little escapade.

"Magic," he said, giving her a dramatic bow.

She was beginning to hate that word.

Siaak straightened his clothing as he stepped away from the weathered Obelisk. He pulled a long silver chain from under his black shirt. Melissa watched him in silence as he touched the object in his hand to the silver chain. A blue iridescent light shone through the gaps between his fingers for a few seconds and dispersed as he shoved it under his collar.

He considered telling her the truth, but remained silent. Instead, he waved his hand indicating she should follow him.

Even without the weird spotlight following his every move like a stalking stagehand, she could see by the bright light from the moon above. Tilting her head back, she blinked at the amazing twinkle of stars above her. "WOW!" She had never seen anything so breath taking as the sparkling view. The jet-black sky hung like a velvet curtain and the stars, like diamonds, were the jewels of the universe. Forever unattainable, but she couldn't resist reaching up. The feeling of being able to touch them made her stand on her toes as she swept her fingertips across the empty space in front of her.

"Keep your head down, you might step on a snake and stay behind me." He ordered.

What happened to 'please or could you'? Men, she hated them sometimes. "Why don't you just grab me by the hair and drag me behind you?"

She shook her fist at his back. If he thought for one second she was going to follow him like a pathetic lost sheep, he had another think coming. She looked around at her surroundings and wished that she could wake up from this horrible nightmare.

She watched him walking away. He was so stupid. He wasn't even aware that he'd left his hostage behind. *Some kind of kidnapper you've turned out to be,* she thought to herself.

Until he shouted back at her, "Are you coming or are you going to sit there for the remainder of tonight? If you think it is cold now, give it a few more hours and you can become a Melissa Popsicle."

She refused to answer him. Let him have some of his own medicine. She could be hard headed, too. She was still calling him every kind of name she could think of when she caught sight of him striding back towards her.

"Holy crap, he's coming back for round two." She tried to turn a blind eye to him. It was somewhat hard not to admire the way his body swaggered with each step he took. His hair swayed in time with each strut of those long legs. He seemed unaffected by the cold. His black shirt clung to his taunt chest, out lining a six-pack that made her blink.

Now, she could snuggle up to that, but something told her he wasn't the snuggling kind of guy. More like ripping her throat out with those ivory steak knives he liked to call 'fangs'.

"Oh shit," she stood up, quickly dusting off her slacks. Should I run? Probably not a good idea right now, she thought to herself as he stopped about a foot in front of her.

She gave him a searching look. Hoping her brown Bambi eyes would defuse the pissed off ticking bomb, she braced herself.

He flashed an amused smile. "Have it your way, but with no provisions, you will die before the next sunset."

Half expecting him to teleport them god knows where, she felt the tension drain away as he turned and walked off again.

She glanced around at her surroundings and panicked. All she could see was sand, mountains of the stuff.

Where would she go?

"You aren't going to leave me out here alone," she cupped her mouth with her hands as she shouted at him so he could hear.

Damn he walked fast! And he wanted her to keep up with his speed walking? Yeah, right!

He stopped dead in his tracks at her accusing tone. His brothers would have dispensed with her by now. Why was he allowing her to live a moment longer than was necessary? He knew why. He wanted to find out why they were lovers in the future. And why she held the mark of his people when she was so obviously human and detested him.

Before Melissa put her hands down, he was in her face. Her mind was trying to rationalize how he could be so far away and in a blink of an eye be standing toe to toe with her. Then, before she knew it, she was hanging over his shoulder staring at the ground as he began walking.

"What the hell do you think you're doing? Put me down you big lug." She banged his back and saw red when she felt the sting of his hand on her left butt cheek. "I know you didn't smack my ass!" She tried to wiggle free and gained another smack.

"Be still Melissa. I am not the type of person who makes idle threats. If you persist in this manner, smacking your ass will be the least of your problems."

Melissa pulled a face similar to his as she copied him word for word as a small child copies its parent or sibling. She was rewarded with a harder smack that made her eyes water. She stayed quiet after that, only because he could leave her in the desert. Dying wasn't her choice of a happy ending.

He wasn't sure what he was going to do with her. For now, he would keep her with him at all times, even if he had to gag her for some peace and quiet. As he walked, he saw her blouse come free of her slacks exposing her lower back to him. One eyebrow flicked up then the other. Without thinking, he tucked the material back into her slacks. His fingers barely touched her skin and he went rock hard.

This was going to be harder than he thought. Just keep walking, Siaak. Don't think about it.

Melissa bit her bottom lip when he tugged her shirt-tail down or up in her case. The second his fingers touched her, heat filled her belly. Damn, he affected her more than she wanted to admit.

Back on the how's and why's she was in this predicament, Melissa found she liked the way his butt looked in jeans. Nope that made it worse. Therefore, she decided to stare at his imprints in the sand, which she noticed faded away as if by magic.

After what seemed like hours, Melissa closed her eyes against the wave of nausea from being upside down for so long. She didn't mind staring at his hot posterior but if he didn't put her down soon, she was going to throw up. As if he sensed her thoughts, he stopped.

"We are here."

"Great. Would it be too much to ask to put me down? Anywhere is good," she used her goodie two-shoe voice hoping he'd gotten fed up with using her rear for target practice. She was answered with a pinch.

"You know, I'm beginning to think you like my ass a bit too much. Whoa!" She landed on her feet so fast her head spun. Shaking it to clear her double vision, she flashed him a bared toothy smile and shook her thumbs up at him. "Great, thanks." Her gratitude came out filled full of sarcasm as she straightened her clothes.

Siaak listened half heartedly, ignoring the sting in her voice.

He knew her bark was more out of embarrassment than any other emotion as he traced the horizon with his eyes.

"What are you looking for, maybe I can help." She cupped her eyes and looked along the horizon. All she could see was the dark sky and silver sand stretching out in every direction.

"Just stand there and be quiet while I concentrate." His arms flew into the air waving back and forth like a conductor in charge of an orchestra.

She imagined him waving a pointer around and thrashing about to the wild tempo of Fantasia, when the earth trembled beneath their feet sending Melissa into frenzy mode. "Oh you got to be kidding me!" she shouted above the loud roar of shifting sand.

A rectangular building shifted into view far off in the distance. She turned around and glared at him. "You got another thing coming, if you think I'm going to walk that far, buddy!"

When he didn't answer and moved off in the direction of his place, she kicked sand at his back. "The least you could do is that teleport thing again or better still, how about a few horses. I don't mind riding one of them." She shouted after him. To her aggravation, he kept walking. That's when she noticed the light drifting past her body, leaving her alone in the dark.

Deciding it best to follow, she ran faster to catch up with him. "You know, for some reason, I bet your place is plastered in playboy posters and littered with empty beer cans and loads of used Puffs." Why she had said that, she never knew. Too late to take it back now.

Then a thought hit her and she graced him with a droll look, "Please tell me you don't have a harem of half naked women in there waiting on you hand and foot!" She stepped up to him and began poking him in the middle of his back. "And if you do, don't get any ideas of turning me into some love slave, either! You won't catch me feeding you grapes or fanning your naked hairy ass, buddy!"

That was it! He had had enough of her rambling crap. He was the one in control, not her. He turned to face her, took hold of her arm with the poking finger and twirled her around like his dancing partner. Chest to chest he locked her in place with his free arm wound tight around her back. Forcing her hand up to his mouth, he placed the tip of her offending finger against his bottom lip. He kept his eyes on hers as his tongue darted out and caressed the soft skin.

Instinctively she yanked on her arm, but nothing happened, he was stronger. Melissa watched his mouth open as he raised her finger from his bottom lip to his teeth. He held the digit tight between his teeth as he let one fang grow.

"Is that supposed to intimidate me?" She wasn't going to let him know how much it turned her on. She'd eat a bucket of sand before she admitted anything to him.

Siaak opened his jaw wider, placed the soft pad of her index finger against the sharp point of his extended fang, and projected his voice in her mind. *These are not for looks Melissa. I know how to use them. If you continue to push me, then you accept responsibility for what happens.*

She heard his voice inside her head as he held her finger captive. She knew he was serious as he bit down just hard enough to give her a demonstration. Her body tensed up at the sharp sting as his fang broke the skin. "What are you?" Her question rushed out as she stared up at him in horror.

"I am a Gahiji! And the last person you want on your ass, lady. Before you, I was happily climbing an extremely tall mountain in Tibet. Alone!"

She snorted at the idea, which gained her a growl of warning.

"If you want me to prove how nasty I can be, then keep it up." He dropped her hand and shoved her away from him. "Now walk and keep up."

"What is a Gahiji?"

She really didn't know how to give her mouth a rest. "It means hunter."He said with irritation in his voice.

And that was it. They didn't speak for the rest of the journey. However, that didn't mean Melissa wasn't forming a series of new questions to his answer. So he was a hunter. Amazing. Not really. She figured he was something like that. Characteristically speaking, he seemed the kind of guy that would have loads of animal trophies on his mantel.

Melissa kept her eyes on the black satchel hanging from his shoulder. *How dare he talk down to me? I haven't done anything wrong. Don't push you. Yeah right! You can kiss my ass you son of a camel! Make me walk, god knows how far! I just want to go home and go back to bed! Hopefully I'll wake up and this will all have been a dream.*

Siaak had to keep his face neutral. Never in his entire life had he been called that. The urge to turn around and tell her to shut up was on the tip of his tongue, when he realized he wasn't even trying to read her mind. It just happened on its own accord. Great, now he had to listen to her ramblings in silent mode, she was going to drive him crazy.

After what seemed like hours to her, Siaak stopped. "This is taking too long."

"You're the one that wanted to go walking. Follow me and keep up!" She copied his order as she made her voice low and gruff, trying to imitate his deep voice.

He opened his mouth and let her see his fangs before he passed a hand over the area in front of them.

Melissa had to tighten her stomach muscles as she felt her body being dragged forward at an astonishing speed. When they stopped moving, she found they were standing in front of his 'home'. "You could have warned me you were going to do some Harry Potter shit!"

"I can send you back and let you walk."

"Gee, thanks, you sure know how to make a woman feel welcome."

Siaak took the first set of weathered granite steps leading up a massive walkway before he stopped. She could tell he was agitated with her. He looked like he was struggling to keep his mouth shut.

"My home is your home. You will be safe here and you shall be treated as a guest." He bowed low before throwing his arm out for her to go on ahead.

"Sure, not like I could run away. Hey! Does your place come with satellite? Oh my god, I'd love a bath," she spoke more for herself than for Siaak's benefit. "I think I've got enough sand in my clothes to build a full scale sand castle." She chuckled and instantly switched to coughing at his look of warning.

Walking on, she could feel his eyes all over her and it reminded her of the episode in the pyramid, as if someone was watching. No, it couldn't be, she thought and sped up.

The mysterious light that followed Siaak's every move, expanded to show her surroundings. Somehow, she knew he had something to do with that.

Show-off.

When she saw his home up close, massive was the word that came to mind. She stretched her neck back as she tried to take in every detail. His temple reminded her of Karnack. Endless steps that disappeared into the sand and towering columns decorated in lotus pedals and papyrus reeds. And enough stone to build a small city. She felt tiny against the backdrop of carved out doorways and statues of gods and goddesses of long ago.

Enthralled, she didn't notice Siaak standing behind her until he reached over her shoulder and pressed his palm against one of five glass orbs embedded in the wall. He waved his hand over them, and each orb filled with swirling black smoke. When he pulled his hand back, a golden door appeared before her.

"Enter. Welcome to my home," his voice low and enticing, made her think of Dracula welcoming her to her death.

When she didn't move he wondered what was wrong now.

He pushed the door open for her and waited. "What are you waiting for, me to carry you across the threshold?"

She was in half a mind to turn around and attack his ankles, when she was met with the most stunning architecture. Black with white veined marble columns as thick as tree trunks stood like polished soldiers in line. She counted six from her vantage point.

She leaned into the room and took note of the huge twin black statues of Anubis standing to attention. Each held sharp realistic looking swords. As her eyes drifted down the impressive statues, she didn't like the growling, snarling jackal statues near his feet. "I see Anubis sent his hounds to greet me."

He was on the verge of actually picking her up again and carrying her forcibly in when she moved. Thank the gods! "Believe me when I say this, if Anubis was here to greet you. First, I would want to know why the god of the underworld would want you. Secondly, I would have to say in all honesty Melissa; there is not much I could do to protect you."

She took another tentative step inside and then did a twirl as she took in the vast openness of the whole room. The floor was made of silver and black marble. She made her way further into the room. She gulped in a mouthful of air at the enormous Black Obelisk. "Wow, you live here and let me guess, your favourite color is," she looked around with raised eyebrows, "black?"

"Yes, I believe I said welcome to my home. Hence the meaning, the place I normally dwell in, when not out searching for people that trespass onto my territory." He didn't mask his annoyance at having to bring her to his home. No human had ever been allowed in the Temple of his people. It had always been forbidden, but now, it was nothing more than a symbolic rule. Like, not talking in a library or scratching your balls in public. His upper lip lifted in distaste at how he had just dismissed his Lor'ship's ruling of long ago by comparing it to a trivial human rule or relieving his private anatomy.

"You will be restricted to your room and only allowed in others unless accompanied by myself. Is that clear?" He paused for an answer. When he was met with silence, he looked back over his shoulder to find his guest on her knees. Her hands were running up and down one of the six central columns. Her eyes closed, taking in every detail as her fingers traced the hieroglyphics of his people.

"What are you doing, Helen Keller impersonations? We already established back in your room, you have no experience in understanding the language and I am not allowed to translate them for you."

"Shush! I don't care if you mock me, but I do care if you refuse to share the knowledge of a race you obviously know more about. It's criminal. It's wrong to keep it locked away. Just–," she looked straight at him, licked her dry lips before flopping back on her heels. "Just allow me to look around. I promise not to touch a thing."

At his stern look of disapproval, she slapped her hands on the floor. The sound echoed around the room. He knew that had to hurt.

"This is a dream come true for me. You have to let me do this, please. Please, I promise I won't speak of it again as long as I live! Cross my heart and hope to die."

Siaak opened his mouth, drew in a deep breath to give his lungs the air he need for the long speech he was about to give her. Then, he stopped. "This is my home. I did *not* bring you here to show you my etchings or to prove that I am not some barbarian that lives in a cave and sucks blood from harmless children." He walked over to her and lifted her off the floor with one hand. "I brought you here as my prisoner. I will make you comfortable until the time I either kill you or punish you in such a way that you will beg for death." He had to keep up the evil dictator routine, otherwise she'd be running all over the place. If he allowed that, she would be putting herself at risk as the entire Temple was loaded with spell points. All of them set to kill.

Melissa shut her mouth around the words she wanted to fire back at him. She couldn't understand exactly what she'd done that warranted his wrath. "And here I was thinking you liked me and wanted to go to the next level. Damn, you give off all the wrong signals. You gotta work on that, buddy, otherwise you'll end up a very lonely old man."

"Walk and stop calling me buddy, its Siaak." He ordered as he shoved her forward. Using a small amount of magic, he kept her steady on the slippery marble floors. The last thing he wanted was her bashing her skull in before he had a chance to do some investigating of his own concerning his little temptress.

Melissa tried to take in every detail of the rooms he directed her through. He didn't bother to give her the grand tour, instead, he sped it up. She looked down and noticed an engraving in gold. It looked like a giant bird but she couldn't be sure as Siaak ushered her on so fast she was contemplating shouting out "fire!"

"Your social skills need some serious improvements."

Siaak kept his face averted. He wasn't going to encourage her silliness by gracing them with an answer or a smile. He found her quite funny, which was a change from the normal humans that ran screaming in terror from him in the past.

"This room will be yours for the duration of your stay. Do not venture outside these walls," he pointed in each direction just in case she confused them with the walls outside. "If you require anything, all you need to do is ask."

"What? Are you going to wait on me or is there some hidden fridge you forgot to show me on my whip around tour of the grand hotel? I could murder a coke, no pun intended, you know."

"Sleep well Melissa."

"Hey, what about my coke, I'm thirsty!" She jumped when a tall fridge appeared by the door. She walked over to have a look. Sure enough, it was stocked full with all kinds of soft drinks, juice and bottled water.

Tucking her hair behind her ears, she pulled out a bottle of Coke and downed it so fast, it made her throat hurt. Screwing the lid back on the empty bottle, she turned toward her door. She resisted the urge to follow him. Even though he was a stranger, she felt safer with him around.

When she realized she was stuck here, she decided to investigate her room. The first thing she noticed was the vaulted ceiling with more of the intricate language she couldn't make head or tails of.

A smile played at her lips as she tip toed over to a beautiful desk and grunted as she tipped the wooden chair onto two legs and pulled. The loud scraping sound made her release the chair immediately as she glanced straight at the door. When there was no sign of her jail warden, she carried on tugging the golden ornamented chair over to the nearest wall.

She realised she had plenty of time to look, without her bodyguard breathing all hot and heavy down her neck. She quickly climbed up, sliding her hands against the smooth wall; she tried in vain to reach the decorative writing. "Damn it," she swore at her inadequate height. Standing on her toes didn't boost her up either. "Shit, shit, shit!" She jumped off the chair and sat down. She glanced around the room again. There was a wide archway off to the rear of the room. Where it led to, she was about to find out.

Standing up Melissa walked up to the oval bed. She held her arms across her chest before she caved in and ran her hand over it. Soft as velvet, it looked inviting with its double row of large square pillows, ranging from deep reds to emerald greens.

Was this how royalty lived? Was Siaak some kind of prince? Prince Jerk off was more like it. Refraining from jumping on the bed, as she wanted, Melissa scooted past it to the double archway at the back of the room.

Popping her head through, she felt a slight breeze that carried the scent of almonds and vanilla. She closed her mouth and took a deep breath in through her nose, letting the decadent perfume fill her senses. The fragrance propelled her forward into the room. Instantly she felt serenity, a calmness that washed away all her problems.

Tall palm trees stood in the corners of the room, lush and green. At closer inspection, Melissa noticed the multibranched trees were planted into the floor. Water trickled softly down the wall from the small alcove above each tree. A constant source of running water had marked the pale aqua stoned wall, carving out long trail lines.

The white water, cascading from the peak of each long dark green leave, smacked the leaves below, making a tap tapping sound that reminded her of a fountain. As the water worked its way down, the soft sand around the trunk soaked it up.

The sound of running water enticed Melissa as she took a few more steps and found out the floor was covered in pure white sand. "Is this for real?" she asked aloud. Not entirely sure, she crept along the sandy floor until a beautiful teal pool came into view. "Oh, now this is what I'm talking about." She peeled her clothes off and dipped in a toe. "Warm too, nice." She took a few steps back and dived in. It felt wonderful against her skin.

As she swam, Melissa realized, the end of the pool seemed further and further away. Swimming down, her hair drifting out behind her, Melissa glanced around the tiled bottom of the pool. Nothing unusual about that, so she went up for air. When she surfaced a few seconds later to the sound of flapping wings followed by a loud squawk, she slid back under the water. This was getting stranger by the minute.

Holding her breath she watched in fascination as the bird swooped down in a graceful curve before flying off. Needing oxygen in a bad way, Melissa resurfaced with a splash. She coughed while combing her wet hair out of her face and paused at a loud short chirp. Looking up at the ceiling, she caught a glimpse of feathers followed by a soft tinkle sound.

The silver and white falcon tapped a small bell once with its beak. The atmosphere in the room altered dramatically.

Melissa hadn't noticed the array of white candles around the room. She rubbed her eyes out of disbelief when the candles lit up on their own.

A second tap and soft music filtered into the room. The bird opened its beak as it leaped off its perch. Long beautiful white silvery wings flapped once as it swooped across the length of the room. On its return flight it squawked loudly as it landed on an ivory perch that ran the length of the entire pool.

Melissa swam sideways and the bird waddled in the same direction, its talons making a clicking sound that sped up in an effort to keep up with her. In the end, it flapped its wings and took off. She wasn't sure where the bird of prey had gone. It didn't show itself again while she was bathing. Feeling refreshed, she climbed out of the pool and walked leisurely across the room naked until a pile of towels appeared at the sound of the bell. "Thank you birdie," she offered her appreciation as she dried off.

Towel drying her hair, Melissa decided to go back to her room. She smiled at the series of chimes from the bell as she stopped long enough to gather up her clothes. As soon as she walked through the archway, the room went quiet. It made her feel like a fairy tale princess.

Even the bedroom had taken on a few alterations since her swim. There was a golden dresser with three polished mirrors encrusted with jewels and a three-foot long stool to sit on. If she were a thief, she would have cleaned him out!

Feeling a little more optimistic, she noticed the heavy ornate chair was back in its customary position. The wall with the beautiful hieroglyphics was now tucked away, hidden behind an amazing wardrobe that ran the length of the wall!

She walked over to the first set of doors and flung them

open. Her mouth dropped open at the footwear stacked on the shelves. From dazzling jewelled sandals to high heels in various colors! It was enough to make her drool until she spotted knee length boots and a shelf of expensive sneakers.

Immediately she threw the other doors wide open and stumbled back at the amazing array of clothing inside. It looked like Siaak entertained a lot to have all these amazing clothes to hand. She shifted through the hangers and coughed at the labels— Armani, Escada, Burberry, Mulberry and Moschino to name a few. Stunning designs for all occasions, but none of them were for sleeping.

The next section was more to her liking. It was packed with Levis, Gap, Old Navy jeans and t-shirts. Shaking her head, she moved down to the double ornate doors. There were delicate silks with fine gold and silver stitching.

Not sure what to look at first, Melissa pulled a red dress out and held it up to her body. "Oh my god, you can see right through the damn thing. Talk about leaving nothing to the imagination." Yawning, she was suddenly assaulted with images of Siaak making love to her in said 'red dress,' on the thick white plush rug, against the massive ivory columns and on the over sized bed. Man! She had watched Sliver way too many times.

Putting the dress away, she decided to put her own clothes back on before climbing up on the massive round bed that was big enough to fit ten people easily. She lay there wondering what Siaak was doing and if she could trust him. Would he try anything while she was sleeping? *If he were going to kill me, surely he would have already done it.*

It was hard to tell what he was thinking or what he had planned for her. She must be crazy to just sit there and do nothing. She should plan an escape. *Yeah and how do you think you'll manage that one, Houdini?* Banging her head against the bed at her dilemma, she tried to stay awake, but found she couldn't keep her eyes open any longer.

He wanted to turn around and go back to her room, strip her offensive clothing off and have one serious sex marathon right there on the floor. He stopped in the middle of his lustful fantasy. Why, all of a sudden, did he want her so much? The mark. Not willing to accept that as the answer, he paused long enough to palm a spell point.

A loud series of clanks echoed through the empty temple, making it sound louder than it was. The powerful hum was barely detectable with the grinding of stone against stone as the symbol retracted in line with the wall. When he felt the slight tremor, he knew the spell was working.

He glanced back in the direction of her room and decided to go on a long patrol. To put some distance between them.

He looked around at his home. Melissa was right. It was very similar to the ancient temple built in Karnak, created by Queen Hatshepsut.

Another royal he had personally groomed for greatness. A fine woman destined to rule Upper and Lower Egypt, she never knew her personal bodyguard was anything other than a mortal man willing to give up his life for hers. None of the royalty, before or after the dethroning of Osiris, ever knew he was a SandWalker. All records, pertaining proof of them, had been eradicated from tombs and temples, to keep their identities a secret.

If Osiris was right, then he had a war on his hands. He still had no idea how he was going to protect the billions of humans that were spread out across the planet. This was why he had gone after Melissa. In all honesty, killing women wasn't his forte. Even though it was always in the back of his mind to do so, it didn't mean he had to like it.

As for the male, he could break his neck. His instant dislike of the man made him snarl. He was less than impressed with his obsessive behaviour towards Melissa. It was boarder line stalking! Even though she had titled him that, he didn't believe in hurting someone to achieve sexual pleasure. The images he gained from Jonathon's mind made his jaw stiffen. His fangs burst free of their housing and he immediately suppressed the reaction to his volatile mood. The next time he saw him, he wouldn't keep his anger in check.

Rubbing his forehead, he felt drained. Keeping his temple camouflaged all the time used a lot of his power. It took more than two weeks to renew two hundred spell points and that didn't include the extra one hundred and forty outside that made up his security system. With everything that had happened, he didn't have days. He would have to recharge only the spell points that would keep Melissa safe. Patrolling the city, however, was another thing entirely.

If Myaten had been around, it would be done in a matter of minutes. Myaten had a way of charging them with a single thought. He, on the other hand, had to touch them. A daunting task for sure.

Thousands of symbols that made up the intricate spells needed to protect the Temple and its Great Library. He had taken on the responsibility of maintaining the building. Not by choice, Sehkem had volunteered him for the role of housekeeper. The second the ancient SandWeaver empowered him with his shashaiti, Siaak had inherited Sehkem's office. Job, title, call it what you will, it was a nuisance.

He could take a vacation as often as he wanted, for months or years at a time, but he could never 'leave' permanently. Not until he found another person to take his place.

Once he was satisfied with making his home as secure as he could, he decided to do some research.

He steered through the maze of corridors filled with statues of warriors long forgotten; men and women who played a major part of his history. He had always paid tribute to each one by lighting the torches of remembrance, a hundred in total. When lit, it was an astounding sight! Each one burst to life with amazing speed, alternating from one to another on either side of him in a domino effect.

For the rooms beneath the Temple, there were polished mirrors that could be tilted in any direction; it made the most of the light that was directed into the rooms carved out of rock.

He had thought of bringing in modern lighting but it would only lead to the discovery of his home. That wasn't an option.

He shut off all the wandering trivial thoughts, in order to deal with the headache he seemed to have acquired. This was another sign that he needed some recharging of his own.

He focused his mind on what he was doing. He knew the inside of the temple like the back of his hand, left, right, straight again and right to a dead end. He pulled his black silk shirt from his waistband as he continued on his path and made short work of the small buttons. Once he had removed it from his body, he reached up and draped it over the back of a chair. Lifting both arms above his head, he aligned his chest dead centre of the locking symbols embedded within the design of hieroglyphics that covered the entire wall. The lock inside the two-foot thick door required a sample of his blood. Not a pleasant process, but then his people didn't care about pain, so he blocked it from his mind.

There was no warning. No sound of the spring loaded

needles that punctured a series of holes in his body that resembled the pattern on the wall. He didn't need one, he had gotten used to it over the centuries. He counted to five and it was over. He could feel the blood running down his chest and back. He had trained his mind to ignore the feeling that made his fangs instinctively flash inside his mouth. Soon he would need blood if he wanted to continue with his mission.

Looking down at the base of the wall, his blood formed a black pool. Like a sponge, the wall with the hieroglyphics soaked up the blood giving the wall a wet look. Siaak knew the route his life's blood would take. The spell required the power contained in his blood cells to pass over each one.

Flicking his eyes up, he saw a trail of dark red filling in the arch of the invisible doorway. Within seconds, he heard a click and the wall shuddered. Dust fell from the ceiling as the portion of wall shook and retracted into darkness. Siaak ducked down as he entered the room. He also happened to be a bit taller than the SandWeaver that built it.

Siaak sighed as he straightened his back and peered around in the dark. "Luminous!" he spoke the powerful word with authority. As he walked up and down the row of bookshelves he was interested in, lights blinked on and off from holes sunk in the stone floor. There was no need to light up the entire area. He knew what he was looking for.

The large room contained all the knowledge that once belonged in the Great Libraries of Alexandria, The Royal Library of Atlantis, Serapeum and Cesarion temples, The Amazonians, a female warrior race that amazed Myaten, The Mayans, Aztecs and a great many more civilizations.

His people were responsible for switching the ancient texts, substituting false documents in their stead. Wars that brought about destruction and sometimes the extinction of an entire race had forced his people into action. A civilization that boasted its own artists, poets and musicians; his people had never been one to stand by and let knowledge be destroyed. Regardless of who started the feud in the first place.

Only he and his brothers knew the real truth behind the destruction caused by the Aurelian during the third century. In order to keep the Libraries safe and out of the wrong hands, safe guards were put into play. Only a chosen SandWeaver or another SandWalker like himself could enter their Library.

Siaak stepped back to get a better view of the scrolls. There were at least five hundred shelves; each contained hundreds of precious documents. Screwing his face up at the prospects of having to look through any of them made him wish for a simplistic approach, like storing it all on a computer. His eyes narrowed in deep thought as he walked down each isle trying to decide where he should start.

His mind kept wandering back to Melissa. The birthmark of his family told the history of their creation. It was hard to come to grips with seeing it on a human. Not that it would free her from him. In fact, as much as he hated to admit it, she would be bound to him for all eternity if she were Egyptian.

He had a responsibility to uphold. He would sacrifice her in a heartbeat if it meant the lives of everyone on the planet. Now, the marker changed all that. He found his instincts rearing to protect her from Jonathon. She was screwing with his morals.

Letting his body levitate, he floated up to the top of one shelf. He removed a handful of delicate scrolls before teleporting all but one to the marble table that sat in the centre of the room. As he began a slow decent, he read slowly to himself. Growling in frustration, he quickly rolled it back up and tucked it under his arm.

After looking through more than fifty scrolls, he decided to call it a night. There was no logical reason, no explanation as to why a human female would have a marker of his people, especially his family.

On his way out the room, he tilted the hourglass containing a small essence of time itself. It was a gift given to him long ago. Over the centuries, the glowing sand particles had dwindled down to a few luminous grains. Once it was gone, he was locked in this time frame, unable to view past events. Being alone was his main excuse for over taxing the hourglass in the first place.

He held the small silver timepiece in his hands, watching one of the grains fall to the bottom. He felt the slowing of time and carefully placed the magical device back on the shelf.

As he walked towards the gym, he decided to check on his little prisoner. He paused long enough to trace the curve of the doorframe with his fingertips. It glowed yellow for a second then faded into the stone. The spell would give her peaceful dreams in order for her to rest through the night and doubled as a silent alarm. If she decided to poke her nose, he would know.

He hesitated when he saw her lying on the bed fully clothed. That was another human trait that puzzled him. He never slept fully clothed. He fought back the urge to undress her with his magic. If she wanted to undress or change clothes, she would have. He had made sure there were plenty of things she could wear. Obviously, she hadn't liked the styles he had chosen. Then he remembered how she had covered herself in front of him in her apartment. Perhaps she thought he would visit in the night and ravish her.

Well, here he was. A dark eyebrow lifted in wonder. She was right, but he wasn't here to seek the pleasure of her body. *Why are you here? You want to see if her marker is there.* He questioned himself as he stood by the foot of the bed watching her sleep. Her hair was spread across the bed in damp curls. The corner of his mouth tilted up in a half smile. She had found the bathing pool. He wondered how Lilly Rose had taken to his little guest. He didn't see any claw marks, so the falcon obviously didn't take offence at sharing her space with Melissa.

He summoned a thick fur blanket to hand and covered her up. He noticed a chill in the room. Glancing at the ancient fireplace, he muttered a spell and the pile of stones caught fire. "Sleep well Melissa."

Four hours later, her eyelashes flickered. "Where am I," she rubbed at her temples as she sat upright in bed. Opening her eyes, she looked around and yawned as she stretched. A dreamy smile on her lips as she felt the soft luxurious blanket against her hands.

Suddenly she ducked down as she remembered the falcon. Looking around the room, she didn't see any birds with miniature bells. Perhaps it was an invisible maid or Siaak had paid her a visit.

Her smile faded as her face grew serious. The image of him looming over her body, dressed in a black cape, hissing as he lowered his fangs to her neck made her hot. It wasn't just his fangs that turned her on. Her Dracula-in-denial was naked under that cape. "I really need to get a grip!" She swept the expensive fur to one side and stood up. Half expecting the floor to be icy cold, she moaned with delight at the warmth beneath her feet. Glancing down she spotted her shoes. "I took them off." An image of Siaak undressing her made her heart skip a beat. Shaking her head, she chided herself as she put her shoes back on.

She reached down to tidy the bed when she felt something touch the top of her hand. Whatever it was burned an image of black fingers across the skin. Yelping, she yanked her hand away and tucked it tightly under her armpit. Looking wildly around the room, she felt the hair on her neck rise. Was it a spirit of long ago? She began to wonder if she had inadvertently tripped one of those spells Siaak had spoken about. Or had he decided to kill her after all?

Her eyes went straight for the doorway. Maybe, if she found her way out, she could flag down a stray camel or something. She moved away from the bed and made it to the doorway before she screamed as her body was picked up off the floor and violently slung against the fridge. She fell to the floor in a slump. How long she lay there was anyone's guess. The last thing she remembered before she lost consciousness was mumbling his name. "Siaak…"

The muscles in his back bulged as he held his body posed in mid air. His strength kept him steady before he let go and latched onto another pole and somersaulted through the air. His long muscular legs gripping the metal hoop kept him from falling as it swung back and forth from a bright orange nylon rope.

Siaak was in the middle of working out where to go next when he felt the alarm go off in his head. "Damn it!"

He knew he couldn't trust her to stay in her room. Hanging from the ceiling where he had constructed metal bars and climbing frames to keep his body agile, he added a few more swear words under his breath. Beads of sweat dripped off his nose and chin as he worked out the fastest way of getting down. It was simple. He let go. The bright blue exercise mats covering the hard stone rushed up to meet him as he fell fast. Counting down, Siaak kept track of his speed and height like a jumper armed with a parachute. Timing it, he teleported seconds before impact.

When she came to, she was instantly dragged around the room like a rag doll. "GET OFF ME!" she shouted while struggling with her invisible attacker. Fighting against an opponent you can see was hard enough, but take away their physical form and she was bound to lose. No defence class could prepare her for this. She certainly never imagined, in her wildest dreams, she'd be the target of a pissed off ghost.

Then again, she never expected to be in an ancient temple with a sexy man that kept offering to do her in the most tantalising voice. Why did she keep coming back to that? Maybe she needed to see a shrink.

Her mind switched gears as she registered something heavy across her chest. A burning sensation crept up her body as she fought to push away the thing that was holding her to the floor. "You won't take me without a fight!" she shouted, hoping she sounded threatening even though she felt like crawling under the bed, if she could get away, hoping whatever it was would just go away and leave her alone.

It answered her with a powerful kick or maybe it was a punch, she wasn't sure which. It didn't matter as she went skidding across the hard marble floor. That was definitely going to leave some colorful bruises she thought as she came to a sudden stop. "Oh shit!" she cried out as she was pulled backward along the floor. Melissa tried with all her might, but couldn't break free. Raking her nails on the floor did nothing to slow her tug of war. Suddenly she was twirled around and heading for the marble base under the bed.

Melissa put her arms above her head just in time to cushion the blow. She flinched and bit down on her lip as the corner stone cut into her forearm. Stunned, she laid faced down and tried to catch her breath. It was hard to think about anything.

Panic set in as she felt an icy cold burn against her ankles. Before she could do anything, she found herself flipped over, staring up at the ceiling. The icy feeling continued up her body making her teeth chatter. She couldn't speak, the extreme pressure returned in full force, closing off her air supply. The last thing she remembered, before she lost consciousness, was Siaak materializing into the room like a black cloud.

Siaak sensed the poltergeist the second he entered the room. They were doomed spirits, humans that had died long ago. It wasn't the first time he'd come across one. Living in different countries had brought him face to face with more than he cared to remember. This one wanted Melissa. She probably resembled someone it knew. And by the looks of things, it was pissed and winning.

He summoned the poltergeist to the physical plane. The shape of a woman snapped into view. She was sat on Melissa's chest, her mouth hovering above Melissa's, ready to drain the life from her body like a leech.

"She is not yours, she belongs to me!" Siaak declared as he circled around the room, waiting for it to attack him. He needed to draw its attentions away from Melissa. Once it became fixated on him, it would lose interest in the human. Then he could fight and not worry about accidentally harming Melissa.

The poltergeist screeched in anger before it shoved Melissa's body behind it. The old woman swayed back and forth. Wailing pitifully, lost within her misery, before her head snapped up. Her nose tilted up as she opened her mouth, showing rotting teeth. She hissed and clawed at him. Her tangled hair fell in a wild mess around her face as she fought to be free again.

He summoned a silver ankh to hand. He mouthed a trigger word and the ankh extended into a dagger. The loop of the ancient cross became the hilt that he gripped in a tight fist as he plunged the silver blade down into the poltergeist's hand, nailing it to the marble floor, trapping her. She howled as if in pain but Siaak knew she was mimicking the remembered emotion from her human life. Without hesitating, he spoke in a different language, his voice soft and lyrical like a mother's lullaby. The woman's face altered for a split second before she snarled and raked her free hand down his chest.

He glanced down to see four long scratches across his naked chest. He dove for her and knocked her back. Digging one knee into her ribcage, he pinned her down long enough for him to complete the sending song. As he spoke the last word, her body exploded into dust. She could rest now.

Siaak crawled along the floor on his hands and knees until he reached Melissa. Her head fell back as he dragged her body off the floor to lay her across his lap. He wasn't a doctor but he knew poltergeists fought dirty. He had 'seen' her go flying through the air before he appeared in her room. She needed x-rays to tell if there was any internal damage or broken bones. And she should count herself lucky considering that it seemed there were more than a few people trying to kill her besides him.

Her pulse was weak and she wasn't breathing. He tilted her head back, opened her mouth as he pinched her nose closed and blew. He kept his eyes on her chest making sure there was movement as he filled her lungs with air. He repeated it four more times until her teeth bit down on his bottom lip. His head jerked at the sudden pain. "Melissa it is me, Siaak!" He stood up, pulling her up into his arms until he was sure she could stand on her own.

She glared at him with accusing eyes for a few seconds before she pushed his upper lip back to show off his teeth, she was looking for his fangs.

"What am I, a horse?" He said while he glared at her from over the bridge of his nose. He felt ridiculous standing there with her fingers in his mouth.

"So it is. Did you just kiss me?" She ignored the horse statement. Looking up at him, she licked her lips and pretended to be offended by his intimate touch.

"You thought that was a kiss?"

"I don't know, maybe you suck at kissing…" she shrugged her shoulders in reply. "Not everyone can be an award winning kisser, so don't worry, I won't tell anyone your dirty little secret."

He ran his tongue around his teeth and inner cheek before he grunted at her below-the-belt statement. If she wanted a kiss he was more than happy to give her that and more.

She saw the look in his eyes and knew she should have shut up. "You can put me down now. Thanks," she said as he let her slide down his body. She eyeballed her bed and stepped behind him. If she was honest with herself, she was damned glad he came when he did.

Siaak wanted to pick her up and show her what his mouth could do, but he didn't want her passing out on him again. "That was a poltergeist. Seems you piss off the dead as well as the living."

"Ha ha, you're a barrel of laughs. Hey, I was minding my own business when you came along. I didn't ask you to kidnap me."

"If you kept your hands to yourself and refrained from stealing other people's things, I would never have bothered you, period!" His voice raised a notch as he watched her. She was shaking again and he knew it wasn't because she was cold.

He placed his hand over her forehead. She felt clammy. His eyes filled with annoyance as her face went white. He put his arms out to catch her body as she slumped forward. He stood there cradling her in his arms while working out his next course of action. Shaking his head, he teleported them to the nearest obelisk.

CHAPTER THREE

"What do you mean, I can't see her?" shouted a male voice.

"Sir, I won't remind you again. Keep your voice down. This is a public medical facility. There are people trying to rest. If you continue in this manner, I will call security and have you removed." The nurse was waving her finger in his face as she walked backward down the hallway in front of him. She had dealt with her fair share of rude and impatient visitors! And she knew exactly how to deal with this one.

Jonathon huffed. He dismissed the nurse with a flip of his hand and a hard, loud tapping of his umbrella on the floor. The nurse muttered something about men and disappeared through a door marked 'private.'

"This is ridiculous, I am her fiancé." Jonathon stood with his hands braced on the curved wooden handle of his umbrella. He glared daggers at Siaak through a pair of expensive Armani glasses.

"Really and here I was under the impression you were just friends."

Jonathon looked up and frowned deeply. "We are the best of friends. I should have been notified straight away when she was taken ill! I promised her father I would keep her safe." Jonathon slammed his free hand deep in his pocket. He wanted to wrap his hands around the man's throat and squeeze.

"Well I think you are doing a poor job of it, Jonathon. I

happen to know she is old enough to take care of herself, do you not agree?" Siaak stood guard in the doorway. He wasn't about to let that jerk near her. He was a liar and a terrible dresser. His eyes watched Jonathon with icy suspicion. Siaak could almost see Jonathon's feathers ruffle with jealousy.

Jonathon huffed again and blew his cheeks out like a blowfish. Each step he took was joined with the tapping of his umbrella against the tiled floor. Siaak wanted to shove it up his snotty ass, but there were too many witnesses. Being in a hospital, they'd only take it back out, defeating the purpose of inflicting pain on mister dickhead. He could always wipe that look of high and mighty off his smug face later.

Jonathon watched as a predatory look passed over the tall man's face. Then it hit him. He remembered him from last night, the man with Melissa. Damn! He was right about them being an item. What other possible reason could explain why he was hanging around here now. He was standing guard like a pit bull. Jonathon narrowed his eyes as a small smile appeared while he tried to gain a glimpse of Melissa through the window.

"How is she?" he asked, his voice full of concern.

"She will be fine. Apparently, she was exposed to bacterial spores from the Black Pyramid. She is on a high dose of antibiotics which they are hoping will make her better."

Jonathon pressed his hand to his mouth, his eyes closed with fake grief.

Siaak glanced down the hallway as he lowered his mouth to Jonathon's ear so only he could hear. "You are a bigger fool than I originally gave you credit for." Siaak let his lips part as he stepped back, in order to get his point across. "I know what you are up to." Siaak's dark eyes enforced his statement as he stared down at the pathetic man. "I will make sure she finds out that you are not all that you appear to be."

Jonathon coughed before he straightened his back. He pushed his glasses back on his nose with his index finger and glared right back. "Tell her I came to see her and give her these." He handed Siaak the bouquet of mixed roses he had tucked under his arm.

Siaak stood there refusing to take them at first and then decided he didn't have to act like the prick standing in front of him. Siaak nodded once before he slipped inside Melissa's room and closed the door, leaving Jonathon standing there alone in the corridor.

Jonathon grumbled to himself as he left the hospital. Once he was outside, he hammered his umbrella on the ground until he broke it. *How dare he dictate to me?* As he strode to his car, his phone went off. He threw the door open and shoved his umbrella inside, almost spearing the leather seats before answering his mobile.

"WHAT?" He shouted.

"Where is she?"

"In the bleeding hospital David! No, you can't get inside her room. She seems to have acquired a bodyguard. I want you watching the front of the hospital at all times. Her newfound friend gave me some fucking bullshit about spores! The bitch had a mask on so I know it's not life threatening. Mores the pity!" Jonathon beamed a fake smile at a group of doctors and nurses as they passed by him. It faded to a sneer as he looked back to make sure they couldn't hear. "I want her brought back to me alive. If he gets in the way, do whatever it takes, do I make myself understood?" he pressed his mouth against the phone making sure his demands were heard.

"Understood perfectly boss."

Jonathon slammed the phone shut and threw it in the backseat with his umbrella. Glancing at his watch, he would have to go by helicopter if he wanted to be on time. It was a shame Melissa couldn't be there to take some small credit for her part in finding the Black Pyramid before the bomb he had planted blew it to kingdom come. He felt a bit better at the thought of being famous. With that on his mind, he left the parking lot and made his way to the airport.

Siaak held his hand over the wastebasket and dropped the bouquet of white and yellow roses inside it. "Those weeds are from lover boy."

"What lover boy are you talking about?" she asked as she found the controller to operate the bed under her pillow. The bed moved up and down as she tapped away at the directional buttons, ignoring the sour look on his face until he jerked the remote out of her reach.

"HEY!"

"You know perfectly well who I am talking about and stop playing with the bed. It is irritating and childish!" He loomed over the bed shaking the small rectangular remote at her.

"Give me that back" She lurched sideways, diving into the air to reclaim the small box. She missed as he leaped back. She pulled herself back onto the bed making her extra large sleeves fall off her shoulders, giving Siaak an ample view of her breasts.

"Thanks!" She saw the look in his eyes as he ogled her chest and won the remote back. She beamed a smartass smile at him and turned the TV on.

"HA, speak for yourself. I'm not childish. I heard you talking to Jonathon. You could have let him in. What did you tell him was wrong with me?" She pushed the thin white gown back in place while avoiding eye contact. As much as she liked it, he set her on edge and right now, she needed to get back to work. She reached for the blue plastic water pitcher that sat on the tray above her lap.

"I told him the doc said you were affected by bacterial spores from the pyramid." Siaak crossed his arms over his broad chest, tapping his fingers against his biceps before he started pacing back and forth in front of the TV.

"Jonathon knows you lied…"

"And that is supposed to bother me in some fashion?"

She groaned and smacked the pillow with her head. "I wore a mask while I was in the pyramid. He was with me. Something tells me, as stupid as he can be at times, he won't forget that minor detail. Men, I swear, what is it with you guys. You see one woman and you go nuts."

He stopped pacing and looked her square in the face. "Did you know he is parading around as your fiancé?"

The pitcher dropped from her hands and froze in mid air as Siaak leaned across the bed and caught it. She desperately wanted to ask him how he managed to do that 'popping in and out of view' thingy. She'd seen him do it before and put it down to her lack of sleep.

He poured her a glass of water and handed it to her as he sat next to her on the bed.

She took the plastic cup and tried to figure out what he was thinking. His face gave nothing away as he watched her. Sitting in the hospital bed, she felt at a disadvantage wearing a paper gown that was so thin she could count the tiny moles on her belly. Not to mention, it was open at the back. "You sure you didn't get the doctor to slip me a little something, because I could have sworn you were standing at the end of the bed just a second ago. How do you do that?"

He waved his fingers at her and smirked, "Magic, re-member?"

"And, I bet my last dollar, that damned ghost was something to do with you. It scared the shit out of me," she said as she put her plastic cup down a bit too hard, making the water slosh onto the table.

"I refuse to take the credit for that. I never make someone else do my work for me." If she was looking for an argument, she wasn't going to get one from him.

"What about his claims on you? Are you engaged to him? Is he your fiancé like he boasts?"

"See what I mean, testosterone all over the place," she paused in the middle of her charade, "fiancé? He's not my fiancé; I told you we're just friends." She fell back on her pillow and jerked the cover over her head.

"No need to conceal yourself Melissa," he spoke softly, "unless you got something to hide." Siaak walked over to her clothes. He unzipped the plastic cover and placed them on the bed. "I will let you get dressed."

She jerked the cover down; it made her hair fly up as she chomped her teeth at him. "I don't have anything to hide. Are you sure you don't want to watch?" She sat up on the end of the bed with her hands behind her back holding her gown together.

"I have already had the pleasure of seeing you naked." He let his eyes travel down her body, the memory of it made him hard.

"Yeah, don't remind me." She twisted her mouth up at him.

"Then why ask unless you want me to stay and give you a hand with the zipper."

"I can't see any zippers…" her voice drifted off as she eyeballed the outfit until he stepped in the way.

"I was referring to my zipper." He said with a straight face.

Her jaw dropped at his outrageous suggestion. He had some nerve. She stood up so fast her gown flew wide open at the back giving him an excellent view of her bare ass in the mirror behind her bed.

"Out!" she pointed at the door and stomped her bare foot in emphasis.

He noted her flushed cheeks and heavy breathing as he strode past. "Let me know if you change your mind." With that, he winked and closed the door.

Weak in the knees, Melissa collapsed on the bed. The woman in her wanted to sample what he was offering, but she knew how dangerous that was.

Shaking her head, she dragged herself off the bed, grabbed her clothes and headed to the bathroom.

Melissa opened the door and stepped through. She paused at the sound of laughter drifting up the wide corridor. Curious, she pulled the door shut after her and followed it until she spotted the nurse's station.

It was overflowing with women. From nurses and cleaners to doctors, they were all standing around Siaak, like flies around a honey pot. She got the feeling he was entertaining the morning staff while he waited for her to get changed. She had expected him to be on guard by the door, afraid she might try to escape when his back was turned.

Instead, he was leaning against the desk with his arms folded across his chest. Deep in conversation with the ladies, Melissa noticed he kept looking in the direction of the main entrance. Was he worried that he might get caught? It left her wondering what he was thinking. What were they talking about? Was it about her or was he flirting with them?

Spearing her hair with her fingers, she wondered what it would take to make him smile like that for her. Silly of course, she didn't know who or what he was. Normal men didn't have fangs, live in hidden temples, teleport from place to place via a statue nor did they use magic. Squaring her shoulders, she hooked her hands behind her back and joined him.

His head swung around as his smile froze on his lips. His eyes narrowed to slits as he watched her watching him. She looked stunning in the navy pantsuit he had picked for her. Her brown hair hung straight down past her shoulders in a style that suited her face and height.

He resisted the sudden urge to meet her half way, to take her by the arm and teleport back to the Temple. What he should have done was dump her body. No not him! He suddenly decided to play hero instead. The last thing he needed right now was her screaming 'kidnapper' at the top of her lungs. There were more than enough women gathered to give him a good pelting if they found out Melissa was his hostage.

Regardless of his intentions, he'd hate to hurt anyone. He played it safe and let her come to him. He offered his arm, raised a dark eyebrow as she took it, and settled herself next to him. Perhaps the doctor *had* slipped her something.

"You look stunning and you smell nice too." He complimented her and then nodded at the hospital staff, "Ladies, thank you for looking after my princess." He winked and felt Melissa tense up at the 'awe's' coming from the women behind them as he guided Melissa from the ward.

"So tell me what you guys were talking about?"

"I was reminiscing about how we met." He scanned the reception area for police or any other official person as she fired question after question at him.

"Really, how amazing. Did this version happen to be the

one where *you* broke into my room, in the middle of the night?"

Siaak struggled to keep a straight face as he teased her. He shook his head no and felt a smile tug at his mouth.

"I know you didn't tell them you groped my naked body before you threatened to kill me. So, what did you say?"

"That I swept you off your feet and we are madly in love." He made kissing sounds as he placed both his hands over his hearts, knowing it was pissing her off.

"Umm, in case you don't know this about us 'humans', wanting to do me isn't being in love." She cut him a dirty look before she looked at her bare wrist. "What time is it?" she asked while he did his Romeo impersonation.

"I do believe it is almost 9:00 am and you are late, Cinderella." He chided as he 'grabbed' her pack from her room and pushed it into her chest. He dropped his arms to his sides and led her to the door.

"How do you know what time it is? You don't have a watch on?" She glanced up at him. Before he had a chance to speak, she placed a finger to his lips. "Magic, yes I know."

Instinctively, she jerked her hand away when his eyes lit up. She turned her back to him to give herself a moment to calm her raging hormones and searched for her cell. When she found her pack empty, she gave him a probing look. "Where is my phone, Siaak?" she glared at him from under her brow.

He shrugged with nonchalance, "Holding up a sandcastle? Before you ask, I have no need of a phone. Why would I? I have so few friends that need one in order to speak with me."

"That helps me how?" She really wanted to whack him with her bag. Shame there wasn't an anvil inside. She imagined him flying up into the air and landing on his head.

"It would be silly, on my part, to allow you to call for help. That would make it all too easy for you to get away. It would upset me greatly, to lose my beautiful hostage." He wiggled his eyebrows at her above a satisfying grin that told her he was more than happy to make her life a living hell.

"By the way," he pointed back into the lobby through the double doors, "If you had looked up, you would have seen the clock on the wall."

"Bite me!" She fired back as she turned to look up at the sky.

He stood behind her and flashed his fangs. She was lucky there were people around. He wasn't in the mood to play nice.

Startled at the sound of screams, they both looked up in time to see a car bounce up and down before it ploughed through the entrance barriers. The yellow and red striped stop arm splintered on contact as the car sped through the parking lot. People jumped out of the way, shouting obscenities at the maniac behind the wheel.

The dark haired assassin slammed on the brakes and whipped the car sideways on to the front of the hospital. As soon as the car stopped, his arm appeared out the window with a semi automatic in hand. He made his mark and fired a wave of bullets at the front of the building.

Siaak saw the man lift his arm and acted on impulse. He whipped Melissa up into the circle of his arms and took cover.

"Put me down!" She demanded as he rolled sideways hitting his back against a brick column.

"Stay still unless you want to get shot!" He warned as he grudgingly let go of her.

She glared at him until a spray of bullets went whizzing by her head. She dropped to the floor and covered her head with her arms as bricks exploded around her. At the sound of glass breaking, Siaak raised a temporary shield around the front of the hospital to protect the humans inside.

"I will be right back–"

She jumped up and pushed him back against the column. "You aren't leaving me here!"

"Fine!" he yanked her close. When the car sped off, he ported them to the roof of the hospital. He tracked the car's movement, calculating his 'jump' and they popped out of view to land on the roof of the car.

The driver spun the white car around in tight circles trying to dislodge them. Sand and smoke filled the parking lot making Melissa cough. "Are you crazy, like I need to ask?" She poked him in the chest with her index finger.

"Now is not the time, Melissa!" He huddled down with her for only a second before he was leaping through the air again. Each time his feet connected with something solid, he launched them up in the air again. It was the only way to avoid the deadly bullets as the driver of the car pursued them at every turn.

Melissa saw the sky one minute, the ground the next. The Tigger bouncing was enough to make her throw up. She had never been one for turbulent rides and Siaak's violent jumping up and down like a deranged kangaroo was making her feel queasy. In the end, she closed her eyes and tried not to dwell on it. After all, he was saving her life.

Siaak could have moved faster, if not for Melissa extra weight, but he couldn't leave her behind. When she snuggled up to him, he almost stumbled.

It was strange how he had gone from killer to protector, all within 24 hours of meeting her. He could teleport them both to his home, but he wanted to be found. Someone wanted her dead and he was going to find out whom it was. First, he was going to get her to safety.

He paused long enough to get his bearings. He'd managed to get them a good few yards ahead of the driver.

People were staring in fascination as he leaped from spot to spot. He knew pictures of his extraordinary display that defied the laws of gravity would be front-page news tomorrow. However, he didn't care.

His head whipped to the right at the sound of screeching tyres. He knew it was only a matter of seconds before their location was discovered.

"When I say *go,* reach under my shirt and pull out my necklace." His eyes scanned the dirt road in both directions. He knew this game all too well. Once he got his hands on the other player, he'd break him in two.

"Go!" his voice boomed. He felt her warm fingers skim his collarbone before she pulled the silver chain free of his collar.

"I've got it!" she shouted with triumph and held onto it for dear life as he propelled them up. Siaak took them as high as he dared without causing her any harm. The speed of their take off made it impossible for her to talk. She hid her face in his chest to keep the wind from taking her breath away.

The car appeared just as he predicted and Siaak 'pushed' her. The last thing he heard was her loud elongated curse. He knew the outcome of 'throwing' a human and not being on the other side to 'catch'. The only thing he could hope for was that she didn't break that pretty little neck when she flew out the other side of the Obelisk.

Siaak twirled around to face the white four-door sedan head on. His eyes tracked the speeding car. Siaak launched his body into the air and landed on the hood with an almighty thud. Smashing his fists against the windshield, he succeeded in cracking it.

A spider web pattern burst across the glass making the driver shake his fist in anger and automatically slam on the brakes. Siaak hooked his fingers around the wipers as his body rose off the hood. His legs swung out and connected with the side mirror. Using it as a foothold, he tried to calm himself down before he did something stupid, like blow the damn car up!

Mouthing a series of words together to form a spell, Siaak jerked his head up and snarled at the man behind the wheel. His eyes flashed fire as his teeth grew, forming sharp fangs. He didn't care about hiding his identity; the man wouldn't live another hour to tell anyone anything.

David saw his life flash before his eyes at the loud explosion that rocked the car. "Bloody tyres!" He didn't have to take his attention off spidy to check his mirrors. He could hear and feel the rims on the right side of the car scraping the ground. Steering was a bitch as the large sedan pull to the right, making it impossible to keep the vehicle in a straight line. Not that he could see to go in a straight line. Visibility was nil as the car threw sand and dirt up into the air.

"Get the fuck off my car–," he stopped short at the menacing growl and sharp teeth. What the hell had Jonathon sent him to eliminate, a fucking vampire? He had taken down hundreds of people in his ten years as a Hitman, but he'd never had a mark sporting fangs and jumping around like a fucking frog on speed. Once he was done, he'd have Jonathon's balls to hang on his rear view mirror like hairy dice for taking the piss. David slammed his foot down on the accelerator pedal. The engine rumbled as it was shoved into gear. It jerked from being pushed to the limit.

Siaak's body hit the windshield with a wallop as the accelerated force pressed him against the glass. He pulled his arm back and ploughed it through the thick glass.

David mouthed 'fuck me' as he dived left to avoid the groping hand. He saw the fury in the man's face and knew he was in deep shit. He spied his guns on the floorboard where they'd fallen off the seat. David flipped off his attacker when Siaak's fingers missed him and took hold of the steering wheel.

The moment Siaak felt the steering wheel he moved his hand up and grabbed the man by his neck. With a loud roar, Siaak pulled the assassin through the windshield headfirst. Without any effort on his part, Siaak threw him over his shoulder.

David hit the ground with a muffled thud. His head and right shoulder took most of the impact as he rolled to a stop. The sand gathered around his body, cushioning his landing and saving him from serious injuries. He rolled onto his knees, chest heaving, as he spat blood from his mouth. With a quick look back, he saw the car with his mark flying away and legged it.

Siaak dismounted with a back flip that sent the speeding car careening off in the opposite direction. A loud crash followed by a large explosion made Siaak furious. It wouldn't be long before the local authorities came charging in to ruin his fun.

Siaak landed on his feet, knees bent, as he balanced his weight with his hands on the ground. His head snapped up as he tracked the hitman's movements. Siaak found him. It wasn't hard as the area was pretty open. No trees and mostly dry sandy ground. Full of adrenaline, Siaak moved like a cheetah, lethal and sleek. Everything became a blur as he picked up speed and gave chase.

David managed to look over his shoulder once before Siaak tackled him to the ground. Their bodies rolled in the sand. David kicked and punched as he tried to free himself of Siaak's tight grip. Nothing worked. He grabbed a handful of sand and threw it in Siaak's face.

Siaak leapt to his feet and held the pendant to each eye like an eyedropper. Similar to a magnet with slivers of metal, the miniature obelisk drew the sand out of his eyes within a matter of seconds. Siaak turned to the man on the ground and opened his mouth.

David couldn't speak as he stared in horror at the double row of jagged fangs. He crawled backwards like a crab. He wasn't going anywhere, fast, as he tried to get away. His heart pounding, he attempted to work out how everything had turned sour. Instead, he stumbled and fell over a pile of rocks. Finding it hard to swallow, his mouth felt dry as he heard the vampire's voice.

"Who wants Melissa dead?"

David looked into the eyes of a monster. He couldn't give a name. That broke the laws of his profession. In his line of work, lies were a part of the job. And he was good at both. To keep his occupation secret, he led a double life. It was so easy for him, like slipping on a pair of comfy shoes.

He could take on the persona of David and know that his job was just that, a job. As Adam, he shed the hellish life he had been forced into. Adam, a football coach, father to twin girls and husband to a beautiful and caring wife.

David's government paid him millions to take out their competitors. He would never be free of their tight leash.

As for his current mark, Stonebridge had approved the hit. It wasn't the first time he'd heard that name. It was synonymous with power and money. If he failed in his assignment, Stonebridge would send someone after him. Either way, he was dead.

Snarling, Siaak lunged at the man. "Answer me!"

David slipped the bowie knife free of his boot and spread his arms wide before he resigned himself to the angel of death. "I was sent to kill you both."

Melissa missed the steps altogether and went sailing through the air. Arms and legs swinging wildly as she mouthed 'oh crap' and landed face down in the sand.

Coughing and retching, she lifted her head, opened her mouth and spat out a mouthful of sand before she flipped herself over onto her back. She made a face of disgust at the taste and gagged again. She longed for some mouthwash or water to rinse the hard bits of grit left on her tongue and between her teeth. Coughing, she managed to spit more out, but every time she closed her jaw, she could hear the crunching sound of sand against her teeth. She hated that! The first thing she planned to ask Siaak was how he managed to walk out of a solid object. She always ended up face down, like she was trying to steal third base.

Standing up, she smacked her clothes with the base of her palms. Most of it had gone up her top and down into the cups of her bra. Looking around, she heaved a sigh of relief. At least she didn't have to worry about attracting a crowd. She removed her jacket and white top giving them both a good shake before she took off her bra. Once all the sand was gone, she folded up her bra and jacket, too hot for that.

Glancing at her wrist for the time, she remembered her watch was missing, too. She wondered how long he was going to be as she walked back and forth. A frown touched her lips but faltered as she wondered if he was okay. Blowing raspberries, she sat at the base of the towering Obelisk with her head in her hands. He would be okay. If he could fight off ghosts then he could deal with Speedracer. She paused, moving her hands up to her hair. Why would someone want to run them down?

Standing up, she turned her nose up at the feel of sand on her rear, so she dusted it off her butt as she began to walk in circles. She stopped when she saw her pack lying on the ground where she had touched down. She stomped over to her bag and yanked it off the ground. Her hands shaking, she looked for her cigarettes. She found one left in the crumpled pack with her lighter.

She was still leaning against the side of the Obelisk, smoking the last of her cigarette when she felt a tremor and witnessed Siaak stepping out of it. She watched him strut down the cracked steps and blinked a few times before she noticed the blood stains on his clothes.

"Are you okay?" she was genuinely shocked, it never occurred to her that he could be injured.

Siaak swung around as his torn clothes mended before morphing into tough brown leather. His hair swung free as a lethal looking curved sword appeared on his back. She was impressed. A 'thank you' was close on her lips until she noticed his brow lowering in an angry glower, which always seemed to be aimed at her.

"I am fine. You are not." He turned his back to her as he twisted and tightened the titanium embellished vanguard on his left arm. He reached up to tie his hair into a ponytail. "It would seem that someone wants our heads on sticks. The Hitman was sent for the both of us." He waited for the million questions to follow as she puffed on her cigarette.

"So what happened to the jerk chasing us?"

"We had a brief discussion, one that I found quiet disturbing. It proved what I already knew. Your so-called friend wants you and me, dead. Apparently Jonathon ordered him to follow you and to make sure both of us disappeared." Siaak didn't offer the rest of the conversation. She wouldn't approve of his methods.

She took the last drag of her cigarette before flicking it on the sandy ground. She blew the smoke up into the air as she stamped the fire out. With a grunt of annoyance, she pushed off the large granite statue and flew at him. "I can't believe you'd sink so low as to blame all this on Jonathon. He's a decent man. Okay, sure, he gets on my nerves. He's a man, he can't help it." She shook her head in denial. She refused to believe what he was telling her. "Jonathon isn't trying to kill me, don't be so stupid, I've known him since I was nineteen. You, on the other hand, mentioned it a time or two."

He charged at her, ramming her body into the weathered Obelisk.

"OW!" Her head hit the hard stone making her vision blur. Instinctively, she pulled her fist back to punch him, as she strained to bite him with her teeth.

Siaak blocked her attacks. His hand clamped around her wrist forcing her arm behind her back with a rough jerk. She sucked air in between her teeth at the sudden burning, cramping pain running along her shoulder blade. Was he trying to pull her arm out of its socket? She gave him a black look as she refused to give in.

The more she struggled, the harder he squeezed. "I am not playing games Melissa. Open your eyes woman! The man wants you dead. Does that not upset you? I mean, if my friends hired assassins to kill me, I would be a little pissed off!"

"You want me dead, too!" She shouted back as she stood on her toes trying to relieve the burning spasm. His fingers squeezed harder at her accusation.

The sound of steel rang in her ears as he pulled his sword free and held it to her neck, just below her chin. "I can do it here and now if that is what you want?" His stance told her, all he had to do was push. The sharp blade would cut right through her neck, tendons, muscle and bone.

"I will be honest with you. My original plans were to kill you both. If you knew what is locked inside that tomb, you would understand my reasons for keeping it that way. I am honour bound to protect you and everyone else on this miserable planet!"

"Let me guess! It is alien and you have a pair of blue tights on under your clothes?" Her voice dripped with sarcasm.

His features hardened instantly. His dark eyes narrowed to mere slits as he felt the sudden urge to shake some sense into her. The square of his jaw, now sprinkled with black hair, ticked with anger as he clenched his teeth together. "You mock me now but when the time comes, you will need me at your back."

The glint in his eyes told her, he meant business. The sneer on his lips, made her feel like shit on his boots. Without thinking, she brought her right knee up and flashed him a knowing smile as it connected between his legs.

He didn't flinch once. Even though he was sure, she'd knocked his balls up into his throat.

When he didn't fall over or immediately grab at his crotch, Melissa made a move to kick him again. She stopped when his sword pressed deep into her neck as he bared his teeth at her.

"I kicked you hard enough to send your boys on a permanent vacation! Why aren't you cross-eyed and turning blue?" She hissed as the blade nicked her skin. *That answers my question!*

She didn't dare move, speak or swallow. Instead, her doe brown eyes turned cold and unfeeling, a mirror image of his. If he were going to kill her right now, she would face him without showing fear. She was innocent. Nothing gave him or anyone else the right to take her life.

He blinked several times at the scent of her blood before he realised he had inadvertently cut her. Lowering the ancient curved sword given to him by Ramses the First, he placed the blade between them in a silent warning. With the expertise of a seasoned warrior, he twirled the hilt with a lose wrist and firm grip. The stained blade spun free from his scarred fingers landing in the sand hilt up. He released her arm but kept his heavy body against hers making sure she couldn't move.

He took in her flushed features, rapid breathing and knew, he had gotten his message across to her. His mouth widened forming a sarcastic smile. Finally, the pin had dropped; she knew he wasn't playing games.

Melissa watched him watching her and wished for a baseball bat to knock that cocky smile off his handsome face. Disheartened by his lack of discomfort, she vowed to improve her aim next chance she got.

"I am not your typical human male, Melissa," he shifted his legs apart ignoring the pain as he stared down at her. His eyes darting back and forth as he watched her from under hooded eyes.

"I kind of figured that one on my own, Count Dracula." She said while rotating her shoulder and flexing her fingers. She bit her bottom lip as the blood rushed back into her cold arm accompanied by sharp twinges and tingles that made her curse his name. He made another grab for her. She shifted side to side in order to avoid being held down again, only she wasn't fast enough.

He shoved his full weight against her, aligning their bodies against the stone block again. Melissa felt his fingers spike her hair sending a tingle along her scalp before he gave a hard yank, anchoring her head against the stonewall.

Unable to move her head she couldn't see what he was doing. She swallowed hard the moment his dark head descend past her line of vision. His fingers stroked her scalp as his lips brushed against her earlobe.

The vision returned, forcing him to accept the fact that she was important to him in some bizarre way. His tongue swept across his parted lips in anticipation. His eyes struggled to stay focused on the lush 'v' of her neck as he felt drawn to the tiny beads of blood across the front of her neck. It reminded him of a ruby choker against the white smooth flawless skin.

Melissa swallowed the large knot in her throat as his hot breath sent chills down her spine. Her stomach muscles jerked in response to a leather-clad thigh separating hers. Her hands grasped the wall to try to balance herself as he pulled his knee up. She drew in a deep breath at the erotic feel of leather rubbing against her crotch. Next thing she knew, Siaak drew his knee up higher, lifting her feet off the stone floor. How could he hold all her weight up like that with one leg?

She heard the little voice inside her head, panicking, telling her this was wrong. The heat of his body against hers opened up a floodgate to her senses. She found herself being assaulted with images of their naked bodies intertwined that left her hot and wanting the real thing.

He pressed harder. He could feel the hammer of her heart as he flicked the tip of his tongue to her skin in his quest to taste her. Salt mixed with blood covered his tongue like honey. He ran the tip of his tongue under his fangs, sucking up the tiny drops of blood. A powerful jolt of energy shot through his system almost knocking him backward.

His eyes grew wide with astonishment. Without thinking, Siaak lowered his mouth, pulled his lips back and pressed his fangs into her neck. He wanted more. He couldn't form a rational explanation why his body was screaming for hers, why he suddenly craved her blood. It went against the grain of his people. Against everything, he was taught. His conscious lost.

As a boy child, Siaak was trained how to create and inject the right amount of poison with a single bite. If she were a threat to his survival, his body chemistry would automatically concoct a deadly poison, injected from microscopic holes at the back of each fang into her body. Instead, without his knowledge, a chemical was released into her blood stream, one that was going to alter her life forever.

She whimpered as his warm mouth settled over her skin. Somewhere in her subconscious, she heard what sounded like words. Unfamiliar, she ached to know what they meant. Fire soared through her body the moment his fangs sunk into her skin. His sucking mouth raised a few moans from her as she instinctively pushed her body toward him. She couldn't explain why she wasn't screaming her head off. Instead, she was fantasizing about him taking her, like the hero in a cheesy romance novel.

He could feel her thoughts of arousal, needing, wanting, the desire to be touched by him, only him. That pleased him more than he realized. At her husky moans, he shoved his hand between their sandwiched bodies. His mouth firmly locked to her flesh, his fangs buried deep as his free hand skimmed up her ribcage. His fingers caressing as his fangs retracted.

His breathless words penetrated her passion-filled head. "I could have killed you…" His chest heaved as he took in her scent. Licking his lips, he wanted to be inside her, to take her the way his brethren took a mate. "I want you. Admit it Melissa, you want me. There is something between us, something that draws us together. I know, deep down, I should put an end to all this!" He rocked his body against hers making sure she could feel him.

Her eyes snapped open as she realized he was manipulating her. "I hate you!" she screwed her face up in anger.

He threw his head back and gave her a cynical laugh. "Good, that is a start my *kepi*." He pulled away with regret. His body burned for hers. He could feel everything she was feeling. Could it be the marker making him want her even more? Was it the bite? He had never bitten a human before. For the life of him, he didn't know why he had thrown caution to the wind and allowed himself to do it. It was as if her blood called to him, whispering his name, filling his mind with lustful thoughts.

"You lied! You are a vampire!" Her voice, raw and filled with rage, she touched her neck and found traces of blood on her finger tips. She held her bloodied fingers up to his face with a condemning look in her eyes. "See?" she shrieked.

He simply stood there looking down at her. His long black hair rippled in the breeze as he formed a reply to the evidence. "I am not a liar, Melissa. You puzzle me." His eyelids drifted shut at the taste of her on his tongue. He steeled himself as he imagined taking her fingers into his mouth and carefully sucking the blood from each digit. "That puts me off guard. I have never bitten a human before now. The desire to be your protector is for reasons beyond my understanding."

"So that gives you the right to nibble on my neck, Count?"

She dabbed at her neck with her fingers and froze in place at the heated look on his face.

"I have lived a long time, keeping the planet safe from Osiris and her kind. She destroys for the sheer pleasure it gives her. My brothers guard her, as we speak; trapped in a spell that slows time. If it is ever broken, I promise you this," his eyes turned hard again as he stared down at her. "I will end your life, because she will not stop until she has tortured, maimed and killed every single person on this planet."

Melissa searched his face for the truth. "Why would you do that?" she asked almost too afraid to hear his answer.

"To keep you from suffering," he replied. For the first time, there was a hint of tenderness in his voice and his eyes.

It was hard to believe what he said. That Osiris was a real person, an evil monster, lurking behind a cleverly disguised version of gods and goddesses.

He nodded solemnly as he let her digest the truth for a little while longer. He took hold of her by the wrist and teleported them closer to the Black Pyramid.

Melissa kept unusually quiet as she followed his footsteps in the sand. For the first time around him, she was speechless. Concentrating on what she knew about the pyramids, she was itching to learn more. Pulling her hair away from her face, she shielded her eyes against the sunlight as she watched him. Her cheeks moved upwards with a hint of a smile every time he looked back to make sure she was there. As if she could go anywhere else, not that she wanted too, she'd get lost without him.

They carried on walking for another hour. He threw his arms out wide stopping her from going any further.

"Why do I get the impression we are lost? To top all that, you made me forget my bag at the last pit stop."

"You expect me to take the blame for your forgetfulness?"

"Yes I do. With all that groping and slurping at my neck, I left it behind. So," she pointed at him, "it's your fault. By the way, I'm thirsty," she swallowed while trying to work up some saliva to restore some moisture to her tongue and lips.

"Hold your hand out."

"Why, you going to bite me again?" She cupped her eyes with one hand to look at him, her upper lip arched as she made a face at him. The other hand she tucked behind her back, like a child hiding a stolen snack.

"No," his voice filled with revulsion. "I did not drink your blood; I told you I am not a vampire!"

"Hey, you were the one nibbling on my neck earlier, Count Dracula. I think that alone speaks volumes about you being part of the walking dead club."

"I was not drinking your blood, Melissa."

Her eyebrows drew up in a show of confusion.

"When I bit you, it was not to feed off you."

"Blah blah, sounds like a vampire to me. You wear black. You fly. You have fangs. If it quacks like a duck, it's a duck. You suck like a vampire, so you're a vampire."

"Grrrr! You drive me crazy, woman. Here!" He shouted as he jerked her arm out and held her palm open. A bottle of cold water appeared. "Try not to choke on it," he stalked off in a temper.

Melissa looked at the water as if it was a bomb ready to explode with the least bit of pressure.

"Drink the damn water! I refuse to take you to the hospital again for dehydration. I will leave your body to the vultures and think myself lucky I am free of your pig headedness!"

"The doctor said it was a combination of dehydration and jet lag! I'm sure imitating a lasso and being thrown around a room by some psychotic ghost didn't help me either!" She defended her fainting episode and short stay in hospital.

Melissa looked at the clear bottle in deep reflection. A shiver went down her spine as she thought about his mouth on her skin, sucking as his teeth entered her body. He hadn't caused her any physical pain, just a throbbing ache between her legs. If he hadn't opened his mouth to give her his little pep talk or warning, she would have let him do her right then and there. Trying to lay the blame on him was easy. However, if he was telling the truth, she would prefer to have him on her team. Especially after having a sample of what he could do with those fangs of his and his hands, she added.

Pushing that to the side, she ran after him. Her shoes were useless for trekking across the desert. Each step she took ended up with a shoe full of sand, making her feet feel like concrete boots. Ignoring the grit that had rubbed her skin sore, even so, she caught up with him. "I'm sorry Siaak; I guess I'm not used to a man like you. Here have some of my water, please." She held the bottle out to him half expecting him to refuse on principle or knock it out of her hands.

Siaak kept his emotions leashed and accepted the water. He twisted the lid off and lifted the bottle. Half way up he paused to salute her before taking a mouth full.

She found herself licking her lips as his slid around the rim. Her mouth opened as his head tipped back. His Adams apple rippled with each swallow. The bottle made a popping noise when he released it. "Thank you for sharing with me."

"No, I should be thanking you." She fell in step with him, "I didn't mean to sound so ungrateful, but how would you feel if I told you I was a goddess? You'd find it hard to believe, surely?" She took a swig of water, screwed the lid back on and slipped it in her pocket.

"Goddesses would never drink water, for any reason. And under no circumstances would you catch one walking. So my answer would have to be, no. I would never think of applying the snobbish title of Goddess to you." He noticed the slight limp she had as she walker faster to keep up with him. He put his arm out to stop her. "What is wrong with your feet?"

"Puff, it's nothing," she waved him away; "a little soaking won't cure. Besides I don't like to complain...um, what are you doing?" As he bent down, she jumped back shaking her head 'no'. "I'm not a sack of potatoes, so don't even think about throwing me over your shoulder again like some caveman."

He flashed a reassuring look as he squatted by her legs. "I believe you enjoyed it, more than you are willing to admit. Regardless of what you think about me, I am not a pack horse." He was graced with a sheepish look from her.

He carefully pulled her shoes and socks off. He muttered something. She had no idea what he was planning until he opened his hands to show her a tube of Neosporin and a roll of bandages. To her amazement, he began to clean each foot before putting ointment on the sores around her ankles and behind each heel before covering them with soft bandages. "What size boot do you wear?" he asked softly.

"I hate to burst your bubble Count, but there isn't a Payless anywhere around." At his low threatening growl and sudden show of fangs, she quickly told him, "six."

He spoke another series of strange words and a pair of tanned boots appeared on the sand next to her feet. He removed the sale tags and carefully put them on making sure not to disturb any of the bandages.

"You know, for someone that keeps calling me a thief, you sure do a lot of stealing yourself."

"I always pay for what I need. Now, come, we must hurry." He replied as he stood up and ushered her in front of him.

Once they reached the top of a massive sand dune, Melissa came to a halt. "Oh, my god, Siaak, its beautiful!" She stood with her hands over her mouth, stunned by the sheer size of the city. It had to be at least three hundred feet tall and well over two city blocks in length. Shame, she didn't have her camera. Her mouth watered at the possibilities of such a find. Then she remembered Siaak wanted to keep everything hush hush, so she hid her regret behind a whimper and carried on walking. Her head craned back as she looked left and right, trying to take it all in and commit as much to memory as humanly possible. "What dynasty was it built in?" She hoped he would at least tell her the answer. He was so tight lipped about everything else that it made it hard to know what to talk about.

"It belongs to my people, Melissa, and it is way outside the dating system your people created."

"Oh, I see. We are back on the 'my people' again." Her voice filled with disappointment. "What is the name of 'your people'? You can fill me in on what a SandWalker is, too. Do you have females in your SandWalker community?" She stood there with her hands on her hips, giving him the schoolteacher pop quiz look.

He carried on walking, as he explained. "A SandWalker is the only words in your English language that refers to my title. Others would call me *Gahiji*."

"Hunter, I remember that part. You know, for a moment, I kind of got the impression of Caine walking the desert in Kung Fu every time you say SandWalker." She teased, but he didn't bite. God, he was hard to kid around with!

"So what do you 'hunt'? Come on Siaak, you have to give me more than that to work with. You kidnapped me and have been moving me from place to place. Tell me who you are, what you are."

He ran his fingers through his hair before bracing his palms against the back of his head with his elbows facing outward. He caught her eyes with his. "I do not trust you with my life or my secrets—" He looked at her once before he glanced up at the bright sky. "I am not prepared to discuss anything about my history with you." He looked back down at her, "do I make myself clear?"

"If you are going to kill me, it doesn't matter if you tell me the truth. I'll be dead. Who am I going to tell then? Oh wait, let me guess, 1-800 physic hotline. Everyone will be rushing to get the latest gossip of Melissa. Hey, better yet, if you bite me two more times, I can have fangs, too, and become part of the walking dead club like yourself—"

"Shut up Melissa." He was close to losing his temper again. "I am not a vampire. There is no hypnotic suggestion in my voice, or glow in my eyes. I am unable to shape shift. Yes, I have fangs, they are part of me." He walked up to her and placed his hand on her cheek. "Open your mouth."

"Why?" she asked not sure what he was planning or if she would like it.

"I want to show you something."

She opened her mouth and raised her eyebrows when he pushed her upper lip back. "Wha are yew dewing?" she tried to speak with her mouth propped open.

"You have canine teeth here and here," he pressed his finger down each tooth before running the pad of his finger over the slight points. "Your ancestors had fangs. It was how you once nourished your bodies." He dropped his hands from her face and began walking again.

"How do you know that? Do you have any proof to back that up?"

"Yes," he touched his chest with his thumb, "me." If you want my pedigree," he paused and took a deep breath, "look me up in one of your books. I am, after all, Egyptian."

"Great. You think I'm full of shit? I wasn't born yesterday, buddy! I know when someone is jerking my chain!"

Siaak let his mouth open as he tilted his head back and roared so loud that she had to cover her ears. "Silence! I care not what you think. Remember who is in charge. If you are lucky, you just might live through this."

He touched the silver pendant through his shirt with a stroke of his fingertips. With his other hand, he reached down and took a handful of sand. As he spoke the summoning spell, the sand fell from his fingertips. The grains of falling sand rose up into the air forming the symbols of his spell, each one locking together to make one giant hieroglyphic that Melissa couldn't read. Boy, she wished she could!

She had never experienced an earthquake, first hand, until the episode in the pyramid. That had nothing on this! The ground rocked and rolled beneath her feet. She cried out as she tumbled back, her arms swinging wildly as she tried to regain her balance. All manner of nasty names came to mind as she rolled backward down the sandy hill. "Son of a camel!" she exclaimed as she stopped rolling and landed on her face. Spitting sand out, again, Melissa crawled to her hands and knees. "I'm beginning to hate this country!" she declared angrily as the rumbling started up again.

In the distance, three giant Obelisks burst free from the sand stretching up high into the sky like skyscrapers. If she didn't know any better, she would have said he had created them.

"Come with me." He took hold of her wrist and pulled her along after him.

"How— how did you do that?" her voice was barely audible as she stared up at the massive Obelisks.

"You already know the answer to that, now step in my footprints." When she didn't move he cursed and reached over plucking her off the ground. He slung her over his right shoulder. "There is no time for this, Melissa." As he made his way towards the three Black Obelisks with glowing hieroglyphics, he leaped from place to place. "The sand becomes unstable when the Obelisks travel through it, I have to keep moving, otherwise we will sink." He kept looking over his shoulder to make sure she was okay. "Hang on!" he chanted another series of strange words.

Melissa screamed as they vanished.

Jonathon pulled the headset off and threw it on his seat as he climbed down from the cockpit. He slammed the door and rapped it with his knuckles to get the pilots attention. He flashed thumbs up, pointed at his watch and waved three fingers while mouthing thirty minutes. The pilot saluted and took off once Jonathon cleared the whirling blades.

He made his way over to the conference tent. A dozen or so camera crews and reporters were hovering like flies around a jam pot. He whistled in a long flat tone. Just about every news channel was present. His eyebrows shot up at the large BBC emblem on two vans. Satellite equipment stacked high on each vehicle, ready to transmit live footage once a time slot had been set aside.

Delving in his front pocket, he pulled out his mobile. The text message from David did nothing to improve his mood. After deleting the message, he went straight to his tent to get changed for the upcoming interviews.

"Put me down, you big ape!"

When she kicked him with her feet, Siaak dropped her where he stood. He drew his mouth up into a satisfied grin when she hit the floor. That was going to hurt. It was her fault. If she had kept up, instead of standing around like an idiot, he wouldn't have to be rough.

"I swear to god, if I land on my knees one more time, I'm going to need corrective surgery just so I can walk straight!" She pulled her pants legs up and rubbed her kneecaps, all the while wishing for some lotion. Her skin was appalling, almost the equivalent to snake skin.

Siaak paid no attention to her moaning and left her on the floor. He proceeded through the low ceiling passages. She hurried after him. As much as she liked investigating one eerie tomb as the next person, she didn't know what was real anymore.

Each spell point he encountered, he ran his fingers over to recharge them. The multiple clanking of the reset symbols helped lead Melissa in the direction Siaak had taken. She was out of breath by the time she caught up with him.

"How many people will Jonathon have invited to this meeting?" he asked as he sent his ghost self ahead and carried on walking. Time was of the essence.

"Well, to be honest, it will be crawling with reporters anyway. That's if they aren't already here. I mean, honestly, how you were going to deal with them all is beyond me. It's not like you plan to kill them off." She said jokingly before her laughter died abruptly. "Please, tell me you aren't going to kill everyone Siaak?"

He kept telling himself she would be gone soon. No more

nagging. No more temptations. He needed to get to his brothers, quick. He needed to release them from the time spell.

What would happen to her? He pushed that thought away. What did it matter to him what happened to her? He assured himself that once she was gone he could get on with life. His jaw jutted out as he became agitated.

Melissa followed him as close as she dared. Part of her knew he was right in what he was doing. However, part of her was worried what would happen to him if the world found out he existed.

"Not now Melissa. Just answer my question. Time is limited. If I am not successful, the possibility of Osiris being found is a much greater risk; one that out-weighs killing off a few nosey reporters."

"What? I didn't say anything, I'm being quiet." Each time he ordered her to do something, it made her want to hit him over the head with a large rock. What was it with good-looking men?

"I thought you said she was trapped with your brothers?" She bent down to squeeze through another opening of yet another tunnel. She had never seen anything like this before. Most pyramids had one particular tunnel or corridor that went in one direction throughout the inner structure. There was one or two that lead off it, but nothing on the scale of this one. She watched him lead the way. His hands trailed over the walls on either side of them, until they lingered in one spot. She did a double take. "What are you doing with your hands?" She resisted a smart-ass commit that had to do with a child's story and breadcrumbs. "When did you change clothes and tie your hair back?" *I wish my hair was up out of my face. God it's hot in here!*

"Recharging spells. She is. Earlier— stand still and wait for the wind." His answers were short and straight to the point.

"What wind? We're inside a pyramid Siaak; there isn't any ventilation or windows." The wind blew across her face. Her jaw dropped open as her hair moved in the strong breeze and stayed out of her face.

He hooked his chin over his shoulder as he graced her with a lingering look that said 'she didn't know everything.'

"Okay you can control the wind, I'll admit when I'm wrong."

He shut his eyes and wished he could control her mouth.

They continued making their way through the maze of corridors. Siaak had put the pyramid on defensive mode when it was first breeched. He had to keep Melissa with him at all times. Some of the traps would cleave a man's head right off his shoulders. Mindful of those traps he pulled her close. "Watch your step and I better not catch you touching anything!"

She raised an eyebrow and opened her mouth, a question on the tip of her tongue.

"I set traps all along the main level leading to Osiris's chambers. There are a few in particular that emit a hallucinogenic mist, trust me; it is not something you would want to sample."

She was still trying to figure out why the pyramid had so many damn corridors like a maze. She opened her mouth to ask and closed it. He had left her on her own again. It was fast becoming a habit and she didn't like it! Looking left, she started to go that way when she heard his footsteps. "Hey slow down for me!"

He was looking through his ghost self when he heard her shout out to him. It was already in the main corridor leading to the exit so he commanded it to wait for further orders once it got outside.

He stopped, only to allow Melissa to catch up again. "We are here," his voice filled with relief. He turned his back to the stonewall and slipped the buttons free on his shirt. Sliding out of it, he balled the shirt up and held it out to her. "Hold onto that for me."

She took it, "what are you doing?"

"I am unlocking the door." He placed his body against the rough stone. His boots stopped at the base of the wall, aligning his shoulders just so, he waited for it. He counted down, reaching zero as the needles shot into his chest and arms.

"What door? I don't see a door."

"There will be one in a few seconds." His voice broke as the needles yanked cleanly out of his body with a sucking sound. He bit down on his lip as his muscles jerked in response.

Melissa covered her mouth with her hands as blood poured from the open wounds. There was no way this was real. She heard a tap tapping sound and looked down. "Oh my god, Siaak what have you done?"

He rested his forehead against the wall. He wondered that every time he did it. His chest heaving as he regulated his breathing. He couldn't move to reassure her. He had to stand there until enough blood flowed from his body to fill the locking spell. "There is nothing to worry about; it is how I unlock the spell that binds the door shut."

Melissa just stood there squeezing the life out of his shirt. She wanted to help him. What kind of sickos were his people? Could he be telling her the truth about everything? If he was, then she was in deep shit. "How long does it take to heal?"

"Try—" he swallowed and started again. "Try to calm yourself, I will heal in time."

He looked like he was going to pass out in her honest opinion. That is if he didn't bleed to death in the process. She had seen those needles. They were long! She was mortified that he could stand there at all. She felt like passing out, too. She could only imagine how he felt. Squinting with disgust against the whole idea, it drew her eyebrows in, forming deep lines across her forehead in revulsion. At the sight of all that blood, she heaved.

Maybe she had never left the pyramid. She must have triggered one of those booby traps and was hallucinating. A vivid picture of her body lying on the floor slumped against the wall; her dead glazed eyes stared back accusingly. That was enough to send her into a stupor.

Siaak knew how garish it looked. It hurt like hell. Worse thing was he'd already done it once today. A loss of blood wasn't fatal for his kind. The only way to replenish it was to feed from one of his brothers or his mate. It wasn't something he relished doing but one's life dictated one's actions to preserve said life.

As soon as the door materialized, he crossed the threshold to keep it open. He paused just inside the doorway, blood still pouring down his chest as he tried to focus his eyes on Melissa. For the first time in his life, he felt sick and dizzy.

Her face froze in shock. He had hoped it wouldn't affect her in such a way. He 'pulled' her close with a little magic and gently pried his shirt from her death grip. He swore at the feel of her cold hands. He held them in his, warming them, before he tried to make her snap out of it. He cupped her chin in his hand and firmly tilted her head back so he could look into her eyes. "Melissa," he spoke sharply. Her eyes moved back and forth before rolling to the back of her head.

"Shit!" He moved his hand back and slapped her cheek. The loud smack made her suck her breath in followed by a harsh cough.

His slap left a pink handprint on her right cheek. He reached out to rub it, but she jerked away from his touch. She automatically covered her face with her arms, warding off her attacker.

Siaak grabbed her arms and hauled her up against his hard chest. His eyes darted to her pulse. His tongue parted his lips in anticipation of tasting her skin before he forced his urges down. His nostrils flared as he caught her scent. And before he realized what he was doing, he traced the outline of her lips with his thumb. Such softness, would one kiss hurt? He pushed her bottom lip down and held it there as he ran the tip of his thumb across it. Running it across her teeth, he forced her jaw open as he replaced his thumb with his tongue and lips.

The second his mouth covered hers, he began to feel his energy returning. Before he realized what he was doing, he had her head between his hands as he delved deeper with his tongue. He had never experienced anything like it before in his life and it made him want it even more.

Her eyelashes fluttered open. As soon as her brain registered what Siaak was doing, she pulled away. "What were you doing?" She wiped at her tingling lips. Giving him the impression, she found the act of kissing him repulsive when he knew different.

He ran his tongue over his bottom lip savouring her taste. "Well the last time I heard it was called kissing."

"I know what a kiss is, that wasn't a kiss," she said as she wiped her mouth with the back of her hand.

"How would you know," he paused to catch his breath before he carried on, "you never allow me to finish." He unrolled his shirt and began tearing it into strips. "Here, press the wounds that are bleeding. It should stop soon." He flinched the moment she pressed the fabric to his open wounds.

"If I had, Siaak, where would it have ended?"

He knew where he wanted it to go, but he knew deep down Melissa would rather jump off a cliff than jump into bed with him.

She looked at his bleeding chest and down at hers. Just as well, she wasn't wearing white. Her navy blouse was smeared with his blood.

"If you'd get my vest, I could clean you up; or you could just rip off a local drug store," she reached out and carefully pulled the soft fabric away from his skin. "You look like someone attacked you with a metal straw."

He managed a brief smile, "Thanks, I think. I will heal soon enough." He paused for a second, his body went still and then he stepped away from her. "My ghost self has spotted a horde of people outside."

"Ghost self," she held her hand up at him as they walked through the magical doorway, "this I got to hear."

Jonathon lifted his red tie up to inspect before pulling the knot tightly up between his collars. "I hope this doesn't take too long, blasted heat–"

The flap to his tent flew open stopping him mid sentence. Light spilled inside as a woman stood there peering in. Her dark glasses hid her eyes from the harsh sun and from him. A large forest green summer hat with a dozen or so corks hung suspended by leather strips around the rim. It sat perched on top of her head until she took it off to fan herself as she walked towards him. "Good'daye Mr. Strathmore," her hand came out offering a friendly welcome.

Jonathon took in the white badge with her picture that hung from her snakeskin belt, a reporter and by her accent, Australian. He smiled and met her in the centre of the tent taking her hand straight to his lips. She flashed a toothy smile and pulled her hand back to wipe it on the back of her shorts discreetly. "Thank you. We're ready when you are." She smiled again and plonked her hat over her blond curls as she left. When she threw the flap down behind her, she grimaced and went to wash her hands.

Jonathon watched her go, admiring her ass, before he grabbed hold of his crotch to give it a good squeeze, the last thing he wanted to be remembered by was a stiff one.

He threw the fridge door open letting the cool air flow over his damp skin, wishing he had air conditioning. Grabbing a bottle of water, he slammed the door shut and went to join his adoring public.

Melissa had no choice but to follow him. She wasn't sure what to expect on the other side. Visions of a half-dressed big bosomed woman chained to a wall with fire raining down in some ill twisted version of hell, came to mind. It made Melissa cross her chest. She wasn't a religious person, but suddenly she wished for some almighty force to stand with her. Especially with Siaak's words filtering through her head. *"If Osiris gets free, I promise I will kill you myself…"*

Whatever this Osiris was, she knew Siaak wouldn't let it attack her. He had said as much, even though it was a promise to end her life. She was hoping it wouldn't have to come to that.

What was it with everyone wanting to put an end to her life anyway? The idea of it was beginning to grate on her nerves. She was a nice person. She just happened to be in the wrong place at the wrong time. If she made it through this nightmare, she was changing her wish list to a simple evening in with a good book and cup of hot chocolate.

She took note of Siaak's footsteps as he swayed back and forth, leaping and twirling through the air. He looked as if he were tap dancing and practicing kung fu at the same time. Where had he gotten the energy? Maybe he had a stash of candy bars on him.

"What are you doing, impersonating Fred Astaire or Jackie Chan?" She shouted out in her normal mocking way.

He graced her with a penetrating glare from under dark lashes that was wasted on her. "If you wish to become human confetti then you can come over here and navigate the controls for the pyramid's security system." He shouted back and turned his attentions to his feet. A low infuriated growl passed his lips at her loud dismissive "carry on" when he almost lost his balance. He had exactly two minutes to finish putting the code in. If he failed, Melissa would die. With her inner voice chatting away to him and the images coming at him from his ghost self, it took all his concentration to put in the right code.

The SandWeavers created these pyramids as prisons. Everything in it was meant to keep the BloodSeekers in and everything else out! The control panel was built into the floor and with each press of his feet, a light tap or stomp configured each square much like a combination lock. Fortunate for him, he had memorized all the codes. Problem was he had to remember the right one. With everything going on around him, he could easily slip up and put in the wrong one. Worse still, he knew what dangers lay beneath the stone floor. Twelve large round blades in constant motion revolving at over 5000rpms would instantly shred flesh and bone. It wasn't a nice way to go. Standing there directly over it like he was, made him glad he could teleport.

Once he reached the other side of the room, he felt the

blades grind to an abrupt halt, making the floor shudder. The mechanism would reset after twenty minutes. He did a few calculations in his head. "Damn, this is going to be close!" He pushed off with his back foot, propelling his body across the room at an astonishing rate. His hearts raced as his arms and legs pumped faster and faster.

Within a blink of an eye, he had reached the other side of the room where he had put Myaten and Kiros in stasis all those many years ago. He felt a rush of excitement wash over him at having them around again. He had been alone for so long that he could easily put up with their constant bickering and practical jokes, even if he happened to be at the receiving end.

It was on the tip of her tongue to ask him if he needed any help, when he turned into the Flash and zoomed across the room in a blur of brown leather. She rubbed at her eyes and blinked in rapid succession as his body appeared between the metal poles.

A chill ran down her shoulder blades making her shiver as he reached out and took the rod closest to him. She had held the one the day before they met. Then it hit her. *Oh my god, it was him!* Part of her was mad at him for making her believe she was going to be eaten by bugs. After all, he had saved her life, twice. She understood why he had done it, well to a point anyway!

She found herself looking at him. Without his shirt on, she noticed his broad shoulders and rippling muscles as he worked his arms up and down. His build resembled that of bodybuilders, or as some people called them, body sculptors. She chuckled at the idea of Siaak as the hulk, until she imagined him in shredded pants. She waved her flushed face and decided not to go there. "Is it safe for me to come to you?" she shouted between her cupped hands.

He looked over his shoulder once, "NO, stay there. It is too dangerous!"

She screwed her face up at his sharp rebuke. "Alright, so what are you doing then?"

"It is a little complicated. I am trying to open a door and allow my brothers out of the time spell around Osiris without letting her out. Any other questions I can help you with, while I try to keep us from blowing up?"

"Okay then, so, what's a ghost self?" She decided to ignore his attempt at sarcasm.

"It is one of my powers." He shouted back making the room fill with an echo that seemed to carry on for ages.

Well that explains a lot, she thought to herself. "Can you elaborate on that; I'm not a mind reader you know."

"I will elaborate," when she saw his head turn, she could well imagine that disapproving scowl of his before she heard him say, "later".

He shook his head making his hair sway across his broad shoulders. He tried to rationalize his reasons for not killing her before now. The only plausible logic was that he had lost his mind. What man could put up with her endless zest for information? Perhaps he should let her loose in the Great Library, which might shut her up for a few months.

"Okay, later is good." She nodded in agreement with herself as she watched him. It wasn't something she had to force herself to do. He had a way of moving that was perfection in motion. Although she had no idea how he could do the things he did. Now he looked like he was meditating or was that sleeping? She couldn't hear any snoring. He had to be meditating.

He shook his head at her humour as his palm rubbed against the metal staff. He imagined it was her mouth.

Can you shut up Melissa? I can't concentrate! He shouted mentally. The chatter stopped instantly. He sighed and thanked the gods for small favours.

Closing his eyes, he focused on the rod he was holding. The power contained within recoiled at his touch. White sparks darted off the metal into the pads of his fingers much like static electricity. It stung like hell but was harmless.

Melissa's head jerked up as Siaak's voice floated into her head. *Well excuse me,* she thought. *I didn't say a damn thing. I've been sitting here being good.*

I know this is all new for you, Melissa. He paused and held his anger in check. *As much as I enjoy telepathy, there is only so much one person can take of insistent chatter. So in other words, shut the hell up!*

Melissa was stunned. She didn't know she could use telepathy.

Siaak hung his head as the 'noise' from her side of the room increased. "Big mouth," he felt like kicking himself for telling her that, right when he needed silence. He knew many humans had the ability, but no means to learn how to use it. So how did she suddenly know how to use telepathy with him? He would get onto solving that puzzle after he was finished here.

Full of excitement, she looked around the room wondering where Osiris was. There were no cells in the room like she envisioned earlier. Perhaps it wasn't in this room.

The image of Siaak bleeding to open another secret door made her lip curl up in revulsion. She swivelled around to search the wall behind her from the spot she had chosen on the floor. She couldn't see or feel anything that looked remotely like a lock, but, then again, the portion of wall he had bled all over didn't have much on it either. She folded her legs Indian style and balanced her elbows on her knees, as she kept silent.

She sat there for what seemed like hours, sweat trickling down her back. She could feel the beads of water rolling down between her breasts making her navy blouse cling to her skin. Reaching down, she scratched through the material before pulling it from the waistband of her pants. Gods, she was hot all of a sudden. Her head fell back as she dug her fingernails into the skin on her hip, 'damn it itches.' She said as she turned her head to ask Siaak something. A burst of blazing light filled her line of sight. "Siaak what's happening to me?" she shouted, her voice shaky, full of uncertainty.

Siaak took time out to look behind his back and cursed even louder as he was assaulted with an overwhelming need to touch her. It made his grip tighten, turning the knuckles of his hand white from the pressure. This was going to have to stop, and soon! He shifted his weight hoping to relieve the tight fit of his leather pants against his erection. He hissed at the need to scratch as he wiggled his hips back and forth. Damn her, after this he was going to lock himself in the Great Library and locate the Tablet of Direction.

Much like a compass, it would lead the wearer to the exact spot or location of what he or she desired to find. His Lor'ship was known for travelling round the world. Knowing him as he did, the information he was looking for could be anywhere. The co-ruler of both sand races was too damned worried about the 'humans' discovering them. They had made a fundamental fuck up, as Myaten would say, by hiding their 'Ancient Knowledge.'

Once the vision ended, his heavy breathing levelled out. They were getting more and more stimulating. With his free hand, he rubbed the sweat from his face to see Melissa lying on the floor. "Melissa!"

"I can't see and I'm burning up!" A scorching heat flowed through her body. She was on fire, her body consumed by invisible flames!

Suddenly, she was thrust into a whirling tunnel of chaotic scenes. Shell shocked, Melissa couldn't believe what she was seeing. Each scene showed her with Siaak. Walking, talking, and laughing! She blushed at the rows near the end of the tunnel showing them making out! How was that possible? Was this daydream a fantasy brought on by the past 48 hours? She didn't know, but gods, she couldn't believe she was seeing this, seeing them together. She narrated what she was seeing to Siaak, up until the tunnel spun away, leaving her in a room frozen in time.

Her face blazed with embarrassment and shock. They were naked and sprawled across a pile of crushed silk draped over some kind of long plinth. Their bodies covered in a fine sheen of perspiration. His upper body settled between her legs. Siaak's tongue posed in mid lick, his intentions were clear to her, especially where he was headed, and it made her burn for his touch. She took a step back when she noticed the fang marks on her double's left breast.

She felt a jolt down her spine and time resumed itself.

Siaak looked up, searching the room. He knew someone was watching. His auburn eyes, burning liquid fire, turned dark as he caught the fresh scent and the outline of Melissa's body out the corner of his eye. Lifting his body up, he managed to catch a glimpse of her eyes before she fled into the safety of the shadows.

Do you like what you see? His mouth parted in a sly smile showing a flash of teeth before he arched his head back. His neck muscles corded under the strain. Before Melissa could utter a single sound of protest, his mouth touched her double's inner thigh, followed by the sinful lapping of his tongue.

Melissa's eyes widened with lustful fear as she felt the same trail down her inner thigh. His eyes bore into hers seconds before he bit down.

Melissa and her twin cried out. With a vertical spin, she found herself back on the hard cold floor as the fantasy or acid trip faded. Never having tried acid in her entire life led her towards the fantasy side of things.

She felt a sticky wetness down her chest and between her legs. Yanking her collar down, she pressed her chin into her neck to see. Sure enough, there were bite marks down the swell of her left breast. Pressing her fingertips against the tender skin her eyebrows rose in astonishment as the bite marks faded away.

How was that possible? Had she tripped a booby switch somewhere? Dropping her shirt, she put both hands on either side of her and lifted her butt off the floor. She gave it a swift once over and found nothing that resemble a sunken tile or depressed block. Maybe she had hit her head. Yeah, that was it.

"Hey you wanna tell me why I'm dreaming of us together, acting out a scene of Red shoe's diaries?"

"Was I any good in this scene?" He asked as he worked.

"I'm not going to answer that."

"Something tells me your answer is 'yes'." When she didn't answer straight away, he continued. "You and I need to have a long talk after I finish here."

"You aren't kidding–" Their conversation stopped when she felt the hair on her arms stand up, she rolled her eyes up. To her amazement, she witnessed her hair branching out.

Siaak mouthed the ancient spell, letting it build up and flow through his body. The white electric pulses danced up the pole, like fat in a frying pan, before arching across the room. The connections bounced from rod to rod completing the circuit. There was a brilliant flash of light followed by a loud sizzling sound as the current ricocheted off the third rod and returned to Siaak's body.

Memories flooded his senses. People dying all around him and at the centre of it, all was Osiris. He used the pain to occupy his mind. He had to keep the spell within the triangle at all costs otherwise, Osiris would be free. With his other hand, he shot a beam of energy at the ceiling. Without much effort, he constructed three clear globes and sent them hovering above his head. He released the staff embedded in the stone floor and jumped to the second rod that made up the left side of the triangle. His left hand curled tightly around it with his other arm still up in the air.

Melissa moved her head back further and saw the translucent rotating globes. She had no idea what he was doing. But, if he ever needed a job, he would make a damn fine special effects engineer.

A jolt of blue lightening hit the palm of his outstretched hand. She wondered how he could manage to stand after being hit by it.

When the bolt dissolved into his body, he immediately tensed up his muscles. The charge set off involuntary spasms on its journey through his nervous system. It took all his strength to keep his feet flat on the stone floor, allowing the energy particles to carry on until his body absorb them. He repeated it once more in order to unite all three staves. His plan was to use the globes like a secondary fence. Taking the surge of power keeping Osiris contained, as he opened a small doorway that would release his brothers.

Melissa witnessed the exchange of energy. The bluish light enclosed within the globes flickering on and off in a steady rhythm. She continued to watch Siaak as he worked each rod followed by the dancing pulsating globes. She had no clue how he used magic and bit down on her tongue to keep from asking. Then, all of a sudden, she heard a loud bang and looked up to see one of the globes had shattered, raining down shards of glass, leaving behind a ball of twirling light. Melissa covered her ears and waited, anticipating a larger explosion.

The shards of glass were drifting down like tiny snowflakes, disappearing before hitting the ground. There were a few that drifted past the metal rods. For a fraction of a second, she saw something. She wasn't sure, but it looked like a man. Whatever it was, Siaak quickly blocked her sight with his body as he moved again.

She could feel the electric current building up in the room, pinpricks against her skin and then an eerie sensation of something crawling along her arms. Nothing was there. After closer inspection, Melissa ignored the feeling and went back to watching Siaak. She was on the edge of her seat as she leaned sideways to see more. She heard a loud zapping sound that vibrated through the room and jumped when the vibration made her body shake involuntarily.

"Melissa, face the wall and cover your head until I can shield you with my body! I lost control of a sphere! Believe me, there is going to be one hell of an explosion!" Siaak explained as he sent the remaining globes down under the base of the pyramid. He had to get to Melissa before the globes blew. When he saw the blackish tint of the rods from cooling down, he knew time had run out.

She turned away as Siaak teleported across the room and threw his body over hers. She hit the wall with a thud and struggled. "Be still!" he shouted.

She could barely hear his voice as the room filled with loud booms! She settled her body against his. Was this the end for them? Before she could speak out, a second explosion penetrated the room from the ground up.

He wrapped his arms around her waist and tugged hard as he felt the floor rise and fall under their feet when the last two globes blew. He knew the backlashes from the spell would cause damage to the structure of the pyramid. The last thing he needed was a wall containing two-ton blocks landing on her or the floor caving in!

He was sure the spell hadn't worked. But having never tried the spell on his own. He blamed her for it! Killing her now would not release them nor would it help matters. The world knew about the Black Pyramid. There was nothing he could do to stop it. Maybe if he put some distance between them, the visions would stop. He could deal with that. 'Liar', he thought.

The sound of rocks falling caught his attention. He shifted his body backwards and pushed off the floor with every ounce of strength he had. Everything seemed to move in slow motion. Melissa felt his arms tighten even more. At this rate, he was going to crack a rib if he wasn't careful. Then they were sailing through the air and landed with a wild bone-breaking skid across the floor before rolling to a stop in a tangle of legs and arms.

Melissa coughed so hard, she thought her lungs had ruptured. Eyes streaming, she waved her hands as if that alone would clear the smoke from the room.

"You okay?" Siaak asked his voice full of concern.

Melissa coughed again and nodded. "I think it's time to quit smoking, what about you?" She joked while trying to ignore his hard body pressed up close to hers.

"I do not smoke."

"That's not what I meant and you know it." Their eyes

locked. His head lowered to her moist lips and all he could think about was savouring them. "I could use a bath," his lashes swept up as he took in the soft brown of her eyes, his head moved closer. "...something to drink..." *And I want to sleep with you,* was on the tip of his tongue as he gently rubbed his lips against her cheek. All he had to do was tilt his head down a fraction and her mouth was his.

"Is this a bad time? We can come back later?"

Nervously they jerked apart at the deep voice. Siaak rolled off her and jumped to his feet. He helped her to stand up before he turned towards the voice.

Melissa saw two dark silhouettes moving towards them through the plumes of grey smoke. They had to be the brothers Siaak kept referring too. Out the corner of her eye, she saw Siaak wave his arms. The thick smoke was sucked backward leaving the circle they were standing in free.

She could see and breathe much better now.

"Melissa, this is Myaten and Kiros, my brothers." The smile on his face told her his feelings were genuine as he introduced her to them.

Melissa looked from one to the other and back up at Siaak. "What are they, Mummies?" Siaak actually cracked a smile at her well-placed joke.

"Those wrappings kept them safe while in stasis." At her raised eyebrows, he stopped. "Yes, another long story, and one I can tell you later. I promise." He walked over to the men and began unwinding. Melissa watched as he carefully rolled away the coffee colored bandages from the tallest man first.

"Do you need any help Siaak?" She moved to the side so she could catch a glimpse of the man's face. She took in a deep breath as a pair of striking green eyes stared right at her.

"I am fine, thank you, Melissa." He quickly removed the

wrappings around Myaten's head and moved over to Kiros who was trying to be clever and do it by himself. "I got it Kiros hold still."

A deep rumble erupted from the thick bandages as Kiros shook his head. She was sure she heard him say something like, "I'll do it my damn self." However, she couldn't be certain.

Siaak carried on as if he hadn't heard Kiros's muffled curses until he had managed to reveal Kiros's chiselled cheekbones, jaw and chin which were covered in fine dark hair. The right side of his face was covered in a strange silver scar. By the time she realized she was openly staring, she quickly cast her eyes downwards— it was too late. His blue eyes were freed of the bandages and his glare cut her down to size before she had a chance to apologize.

She suddenly felt out of place. All she wanted was to go home. To sleep in her bed, but reality told her that wasn't going to happen. Not sure where to look, she caught a glimpse of the blue eyed sandy blond haired man as he gave her the once over. As if she had suddenly grown a third eye or something, Kiros turned away as he continued to uncover his arms. He looked like a boxer taking his gloves off with the wrapping hanging from around his wrists. It reminded her of the boxing hand tape her brother used when he boxed in high school.

Melissa watched with fascination as Myaten moved into her line of sight. He flashed her an award winning smile as he ruffled his black hair making it stand up on top before his wrappings began to unwind on their own. Thin strips of fabric floated down to the floor and when Melissa glanced up her eyes bugged out. "Oh my god, Siaak," She slapped her eyes shut with her hands. "You could've warned me they were butt naked!"

Myaten graced her with a sexy smile that lit up his eyes as

Siaak planted his body between them. "Myaten, you did that on purpose." Siaak accused as he braced his arms across his chest and waited for a damn good explanation.

"Hey, I just woke up, don't blame me." Myaten turned and strutted off into the white cloud and vanished.

Dressed in black jeans and a black hoody sporting a white Chinese dragon, Kiros bowed low before embracing Siaak with a hard hug and a loud smack against his back.

Siaak winced; the holes through his chest hadn't healed yet. He pulled a face at the pain as a few on his chest and back tore open when he rescued Melissa. Before he could object, Melissa was at his side, like a good Samaritan. She began to explain to Kiros what had happened.

"He needs medical attention. I don't care what he says. I'm taking him to a hospital. Will you help me?" She pleaded at the strange man that looked nothing like Siaak. How they could be brothers was beyond her.

"Melissa, there is no cause for panic. I will heal in a few hours. Besides, Jonathon is giving his speech. The world will know of the Black Pyramid soon and my place is here."

"We can move Osiris to another location, Siaak." Myaten walked out of the cloud fully clothed. He looked as if he'd had a shower. His black hair was styled and gelled to the max in the latest fashion. He was sporting combat kakis and a bright orange tank top that said 'lick this'. How could he have possibly done all that in the last few minutes? And where had he gone to do it?

With Siaak being able to teleport, she figured it wasn't beyond the realms of possibility for his brothers to have special powers. She wondered what they could do, but figured right now wasn't the best time to ask.

Myaten walked past their little group, until he was

standing near a series of hieroglyphics. Melissa swore she hadn't seen those there before their release.

He licked his index finger and traced the surface of the sun disc at the top of the cartouche. He glanced at Melissa as he pushed it into the wall with his middle finger. The smoke was filtered from the room in next to no time, sucked out through hidden holes in the ceiling. As Myaten rejoined them, the sound of stone moving reached her ears.

"What about rearranging the rooms inside?" Kiros asked as he stepped back to have a good look at his older brother. "You do need blood, don't argue, Siaak."

Siaak raised his hand making a cutting motion across his throat, "No, now is not the time." He murmured out the side of his mouth.

Kiros's frown deepened, "But you are weak," he bent down on one knee and pulled his hood from his head as he tugged his collar down baring a deeply tanned shoulder. "It is my duty, as your brother, to restore your energy."

Melissa cocked an eyebrow at that and gave Siaak a knowing look that said 'I knew it!' She patted his arm as she stood on tiptoe and reached up to whisper in his ear, "What you got to say now, Count?"

Myaten looked from one to the other and flashed a big smile. "I bet Kiros you'd find your woman in this century."

"Find your woman?" Melissa clenched her teeth. Her hands braced on her hips as she glared daggers at them. "You wanna explain that one to me, Siaak?"

He stared silently at Myaten before he looked at Melissa. "I have no idea what he is talking about."

"Don't go there Siaak. Don't lie to me."

Siaak pushed her away. "Myaten take her home, I'm too weak to do it myself. She needs food and rest."

He nodded without question and reached out for Melissa.

She stepped out of his way. If looks could kill, he'd have died right there on the spot. "I'm not moving from this damn spot until one of you explains to me what is going on here!" She looked at each of them in turn.

"Why won't you go to the hospital? And if you aren't a vampire, why is he," she pointed at Kiros who was still on his knees offering his bare neck to Siaak. "...shoving his neck in your face? And don't even try any gay shit on me. It won't work either. You've been fucking me with your thoughts, teasing me from the beginning, so don't try to hide it now because your brothers are here."

Myaten choked on air. Kiros managed a slight smile that never quite reached his blue eyes.

Siaak rubbed his temples, how was he going to explain to her that all of this was foreign territory to him? "I am not hiding anything from you, Melissa. We are SandWalkers and as such, we feed from one another. It is how our race eats and how we replace lost blood."

"So you drink blood, which makes you vampires!" She raised her arms in triumph.

"I do not recall telling you anything about myself, Melissa. Our species do not drink the blood of another living creature. It is forbidden outside our people, a taboo subject, one that is considered a crime punishable by death."

Melissa laced her fingers together as she stood looking from one face to another. "How do I know you speak the truth, Siaak? You bit me and I felt drained…"

"I can only apologise for that Melissa, it will not happen again. I vow on my life—"

"Only because your brothers are here and can feed you." She uncrossed her arms in a cutting motion. "Look, I don't care what you guys do. If you want to neck amongst yourselves, then be my guest. All I want to know is what this Osiris is. Why have you kept her, it, locked away inside this pyramid? You took me against my will and threatened to kill me for trespassing when Jonathon and I explored the inside of the Black pyramid. You owe me an explanation."

Siaak opened his mouth to speak when he was cut off.

"Osiris is the leader of the BloodSeekers. She's very dangerous and, if let loose in this era, she'll cause massive destruction and chaos not seen since Hitler tried to rule the world." Myaten spoke with such sincerity that Melissa found it hard to form a decent argument in return.

"He speaks the truth," Kiros added as he stood up.

"So what now, Siaak," she looked around the room, not sure what was going to happen to her. In the past two days, her life had been turned upside down. He wanted her to forgive everything he had said and done by accepting his apology. No, he was going to have to do more than that!

"You need to go home and get some rest. Myaten will see to it..."

"At least have the decency to do it yourself," she fired off at him. He shook his head 'no' at her idea. If he went back with her, he would regret it.

"I'm not going anywhere without you. What about the person in the car park that tried to run us down? He might try it again, then where will I be? You said you'd keep me safe," her voice filled with resentment and anger.

He looked down at her, itching to run his fingers through her hair. Wishing things could have been different for them. He captured her face between his hands and whispered. "I killed the assassin." He searched her brown eyes, half expecting her to blow up at him. He didn't mind her ranting about ethics and how it was wrong to kill. It showed she was a good person. Instead, she stood there just staring at him as if she'd lost control of her faculties. "Are you going to kill Jonathon?"

Her voice wasn't full of the normal rancour or accusations he had sampled in the last two days concerning her 'friend'. He had to wonder if she had finally accepted the truth. At his stiff nod, she closed her eyes and swallowed the lump in her throat. She knew she had to ask him one more question. "Are you still planning to kill me?"

Her pulse raced when he didn't answer. Would he tell her the truth? He had no reason to lie to her. He had saved her life on more than one occasion. Yes, he had killed but that didn't make him a murderer did it? Surely if it was self-defence, that meant he was one of the good guys. Policemen did it. They didn't go to jail for killing to protect the innocents or themselves.

Her mind filled with all the questions she would be faced with upon her return. Where had she been for two whole days? There was her short stay in hospital. How was she going to explain her way out of that one? She could say she lost her way out in the desert and Siaak had found her.

He would have to face the same reporters that were gathered outside, getting ready to tell the world about the Black Pyramid. Would he want that? To be labelled a hero and be subjected to the intense speculation of opinions brought on by the big shots that ruled daytime television. She knew the answer to that one as well.

Then, there was Jonathon. He would know she was lying. He really wasn't her friend. After all these years, why had he changed? Then it hit her! He wanted to be Howard Carter! He wanted famed and fortune. Siaak's words drifted back to her.

"Tell me something, do you want fame and fortune out of this find..."

She had been so stupid. He wasn't going to kill her because she wasn't in it for the glamour and status it would bring her, Jonathon was.

"No. I am letting you go."

Her eyes flew open at his declaration. "What about the dream I had of us? What does it all mean?" She really wanted to know as she pulled him along with her. It was silly, all this time they had been alone. Now when she wanted privacy the most, she had two brooding men staring at her as if she was going to attack Siaak with a meat cleaver.

Siaak sent his brothers a quick message asking them to give them some time alone. Siaak waited for Myaten and Kiros to go on patrol before he spoke. "I have no idea what the visions mean other than the obvious, Melissa."

The sudden explosion of heat within his eyes made her feel uncomfortable. He had a knack of staring at her in a way that made her feel like he was crawling under her skin. The power within those amber eyes flickered with untold secrets.

She felt drawn to him. Was he using magic on her? It was hard to tell. She wanted to stay with him. She wanted him to teach her to read the beautiful writings that littered the walls of his home. She wanted him to make love to her. Who would have thought that? Two days ago, she wanted to push him in front of a bus, shove sticks of dynamite down his pants! What was wrong with her?

"Why do I get the feeling, this is your way of saying good bye, Siaak?"

Siaak lifted his hand and gently raked his fingers against the curve of her neck. He needed to feed soon; otherwise, it might be good-bye, forever. Shaking his head, he summoned Myaten to the room. Myaten came up behind her and at Siaak's sharp nod they vanished from sight.

Siaak wanted to go after her. Something inside him demanded it. Instead, he ignored the urgent need to have her in his arms, to hold her close.

His head jerked around as Kiros entered the doorway. Siaak crossed the room in one stride, his body flying to meet Kiros with his mouth open wide.

Kiros raised his arm to lower his cowl when Siaak jerked Kiros's wrist up to his mouth and sank his fangs into the deep vein that ran the entire length of his arm. To replenish his blood loss took no longer than four heartbeats between them. Siaak's fangs retracted and shifted to the front of his teeth as he began to feed on the real source of energy that could only be gained between two SandWalkers.

Siaak felt his energy returning. The holes in his chest had healed now. The only indications of the wounds were the bloodstains on his skin. Once his energy was replenished, his fangs automatically retracted. The tiny marks closed up and faded away before Siaak lifted his head. "Thank you, Kiros, I needed that. I was dangerously close to proving her right."

Kiros nodded "Well, in a way, she is right."

"Please, not you too; it was bad enough with her commenting on my fangs and sucking her dry."

Kiros threw his head back and roared with laughter. Still laughing at his older brother, Kiros clapped him on the back. "So tell me, who is this Jonathon?"

Siaak's ghost self witnessed the media coverage of the most astounding find since Howard Carter's discover of Tutankhamen in nineteen hundred and twenty-two. It was too late for him to do anything, so he stood in with the crowd to see what crap came out of Jonathon's mouth.

Flashes of light sprinkled from the crowd of reporters from all over the world. Pictures were taken as live footage of the Black Pyramid was beamed all over the world via satellites.

Jonathon put on his professional face as he stood in front of the cameras. His coy laugh turned into a cough, disguising his total amusement with the media. They were so predictable and easy to manipulate. "At the back, in the red shirt," he placed his hands on the table waiting for the barrage of questions.

"James Quinn, World News. How did you find it?"

Jonathon fought back his sarcastic nature and beamed a fake charming smile. "Well, I have to be truthful Quinn, it was a complete fluke. The United States Military were testing some new sonar for their desert ground vehicles. I don't know all the particulars, but that is how it was found. You in the front row," he pointed to a woman in a white summer dress.

"Thank you." She held her Dictaphone up before she spoke, "We were told two people excavated the pyramid, an American woman and yourself. Is that correct?"

His icy glare turned to one of sudden sadness. "My colleague has, unfortunately, disappeared. She was last seen at a private hospital being treated for dehydration. I have informed the local authorities and I've been assured that they are doing all they can to locate her."

He wiped his brow and quickly opened his bottle of water. He took a few mouthfuls before he was ready to take another question.

"Is the Black pyramid cursed?"

"Is it an alien ship?"

Jonathon spat his water out. "Who concocted such a ridiculous idea?" He was met with more flashing lights and blinked at all the microphones being pushed into his face. "No. There is no such thing. We live in a time where people are highly educated. Don't let the myths of the past convey those same narrow minded views." He glared at everyone as he shook his head in rejection "It is not an alien space ship either, nor a government plot to hide information!" He held up his hands, "that is all I'm prepared to answer. If anyone wants a more in depth interview, book an appointment with my secretary. Good evening." He threw his arm out to show off the black monster behind him before making his exit.

Back in his tent, he tried calling David. There was no answer, which told him one thing; he'd have to find another method of disposing of them.

Melissa remained silent as Myaten teleported her outside. "You know, I can call a taxi or a camel. It's not far, really." She snuck a glimpse over her shoulder, hoping to see Siaak coming after her. After the fourth time, she stopped looking back.

Myaten laughed at her humour as he shoved a pair of Ray bands over his eyes. "I like that, very funny. My brother's wishes are my commands. I don't mind taking you home." He carried on walking until they were well past the Giza pyramid.

She was beyond the point of sweating, her wet hair plastered to her neck and jaw. Not to mention, her pantsuit was soaking wet and clinging to every inch of her body like a second skin. Thirsty didn't describe the craving she felt, even her skin felt dehydrated. She was positive she could drink a gallon of water. If Siaak had been there, he would have made sure she wasn't suffering like this.

"How long does this tour take?" she asked sarcastically when she tripped up. "Who in their frigging mind leaves a bag buried out in the middle of nowhere- wait a damn minute? That's my bag!"

Falling to her knees, she clawed the sand off the expensive backpack. The zipper gleamed in the sunlight as she grabbed hold of it and pulled. "Oh thank you, God!" she said shaking two bottles of cold water in her hands as she danced around kicking sand in her excitement. She flopped back on her butt cradling the bag between her legs. Sipping on the cold water, she reached inside the bag again to find a pair of sunglasses, a hat, and a tube of sunscreen along with fresh fruit. "Would you like some? She asked offering him an orange. He took it and thanked her. "Either I am going crazy or I think this is my bag. Only thing is, it didn't have all this in it." Looking up at Myaten, she waited for an explanation.

"You had need of it; otherwise Siaak wouldn't have sent it to you."

She wasn't sure if she could deal with that. After all, he had sent her away.

Myaten didn't give her time to dwell on it. He turned without another word, peeling the citrus fruit as they continued on their journey.

Melissa popped a grape in between her teeth and savoured the sweet juice as it burst inside her mouth. She offered some to her silent tour guide, but he was so intent on taking her home that he hardly spoke to her.

She couldn't guess how long they had been walking. She was thankful for the fashionable sunglasses and the wide brimmed hat that kept her head cool. She was applying some sunscreen when she ploughed into Myaten's back.

"Take my hand, please," he offered politely. She knew

better than to argue. She really wanted to go back to the hotel room and have a shower. Then, she was going to give Jonathon a piece of her mind!

She offered him her hand and held onto her pack so she didn't leave it behind again. Hoping she'd see Siaak again, she closed her eyes against the sudden jerk and away she went.

She was slowly getting used to the feel of being teleported here, there and everywhere. The change in temperature was more a shock to the system than popping in and out of view. Hot to cold made her body go into shock.

"Don't worry, I've got cha."

Melissa didn't make the same mistake twice. She held on for dear life, hoping this would be the end to her wild ride.

She tried to open her eyes and wondered who was screaming. As her consciousness rejoined her body, she realized it was her, as she crumpled to the floor in a heap.

Hours came and went before she stirred. She blinked trying to focus her eyes on the blobs of color. "Where am I?" She moaned as she pushed herself up to a sitting position. Shifting around on the floor, she waited for the blobs of color to focus into something she could recognize.

Moving her arms out to keep her balance, she dropped her bag and jumped out of her skin. She had no reference of time. She wasn't sure how long she had to get her story straight before her run in with Jonathon. While she waited, she decided to go over it in her head.

Instead, she found herself thinking of Siaak. Will I see him again? She didn't think so. The prospects of having to lie about him made her angry.

Rushing to her feet brought on a wave of dizziness. In order to keep from falling over, she reached out, smacking her hands on something hard. She managed to hang on.

"Myaten!" she screamed out his name.

Shaking her head, she lowered her face. With a rush of heat up her body, everything merged into perfect clarity. Looking around in total shock, she couldn't believe it! The bastard had taken her all the way home! Panicking, she ran for the phone. Squeezing the receiver in her hands, she stared at it in horror. He doesn't own a phone. "Damn!" She slammed the phone down as she made her way back through the house in a huff.

"How could I be home?" She glanced down at herself and realized that during her trip home, she had wet herself. Great! She thought, as she walked with anger in her stride. Slinging her arms out by her head, she couldn't believe this shit! She was so mad she could spit nails!

Once she stepped in her bathroom, she stripped off. In the shower, she scrubbed her body in angry jerks until her skin turned a deep red. It was then she noticed the faint lines on her left hip. Water dripping off her chin; she wondered where that had come from. She stretched up to put her soap and wash cloth away when it began to burn.

It was the only warning she was given before she was hurdled back against the tiles. Her body was engulfed in heavy petting. Invisible hands stroked down her body and paused at the mark on her hip before continuing.

Melissa cried out in dismay as she was flung around to face the tiled wall. Her cheek hurt under the pressure of a hand against the back of her head. She didn't know what was going on. She felt the hair on the back of her neck stand up as something heavy pressed hard against her back. This wasn't good! "Siaak, where are you? I need you!" She sobbed against the wet tiles, her body shaking with hurt and fear. "What is happening to me…please, someone, help me before I lose my mind…."

Instantly, the pressure evaporated and the burning turned to an itch. Melissa stood against the wall, too afraid to move. Was it another poltergeist? If so, she had no hope in hell of fighting it off—

I want you Melissa...I need you to come to me... Siaak's voice interrupted her thoughts of terror.

Melissa felt herself being tugged around to face an empty space. She reached out with her fingers and shivered as her hands past through empty air. "Siaak?" she spoke his name softly. Not sure if what she had just experienced was real or a figment of her hidden desire to have sex with him. She stood there with the water running down her body waiting for him to touch her again, but nothing happened.

Turning the water off, she climbed out and found herself staring into nothing, like some stupid love sick puppy. Nothing seemed to take her mind off Siaak. She wandered into the kitchen leaving a trail of wet footprints behind her as she sat down.

She struggled to get up. It wasn't until she spilled hot coffee on her hand that she snapped out of it. What had he done to her? Running cold water over her hand she relaxed, it wasn't a bad burn. Might hurt for a little while, but it wouldn't blister.

After she cleaned up her mess, she poured another cup of coffee and opened the fridge to find it empty. "No milk, great." *Of course, there was no milk stupid, you were in Egypt!* Palming the door shut, she dug through rows of tin cans until she found some powder milk.

After heaping half a bag of sugar in her mug, she made her way to her bedroom. It was like a match box compared to the one at Siaak's. She sat her mug down on the nightstand by her bed and stared off into space. The chime of her grandfather clock broke the trance. Her hands went to her face, she felt flushed almost feverish. Crawling across the comforter, she flipped over, sunk into her pillows, and cried. Her last thoughts were full of dread and disbelief, why did she feel so alone?

Siaak paused in the middle of retrieving a silver scroll from the top of a glass shelf in his office, when Myaten appeared behind his back. "Is she okay?" Siaak asked without looking at Myaten.

"She's pissed at you if that's what you want to know?" Myaten answered truthfully. No point in hiding it from him. "And I don't think she likes me that much now, either." Myaten walked ahead of his brother nabbing an apple on the way. "Oh! The next time you get a brain wave…," he rubbed the shiny red fruit against his jean-covered thigh. "…don't come to me."

Siaak nodded, "Yes, it would seem I owe you both an apology." Siaak tucked the silver scroll under his arm and sat down behind his desk.

"You can have tonight off. Kiros is keeping watch. I, on the other hand, will go and apologise to Melissa. I have not exactly been overly nice to her and I am against the idea of her being anywhere near Jonathon Strathmore."

"I take it, you don't like him?" Myaten teased as he tossed the apple into the air sending it spinning around before he reached up and caught it square in his palm.

Siaak graced him with a callous look. "I would have ended his life just like that!" He clicked his thumb and finger together making a snapping sound before he slapped the palm of hand down on his desk in frustration, "…she honestly thinks he is her friend and I have been unsuccessful in making her see sense. However," his eyes turned jet black, "I can make his life a living hell and he will wish he were dead."

He sighed, "I wish we were back in the old days, Myaten. I could have thrown him to the BloodSeekers and let them deal with him."

He stood up, tapping his fingers on the desk as he walked around it. "No, I have to bring her here. I could never live with myself if I allowed that bastard to touch her! I can collect her things from the hotel later."

Myaten opened his mouth placing his teeth against the skin of the apple to bite into it and paused. He held the fruit in his hand as he pointed at Siaak. Myaten didn't know what he was talking about. "What hotel? Siaak, you never mentioned a 'hotel' you said, "take her home." He put the apple back in his mouth and bit down.

Siaak placed the silver scroll down on top of his desk without making a sound before he sat back in his leather chair, "Myaten where did you take Melissa?"

Myaten took another large bite and chewed. His jaw working overtime as he made sure he chewed it up before answering, "I took her home like you asked."

"I did not mean literally "her home" I meant to take her back to the hotel."

Still chewing he gave his brother a nonchalant look. "Well, then I guess I'll go back and get her, but you get to do all the explaining."

"NO, you stay here. I will go and get her myself."

Myaten sucked in the last piece of apple, surprised at his brother's unusual concern over a woman. It caught him completely off guard. A fit of coughing made his face turn beet red. In order to dislodge it from his throat, he fisted his chest. "Now I know you're serious about her." His face screwed up as he managed to swallow the lump of fruit.

"I promised I would protect her." He stopped at Myaten's raised hand, 'What?'

"No that's not officially true big brother. You told her you would kill her before Osiris could torture her to death."

"That is the one thing I hate about you, nothing is ever a secret around you." Siaak didn't mask the irritation in his voice. "You can do *my* patrol while I am gone, so no running off to play pranks on Kiros."

A mischievous twinkle lit up his green eyes as he flashed from the room, his apple core bounced off Siaak's desk and landed in the trash can.

Siaak was more than angry with his brother, he was livid. A simple mistake, yes, but it was Melissa's life at stake. And make no mistake, he would not allow Jonathon to harm her.

Standing up, he walked across the floor, a brief touch of his pendant and he teleported straight to Cairo International airport via the only fully functional Obelisk there.

Reaching out across the wide expanse of water that separated his homeland from hers, he blinked out of existence, and then back again. What was he thinking? She was safer there than here with him. Laughing aloud, Siaak was pleased that he had inadvertently foiled Jonathon's plans to kill her. He would never think to look for Melissa in the good old US of A.

As he made his way home, he flashed to her hotel room long enough to gather her things. Standing in her room, he remembered how they had met. She almost took his head clear off his shoulders. Smiling at that, he waved his arm around the room and all her things appeared in a heap on the bed. His eyes darted over her personal effects. How had she managed to pack all of that in two suitcases?

His eyes drifted over shoes, clothes, magazines, makeup

and other personal effects. Picking up one of the various colored bottles, he pressed it and a mist filled the air, instantly he recognized her scent. He capped the bottle and placed it on the bed.

His knuckles skimmed over her soft white robe and the pile of silk panties, he picked up a thong with his thumb. It was nothing more than a strand of pale pink lace. Without thinking, he placed it over his nose. Her scent was faint, and as he stood there next to her bed, he felt his mark burn. He hissed and dug the heel of his palm into his hip as he doubled over in pain.

Everything went dark around him. Then he felt hot water against his skin. The scent of clean soap met his nose before her naked body shimmered into view. Without thinking, he shoved her against the wall and allowed himself the pleasure of touching her wet soapy body.

She had cut him deep. His need for her had become an obsession!

With that, he flipped her body around and rammed his hard erection against her. He wanted her to feel, to know how much he wanted her. He was so hard and ready for her. His fangs burst free as he held her head still. Then everything came to a sudden stop.

She was crying. Why was she crying? He moved away from her. Disgust written all over his face, he waited for her to shout at him. He heard his name on her lips. It tore at him. The fear in her voice made him call out to her. 'Melissa, come to me..."

The last thing he saw was her reaching for him and then he found himself standing at the foot of the bed. His hair wet and plastered to his face as well as his clothes. The marker on his hip itched so much he felt like digging into it with a knife, if he had one.

Not sure what just happened, he gathered up everything and returned home. He stored her bags in her room and left it as quick as he had entered it.

CHAPTER FOUR

Melissa woke to a loud persistent ring, *damn clock; I was having a wonderful dream,* she thought as she opened her eyes. She laid there with her head on the pillow not batting an eyelash. Listening to the sound of the alarm clock from beneath the white cotton blanket, she flicked her eyes in the direction of the annoying sound.

Her head and arm poked out from under the cover, making her hair stand on end. In one fluid move, she swiped the small digital alarm clock off the nightstand, yawned and threw the cover back over her head. Smiling with smug satisfaction, her eyelashes drifted down as she fell back into a deep sleep.

A few minutes later... *What's that sound? The phone? No, can't be the phone. I'll ignore it.* She stretched, yawned and scratched exactly in that order, the morning rituals to waking up. She lay there for a while, her eyes barely open. Her arms slid across the crumpled cotton sheet, the familiar lemon scent made her smile at first until she realized something important.

I'm home. I'm home? "I'M HOME!" she sat upright and fell off the bed hitting the floor in a giant heap. Fumbling around for the end of the blanket, she grabbed it with both hands and dragged it off her body with a loud angry shriek.

Immediately her attention was drawn to the built in

aquarium above the bed, the bubbling sound barely audible against the loud insistent ringing of the phone. Her eyes settled on the phone and then she spotted her black coffee mug. That's when it hit her. "It wasn't a dream. The bastard sent me home!"

She grabbed a pillow that had escaped the plunge off the bed, pressed her face into it and screamed as loud as she could. When she was done, she tossed it to the floor behind her bed. She climbed to her feet and gave the quilt a few kicks before turning her anger on the irritating phone. The small display screen showed unknown caller. Baring her teeth at it, she kicked another pillow across the room to land with a soft thud as it hit the wall.

She flopped to her knees scraping them across the carpet as she covered her mouth with her fingertips. Gods she was losing it. How long she sat there was anybody's guess. Suddenly her eyes opened wide as she realized she was drifting off again. "I'm in a bad way, I need some serious caffeine!"

She got back up and marched through her house stopping long enough to pee, flush and wash her hands. She would tackle her teeth after she started a pot of coffee. Then she remembered she didn't have any milk. So she back tracked to the bathroom.

Grabbing her toothbrush in one hand, she slammed it against the side of the sink. *"How could I be so stupid?"* She squirted some toothpaste on her brush and waved it around furiously as she imagined stabbing Siaak with it before turning it on Myaten. Then she smirked, somehow fluoride toothpaste didn't seem a fitting end to the two little conniving male shits! She envisioned a pool of acid with them both dangling by their legs. Laughing evilly as she slowly cranked the wheel, releasing the tension on the chains that was tied around their ankles. She stood there with a wicked smile on her face as she enjoyed their screams, begging for her forgiveness.

She was torn out of her evil plotting by the phone. Swearing, as she was enjoying her revenge fantasy, she snapped her teeth together. Growling she cleaned her toothbrush after she attacked her teeth and gums. Rinsing her mouth, she stooped over the sink to make sure she removed all the left over foam. Lifting her head to look in the mirror, she almost jumped out of her skin. Siaak's image stared back at her. His mouth moving as he faded from view. She was pretty sure he mouthed 'phone', but she wasn't sure of anything anymore.

"I'm going crazy," her voice just a notch away from hysteria as she threw her arms up in the air.

Out the corner of her eye, she caught sight of the offending pantsuit. She dropped her toothbrush in the sink and walked over to the tub. She reached down and grabbed the outfit off the floor where she'd left it last night. Huffing and puffing, she balled it up before dumping it in the hamper basket. Even though it was out of sight, it made her think of him. She kicked it, imagining it was Siaak's balls, not that it made her feel any better. All it did was put a nice hole in the wicker. Shaking her hair out behind her, she finished up in the bathroom and decided to get dressed.

She was going out to get some fresh air and milk. Keys in one hand, doorknob in the other, she paused when the phone rang again. What was it with the constant ringing? If it was so damn important the caller could leave a message, she wasn't going to answer it.

She didn't feel like talking to anyone and besides, she was supposed to be in Egypt.

Standing on her doorstep, she looked around her front

yard thinking the grass needed mowing. For the first time, she took in how green and lush it was. She put that down to being in a giant sandbox for a week. It was bound to make anyone appreciate dirt, grass and weeds. Yawning, she tried to shake the lethargic feeling. She couldn't understand why she was so damn tired. It was like trying to move through thick sludge. Each step she took seemed to take forever as she made her way around the side of the house to the garage.

Once she was in her car, she pressed the remote to open the garage door. As she sat there in the driver's seat, she felt a tingle near her hip but ignored it until she pulled the sun visor down and saw Siaak's eyes staring right back at her. She palmed it shut and sucked in a deep breath. "Yes! I'm losing my marbles." She spied the rear view mirror and instantly turned it away. And with a push of a button, the side mirrors folded in toward the doors. If this carried on, she'd have no choice but to see a therapist. With that on her mind, she paid little attention to where she was going until she pulled up to her favourite mini market and parked the car.

She always found shopping therapeutic, but somehow even that couldn't take her mind off what she now knew. Part of her wanted to call her best friend Brenda, but what would she tell her.

Brenda while I was in Egypt, I helped solve the secret behind the Black Pyramid. Oh! And a man named Siaak, the keeper of the pyramid took me hostage for a few days. He offered to do me more times than I can remember. Saved my life because I'm marked by a former friend of the family and, did I mention, he's a vampire? No? Well he is and, to be totally honest, I let him bite me.

"Do you need any help?"

Melissa looked up, her cheeks flaming as she realized she

was standing in the middle of the isle staring at the floor. "No, thanks…" she beamed a gracious smile and quickly added a bottle of Coke, some Oreos and a gallon of milk to the few items already in her basket. At the cash register, she glanced up at the security mirror.

She dropped her basket. It made a loud whack as it hit the floor. Staring right back at her was Siaak, his mouth moved as he raised a finger in her direction. She whirled around but there wasn't anyone standing at the back of the store. "Yep, I've lost it for sure! Melissa, honey, you've gone stark raving mad!"

She grabbed her basket off the floor and managed a tight smile at the suspicious look on the woman's face behind the counter ringing up her groceries. *Even she thinks I'm off my rocker,* Melissa thought as she paid for her items and almost ran back to her car.

The drive home seemed to take forever. All she could think about was Siaak. Standing by her front door, she could hear the phone ringing. She just managed to unlock the door, drop the bags by her feet and make a mad dash for the phone. "Hello, hello, who is this?"

No answer, just silence.

Melissa put the phone back on the base. Staring at it for the longest time, she shrugged her slender shoulders. But each time she turned in the direction of her kitchen, she whirled around to glare at the phone, expecting it to ring again. When it didn't, she left it.

After she unpacked her groceries, she put a new pot of coffee on to brew. As she stood watching the coffee drip into the glass pot, she realized just how boring her life was. She wanted to go back. No matter how hard she tried to deny it, she wanted to know more about him.

She banged her fist against the counter top "I don't have

my passport! So I can't go back. Bastard. He made sure I was stuck here." She couldn't register it stolen, and try to explain to the authorities how she got home without it in the first place. Well, she could if she wanted to end up in a rubber room with a cocktail of drugs running through her veins.

While she waited for the coffee to finish, she slipped on a pair of grey cosy pants and a baggy t-shirt. Then grabbed the laptop off the nightstand, switched it on and while it was loading up, she made a quick cup of coffee. "That's good," she said out loud. So there she sat, cross-legged on top of the bed, alone, staring at a blank screen. She looked over her right arm, willing the phone to ring and hoping it would be him.

Minutes went by and then she jumped at the first ring. Her skin turned goose pimply down both arms and the hair on the back of her neck stood up making her shiver. Reaching across the nightstand, she picked up the receiver and swallowed once before placing it next to her ear. "Hello," she tried to make her voice sound normal.

"For someone that carries a phone with them, it sure takes you a fucking long time to answer!"

She slammed the phone down. How did he get her number? Better yet, why was he swearing? She should be the one cursing like a sailor. He tricked me! The phone started ringing again. She choked. The caller display read: PICK UP MELISSA. How could she forget! It was the magic thing again. Sighing, she jerked the phone off the bedside table, "what do you want?"

"I wanted to hear your voice."

"What happened to, Oh! You can hear me from anywhere in the world?"

"I did not want to scare you."

"And seeing you in every god damned mirror isn't scary, Siaak? I thought I was losing my mind.

When his words broke up, she had to strain to make out what he was saying. "Siaak, I can't hear you."

"I said there is a sand storm heading our way. I will be unable to keep the connection for too long, it drains my powers."

She sat up and blinked as his words entered her mind. She cleared her throat as she quickly ran her tongue over her lips and spoke, "You aren't using a phone are you?"

"No."

Her hands began to shake. Was it the sound of his voice inside her head or the fact that she was talking to him on a phone connected to thin air?

"Melissa, I am sorry. Myaten mistook my words and returned you home. I want you to know that I was coming after you."

His confession made her heart do a funny dance inside her chest. Squeezing her eyes shut she opened her mouth to speak, but nothing came out.

"I got to the airport and realized that Myaten did both of us a favour. Jonathon will never know where you are and I want it to remain that way. You are out of danger if you keep yourself hidden away," from me, he wanted to add, but knew that would make matters worse. She was already frightened of his magic.

"Tell me that was you in the shower with me."

"It was," he gave a long-suffering sigh before he apologized again. "I refuse to make excuses for my behaviour, but I will only apologise for terrifying you. I truly believed that I was with you in a vision. It never entered my mind that I could interact with you from a distance. Like you, this is foreign territory to me. And I have never experienced anything like that before with another woman—"

To her dismay, the connection died and she let the phone slip from her hand into her lap. Running her fingers through her brown hair, she felt her whole body relax at his honesty. Covering her eyes with her hands, wondering where this never-ending nightmare was leading, she heard his voice inside her head

When Jonathon is dead, I will come for you.

She needed to get a grip before she went bananas. Taking a deep breath, she put the cordless phone back and logged into her computer. Maybe if she did some investigation of her own about the mysterious symbols, she might find out more on the SandWalkers.

Jonathon finished off his scotch in one gulp, took out a few notes, tossed them at the glass and walked from the bar. Hands in his pockets, he strolled leisurely across the lobby and up to the receptionist behind the help desk.

Flashing a friendly smile as he gave the tall brunette the once over, "Do I have any messages?" He made sure she knew he was interested as he leaned over the counter licking his lips.

The receptionist perked up instantly. She had seen him on TV yesterday. Running her hands over her hair and down her uniform to straighten it, she smiled shyly. "I'll check for you." She turned around and walked to the back office.

Jonathon watched her walk and puckered his lips; 'he'd love to have a bit of that'. He tapped his nails on the marble counter as he looked across the lobby. When he heard her heels on the floor, he turned in time to see her round the corner.

His eyes balked at the stack of mail she managed to carry up to the counter.

"These came in during the morning delivery, Mr. Strathmore, would you care to have them delivered to your room?"

"Yes," he wasn't going to try to juggle that all the way to his room. "Say, are you doing anything this evening, umm... Brandi?" He read her badge as he put on his most engaging smile while toying with the idea of a good romp in the sack.

"I finish at seven; I can meet you here at eight?"

A wolfish smile spread across his face making his blue eyes light up, "That's perfect my dear. Now I need you to do me a small favour."

He stood in the middle of her room wondering where her shit was, as he tapped the plastic card key against his palm. He pushed the bathroom door open with the tip of his trainer, it was empty.

All the drawers and wardrobes looked as if they had been cleaned out. Scratching his head, he never told David to sweep her suite. Shrugging, he turned on his heel and headed back to his room.

He was just clearing up when he realized that the best way to cover his ass was to report Melissa missing, especially since he'd been recorded live saying just that.

Using the telephone in his room, he dialled double zero for the hotel operator. "Connect me to the local authorities please." He held the phone to his ear as music filtered down the line. He hated being put on hold.

In order to waste some time, he went through his wardrobe and pulled out a few outfits for his dinner date. He envisioned Brandi sprawled across his bed. Her mocha skin, soft and inviting.

"Is the call emergency related?"

Jonathon jerked his head back and rolled his eyes as he began to pace back and forth. "That depends on what your description of an emergency is." Jonathon talked over the man's polite request.

"Sir, I need to know the kind of emergency so that I can put you in the right department."

"Police," he barked out. The phone clicked as his call was transferred.

"Hello, you need translator?" The thick accent made the words almost impossible to understand.

Jonathon slung his head back ready to go into one. He opened his mouth and spoke in Arabic. "I would like to file a missing persons report." His dialect was perfect in pitch and pronunciation, which caught the police officer off guard. He gave the male officer the short version of Melissa's disappearance, her description and the man he saw her with last, before he ended the call.

Jonathon pinched the bridge of his nose as he tossed the Razor phone on the couch. "Two fucking hours," he kept saying as he stomped into the bathroom to shower and get ready for his date.

Dressed in black slacks that hugged his narrow waist, he glanced in the mirror to make sure he looked the business. The white silk shirt made his new tan stand out. Flashing a dashing smile, he loved the effect. Perhaps he would invest in one of those tanning machines his sisters were always harping on about. Rolling his shoulders back, he turned sideways to view his profile. Not bad.

Shoving his hands inside his pockets, he questioned his choice in shoes. Changing the white Italian loafers for black suede shoes, he nodded in agreement.

Putting his arms in the sleeves of his white dinner jacket, he grabbed a red rose from the vase on the table by the door as he stepped into the hallway. Crossing the hallway, he laid the delicate flower outside Melissa's room. Raising his foot over the flower to destroy it, his body went ridged when the elevator chimed. He quickly bent down and covered his face, hiding the brief smile. Sniffing, he lifted his face away from his cupped hands and looked around. Two old women graced him with caring, thoughtful smiles.

"Mr. Strathmore, can we say how awful we feel at the news of your friend's disappearance.' The other one nodded in agreement and offered him a tissue.

"Nothing wrong with grieving, it shows that you have a good heart." They scuffled past and waved before entering their room.

Jonathon wiggled his nose at the heavily perfumed tissue. He blew his nose on it and was gifted with a series of sneezes. Bloody old cows, he thought as he looked over his shoulder and stomped on the rose, making sure it was ground into the blue carpet.

Standing in the elevator feeling quite pleased with himself, he pressed for the ground floor as the doors slammed shut. He relaxed his shoulders and flicked off imaginary lint as he shoved his hands in his pockets.

As soon as he stepped from the lift, he spotted his date in the lobby talking to two men in immaculate white uniforms. As soon as she turned and graced him with a smile and a wave, two sets of eyes raked him from head to toe. He hated cops regardless of what country they were from.

He approached them in a leisurely stroll, he had nothing to hide. His last text message from David had said he was in position, target in sight. Nothing in four hours, strange, but none the less, he trusted David's abilities and knew he'd come through.

"Mr. Strathmore?" the tallest police officer addressed him with a stiff nod.

"Yes."

"My name is Adam Klein, I'm a translator from the American Embassy," He put his arm up to stop Jonathon, his face showing no emotion. "I know you speak perfect Arabic as well as Cairene Arabic, but in these circumstances, protocol dictates my role in making this investigation run as smoothly as it can." Adam turned to his partner. "This is Adjo Ahmose. He was born in Alexandria and speaks four languages: English, French, German and Italian. Now, if we may, there are a few things that need clearing up."

Adjo removed his black beret, tucking it under his arm as he pulled a pad from his front pocket.

Brandi gave Jonathon a timid smile as she began pacing in small sexy circles. Her black high heels clicking with each slow deliberate step she took. He wasn't making much of an effort to listen to the questions as his eyes caught hold of her ass in that tight skirt. Oh how he planned to tear her ass up later.

"Mr. Strathmore! I think your evening plans can be set aside for a few minutes of your time." Adjo glared at the Englishman as he jotted something in his notepad.

Turning his back on her, Jonathon looked the Egyptian officer in the eyes, "I answered all the questions on the phone. Can't this wait till tomorrow? I've had an extremely long day and wish to relax in the company of my date. Is that too much to ask?"

Both men pulled up short at his manner, their eyes filled with surprise and instant dislike. "Sir…surely you must be anxious to find your missing friend? After all, you called us." Adjo leaned sideways to look past Jonathon's shoulder and spotted the attractive woman standing off to one side, waiting patiently.

Adam and Adjo spoke briefly and nodded in silent

agreement, "I think we got all we need, enjoy your evening. Oh, but before we go, don't make any plans to leave the country Mr. Strathmore." Adjo tipped his head, placed his beret on his head and walked to the entrance of the hotel.

Jonathon couldn't believe his luck. Well he didn't mind being stuck in the country. He blew a kiss at Brandi as he waited for the officers to exit the building.

Taking her by the arm, he gave her a look full of promise as he led her towards the bar. Her flirtatious manner told him that he wouldn't have to bother getting her drunk tonight. He was definitely going to enjoy himself tonight.

His back supported by a tall column, one knee rose up in the air, his bare foot braced on the base of the wide stone support as he stared into space. He concentrated all his energy into one message. Not sure if she would get it, he could only pray to the gods that she wouldn't find telepathy scary and refuse to accept his oath as fact.

The connection to Melissa severed, just as well, he thought as he combed his fingers through his hair. It hung down his back spilling over his chest as he turned his head to look at the scrolls spread across his desk. Try as he might, he still hadn't found any reference to how a human could have the mating mark.

Myaten didn't have an explanation for it. However, he took the time to remind him of his obligations to Melissa, before he went on patrol.

Rubbing through the material covering his left hip, his fingers itched to trace her mark. He knew all too well how he'd do much more than that if given the opportunity.

Dropping his bare foot to the floor, he stepped away from

the column and sat down behind his desk. His eyes scanned each one, from right to left until his mind was overflowing with tales of long ago. He definitely wasn't searching in the right place. There had to be some kind of record to explain the reason for his behaviour. He had thought of discussing it with Myaten, especially after his comment concerning Melissa.

"So you found her. I bet Kiros you'd find your woman in this century."

The look on her face told him, she wasn't amused to say the least. He could understand her lack of enthusiasm. If he wasn't insulting her, he was offering to fuck her brains out. Shaking his head in disbelief at his rough animalistic behaviour in the shower, he was surprised she had talked to him, period. He was lucky she wasn't cowering in a corner having a mental break down.

Totally pissed off with himself, he shoved the precious scrolls off his desk. Snapping his fingers, they froze in mid fall. Gods, he needed to get his perspectives in order. He carefully rolled, tied and slotted them back in their cases before depositing them back on their shelves. Melissa was important, but he needed to collect himself and focus on the immediate dangers.

Standing in the Great Library, he thought about the sand storm that was coming. A by- product of sand particles induced by a static electric field and friction. His magic had created it when he released his brothers from the time spell.

The negative charges from the electrical pulses travelled through the pyramid causing the sand to loosen and rise up with the wind for miles opposite the pyramid. Natural sand and dust storms would only rise if the right conditions were applied. The wall of dust not sand could reach up as high as twenty thousand feet, he had seen with his own eyes, cities covered within minutes.

Right now, Kiros was preparing the pyramid to keep it from being pulled apart from the devastating effects of the storm. Myaten was making his way to Cairo. From there, he would raise a shield over the city until the storm passed. Their plan was to stretch the shield to include the pyramid if it needed it. In order to do that, all three of them would have to merge their powers.

Formulating more plans, Siaak left his desk to begin his long patrol around the temple. He couldn't allow the scrolls contained within to be damaged or worse, destroyed all together. Once he had reinforced the spell points to keep the Great Library safe from the destructive forces of the storm, he would join his brothers.

Not really thinking of his routine, he walked by her room. He would always think of it as hers regardless that she had used it for one night. He couldn't help thinking back to that night. A smile played at his lips, she was a handful, one that made him stop and walk backward until he was in line of her doorway.

There were no doors to open and close, no need for privacy, as he had always lived alone. His head turned and then his body. Before he realised it he was in her room holding her bathrobe up to his face. Taking a deep breath, he inhaled her scent. It brought images of her. Having a shower, drinking coffee, sleeping. With that in mind, he wished for her company even though she drove him batty.

Chuckling at the term 'batty', it reminded him of what she thought he was…a vampire. What was it going to take, to convince her otherwise? The evidence was stacked against him. He had bitten her. The taste of her blood in his mouth was down to two things. The sucking pressure of his mouth against her skin made the tiny blood vessels rise to the surface.

When he bit down his fangs grazed them open, producing blood around the wound. Making it look as if he had sucked her blood. The mere thought made him feel disturbed.

He stopped walking. How could he have taken even a small amount of her blood and not have been violently sick? Shaking his head, he was definitely going to see her again. He needed answers, besides; she still owed him a decent kiss for saving her ass, twice.

Myaten felt the wind whipping up around him. The hair on his body began to stand up with the electric current that he felt around him in the air.

The storm was approaching fast. He could see it off in the distance, a sheet of dancing sand and dust. The people of the surrounding cities had no time to take cover, even if they knew what was about to happen. It was up to him to see to the lives of so many.

Worse part of it all, he was like Nostradamus, someone that could see visions of the future. He knew things thousands of years before it was supposed to happen. Only difference between them, Nostradamus was a human man and even though he made predictions of future events, it was never written in stone.

Myaten saw people, places and knew when major catastrophes would take place. At the risk of the universe, he never tampered with the fate's powers. He hated watching movies or TV shows where the hero could go back in time to fix past mistakes, disregarding all the rules. He never had and never would play god.

Setting himself above Cairo, he wove a protective spell that appeared in his cupped hands. The small globe of green light, that resembled a tiny marble, pulsated with energy as it grew, tripling in size, engulfing his hands and then his body before it zoomed along to shroud the surrounding cities in its protective shield.

His eyes flickered up; he braced his mind and body against the backlash of the storm.

"It's coming Kiros!" he shouted.

Kiros heard his brother's mental shout. Standing with his arms above his head, he concentrated all the power within his body. Building a smaller shield that would enclose the Black Pyramid and Giza. No sooner had he raised the shield, he felt the cloud pass over. He just hoped he could ride it out, some storms lasted for hours and he had never tested his capabilities in such a manner before.

The storm hit with such force that it blocked out the sky. And swallowed up the pyramids and surrounding buildings in the blink of an eye.

Myaten's shield held as the destructive cloud collided against it. He dug his teeth into his bottom lip as he pushed his arms out. With that action, he mentally reinforced the iridescent, bubble, shaped force field as he held it up, all on his own.

Mother Nature was strong, but he was stronger. Summoning another spell, he lowered his hand to the small, black, leather pouch that appeared on his belt. Reaching inside, he took a handful of the precious dust and sprinkled it around his body. The moment he felt his shield lock into place, he lowered his outstretched arms.

He gathered up the wind and spread the sparkling sleep powder over the city. With everyone in a deep sleep, he didn't have to worry about witnesses.

Myaten looked around as his body revolved in rapid circles. With each group of people he detected outside the force field, he had to quickly weaken it to allow them to come through. His arms shot out in different directions, his fingers curled in against his palms and with a yank, he pulled them through the field and watched as the sleep spell worked instantaneously. They wouldn't remember anything once it wore off.

He glanced up as he sensed a surge of power, seconds later, Siaak shimmering into focus.

"Took you long enough," Myaten teased as he yanked on a stray group of tourists near the Giza pyramid, why they were out so late, he didn't know.

"I was having a hard time finding shoes to match my kilt." His mouth broadened into a relaxing smile.

Myaten almost dropped the people he was teleporting through the shield. He laughed at Siaak's small joke. It was about time he removed that proverbial stick from up his ass. Seems the woman had rubbed off on him a little, about damn time too.

"I need some help here guys!"

Myaten nodded and took the helm as Siaak flashed straight to the Black Pyramid. Kiros was down on his knees, his arms above his head struggling to keep the shields up, while feeding constant energy to the prison around Osiris.

The electrical pulses within the sand storm were draining the power from the magic points. Seventy-eight magic points formed a grid around the brickwork that made up the structure of the building. Once the grid was powered up, the end result was a complex force shield. Now the force field was failing.

Siaak sent his ghost self to investigate and found that twenty-two magic points were completely drained. As a result, two sides of the pyramid would need major repair.

Combining their powers, Siaak gathered it up, aimed and directed the energy at the tip of the pyramid. Both men concentrated as they made short work of recharging the remaining points and restored the grid to full strength. The thin gleaming bluish beam climbed up the sides of the pyramid and fused the large hole that had left half the pyramid unprotected.

"Cutting it a little close Kiros..." Siaak kept his face neutral. Kiros hated it when people showed any concern for him.

"I am finding that a lot of my powers seem to come and go in this time." He swept his fingers through his sweaty hair that was plastered to his neck, jaw and forehead. "I only called for help in order to keep Osiris within the prison."

"Perhaps Myaten can take you back in time to let you feed upon another SandWalker?" Siaak left the ball in his court as he whacked Kiros on the back. "Osiris is contained within her prison and the storm will pass in a few minutes, so join us when you can." And with that, Siaak jumped.

"Is he okay?" Myaten asked softly, his voice full of worry. Even though none of them was biological brothers, they cared for each other like blood family.

"You know Kiros, stubborn beyond all reason." Siaak looked Myaten straight in the eyes and gave a stiff nod before he joined his power to Myaten's.

"Are you upset with me about your woman?" Myaten figured it best to clear the air. He felt like shit. And he should have taken more notice of her reactions after he dropped her off. The shocked expression on her face. Her tense body and the fact that she had called him just about every vile name there was between A and Z. And a few he was sure she had made up before she fainted.

Looking over at Siaak, he half expected him to settle into one of his long drawn out silent observing moods. Instead, he shook his head no.

"So what are your plans?" Myaten asked, as they landed on the roof of Cairo Museum.

"I plan on keeping the people of this planet safe."

"There you go all comic book hero on me. I meant, your woman?" Myaten shifted his position so he could look his old friend in the face.

"Why do you insist on calling her 'my woman'?"

Myaten raised a dark eyebrow at him and for once, he felt sorry for Siaak. "You would have killed her, otherwise, and besides, I know she's your woman."

"We shall see, Myaten," he closed his eyes and flicked his tongue against his teeth.

Myaten knew it was his way of avoiding the subject. Therefore, he left it and focused his mind on more pressing matters.

They made their way across the populated cities, extending the shield as they leapt in different directions across uneven rooftops of shops, banks and hospitals, keeping ahead of the sandstorm.

Once Kiros joined them, Siaak kept to the rear making sure the storm was dissipating and waking up the populace.

Myaten branched out towards Memphis. Once the storm had passed, he rejoined Kiros on the banks of the Nile near Beni Suef. They exchanged information before carrying on towards the next populated towns.

Myaten enjoyed the power boost, but over the next few days, he'd feel the drag. It was almost like having withdrawals. This was another reason why they were glad they didn't do it very often. He'd end up sleeping it off and if need be he could always take some vitamins.

Vitamins to them were power personified. Similar to what they took out of each other when they exchanged blood, only it took less time to settle in their systems.

The shield gradually switched from a pale yellow to an emerald green, proof that their combined powers had pushed it up to full strength. He figured another hour before the sandstorm hit Karnak. They would concentrate all their resources to keep the Temple from being pulled apart. The sandstorm wouldn't destroy the ancient building, it could, however, weaken the structure to the point of making it impossible to house the libraries contained within.

There wasn't any place on Earth to hide them should that happen. There was too much to risk, all the written records of the ancient world containing knowledge that would astound the populace of today.

As soon as the storm passed Qena, Myaten teleported everyone into position around the Temple, giving them time to merge again.

The storm had lasted almost five hours. Travelling more than five hundred miles since it began.

Once the cloud appeared, they braced themselves for the collision. It hit like a freight train, instantly changing everything around them. Visibility dropped to zero. Impossible to teleport, the men couldn't fight the storm. All they could do was ride it out. Keep their formation; protect the Temple and its treasures.

The wind whipped sand around in whirlwinds, slamming

them into the protective barrier, palm trees bent over, their leaves touching the ground at the G-forces of Mother Nature. Piles of sand began to build up around the shield. All three of them locked down, feet braced in the sand, arms out as they blasted the sand off the Temple.

Half an hour later, the men filled with a sense of victory were on their way, following the storm until it reached miles and miles of unpopulated desert then they split up. Siaak went back to the Temple and Kiros returned to the Black Pyramid. He needed to access the damage. The only comforting thought to Kiros was that, at least in this age, tomb robbing wasn't heard of very often.

Myaten took flight and watched from above. He couldn't live with himself if a stray animal got caught up in the deadly storm. And he knew that one of the ranchers was constantly letting his cattle free at this time of year.

He sniffed and looked up at the same time as an airplane flew past, knocking him from the sky. "Damn airplanes," he swore as he fell like a rock. Tucking his head and knees into his chest, he rolled as he hit the ground with a thud; the sand acting like a crash barrier stopped his forward momentum.

He just lay there, wishing he could be in Vegas surrounded by women and loud music instead of sitting in a pile of gritty sand. Spitting sand from his mouth, he flipped over and stared up at the moonlit sky. Standing, he thrust his powers out and blasted the sand from his body. Shaking his fist at the loud plane, he suddenly remembered that Siaak wanted him to pick up Elizabeth and Mark.

Elizabeth grabbed hold of her seat as the plane shuddered and lost altitude for a few minutes. Her mind played over a million and one reasons why that happened and none of them was good.

She pulled the visor up on her window and looked out. She was met with the most stunning image. The plane passed a white puffy blanket of clouds as the pilot announced they would be landing shortly. She drew in a deep breath of appreciation at the sight of the moon showering the desert in silver light. She caught her breath at the reflection of their plane off the golden cap of the Black pyramid as they passed over. Shaking her head, she shoved the visor back down and huffed. She still didn't let go of the arm rests after that.

"For someone that loves to travel, you don't do planes do you, Beth?"

Beth rolled her head on her seat and flashed a fake toothy smile. "What gave it away, the permanent handprints on my seat or the fact that I'm wearing a concealed parachute?"

Mark sat relaxed in a reclined position smiling, "Here, hold my hand."

Her eyebrows drew in as a devilish gleam entered her eyes, "Well, you asked for it." She took his hand and squeezed.

Mark didn't utter a word as she cut off the blood flow to his arm. "You know it's only wind turbulence." He shut up at the look on her face.

As soon as the plane landed, Beth was up, bags in hand, waiting by the door. The Stewardess frowned and pointed to the seat belt light as the plane rolled to a stop.

Mark covered his eyes and waited for the bitch slapping to begin. There had to be a wanted list with her face on it. Warning all Stewardess's of her phobic tendencies. The last plane she flew on, apparently she broke the Stewardess's' wrist in three places. And all because she took Beth's bag and told Beth to sit down until the plane came to a complete stop.

Mark watched as Beth flew out the door as it opened. He quickly grabbed his leather bag and apologised, as he pushed past other passengers to dart after her.

Beth held the phone to her ear and tapped her foot as she glared daggers at the silver digital watch on her wrist. "Jonathon! Where the HELL are you? The plane landed forty-five minutes early. Get your English butt over here and pick us up or I swear I'm going to kick your sorry ass all the way back to jolly old England!" She slammed the phone shut and shoved it in her pocket. "What?" she answered Mark's questioning look as he pointed over her head.

Beth turned around and let lose a lustful whistle directed at the man standing in the waiting area holding a sign above his head. There weren't many people milling about at this time of night. Even in a crowd, he would have stood out like a sore thumb. Extremely tall and well packed in all the right places, well she was a woman after all; it was in her genetics to have a good long ogle.

"Stop drooling." Mark slapped her arm as he handed her bag over.

"Why you interested," she wiped her mouth with an imaginary tissue.

Mark jerked his head up and snorted, "Just because I dressed up as an Indian for Halloween doesn't make me gay, Beth!"

She smiled, "Yeah, alright you tell me that the next time you and your room mates dress up as the village people, get drunk and end up in a naked pile in your living room."

He dropped her suitcase inches from her feet and fluffed his hair as he walked by.

She huffed as she pulled her two suitcases behind her trying not to laugh at Mark's outrageous walk.

FIFTEEN MINUTES EARLIER

Myaten looked around before he stepped out of the shadows and pushed his glasses in place. Last thing he wanted to do right now was draw attention to his self.

Siaak wanted them protected at all costs. He knew Jonathon wasn't going to allow them to live much past their usefulness. Therefore, it was Myaten's responsibility to meet them and escort them back to the Temple where the SandWalkers could keep them under surveillance.

He turned the corner and spotted a black stretched limousine parked in the loading/unloading zone. The driver stood with his elbows balanced on the hood of the luxury car, smoking a cigar while staring at the entrance to the airport.

Myaten wondered whom he was waiting for. "Excuse me," Myaten cleared his throat as he approached the driver.

The man chewed on his cigar and ignored him. Myaten spoke louder.

"Excuse me, is this transport for hire?"

The driver plucked the large Cuban cigar out of his mouth and turned slowly. With a subtle hint, he pulled his jacket open and gave a cocky smile. "What do you think?"

"I'm guessing private," Myaten answered when he saw the gun strapped to the driver's ribcage.

"Good, now fuck off!" The driver flicked his ash before turning back to guarding the car to wait for someone that was obviously important or on the wrong side of the law.

Myaten would have to find out. He waved cheerfully as he passed and was awarded a polite middle finger. Myaten smiled and nodded, when he really wanted to walk back over there, break it off and shove it up his ass with that disgusting cigar.

Once inside, he immediately took in the sprinkle of

humans. Not many people flying at this time of night. Most of them were cleaners and staff.

He didn't have to worry too much if he was stopped by the police. He held four passports, two licenses, one of which was an international license giving him permission to drive outside the US.

Basically, he had enough info to keep them at bay.

Looking up at the monitors, he scanned the display for the inbound flights from England. It had already landed and the passengers where in customs. He glanced at his watch as he took a spot near the waiting lounge. He couldn't go any further without a ticket.

He hated waiting. It drove him insane. Ironic that he could control time, travel in it and yet here he sat twiddling his thumbs wishing time to hurry up.

Shaking his head, he bit on his lip as he remembered an event from his past The last time he played with *time*, where it involved humans, he had to sit through a Siaak lecture. He'd inadvertently caused a black out that lasted for a day or so. Utter chaos! And he'd never forgiven his self for it. And to try and justify the whole thing, he'd gone against his teaching and gave the humans penicillin. He wouldn't interfere with the dates of when the true discovery was. Therefore, that meant going back to the late eighteen hundreds. Okay, so it was a kick-start into the right direction. It made him feel better, even if it earned a tongue-lashing from his mentor.

The real problem was the humans. He'd been around them way too long, but the truth of the matter was, he loved them. He enjoyed the lifestyle they had created for him. Being a Casino owner gave him everything. The nightlife he enjoyed, the money, not that he really needed it, but it was still worth it. And it gave him friends that he could count on.

Speaking of friends, he took out his phone and connected to the internet. He checked his emails and read all his offline messages on yahoo and MSN.

He gave a lopsided grin at the ton of messages from Rachel. He enjoyed her company. They spent many a night chatting about anything, books, movies, games and their ultimate passion, anime. If he went missing for too long, she'd worry. He quickly emailed her explaining why he hadn't been on for a couple of weeks. He couldn't tell her the truth as much as he'd like too, he knew the rules.

As soon as he saw people exiting customs, he shoved his phone in his back pocket and grabbed a bit of cardboard and a giant black marker.

Myaten noticed a man and woman arguing and knew it was them. "Excuse me, I'm Myaten Sands, would you happen to be Mark and Beth?' At their relieved looks, he continued. 'Melissa made reservations for your stay and I will be your driver and tour guide." He offered to take their bags, but Beth stood there not moving an inch.

"Jonathon said she was missing," she looked up at Mark as he rubbed her shoulder in a display of soothing reassurance. She patted his hand, smiled and turned back to scoff at the attractive stranger.

Myaten ignored her attitude. "If you'll follow me, I can explain," he looked around the lobby as he folded the small sign up and shoved it under his arm. Interpol made regular visits here and with a clean sweep of the place, he spotted two undercover agents walking from customs. He didn't want their attention drawn to them. If anything happened to keep him from bringing them back to the Temple, Siaak would have his ass in a sling.

"How do we know you aren't a serial killer and as soon

as we get in the car we get hacked to pieces?" Beth put her hands on her hips and refused to move an inch.

Myaten did a double take at her comment. "Serial killer? Honey, I think you've watched The Bone Collector one too many times." Myaten let his eyes drift down and back up her body in a silent, hot caress. "The only screams coming from my back seat would be yours, out of sheer pleasure."

Beth tilted her head to one side and closed her mouth at his outrageous remark, like she'd have sex with a total stranger and in the back of his car.

"I'm in." Mark sided with Myaten. "Anyone that can make her shut up is a good guy in my books."

Beth scrunched her face up as she pursed her lips. "Take that back or so help me god, I'll shove my phone so far up your ass, you'll be saying 'welcome Motorola' every time your lips move."

Myaten uttered a long whistle. "Is she always like this?"

Mark nodded and made a run for it.

Myaten saw the evil glint in her eyes and knew she wasn't joking in the least. He put his hands over his rear as he walked, succeeding in making Beth laugh out loud. Even so, she took her sweet ass time getting from the lobby to the front doors, where Mark was waiting outside by the loading/ unloading bay.

Myaten touched the key hole with his thumb, rotating the locking mechanism until he heard a soft click. He quickly stowed their luggage before opening the back door and waved them in. He climbed in the driver's seat and pulled away from the curb. He sped up as the image of the chauffeur filled his rear view mirror. The man ran into the street waving his gun as if that alone would make Myaten turn the car around. Only to run him over, but seeing as he had witnesses in the car, he'd have to forgo his playtime.

The enraged driver glanced over his shoulder at the sound of heels. Damn, he was going to find it hard explaining this to his boss. Placing his gun back in his holster, he phoned for another limo, while he informed Mr. Ambers on his daughter's whereabouts.

The sleek black limo was the perfect choice. The only visible trace of it was the white glare from the headlights and amber light strips along both sides of the luxury car. Myaten was glad he'd stolen it. And was smiling from ear to ear, until he looked up.

Shaking his head, he watched his passengers fumbling around at the locks. "It's for your protection. Melissa is safe; that I promise you. Luckily for her, my brother happened along otherwise she'd be dead."

Jonathon opened his eyes to find Brandi face down on the table. He grimaced at the pool of half dried drool around her mouth along with her dinner plastered to one side of her face.

Rubbing his eyes, he raised his head from his own dinner. Disgusted he grabbed a napkin and wiped the mask of dried caked-on food from his face. Swearing, he got up from his seat and ran towards the bathroom. He stopped and looked around to find everyone was asleep. That was strange. He had never seen anything like it before in his entire life. How could a whole restaurant, full of people, fall asleep?

Gas leak perhaps? He spotted lit candles dotted around the tables and knew it wasn't gas or they'd have body parts everywhere! The image of that made him screw his face up in distaste.

Outraged, he went in search of the manager. He'd slap a

lawsuit on them so fast it'd make their heads spin as well as having the place shut down, permanently.

Leaving the restaurant, he walked across the lobby. He stopped dead in his tracks at the silence. There was a security guard laying face down, both arms above his head. His torch had rolled across the floor not far from a set of keys he had obviously dropped when he fell.

Jonathon bent down and grabbed the keys. He walked over to the security guard and crouched down to feel for a pulse. Well, the guard wasn't dead. He had been up and walking around, so whatever put them down like this couldn't possibly be poisonous.

Jonathon stood up and dropped the keys, not caring where they landed, as he carried on with his investigation. Something was going on and he was going to find out what it was.

Ramming his hand into his front pocket, he found his phone. "Bollocks! No fucking signal!" He shoved the useless phone back in his pocket and raked his fingers through his hair. That's when he spotted a phone on the wall. Mouthing 'yes' between clenched teeth, he dashed across the large granite floor. He quickly yanked his cell phone out to flick through the phone book. Picking up the receiver his smile fell flat, no signal. "What's with this place?" he slammed the phone down so hard it rang through the lobby.

His nose flared as his face contorted with anger. As he flipped his body around and slammed his back into the phone box, his elbow flew out and smashed the glass. He clenched his teeth as pain rode up his arm. He ignored the backlash of pain from his outburst.

"Calm down," his eyes glanced wildly around the room. His shoulders shook as he felt sick to his stomach. Shoving his hands deep in his jacket pockets, Jonathon started pacing. He always paced when he was anxious. He didn't know what the hell was going on, but he was going to find out. Whoever was responsible was going to pay.

Glancing at his wristwatch, he tapped the crystal. "Well I'll be damned, it's stopped." Tipping his head back, he noticed the giant silver digital clock on the wall above the receptionist's desk. It had stopped, too. He raised his arm to compare the timepieces. One eyebrow drew up in question. He couldn't explain how his watch and the clock had stopped at the exact same time.

Covering his mouth with his shaking hands, he walked back to the bar. With a handkerchief, Jonathon covered the bar tender's forearm and lift it up to check the time. "Damn! Eight o'clock!" He needed a drink. Reaching over the bar, he picked up a bottle of scotch and took a long swig. "That shit will kill you!" He shook his head and coughed at the fierce burn that trailed down his throat.

Shrugging his shoulders, he decided to go and find the men's washroom. He took the scotch with him. In the bathroom, he scrubbed at the bits of dried food on his cheek and forehead. He dabbed at the large red wine stain that ran all down his white jacket and silk shirt. It wasn't coming out. In a fury, he yanked it off and threw it at the sink.

Leaning over the counter, he caught a flash of white in the mirror. Glancing up at his reflection, he saw a beautiful woman in a white dress staring at him. One minute she was smiling, offering him her open arms and then she was hissing and clawing at him. At the sight of her transformation, Jonathon ploughed his fist into the mirror shattering it and cutting his hand open at the same time. "Fuck!" he hissed as he felt the glass slicing through his skin. "Son of a bitch!"

He flexed his fingers to see how deep the cuts were. He quickly put his hand under the cold-water tap, but nothing happened. There was no water!

At closer inspection of his hand, he found four white scratches. He grabbed a towel just in case it started bleeding. Wrapping it around his right hand, he left the bathroom and went back to his room.

Beth moved to the edge of her seat making the leather creak as she tilted forward. "What was that? Did you say Jonathon tried to kill Melissa, because I know I heard you wrong? That man doesn't have a mean bone in his body."

She pulled her phone out of her purse and dialled Melissa's cell. No answer. Her head jerked up, "Okay, what the hell is going on here? Where is Melissa and you'd better tell me before I smack you in the back of the head with my phone!"

Mark sat nestled in his seat. "I'd answer if I was you, she can throw a mean cell phone! AT & T didn't get its reach out and touch someone logo by accident. She actually smacked the president of the company with her phone. I'm telling ya, she's mean." Marks eyes rolled over to the woman opposite him, he flashed a boyish smile.

"Shut up Mark, before I make you eat yours!"

Mark closed his mouth and shrugged. He knew better than to argue with her when she was in a bad mood. He wanted to know where Melissa was, too. After all, she was his little sister.

"What's your name again...?"

"Myaten."

"Myaten, if you know anything, please tell us! I've been worried sick since we lost contact a week ago. I'd really appreciate it, and it'd save us both a pounding too."

Beth flopped back in her seat glaring at their driver and

then slammed Mark in the rib cage with her thirty-pound purse. "Shut up Mark!"

Myaten kept his comments to himself as the small woman in the back seat smacked the shit out of Mark. "She is at home. And before you start asking me how, I'll explain. So stop beating up the poor guy and listen."

Mark found the stranger's story hard to believe. "So you're telling us that she's at home in Kentucky? When did she leave and why did Jonathon say she was missing? This doesn't add up Myaten."

"Call her at home and see for yourself." Myaten steered the long vehicle around a steep curve easing it into the other lane before he took a hard left. He wasn't taking them to a hotel. These two humans were under their protection now. He spotted the Obelisk ahead, closed the glass partition behind his head and drove straight for the tall stone statue as Siaak held the portal open for him.

Melissa stood in the shower, wishing Siaak would make another appearance. She was being silly. Waiting for over an hour, hoping that something would happen, so far, nothing had.

The phone rang making her jump out of the tub. She barely managed to stay on her feet as she went sliding across the wooden floor. Cursing, she managed to get to the phone without breaking her neck, "This better be good— Oh, Hi, Mark!" She was more than surprised to hear his voice. "You are WHERE? No…no I thought I heard you wrong. Yes, I'll speak to Beth." She pressed the speaker button and while they decided on who was going to speak first, she went and switched the shower off.

"Hey, can you hear me?" Beth's voice shouted from the speaker.

"She's not deaf, Beth." Marks voiced sounded irritated and tired.

Melissa blew a strand of wet hair out of her eyes. "Yes, I can hear you both. I take it you guys landed in one piece?" She towel dried her hair and stopped at the exaggerated intake of air.

"Honey, I tell you I ain't seen a man this good looking since American Gladiators. If I'd known, I'd have flown the plane myself..."

"Give me that phone, what is it with you and Myaten? Stop drooling all over yourself. Melissa, are you okay? I've been worried out of my mind. Where is your cell phone? I've called you a hundred times or more. And all I get is your voice message."

"Ask Siaak when you see him." She bent down to wrap the towel around her head when she heard them arguing again. "You two quit it."

"Who is Siaak?" She heard Beth ask before the phone was snatched away.

"If you want to talk to her, use your own damn phone, Beth," Mark demanded.

"Fine, hurry up so I can call her!" Beth snapped back.

"I'd have thought by now, you two would've figured out how to get along..."

Mark cut her off, "I've got to go, but before I do, who's Siaak?"

"You'll see soon enough. Give him a message for me…"

She turned the speakerphone off and hung up after saying bye to everyone.

Mark held the small touch phone to his chin. He took in

Beth's index finger pressed hard against her nose and mouth. When he mouthed 'what.' Her head flew forward in the direction of their driver, to show him, the glass partition was shut.

"Where are we going?" He tried to shift his weight forward, but his body wouldn't budge. However, he managed to turn his head to look at Beth and suddenly found he was clutching his seat belt as the car began to fall. The last thing he saw was Beth's head bobbing up and down and then darkness surrounded him.

"So you are the infamous pyramid experts?" Siaak crossed his arms over his broad chest to stare down his nose at them. His eyes were like red, hot, coals as he raked their new visitors over with a look of uncertainty and disapproval.

Myaten stayed behind in case they decided to run, not that they'd get far.

"Who are you and where the hell are we?" demanded Beth. She felt herself drawn to the beautiful architecture of the building. She reached out and ran a hand over the carvings on the wall nearest her.

"Excuse my brother's manners; he was raised in a sand pit." Myaten indicated with a nod in Siaak's direction. "Siaak, this is Elizabeth Taylor and Mark Ambers."

"And, I better not hear the word Cleo or anyone humming walk like an Egyptian."

Siaak continued to stare her down before he spoke. "You do not look like Cleopatra, although with the temper, I am willing to bet you have fangs like her."

Mark turned his head away and stifled his laugh with a loud cough as he met Myaten's green glittering stare.

Beth's eyes narrowed as she frowned at the men in the room. "I mean it."

"What is your purpose regarding your journey to Egypt?" Siaak let his lips part to show his pearly whites. If need be, the fangs were next.

Beth looked at him with raised eyebrows. Her eyes moved back and forth between Myaten and Mark. "Is he for real?" She smirked at Siaak's proper English. "Honey, you sound like you're trapped in a time warp. What's with the regal stiff lip anyway? I mean, are you some King we don't know about?"

Siaak supplied her with a stiff nod before he offered his hand. "As a child, I was taught by the best linguistics teacher in all Egypt. She felt contractions murdered the English language. As for you, I am not the kind of person that ridicules or teases others. I, more than anyone, understand your devotion to Melissa," he took her hand in his and patted it softly, "she is safe, I will not allow anyone to hurt her, I swear on it."

He dropped her hand and stepped back. "You and Mark are welcome into my home, but I must advise you to stay in your own rooms. My home is warded against the creatures of the desert. I would feel regret if either of you were hurt." He graced her with an elegant bow and moved to leave.

"WAIT!" She had no idea why she was here, or why she suddenly felt that Siaak was telling the truth. But all she knew, was that her friend was in danger and she would do everything within her power to help.

Siaak paused inside the doorway, 'Was there something else?"

Beth looked as if she was struggling with what to say when she finally opened her mouth and tugged her purse over her shoulder. "Thank you." She followed Myaten as he left the room.

Mark stopped short as he gathered up their bags. "I still don't understand all of this."

"I shall explain everything to you in due time. Sleep well, Mark Ambers."

Mark frowned and watched Beth turn and glance in his direction. The look on her face made him wonder if he had acted too soon. He felt the hair on the back of his neck rise and knew Siaak watched them from the archway.

"You can stay in these rooms." Myaten showed them into the bedrooms opposite each another.

"I'm afraid we don't have TV or any other high tech equipment here."

At Beth's audible groan, his mouth moved into a lopsided grin. "Believe me, I know how you feel. I put my iPod down some place and," he frisked his body, "for the life of me, I can't find it." He rolled his eyes in a show of frustration.

"Please-please tell me I don't have to share a bathroom with him!" She pointed a finger at Mark who poked his tongue back.

"There are bathrooms in each room. Don't even ask how they work or I'll have to go dig up a magic book this thick and read it to you." He moved his arms out as far as he could get them.

Mark smirked as Beth clicked her tongue at them both. Myaten slapped the empty doorways with his hands in a rad-a–tap-tap before he turned on his heel and waved bye at them.

Mark turned his back to Beth as she dragged her heavy suitcase behind her. What had they gotten themselves into? Better yet, what had his sister gotten them into?

He whistled in appreciation as he took in the grandeur of his room. His bed or mattress sat on a round black and red veined marble plinth. It stood about three feet off the floor, god he hoped he didn't roll over in his sleep, he might crack his skull open.

He noticed, straight away, the lack of windows. And wondered where the cool breeze was coming from. He licked his finger and pointed it above his head. Wow, it seemed to come at him in all directions. Did they have air conditioning in Egypt? He figured, with the heat index of one hundred plus, it would be hard to keep the machinery from overheating.

Then he remembered that Beth *was* staying at a ritzy hotel. She never went without the comforts she was accustomed too. Coffee and air conditioning, she didn't need much else.

He placed his bag on the bed and was unzipping it when he felt someone watching him. He looked under his arm and saw a pair of feet standing in the open doorway.

"Come in," he raked a hand through his brown hair making it stand up.

"I apologise for my intrusion," Siaak said as he stood in the doorway. "I know it sounds strange of me to ask, but how is Melissa? Myaten said you spoke to her on the phone earlier on the way over. That you had a message for me." He really wanted to reach out to her, but was afraid he might hurt her again.

Mark knew that look and had seen many men eager to know such details, especially when it concerned a woman. Mark flopped down on the bed and stared at his fingers before looking up at him. He didn't know who to trust. It has always been like that for their family. With their lifestyle came certain aspects that made it hard to believe and trust other people. He had never met Jonathon, but if Siaak had saved his little sister's life, he had no choice but to side with him, for now. "Yes I spoke to Melissa. She mentioned you and asked me to give you a message."

Siaak stepped into the room, he hadn't meant to speak with Mark until the morning, but, somehow, he felt the need to talk with him. He resembled Melissa in many ways. Mark had a way of tilting his head to one side as he inspected things in passing. It was like he was trying to uncover its secrets by staring at it.

"You like my sister don't you Siaak?" Mark asked as he bounced on the bed. He half expected his butt to collide with the hard base; instead, it was soft, very nice.

"Yes I do, she drives me insane with her insistent chatter, but I must confess I miss it now." Siaak took another step into the room. "What was her message Mark?"

Mark hung his head and rubbed his eyes before he looked back up. "She said to tell Count Dracula 'Hi' and that the next time she sees you, you better be wearing steel under pants. Something tells me she's a little upset with you."

"I am afraid we got off on the wrong foot. She is very displeased with me." Siaak said as he smiled at the image of her over his shoulder, "She has every right to be." He wasn't going to voice his desires aloud.

Mark stood up and pulled out his overnight pack. Holding his electric shaver, he glanced around the room, no electric sockets. *Great*, he thought.

"So how did you two meet?" his voice drifted off as Siaak held his hand out for the shaver. "There's no place to plug it in," Mark quickly added, pointing out the obvious.

Siaak nodded as he took the razor and charged it with his powers and handed it back, "try it now."

Mark raised a curious eyebrow as he turned it on. The familiar buzz with the green light meant it was plugged in. Impossible! It wasn't a cordless shaver. "Thanks, um you wouldn't mind telling me how you did that?" Mark threw it on the bed and quickly shoved his hands deep in his back pockets before he turned to face Siaak again.

"Magic," he said, "it is a long story."

"I'm wide awake and I'm not letting you get out of telling me how you did that magic trick." Mark sat back on the bed, his legs dangling off the side as he stared at his possessed shaver. He poked it with his finger before looking back up at his towering host.

A sheepish look crossed Mark's face as he caught sight of Beth behind Siaak. She knocked on the wall inside the doorway. "Can anyone join this pyjama party?" she asked. Her hair had been brushed back into a long ponytail that hung over her right shoulder. She had removed all her makeup and was dressed in her bat pyjamas with a long black robe that flew open as she walked.

Siaak stepped aside as she entered the room giving her a graceful bow from the waist. Once she was settled next to Mark on the bed, he began his long story.

CHAPTER FIVE

Melissa drove slowly. The land had grown wild and the driveway was overrun by weeds and broken branches. *When 'was' the last time anyone visited?*

Switching the engine off, she leaned over the steering wheel to peer up through the windshield. "Feels all welcome like," she said with sarcasm as she unclipped her seat belt and quickly shoved the door open.

Stepping out of the car, she took a deep breath and stretched her cramped body. Country air, nothing better in the world! Shame you couldn't can it and laughed the silly idea off as she looked around.

Digging in her back pocket, she pulled out a skull and cross bone key. Tapping it against her palm, she stopped for a second. Holding the old key in her hand, she looked up at the sky and closed her eyes. Wishing her brother could be here with her like back in the old days when they were kids, they'd had many adventures here.

Moving on, she cleared some of the debris from the path. The gravel crunching underneath her boots, as she walked around to investigate the six-foot steel gate blocking the entrance to her parent's cabin. She remembered when her parents had it installed. Her father's promotions through the years were enough to put him behind fort Knox. After her father passed the BAR, he quit his job as a law clerk. He scored the highest and was soon the top-notch criminal lawyer every firm wanted.

His winning streak was unstoppable and soon he was up for promotion again. Last, she heard he had been made a Federal Judge appointed by the President himself. The title didn't impress her. Growing up under the ominous presence of their father made life hard in every sense of the word, especially for Mark. Her father pushed and pushed until Mark had left home after exchanging some seriously harsh words about his 'future.'

Daddy wanted Mark to follow in his footsteps, but Mark wasn't interested. Her big brother wanted to travel the world after college. See if he could get a few assignments on a small number of digs in Greece and New Mexico. He didn't care, as long as he didn't have to stay in one place for too long. But no matter where he went, father always seemed to know the exact location.

Melissa remembered that night. Sitting huddled in her box window, holding her Raggedy Ann doll in her arms, listening to their loud voices. Her Father's deep patronizing tone followed, *"...if you leave, boy, don't come back!"* then silence.

Tears slid down her cheeks at the loud revving of Mark's old jeep. He was leaving she smiled. He was free and that made her happy. Her lips trembled, but now she was all alone.

From that day onward, she made damn sure she caused as much trouble as she could. She wasn't 'Daddy's little girl' anymore, not after that! She loved her brother more than life itself and hoped Mark made his dreams come true.

Now she found herself standing in the one place she always refused to visit after she left home. Glancing at her watch, she had about six hours of daylight. The last thing she wanted was to have to turn around and go back home. Even more so now that her Peeping Tom could look at her through every mirror she owned.

Thinking of Siaak, she couldn't suppress the tingly feeling that flooded her body. "Damn," she itched so bad it wasn't funny. Scratching through her jeans, she flipped her hair over her shoulder as she tried to concentrate on the lock. Once she had managed to clean the dirt from the key hole, it took a good ten minutes to get the darn key in. The lock was jammed tight. She was rewarded with scraping her knuckles as she yanked on the thick chain out of frustration. Cursing the stinging, she waved her fingers as she kicked the gate with her boot.

Returning to the car, she opened the trunk and took out a can of WD-40. She sprayed the heck out of the lock. She gave it a few minutes and tried again. "Yes!" she shouted in victory. The key turned and the lock popped open. Twisting the large black lock, she pulled it free of the looped security chain. After unravelling the braided chain from the centre of the double gates, she pulled it free. With a grunt, she swung the long chain up over her head to land over the gatepost.

Crossing her fingers, she hoped the damn things opened. Pressing the small button on her keychain, she aimed it at the gate. With a drawn out squeak, the gates parted at an agonizing snail's pace. She didn't care, she was just happy to be on her way.

Back in the car, she sped up the drive. Over hanging branches smacked against the windshield making her duck, she laughed in spite of being jumpy. She had a right after the last few days of being chased down like some criminal.

As she pulled up near the house, she switched the car off and just sat there staring. The cabin was in need of a lick of paint. Not to mention, the overgrown grass in the front yard that resembled a field. She used to have a teddy bear picnic out on the immaculate blue green grass when she was a child, now she could hide in it.

Where were the caretakers? Looked like nobody was home. It was for the best. She really didn't need anyone running off to tell her Mother and Father where she was.

She left the car door open, the warning ding sound drifted off as she approached the steps leading up to the porch. Reaching into the cracked pot plant, she retrieved the front door key. Holding the screen door open with the toe of her black boot, she made short work of unlocking the front door.

As soon as she walked in, she was bombarded with good and bad memories. Pictures of her and Mark at various stages in life filled in spots on the walls between family portraits and her father's countless awards.

She pushed the door back against the wall and began opening all the windows to let the house air out. In the kitchen, she took stock of what supplies were needed. She hadn't come to a decision on how long she was staying, so she quickly unpacked the car and took her spare suitcase to her old bedroom.

Climbing the dark oak stairs, she ran her hand over the knotted railing as she tugged the heavy case behind her. She wished she had her new suitcases, but they were still in her hotel room in Cairo. There was no way she was calling to ask them to return her luggage. Writing them off as a lost cause, she reached the top of the stairs. The familiar creaking greeted her as she turned right and walked down the hallway. The curtains swung out across her path enveloping her in the scent of apple blossom from the back yard. The sunlight shone against the walls and across the ceiling as she made her way toward her old room.

Standing in the doorway, her eyes drifted over the single bed covered in white lace. Her dressing table, with its princess mirror and stool in matching white, stood opposite her bed. Her eyes flickered over the bronze and gold medallions and other numerous trophies she had won for gymnastics. It was exactly as she had left it, except for a few layers of dust.

Dropping her suitcase inside the door, she took a step and paused. Shaking her head 'no', she picked her case up and went back downstairs. She'd sleep on the sofa bed. Her room held too many memories.

She quickly unpacked her things, when she realized she hadn't called her Mother to at least reassure her. Jonathon had reported her missing after all. Even after all that had happened in the past, they loved her and would be worried to death. But what if Jonathon had tried to contact them? She would never willingly put her parents in danger. Although, her Father being a judge, they had dealt with death threats more times than she could count. That didn't mean she wanted them to now, especially over her.

It was best she didn't call anyone. That also meant she couldn't call Brenda.

This was starting to piss her off just a little.

After putting her things away and unfolding the sofa bed, she went back upstairs.

Walking through each room, she carried an armload of bed linen. She covered all the mirrors with sheets and pillowcases. Just in case Siaak got any crazy ideas that, he could peek at her whenever he felt like it.

Standing back, she smacked her thighs and surveyed her handy work. "Not bad," she said and jumped at the sound of a ringing phone. Her hand flew to her throat. Listening for the ringing, she spotted the phone in the living room.

She picked it up and found a dial tone. Poking her tongue out, she put the receiver down with both hands. Nope, not that phone, she thought as she walked by her purse. The ringing got louder. It couldn't be. She hadn't even activated it or registered it with a network. She picked up her purse and reached inside. When she pulled it out, her mouth fell open at the flashing name on the small LCD screen.

SIAAK

Melissa held it in her hands for the longest time waiting for the ringing to stop. It didn't. Twisting her jaw in irritation, she felt like tossing the new phone on the floor. Now she understood what drove Beth to phone murder on a regular basis.

Standing, she left the phone on the chair in the living room. She went to the kitchen, poured a drink and drank it down. Putting the glass down, she ignored the insistent ringing, the Yankee Doodle Dandy tune was driving her nuts.

Each time she walked by it, she crossed her arms over her chest, holding herself back. Fighting the urge to answer it, knowing he wasn't going to say what she wanted to hear.

Answer the phone.

How could three little words make her skin turn cold?

In addition, immediately she felt a gentle touch at her cheek. Like the rush of warm air.

Was that him? She didn't know anymore. Could he do that from a distance?

The shower episode answered that stupid question.

She didn't have a clue really. And why would she? It wasn't like she knew any witches. The Addams family didn't live next door to her. So perhaps it was one of many abilities he could use.

She did know the history behind magic and sorcery. In

the seventeen hundreds, countless men and women were burned at the stake for supposedly wielding 'magic'.

Of course, there was Houdini and Copperfield being some of the great illusionists, not really magicians, just sleight of hand entertainers. But she knew Siaak was different.

She resisted the small smile that tugged at the corner of her mouth.

He had used telepathy again.

It felt weird.

His voice inside her mind, it was like listening to headphones with the volume turned down low.

She ran for the phone and answered it. "Hello." She swallowed anxiously. Why was she nervous all of a sudden?

"Hello Melissa."

She closed her eyes at his voice, it sounded deeper on the phone.

So Sexy.

Shaking her head, what was wrong with her? God, I need to get a hold of myself, quick.

"H- how are Beth and Mark?" She switched the phone to her other ear and sat down on the edge of the windowsill.

"I desire to talk with you. I do not wish to waste my time discussing how my unwanted guests are but since you ask, they are well and sleeping. I am keeping watch tonight, so they are safe."

"So what did you call me to talk about then?" she asked while playing with the silver buckles on her boot.

"You covered up all the mirrors in your home, are you trying to hide from me?"

"I'm not at my house, I'm staying somewhere else and I'm not hiding from you." She lied as she crossed her fingers.

"Why?"

"Because I felt trapped, I needed to get out." She dropped her legs to the floor and stared at them as she shifted her feet back and forth on the carpet. She resisted tapping them together as 'there's no place like home' filtered through her head.

"Remove the drapes so that we can see each other."

"Why, you afraid I'm with someone?" She covered her mouth with her hand. Why she felt it, necessary to taunt him she had no idea.

"I know you are alone Melissa, take down the drapes so I can see you properly."

"Okay buddy, what am I wearing? Prove to me that you know I'm on my own. I could have an old boyfriend here with me. Perhaps I'm throwing a big party and afterwards we'll have a big orgy." She felt guilty when he let out a big sigh of aggravation.

"Melissa, this is a tiresome game you play. Have it your way then. You are wearing a soft pale green top and jeans and a few minutes ago you were playing with the silver buckle on your black boots."

His voice lowered to a whisper as he continued.

"If you were with someone special, I would detect your excitement. I would see the faces of the people around you if you were having a party. The atmosphere around you is quiet, no music. In fact, it is too quiet where you are. Now take at least one drape down so I can see you better…please."

She shuddered at the silky tone of his voice.

Before she even realised what she was doing, she was staring at the full-length mirror in the hallway downstairs. Reaching up, she pulled the pale blue sheet off it. And just stood there holding it to her chest as he looked straight at her.

It was amazing!

She could see into the room he was standing in, the candle light flickering behind his head and shoulders with a stonewall off to his left.

She loved the chain around his neck. The strong silver links could never be broken, just like the man that wore it. He was wearing a white tank top and jeans. His hair was short. "You cut your hair Siaak."

"It would seem, I was behind in the hair styles, I blend in more now," he confessed before yawning.

Not with those pearly fangs, you don't, she thought to herself.

"Remove your jeans; I need to see your mark again."

"Hey! You got one look for free, I'm not stripping my clothes off so you can ogle me from afar. I can't even slap you properly!" She froze as his hands reached for the top button on his jeans.

God, he looked fine in denim.

She flinched at the slight click of his fastener. When the material fell open, her mouth did too, especially when she saw a scattering of dark hair.

Her eyes locked in place with her mouth frozen in an O when his hand moved pulling the zipper down. The metal sound caused her to shiver as she wet her lips. "What are you doing?" Her mouth went dry as he pushed his Wranglers over one hip and then the other by sliding his fingers down underneath the waistband and pushed.

"I've died," she gasped, "and gone to heaven."

Siaak liked the husky lilt to her voice. The sudden need to touch her was foremost in his mind. He liked how he affected her, it made him want to step through the mirror and make love to her in front of it. "I want to show you something."

She stepped closer and bumped her head on the mirror. Her

cheeks turned red, she had never felt so damned embarrassed in all her life. She took a deep breath and snatched a look in the mirror, half expecting him to be on the floor rolling around in hysterics. Instead, he was staring at her with those dark penetrating eyes. She breathed a sigh of relief that he wasn't amused at her clumsiness.

It seemed so real. The way he was standing there in front of her, as if she could reach out and touch him. Looking up at him, she placed her fingertips on his cheek. Very strange, she could feel hot air coming off the surface, but it was stone cold to the touch. "I can't touch you?" her voice filled with regret.

His eyes locked with hers, as he mouthed a no at her. "Look at the birthmark on my left hip, Melissa. Tell me what you see." His voice whispered from the phone against her ear.

Melissa stared at him before she stepped back and squatted to look at him. Her eyes trailed along the dip of his waist, over his hip when she saw it. Swallowing, she reached a trembling finger up to trace the mark. "It looks like mine!" the words flew from her mouth in a bewildering whisper.

Standing up, she looked into his eyes; she understood why he had shown her his birthmark.

She reached down and pulled the hem of her shirt out from the waistband of her jeans. She undid the fastener and quickly unzipped them before she got cold feet. She kept reminding herself that he'd already seen her in her birthday suit.

Siaak kept his face focused on her right hip as he watched her do a little squirm and wiggle to push her jeans down. He was right; it was just as he remembered. Her mark was exactly like his. He placed his hand on the mirror and spoke. "Thank you, Melissa. When I know it is safe for you to return, I will come for you."

"Siaak tell me what all this means…"

He winked as his image faded from the mirror.

"NO, don't go!" she cried. Reaching up to touch the mirror, she freaked when the palm of her hand sunk into the glass. Jerking her arm back, she stumbled backward until her back rammed into the wall.

How was that possible?

She stared at her left hand, palm up. Shaking slightly, she noticed a faint red tinge to her skin, making the veins glow neon blue. God that was just *too* weird.

Sliding to the floor, she rested her back against the wall. With a slight tilt of her head, Melissa watched her reflection. She imagined him being gentle, but she knew he could be rough. The memory of his hard lean body pressed against hers made her shiver.

Reaching up, she touched the area where he had bitten her. And suddenly, his image blinked onto the surface of the mirror.

He was in a stone room surrounded with books and talking to Myaten.

This was extraordinary! How could she possibly see him?

Shaking her head in denial, she got up off the floor. *It had to be some kind of spell.* It had to be the hallucinogenic drugs Siaak warned her about in the pyramid.

While she continued to argue the point of reality and fantasy, she made her way upstairs. Just before she stepped in the shower, she blew a kiss at the mirror and covered it with a towel.

Myaten was on the verge of losing his temper. His touch screen IPod was missing, again! He was going to kick Kiros's ass if he was behind it. The last time Kiros borrowed his favourite mp3 player, it ended up in a Roman fountain. He'd lost all his playlists and had spent ages downloading them from a piece of shit computer, that had duct tape wrapped around it.

Walking and rattling the ice in his glass, he raised the orange juice to his lips, until he heard Siaak's deep voice. He was talking to himself; this was fast becoming a habit. And talking to oneself was way out of character for Siaak.

Myaten stopped. His green eyes slid back and forth at the conversation Siaak was having. Normally he wouldn't eavesdrop, but Siaak wasn't being himself lately.

Myaten was hoping he'd go with the flow and accept the woman as his mate. He should have known better. Siaak did everything by the book, not that it was a bad thing, far from it. He just needed to loosen up a bit.

When he entered the room, he skidded to a halt. His nose twisted up at the sight of his brother-in-arms and the fading image of his lady in the mirror. Both of them had their pants down, literally! "I've seen it all now, its phone sex, Siaak, not mirror sex, get it right bud."

Siaak didn't bite at the joke; instead he looked longingly at the mirror. If Myaten hadn't interrupted he would have 'jumped'. "We were comparing our marks. It would seem there is a possibility she is my mate."

"Yeah I can see that and a few other things I could've gone the rest of the day *without* seeing." Myaten teased.

Siaak clamped his teeth together, and bit back a reply. As he pulled his jeans, back up he did the zip before turning to look at Myaten.

"Since we are on the subject, where is your mark?"

Myaten coughed on his orange juice. His face turned sour

as it went up his nose. He glared at Siaak. "I'm not going to show you. Let's just say, only the right woman will ever see it." Shaking his head in wonder at Siaak, Myaten plopped down on the arm of an Isis statue while letting his legs dangle over as he contemplated what he was going to say next.

"Why do I get the impression you are holding something back, Myaten? If you know what this woman means to me then tell me!" Siaak gnashed his teeth together making his jaw hurt.

"You'll find out in due time, Siaak." Myaten looked him square in the face. "She has your mark. You know very well what that means, so I advise you to stop trying to deny it! It is your responsibility to make sure she is made aware of who and what we are. If you can't, or won't accept her as your mate, then you don't deserve her. What you need to do is learn to relax. Spend more time getting to know Melissa, regardless of her human side."

"I wish I had your power," Siaak covered his face with his hands and let out a long sigh of frustration; "I would go back and do it differently."

"No, that's not the answer, Siaak. Believe me when I say this, it only causes more heartache in the end. You risk changing the lives of those you care most about. I will tell you this much. As soon as I meet, the woman I am destined to be with, nothing on this earth will keep me away from her. I will do everything in my power to keep her safe. Most importantly," the ice in his glass moved around as he rotated his wrist in a circle, "I will give her the chance to choose me because she loves me, not because we are preordained mates." Myaten gave Siaak a piercing stare full of emotion within those deep dark green eyes of his.

"What about Kiros, has he mentioned anything about his mark on a woman?"

"No. That's why he wears a cowl, to hide it since you brought us back. People stare and it makes him uncomfortable. Not that I blame him, I wouldn't want people staring at me in revulsion. I get enough from the men as it is, without making it worse."

Siaak wasn't sure if he found that funny or sad. "If you need me, I will be on patrol." Siaak gave the mirror a fleeting glance as he left the room.

Myaten held his glass in his left hand as his arm dangled around Isis's breasts. He ran the rim of the tumbler over the stone nipple. "I promise you one thing old friend, I'll be there to guide you in the right direction." He jumped down and landed on his bare feet with a soft smack. A smile appeared on his face. Sometimes knowing the future was a great thing indeed!

Jonathon woke up with a start.

"Housekeeping…" A few seconds later, a slender young woman in a red dress and white apron entered the room. "Oh, sorry Mister Strathmore, I figured you would be out having breakfast. I will come back later." She offered an apologetic smile before she spun around and left, taking her cleaning trolley with her.

When the door closed, he let his head flop back on the arm of the sofa. God his hand hurt.

He reached over for the remote with his good hand. It had fallen between the cushions. As he sat up, he scratched at his jaw and turned the TV on. Tossing the remote on the new coffee table, he stretched making his shirt ride up his chest when he stood up.

He'd only just walked into the bathroom and turned

on the water to wash his face, when he stopped dead in his tracks.

"Just in....there has been reported sightings of the American archaeologist supposedly missing. Her colleague, Dr. Jonathon Edward Strathmore, reported..."

"Fucking bitch!-I'll kill her!" Jonathon stormed out of the bathroom with water dripping down his forearms as he stared at the large screen in disbelief. Pictures of her looking at phones in a department store appeared on the screen. It was followed up with more of her at a gas station and a mini mart.

"Therefore, it leaves us to wonder what possessed the good doctor to report her missing. When it's obvious all he had to do was pick up a phone and call her."

He reached for the remote to turn it off, when a picture of David flashed up on the screen.

"If anyone has any information on this man, the police are offering a reward surrounding his death..."

"Fuck me! What a wanker! I can't even hire a decent Hitman!" He shouted as he threw the remote at the wall above the expensive television. "I swear to god! This is fucking utter rubbish!"

While he cursed Melissa into the ground with a metal spike through her friend's skull, he yanked his jacket off the chair and pulled his mobile phone out. He slid it open with the side of his thumb and wiped everything off the phones memory. Then proceeded to take the back off, and remove the Sim card, which he broke in half before he tossed the phone to the floor and stomped on it. All he managed to do was chip the paint and crack the screen. Roaring in frustration, he swiped it off the floor, walked over to the window and threw it as hard as he could. He nodded with smug satisfaction as he strutted back to the bathroom, his spirits lighter as he decided what he would do.

Kiros sat hunched over in his saddle. His black Arabian Stallion shifted its weight slightly as it lowered its head to drink from the water bucket on the wall in front of him. Tapping the ends of his reins against his brown leather clad thigh he was bored enough to go to sleep in the saddle. His head turned and his eyes zoomed in on his target. What are you up to now, he wondered to himself. He sat up and pulled the reins tight, making his horse respond immediately by turning to the left.

Kiros wasn't happy to be tracker of the day. Since Melissa had gone home, Siaak had them following the English doctor everywhere he went. Kiros would rather go to see one of those moving pictures that Myaten was always talking about. They had been discussing one the other night. Myaten called it a comical movie. No, that wasn't right or was it? A comedy, yes that was the word he had used.

His thoughts changed when Jonathon came out and got into a taxi with what looked like sacks, no luggage. Gods, he hated the different words now.

Nudging his horse into a trot, he felt his cowl slip from his head. As he encouraged the animal into a gallop, he didn't have to worry about anyone staring at him as he sped by leaving a trail of dust in his wake.

He's left the hotel and going to the airport, Siaak.

I am on my way. Return to the pyramid, we seem to have visitors again. Myaten will join you.

Kiros brought his horse to a halt and made it pivot around on its hind legs. With a loud 'YA', Kiros kicked his mount into a full gallop. Now this was going to be fun! He thought as he rode in the direction of the pyramid.

"I have to leave. You two shall stay here until I return." Siaak ordered.

Beth's brown eyes shifted up from the scroll she was reading. "Is it Melissa?"

He didn't answer until Mark joined them in the room. "I do not believe so. Jonathon is on his way to the airport. If he has found out Melissa is alive, he will go after her."

"More like, send someone after her." Mark added.

Siaak felt his temper flare at the mere thought. "I made a vow to Melissa. If Jonathon so much as touches a single hair on her head, I will kill him!"

Beth blinked and turned to look at Mark before opening her big mouth. "You like her don't you? Oh, my god, I-"

Mark quickly put his hand over her mouth to stop any further embarrassing comments. "Ignore her, we all do." Mark eyeballed her with that look that said 'shut up' before he pulled his hand away.

Beth huffed and glared daggers at him. How she managed to keep her mouth shut was beyond her.

"I will be back as soon as I can." He turned to leave and hesitated for a second. He flashed a golden oval serving plate to hand. "Here take this." He handed it to Beth. Before she could question Siaak, two goblets appeared in his fisted hands. Mark took them and was about to ask what they were supposed to do with them when Siaak hurriedly explained.

"If you are hungry or thirsty, speak aloud your request and it will appear." He left them standing there with shocked expressions on their faces.

Siaak strode across the black marble floor. His boot heels echoed with each step he took. His arms swung by his hips in wide angry strokes. He was headed towards the Obelisk inside the Temple. It was one of the last Obelisks created and the hardest to control. He knew where he wanted to go. Arms out wide he walked head long into the statue.

The minute the stone recognised his necklace he could feel it dragging him forward. His bones and muscles felt like elastic bands being stretched to near breaking point as he was yanked from one space and thrust into another. The time it took to blink, Siaak found himself standing outside Cairo International airport. He felt the cold limestone through his shirt, making his skin burn as he fought the magic of the Obelisk. He rolled off the five foot wide stonewall that supported his weight and continued walking at a hurried pace.

He wanted blood. The man deserved to die in the most atrocious way possible. Decapitation was at the top of his list, followed closely by slitting his throat or burning him alive in a sandy tomb. The scent of blood would bring a swarm of insects to eat him alive. He liked that idea even better.

He walked through the busy airport feeling ill at ease. He hated large groups of humans, made him feel claustrophobic. This was ridiculous.

Standing there in a sea of people, he sent off ten of his ghost selves. He was one of a few who could pull off the nifty trick. The only down side to it was he couldn't move a single muscle. Being paralyzed totally sucked, but hey, it was easier and cut down on time wasting.

Standing near the bottom of an escalator, he watched people rushing around him. Some stared as they wondered what the hell he was doing. He paid them no mind as he waited for the ghosts to seek out Jonathon. Within a few minutes images poured in like snap shots on flicker; filling his vision in rapid succession as they searched the airport for him.

Then he found him!

Siaak summoned his ghosts back. Each one reconnected with a surge of light. It took immense power to guide them back into his body. Making him tingle with surges of magic until the last ghost merged with his body. Using the power rush, Siaak made his way through the airport. It wasn't long before he caught up with Jonathon. Siaak took cover behind a potted tree. When no one was looking, he 'jumped' straight to terminal C.

Jonathon was in a queue of people boarding a plane bound for France.

Siaak stepped out of the dark corner and slid in line with the other passengers of flight 208. He wasn't going to let him get away! Standing behind the little weasel, his eyes bore holes into the back of Jonathon's head. Siaak shifted his stance. Putting all his weight on his right foot, Siaak intended to trip him over with his left foot. Any onlookers would assume Siaak had tripped and accidentally knocked Jonathon to the floor. Siaak moved his leg forward and that was as far as he got.

Two airport security guards shoved Siaak aside and surrounded Jonathon.

Siaak watched through narrowed eyes, as his prey was carted off swearing and shouting about how important, he is. That if he wasn't allowed to get on his plane, there was going to be serious repercussion! Siaak wasn't sure what the Englishman was up to, but he wasn't about to lose sight of him, either. He sent his ghost self ahead and followed at a slower pace.

"What the hell is going on here?" Jonathon questioned the guards as he was dragged down a long corridor. Two surly men dressed in dark, plain uniforms, met them half way. Jonathon didn't bother to fight them. He knew from previous encounters with them, it was easier to do as he was told. They took him to a private room, shoved him inside and slammed the door after him.

Looking around, he wasn't sure if he felt relief at being on his own or not. The small room was less than hospitable. The drab green mint colored wallpaper was peeling in places. Definitely wasn't his taste in décor. Lucky for him, there was a small table with two chairs. He took one and sat down. Looking over his shoulder, he noticed there one small window. It had thick steel bars that ran diagonally over the pane of glass. He snorted, like anyone was tiny enough to fit through it in the first place.

About an hour later, the door swung open. In walked a tall man with glasses. He shut the door quietly behind him before crossing his arms over his chest.

Jonathon should have known it had something to do with him. The man was beyond obsessed with the goings on about his daughter. Jonathon watched Robert watching him in that suspicious disapproving way of his. His tailored navy suit was pristine and the gold chain that hung suspended around the knot of his tie was a conservative way to show he had money.

"Where's my daughter, you bastard?"

"Hopefully buried in some sand pit," he muttered.

Robert dropped his arms and walked up to the small table. His steps slow and meticulous until he stopped behind the unoccupied chair, his fingers slid over the back.

Jonathon noticed the manicured nails and the bright red square jewel set inside an old college ring.

"You tone deaf or something? I, said, where is my daughter?" He pronounced each word slowly insulting Jonathon's intelligence.

"She's at home."

"You think I'm a fool? My daughter came here with you and I allowed it. I might add, you reported her missing," he kicked the chair; it went skidding across the floor and hit the wall where it rocked in place.

Jonathon's eyes followed it before turning back to the furious man. Robert didn't scare him in the slightest.

"I checked for myself. There is no record of her on any inbound or outbound flight, anywhere in the world! Do you know how that makes me feel Jonathon?" Robert stood up sliding his fingers into his pants pockets.

Jonathon knew that too, he had checked early that very morning. Even the police had verified that their search for her was uneventful. It was like she had dropped off the face of the earth. He knew differently from the pictures of her on the TV.

"Pretty pissed off, but look... all I know is she was with a man the last time I saw her and, this morning, she was supposedly in the states, so search me."

Robert reached over and grabbed Jonathon by his lapels, dragging him over the top of the table. The small table rocked as Jonathon struggled to keep from falling off.

"What, man?" Robert said between clenched teeth.

Jonathon quickly raked his memory for the man's name. "I don't remember his–" Jonathon's excuse was cut off as Robert slammed his right fist into his left kidney, twice. His face turned red as the pain rode up and down the entire left side of his body.

"Name now or I'll have your balls next." Robert lowered his head until his frosty blue eyes were an inch from Jonathon's.

"His name is Siaak, he didn't give a last name, said he was an old friend of Melissa's."

"He lied. I know all of my daughter's friends."

"Well maybe he's her lover."

"I know all of those too."

"A fellow teacher perhaps," Jonathon was running out of time, he could tell by the red stain creeping into Robert's face. He was about to blow.

"Unless you can give me a full name to go on, I guess it's a ball sling for you." And to show he meant business he reached down and grabbed a handful and squeezed. Jonathon screamed as Robert smiled with satisfaction before calling his men for his 'tool kit'.

Siaak watched via his ghost form. Impressive, but tame in comparison to what he could do to him.

So Melissa's father monitored everything she did, over protective perhaps. It was never a good thing when a parent refused to let their children go completely. He knew from his short time around Melissa that she didn't take orders easily. He also knew that Robert wouldn't accept his daughter with a man like Jonathon, especially if he found Jonathon had taken out a contract on her life.

Would Robert actually kill the archaeologist if he found out about the hired assassin? Maybe he should drop a hint. If he played his cards right, Siaak might not have to kill Jonathon after all. By the looks of things, her father wasn't the type to play games. Siaak could respect that.

Robert shut the door and walked at a slow pace down the corridor while tucking his shirt back in his waistband. He would find his daughter at all costs. If this man had hurt his daughter in any way, he would see to it that he paid with his life! No one would take his little girl away from him. Ever! Robert straightened his tie and smoothed the creases out of his Armani suit. As he bent down to wipe some blood off his shoes, he knew someone was watching him. The Federal judge looked up and caught a glimpse of a man standing further down the hallway.

Siaak held Robert's searching look as the older man stood up and walked right by him, how ironic. Robert didn't even know he was standing within a few feet of the man he was desperately hunting.

Robert stopped at the security desk and began giving orders to one of the guards. His face showed no emotion, it wasn't a surprise to Siaak. The man held power. Siaak could see that in the way he ordered the security guards around, as if he owned them. He wanted to know what Robert was up too. So he commanded the air inside the room, directing it towards him bringing their words to his ears.

"Tell me who that man is?" Robert asked. "Don't let him know you are looking."

The head of security radioed in the man's description by talking into his hidden microphone. "Sir, he's not an employee of the airport, probably a wayward traveller, we'll escort him downstairs."

Robert dismissed the stranger as unimportant. "Leave it. I want Mr. Strathmore watched at all times. Put surveillance equipment in his room. I want to know how many times he takes a piss. Do I make myself clear?"

The guards nodded enthusiastically and quickly departed in order to carry out his orders.

Siaak waited for the right moment to make his move. Keeping to the shadows, as soon as no one was looking, he slipped into the interrogation room.

Jonathon rolled his head to one side. His knees pulled up to his chest as he tried not to move. When he saw Siaak, his face froze in a scowl of contempt.

"Where is Melissa?" He spat while trying to keep the pain from showing. He didn't want Melissa's lover gloating over how he was rolling around on the floor holding his swollen balls between his hands and whining like a baby.

Robert had done a nice job. If Jonathon didn't understand that Robert wasn't messing around now, then he was utterly stupid. Jonathon's face was a bloody mess. A broken nose, one dark puffy eye and a long gash down the left side of his face. The blood pouring down his forehead was from some serious blows to his head. He really needed to see a doctor. Oh well.

Siaak raised an eyebrow as he moved his head back, nothing special– a slight tilt, an unthreatening gesture as he locked eyes with Jonathon. For Siaak, that one small shift empowered with his magic picked Jonathon off the floor and threw him across the room.

"Safe from you," Siaak placed his arms behind his back as he walked up to the man hanging on the wall. The SandWalker whistled as he stared at him. A mocking smile lifted his lips before settling behind a mask of solid loathing. He could never understand why humans felt greedy, the hunger to control others, but underneath it all, the need to obliterate that which they could not obtain for themselves. Insatiable greed was what ate at Jonathon. He wanted Melissa; he wanted to teach her a lesson. Siaak could see it. Like a black plaque across his soul, smothering all the good out of him.

Jonathon tried to move, but nothing worked. His mind screamed out. Move your arms, your legs. Fucking move! But no matter how hard he tied to force his limbs to move, he couldn't. He refused to grace his attacker with an answer of any kind until he went sliding back and forth along the wall like a ping-pong ball.

"What are you?" Jonathon screamed with rage.

Siaak raised an eyebrow at him and smiled. Raising a finger, he rubbed at his teeth as if there was something stuck there.

Jonathon felt his eyes drawn to that simple action. A flash of sharp teeth, no those weren't teeth they were fangs. Suddenly, there was a lump of fear lodged deep within him that he couldn't swallow down, no matter how hard he tried.

Siaak dropped his hand away and rubbed at his jaw, he needed a shave. He took his time, acting as if he hadn't heard the man's question.

"You don't have the balls to kill me." Jonathon declared with a sense of surety that made Siaak wonder once more, how Melissa could be friends with someone like him.

"I am seriously contemplating it. Give me a good reason not to." Siaak snapped his fingers and the table and chairs moved in reverse like rewinding a scene in a movie. Siaak took one of the chairs and sat down. Crossing his legs at his ankles, he sat back and gave Jonathon his full attention.

"You are fucking with me-right?"

"Somehow that seems a feeble answer. Would you care to give it another try?" Siaak said from his chair as he inspected his nails.

Jonathon wished he could get down from the wall and punch Siaak's lights out. If he had a gun, he'd blow his god damn brains out. But some inner voice told him that wouldn't kill him.

"You're some kind of magician, a hypnotist. Yes, that's it! I'm not really hanging up on a wall. You're just manipulating me, making me believe I am. Maybe if I concentrated, I can get down."

Siaak had to give it to him. For someone that was so

smart, he could be so fucking juvenile at times. "You really must stop believing that bullshit. You are hanging three feet off the floor suspended on a wall in an interrogation room, trapped here for as long as I want." Siaak spoke as if he were having to describing it to a five year old.

He stood up and walked away from the table. Siaak made sure he took his time closing the gap between them. Jonathon got the measure of who was in control. He was fed up with playing games. If Jonathon thought Robert was tough, he hadn't seen anything yet.

"Now tell me," he paused as he put a hand out, the table zoomed across to him so he could stand in front of Jonathon, "why are you after Melissa?"

Jonathon worked his jaw as he tried to move his head to look at Siaak.

"For the same reason you are!"

"Please, can we get past the fucking part, I knew that the moment I saw you."

"I saw the way you two were together. She couldn't take her eyes off you. I mean let's face it, she's very attractive." Jonathon didn't expect any reaction from the man. What he was hoping was to make Siaak so angry that he'd release him from the wall. Once down, he could make a run for it.

"What would you like to know, Jonathon? Does the idea of us being together make you cross?"

Jonathon snapped his eyes shut trying to block him out.

Siaak took part of a vision of him and Melissa and projected it in the room like a hologram. "Can you picture it Jonathon? Open your eyes and see for yourself."

Jonathon felt his head being forced down and his eyelids pulled open. NO, it couldn't be real. Melissa was all over Siaak. Her back to his chest as his hands cupped her breasts before slipping inside her shirt. Her arms curved around his neck pulling him closer as she moaned with pleasure.

Jonathon licked his lips as Siaak's hands moved seductively down her body towards her panties before the image of them vanished from the room.

"You bastard," Jonathon shouted as he tried to free his body from his invisible bonds.

Siaak lifted his head and allowed him to see how much he really didn't care for Jonathon or his attitude."I am waiting Jonathon," he brought his arm up, "you are wasting precious time," Siaak tapped on his bare wrist as he jumped down from the table and grabbed a seat.

Jonathon hated the man. It was all he could think about. It had become a fixation. Smiling to his self, Jonathon chuckled. It started low almost soundless and turned into a loud mad cackle. "I know that Robert thinks you kidnapped his daughter and he'll stop at nothing to get her back. I suggest you cough up and tell me where you are hid–"

His voice stopped as his airway became constricted. His eyes narrowed as he glared at the area above Siaak's head.

Siaak stood up so fast he knocked his chair flying. "I am done with you!" His right arm shot up into the air. Jonathon's smug face crumbled. The fear he felt was evident in his wide-eyed stare.

Beads of sweat ran down his face. The unnatural red tint of his skin slowly turned purple. His veins enlarged inside his body as his heart pumped faster, trying to supply the body with rich oxygen filled blood.

"You ever come near her again and I will kill you!" Siaak stepped closer, his eyes full of malice, his mouth open wide as his fangs grew with his full-blown wrath before retracting as Siaak teleported out of the room.

Jonathon closed his eyes. He wanted to scream. Desperately struggling, trying to free himself from the invisible force holding him to the concrete wall, he wasn't prepared for the sudden drop when Siaak let him go. He hit face first on the floor making his eyes water. "Mother fucker!" his hands went straight to his nose. Dabbing his fingers near his nostrils he pulled his hands back to check for more blood. When he managed to crawl to his knees and stand, he noticed blood all down the front of his shirt. He cursed.

CHAPTER SIX

Melissa woke up to a loud banging. "I'm coming…I'M COMING! GODS!" she shouted. Forcing her legs from under her, she swore at the cramp in her legs as she tried to stand up. Instead, she fell over and ended back in the chair. Accidentally knocking the lever with her hand, making the footrest pop out.

She'd slept in her dad's Lazy boy all night sat upright. Rubbing her legs, she hissed at another series of cramps. She had tried to stay awake as long as she could to stop thinking about Siaak. It hadn't worked. But then again, watching romantic movies until two am probably wasn't the way to go. She had dreamed of them making love on a bed of sand, of all things. She felt giddy as her body flooded with desire. It felt so real. His hands and mouth all over her body, just thinking about it made her go hot.

Fanning herself, she pulled on her blouse shaking it against her chest. There was an obvious attraction between them. She made up her mind; if she ever saw him, again she was jumping his bones.

Looking up, she frowned as she realized she had left the TV and DVD player on. Reaching her hand under her butt, she found the remote and switched everything off. Rubbing the sleep out of her eyes and yawning, she paused at the sound of breaking glass. Her head jerked up, the sloshed disoriented feeling evaporated as her heart began to pound.

The sound of something bouncing on the floor made her glance at the ceiling. Part of her hoped it was Siaak when she heard footsteps but then he wouldn't break in, well not like that anyway. "Oh shit!" she said as she leaped out of the chair into a dead run. In the kitchen she threw open the closet door and pulled out two boxes of shotgun shells, twenty-four in each box.

Filling her pockets, she had enough shells to do some serious damage, but no gun. Racking her brain, she tried to remember where her Dad kept his precious guns. Then it hit her. The shed!

As she turned to exit the kitchen, she spotted four stainless steel knives. An evil smile spread across her face as she slid the butcher's knife free and held it in her right hand, hiding the blade behind her wrist she listened for a few minutes before she snuck back into the living room. She kept her movements slow and silent. Inching along the floor, she clamped her hand over her mouth. Clouds of grey smoke crawled across the floor. She pulled the knitted throw off the couch, winding it around her nose and mouth as her hand slipped into her purse for her cell phone. Grinning in triumph, she darted for the front door. Once she was outside she dropped the blanket and high tailed it. Her heart hammered loudly in her ears, drowning out everything around her.

Am I going to die? Where was the police when you needed them? Saying that, where was her hero when she needed him? "Siaak, you bastard, I need your help!" She slid her phone open, Fuck! No signal! Disgusted she shoved it in her back pocket and resisted the stupid urge to look back. Squeezing the round, metal, knife handle, she could hear her

Mother's voice, 'don't run with a knife in your hands, you'll stab yourself'. Knowing her luck she'd probably would get stabbed with it, but not by falling over.

Instinctively she knew her only chance at living was if she got to the shed. Running, she crossed the lawn. The over grown grass slowed her down a bit, but she was determined. Whoever was after her wasn't getting her without a fight. Her chest heaving from all the running, she made a promise, if she lived through this, she was going jogging every morning.

She reached the shed and almost did a dance. It was unlocked. She threw the door open and stood there until her eyes adjusted to the dark. She looked around trying to remember where her Dad had kept his shotgun. Then she saw it on a metal shelf that ran along the wall. She grabbed the handle of the long storage box and pulled it off the shelf. She dropped it on the floor and flinched as the metal casing made a loud bang when it hit the floor. Without taking her eyes off the door, she opened the box and pulled her Dad's AOC sidelock twenty-gauge shotgun out of its weatherproof sleeve.

Dropping to her knees, she pulled all the shells out of her pockets before thumbing the safety on. She lifted it up into the air then brought the butt of the stock down against her left thigh. God, it was heavy but then it had been built to her Dad's specification. He'd had to use it a lot when entertaining the upper crusts of society from London, the normal posh array of clay pigeons with bird and fox hunting. Her Dad was an animal activist and pretended to be a horrible shot, when in fact he was the best in his country club. He usually helped the local games keepers to keep the population down, but other than that, he would never hurt an animal.

Her eyes slipped over the gun as she got re-familiarised with it. She positioned the trigger and trigger guard on the other side of the shotgun, facing away from her. She took a single shell, placed it against the loading flap, just ahead of the trigger guard. Using her thumb, she pushed the shell straight up until she heard and felt the distinct "click" as the shell passed the magazine catch. She loaded another three shells without looking at the gun.

Her eyes stayed firmly fixed on the door, as she yanked on the slide. Pulling it backwards with a hard jerk, she gritted her teeth as she yanked it back. Smiling she positioned it over her right shoulder, her finger curled round the trigger and, with her father's endless lessons, she'd take down whoever was after her.

He had scoped out the area before putting his men in place. Being S.A.S., he was trained in all methods of combat. He had nerves of steel and killing was like stripping wallpaper. He could do it with ease and make sure everything fell into place with perfect precision.

Tapping the headset, he gained the attentions of his partner. "Target is on the run, I repeat target is on the run." He watched as the woman flew from the house and ran at neck breaking speed towards a brick shed across the wide lawn.

He raised his special forces binoculars to his eyes, the digital lenses rotated back and forth, as he went through the different settings. He saw his men making their move by walking in a half crouch across the porch before jumping down the steps. His entire unit spread out, hand signals directing their actions. The black special ops chopper hovered above the house, its blades swishing in silent mode. The last thing he wanted was witnesses. Her Majesty would have his fucking balls for desert if she knew he was doing this without permission from his senior officer and worse still, for a stupid favour.

"Target is in shed, Hasbro keep your men tight." He kept a firm grip on his binoculars and the infrared picked up four, five then six heat signatures. He could see two in the shed. Suddenly, another one sprang up out of nowhere. He dropped his binoculars. That was impossible! "Fall back, god damn it!" He heard the familiar spray of bullets. The binoculars shook in hands as he witnessed a man leap out of nowhere. His arms wound round Hasbro head, with a jerk, Hasbro slumped and fell to the ground. Before he could blink, the man vanished and reappeared behind Lucas followed by Simons. Standing he slipped his binoculars over his eyes and grabbed his gun. He had a job to do and he wasn't about to fuck it up.

Mark couldn't believe he was standing in front of his sister with his arms above his head and their Dad's gun aimed at his head. "Hey, it's me!" He shouted when the gun went off. His life flashed before his eyes as he found himself eating dirt.

"What the hell are you doing here Mark?" She shouted before lowering the gun. "I could have killed you!"

He spat dirt and grass from his mouth as he rolled over and flopped onto his back. His legs and arms turned to jelly. Next time he saw Dad, he would thank him, personally for teaching his baby sister how to shoot.

He knew Siaak had something to do with him and the ground and minus a large hole in his head. There was no other explanation for his sudden escape from death's grasp.

Looking up he spotted the six-foot giant standing in the doorway, his back to him. Mark had seen people die before but never like this. The man was killing to protect his sister. He didn't hesitate.

It was strange, one minute they were all sitting at a large table talking, making plans to bring her back, the next thing he knew, Siaak was dragging him towards a large Obelisk. The man didn't waste any time! He had sent him to find Melissa while he took care of the enemy.

Melissa lowered the barrel of the gun and quickly crammed the shells back in her pockets. "I ought to shove this gun right up your ass!" she shouted at him. She was so angry, it wasn't even funny. Shaking she realised what could have happened. She had almost killed her brother.

Dropping the shotgun, she ran towards him. Falling to her knees, she hugged him as hard as she could. Her heart hammering as her mind filled with dread at what could have been.

Siaak turned to see what was keeping them. "I suggest we leave the family reunion for later."

She helped Mark stand and retrieving the shotgun, "here Mark, take this, there are three shells left in the gun, but I've got plenty in my pockets."

Siaak raised an eyebrow at the weapons. It was hard to envision her with a shotgun and butcher knife.

She let go of Mark and glared at Siaak as she walked past.

Siaak pulled her to a stop by grabbing her wrist. "There is no need for you to have that…"

Melissa tried to pull her arm back but instantly found she couldn't break free from his tight fisted grip. She reacted on pure instinct. Her right arm went flying through the air. A flash of silver and before she realised what she was doing she held the knife to his throat, "maybe I should cut you and let you see how it feels."

He didn't move, instead he let his eyes trail over her face, down her neck to the swell of her breasts and back up to her arm that shook slightly. He felt the blade against his skin. He didn't blame her for lashing out, she had been pushed too far.

"Sis…? What the hell are you doing? He saved your life and mine, so put that damned knife away!" Mark ordered as he stomped over to them.

Siaak put his arm up and motioned for Mark to stop. "This was not exactly how I envisioned us, especially after the other night. I was sure you would want to show your handsome hero how much you appreciate his selfless action of placing himself in danger, once again, to save you. Perhaps you would feel like gracing me with a warm affectionate hug or even a long passionate kiss. After all I made sure I brushed my teeth and showered just for you."

She opened her mouth ready to tell him where he could go when he grabbed her arm. He applied just enough pressure to her wrist to immobilize her fingers. The knife dropped to the floor as he wrapped his other arm around her and yanked her behind his back.

He sensed someone was near. He had to act fast. He pulled her with him into the shed and ordered Mark to stay with her. His head lowered long enough to kiss her long and hard before he slammed the door and sealed it shut with his magic.

She stood there reeling in the taste of him before it dawned on her. She looked at her brother. He didn't even try to hide the cheesy grin on his face.

"Don't you dare say one word?" She waved a bullet at him, "or I'll shove one of these in each orifice."

Mark struggled with control over his quivering mouth and was losing badly. He shook his head as he bit down on his bottom lip to steady it. His eyes watering as he fought back. "No I'm good….really."

The look on her face after Siaak kissed her was priceless. If he didn't get out of her way, he was going to end up with eight rounds of ammunition up his ass and the trigger being his sister's foot. He coughed and held his hands up, "I'm better see and I'd never laugh at you sister dear."

He stared back at her with a more composed face. The moment she turned away, he stuffed his hand in his mouth. He had never seen his sister so angry.

She was definitely affected by Siaak, possibly in love; he wondered how long it'd take before she figured it out for herself?

"Stop it Mark!" she said as she reached for the door handle.

"It's locked!" She grabbed the handle with her hand and turned it left and right. It wouldn't move. It was stuck. "Hey let me out!" she banged on the door with her heels of her hands and then kicked it with her shoes. The door didn't budge, that pissed her off even more.

Siaak heard static and conversations in between bleeps of long-range radios.

STAND DOWN. PUT YOUR ARMS ABOVE YOUR HEAD. IF YOU RUN, WE WILL SHOOT TO KILL.

The voice of the pilot amplified over the loud speaker could be heard for miles. His threat ignored as Siaak growled low in his throat.

He heard Melissa swearing in between loud heavy booms as she hammered something against the door. She wouldn't get it opened, not while his magic kept her safe inside the small man made building.

He would have to get rid of the helicopter though. He wasn't going to put the lives of Mark and Melissa in jeopardy. If trigger-happy fired a missile at him and hit the shed, he would never forgive himself.

Looking up he locked onto the whirling blades of the impressive flying machine. He threw his arms up and blasted the black Huey out of the sky. The ear-piercing shriek of metal, soon followed by an impressive explosion, turned the flying weapon into a fireball that seemed to hover for a few seconds before falling from the sky.

Siaak gritted his teeth, digging his feet into the ground and pushed the burning helicopter back. He pictured the lake behind the house and teleported it there. It was the safest way of extinguishing the flames and preventing a forest fire.

Dawson saw the explosion from his hiding place. He whipped off his binoculars and tapped a signal into his mic. "… requesting backup…men down…send in reinforcements…" This had gotten way out of hand. He waited for a reply, but all he got was static. He would deal with this situation on his own. Standing up he walked toward his target.

Siaak sensed him before he was passed the clearing of the woods. Siaak watched him knowing he was trying to figure out what he was. Dawson needed to know if he could kill him with bullets or a well-placed grenade. Well he was about to find out the hard way. And it would take more than that to put him down, especially for good.

Dawson weighed up his opponent. Whatever he was, he wasn't human. John had been his buddy for a long time and he hadn't said the man was this dangerous or that he had special powers.

How was he going to explain the death of four SAS officers, Hasbro, Lucas, Simons and Mallard, good men gone because he owed a favour?

He tapped the mic and spoke in code, "Firebrand stand down, target acquired, I repeat, I have the target."

Another helicopter zoomed into place. The nose of the military camouflage machine rose into the air before it lowered its guns. All of which were aimed right at Siaak. The pilot wasn't letting him out of his sights as he directed the air craft to pan round him.

Siaak stood there, he didn't challenge the men. They were innocent pawns. None the less, they were going to hurt Melissa and for that, they would all die.

"Hands above your head mate!"

Siaak didn't move. His mind reached out to Myaten. *"…protect her with your life…"*

Siaak casually glanced down at the sudden stings all over his chest and legs. And within a few minutes, he felt his knees buckling. He reached up and yanked three darts from his neck before pulling six more out of his chest. He roared in anger, his mouth opened wide showing off his elongated fangs. "Protect Melis…s…a," he mumbled before he landed face down on the ground.

Another man approached the target before radioing it in. "Target is down."

As soon as Myaten heard the emotional order from Siaak, he flashed straight to where he had tagged Siaak during his brief message. He fell to one knee and ran his fingers over the soil. When he raked his nails through it, he discovered three used trank darts.

Glancing further up the lawn, he could see where the helicopter had landed mashing the long grass down flat like a crop circle. As he stood up, he followed two thin trails that started from the patch of earth with the trank darts and ended near the circle of grass. It was more than enough evidence to suggest someone being dragged away.

Siaak

Looking up he saw the helicopter rising into the sky, the

sun reflecting off the metal shell of the flying machine. He heard the pounding and shouting coming from the shed behind him and knew that Siaak had put Melissa and Mark there to keep them safe.

With a wave of his hand, the magic shield dissolved and the door flew open. Melissa fell forward onto the ground. He watched her get up and immediately looked around for Siaak. "Where is he?" she asked as she strode across the lawn to stand with him. She was ready to do battle. He liked that about her. Siaak needed a mate like that.

Myaten pointed at the fading helicopter, "I believe he's in there." He threw his head back and concentrated his magic. Lifting his body up off the ground, he began to twirl as he spoke aloud.

"Externas– expellees, wind destroy!"

He like Siaak controlled the wind. He directed it across the sky around the loud apache. The howling winds grew louder as he summoned them to his aid. Faster and faster, he pushed at the metal beast knocking it back, keeping it from escaping him. He couldn't risk destroying it, at least not with his brother onboard it.

He could feel him, his thoughts of Melissa and how he'd broken his vow. That made Myaten furious. He yanked on the helicopter and watched with satisfaction as it lurched to one side, the blades spinning in jerks as the wind pulled at them.

Siaak felt the rumble of the engines as it fought to stay airborne. He lifted his head and looked at the man holding a gun between his eyes.

"Wh–what do you want with Melissa?" his mouth was so dry that his lips stuck to his teeth. He tried to moisten them with his tongue, but it felt like a thick wad of cotton in his mouth.

The drugs were making it hard for him to focus. His eyesight blurred putting him off balance. "What did you give me?" his head fell forward making the gun dig into his skull but he couldn't feel it as he slipped into darkness.

Dawson watched John take the gun and backhand the prisoner across the head knocking him to the floor of the helicopter. A dark pool of blood spread out from his head.

"Hey! He's out cold! Leave him." Dawson put himself in the way, blocking any further attacks from John as he thrust his hand out. "Give me your firearm!" Dawson ordered.

John released the safety and pointed the berretta at Dawson, "Move! I won't think twice about shooting you too." John turned his frantic eyes on Dawson, he felt edgy. If he gave Dawson the gun, he'd be powerless. Shaking his head no he locked his elbows as he held his arms out with the gun aimed at Dawson's head.

Dawson had seen it before. Madness eating away until there was nothing left keeping you alive. "You told me he had kidnapped your fiancé, that's not true is it? Answer me Jonathon!"

Jonathon began to panic, his eyes wondered around the small compartment of the helicopter. "He took her from me, she belongs to me!" His lips parted forming a sneer as if he had a bad taste in his mouth. It made his nose lift as his eyes bored holes into the man sprawled on the floor.

Dawson felt a sick feeling in the pit of his stomach. Men had died today over what? Petty jealousy! "NO! Put the gun down John, I won't allow you to kill another man today."

Jonathon blinked as if he hadn't heard him correctly. "He's not getting away Dawson, he can't have her." His words barely a whisper as he stared off into space.

Dawson looked down at the dark hair man lying near

his feet. What had he done? He had let John trick him into going after an innocent man. A very strong, athletic man that has super human powers, he thought to himself. He had seen how he appeared out of thin air. The way he had blown up the helicopter.

It was all coming together, a very brilliant plan. If he offered this man to the 'lab techs', he was sure it would appease his superiors. The most he would get was a charge of misconduct and theft of military transport. Then there was the loss of some very good men. That he would never forgive himself for, or Jonathon.

"You're right he's not getting away," Dawson saw his co-pilot creep out of his seat and come up behind Jonathon, he raised his gun and brought the butt of it down against his head. "And neither are you!" Dawson said as Jonathon hit the floor.

Myaten locked onto Siaak as the helicopter spun around in mid air. Just as Myaten moved in to 'grab' his brother, the flying machine dropped altitude and he missed.

The loud boom of an engine engaging drowned out all sound, stopping its stomach curdling downward plunge. It shot across the sky. A bit too close for comfort, as far as Myaten was concerned! He stood like a mountain, daring the flying beast to come near. His hair and clothes whipped back and forth in the burst of turbulent wind in its wake. He was fed up with this cat and mouse game.

Myaten watched in fascination as the blades crossed and lowered in a downward tilt before being concealed within the body giving the machine a sleeker look. The helicopter was changing right before his eyes!

"Fuck me, it's a transformer!" He laughed and cursed as two side panels cracked the metal skin of the helicopter's body and slowly extended outward before locking into place. A loud clicking of gears followed by a deafening burst of engines kept the giant fighter helicopter hovering in place as it locked onto multiple targets and fired.

The first thought in his head was the sound of Siaak's voice ordering him to protect Melissa with his life. Siaak had never asked anyone for anything. He was going to make sure he got it.

The loud whoosh of hydraulics followed by a spray of red tipped missiles caught Myaten's attention. Heat seekers, there was no mistaking the low cost standard issue for most military armies around the world. Their enemy was upping the stakes to gain freedom.

This was going to be fun.

Myaten ground his teeth together and roared as he took off from the ground. He rolled his body left then right, swerving two missiles followed by three more in his upward approach.

Slamming his hands together, he ignited a time globe. Everything moved in slow motion for the humans but his body and mind were free from the effects of the time spell. Years of practicing with his mentor, Roris a legendary SandWeaver long buried beneath the sands of Egypt, had honed his skills to perfection.

Silver netting flew from his fingertips like spider webbing. Shimmering in the sunlight, it flew across the sky towards the flying projectiles. He kept his concentration fixed on the heat-seeking beacon. With a single thought, he dismantled the detonators.

There was no way he could 'catch and throw' all the missiles that went in every direction. Two of which were headed straight at the shed.

Bringing his arms over and around his head like he was swinging a baseball bat, he built up his momentum and let the net go with the missiles inside. He heard the unmistakable sound of more missiles flying through the air. "Oh don't you people know when enough is enough?"

He leaped, knocking Melissa to the ground, using his body as a shield while he teleported Mark from his spot inside the shed to a safe place by the cottage. The shed exploded turning it into a dangerous expanding cloud of shrapnel. Myaten hissed as shards of glass and metal sliced into his back and legs along with a good pelting of flying debris from the small building.

Myaten stirred and lifted his head; his eyes homed in on Mark's running figure. Myaten didn't need to look up to know what he was running from.

As he rolled off Melissa, he saw the impact a second before the house blew up in a flash of orange. "NO!" He shouted. His hand reached out and yanked Mark from the backlash of flames that was close enough to score his clothing. The fire screamed as it spread out, consuming everything in its path.

Melissa grabbed hold of her brother as he appeared out of thin air. "You okay?" she saw puffs of smoke from his clothes and immediately she yanked his shirt off, threw it to the ground and stomped on it.

Mark nodded. He couldn't speak. What had they gotten themselves into? He looked down at his sister who was busy inspecting him for second or third degree burns when Myaten grabbed them both and smiled.

"….*Kiros, I got Melissa and Mark coming your way, get ready to "catch" when I send them…*"

Thousands of miles away, Kiros jerked his head up, the cowl slipped from his dark hair as he turned in the direction of his brother's voice. His lips moved out of habit as he answered back.

"I'm ready." He braced his body against the stonewall where he stood after Myaten spoke to him. His brother was known for throwing hard and extremely fast. And catching two humans at the same time wasn't going to be easy for him.

He held his arms out as he sensed the portal opening before him.

A rush of cold air followed by the smell of sulphur made his nose twitch. With a loud grunt, his back muscles pulled tight as he caught Melissa first. He let her slip from his arms as he felt his brother's second throw.

Before he had a chance to blink, Mark was there, his back facing Kiros. The young SandWalker almost dropped him. Myaten didn't say Mark was hurt. Kiros frowned, but managed to catch Mark before he hit the floor.

"What happened?" he asked Melissa as he lifted her brother off the floor and carried him to the lounge bed made of solid marble with gold embellishments and thick red pillows.

He noticed the burn patches on Mark's jeans as he lifted the human's long legs up and positioned them outstretched along the lounge bed. He raised an eyebrow in surprise at scorch marks on his bare back and chest.

She gripped her hair, pulling in frustration, as she stared at her surroundings. "I'll be damned; you guys have done it to me again! Send me back, NOW!" She raced up behind Kiros to shove him out of frustration and anger. She stumbled and met the wall with her shoulder. Cursing she turned on her heel to find Kiros across the room staring at her with an icy glower.

"Don't try that again, human." His voice was full of contempt. He didn't like to be touched unless he was asked.

He reached behind his neck and pulled the cowl over his head as he turned slowly to look at her. His blue eyes glittering, like chips of ice, as he passed judgement over her actions. Humans caused nothing but trouble, just like the evil one he guarded. Why Siaak felt the need to keep in contact with her was beyond him.

"Send me back! Siaak needs me!" She disregarded the look of revulsion that he didn't bother to mask. "Siaak was captured by some…"

Kiros clasped his hands together behind his back as he cut her a look from underneath his hood. "I know what has happened to my brother. Myaten informed me…"

"Then you have to go and help! Take us with you!" She took a gulp of air making her chest rise and fall rapidly. "We can get him back…"

Kiros pulled his cowl back letting her see the look of distrust he felt towards her and all her kind. "I'm not allowed to leave my post. I, more than anyone, wish the swift return of Siaak." Kiros worked his jaw. The muscles twitching in time to his outrage, how dare she order him? How dare she presume he would not attempt to free Siaak or care about his health and well-being?

"Myaten will find Siaak and bring him home. Of this, I am sure. If he had not been watching you…" he took a few steps closer to her, the hem of his black cape dragging across the marble floor behind him until he stopped. "…letting his guard down, trying to figure out what you mean to him, why he keeps having the 'visions' and," he lowered his face to hers forgetting that she would see his mark. "…if Siaak was not consumed with the knowledge of your matching mark, he would have killed you for breaking into the pyramid. He would not be a prisoner."

He let his icy blue eyes brand her with their fire before he turned his back to her and walked to the centre of the room. "I can send you back if I want a fight with Myaten, which I don't. He gave an oath to protect you and him," he nodded in Mark's direction. "I owe Myaten my loyalty for life; you on the other hand, I owe nothing." He turned to grace her with a hard look that told her he meant every word as he left the room.

His words echoed inside her head. He was right to a certain degree, but she didn't have time to worry about what other people thought of her. Lowering her head, she looked at her brother. He would have died if not for Myaten. She owed him big time.

For the first time since she was thrown across time and space, she had a good look around the room inside the Pyramid.

The room was filled with rich dark colors of reds and gold. She hadn't expected the kind of luxury she had sampled in Siaak's temple. The last time she had been inside it, Myaten had escorted her off the premises.

Hanging her head, she pushed the thoughts from her conscious. Her brother needed her and if not for her, he wouldn't be in this mess to start with.

He was out cold. She wasn't sure if that was due to shock or Myaten tossing them across the world.

Sitting down in a chair that faced him, she took his hand in her lap. "I'm sorry I got you into this Mark." Her voice was edged with regret. She had never meant for anyone to get hurt. "I feel like I'm stuck in a fairy tale. I don't know if you'd believe it or not. Then again, I'm not so sure what to believe anymore."

She put her face in her hands and prayed that Mark would be okay. "Wake up, please," she lifted her head to stare at her sweet brother. He had always been her rock. Someone she could depend on when her life got too tough.

Standing up, she rested his hand over his chest and gently pushed a stray hair away from his brow. Then she took a step back. She couldn't understand why all this was happening. At least he wasn't dead and that, she owed to Siaak.

That made her think of their kiss in the shed. That was the last thing she expected. Had he done it to put her off guard? He did lock her in. Probably to keep her out of his hair while he went and played hero.

Then her mind shifted gears at the realization that Siaak was gone. God only knew, what would happen to him now. He had been captured. If they found out what he was, she knew what they'd do to him. And who would have the power to enlist a military force? What did they hope to gain by taking Siaak?

"What in the name of all that's holy happened to you guys?"

Melissa whirled around to find Beth standing in a doorway that hadn't been there earlier.

Melissa ran over to her old friend and hugged her tight. "Oh, my god, Beth! I'm so happy you're here." She dropped her arms and paused as she looked at her friend in wonder. "How did you get here?"

Beth flashed a wicked smile as she pressed a finger to the side of her nose. "It's magic."

"OH! Don't you start! Now why are you hanging around? You should have high tailed it, when you had the chance too!"

"Honey, open your eyes. You ain't gonna tell me you ain't see the muscle walking around here?"

Melissa snorted, "Yeah I saw and I got escorted from the

building by Myaten. I hope he wasn't captured too." She looked around the room half expecting one of them to walk out of a wall or something.

"You don't know the half of what I've seen." She waved her hand at her face like a fan. "These guys strut around like peacocks showing off their feathers…"

"I don't think I wanna know," Melissa said as they walked over to where Kiros had put her brother.

Beth stared at him for a second before she whistled over the scorch marks on Mark's body. "Boy, he's been in the wars," her eyes raked Melissa for info, "so, spill the beans woman, or am I going to have to get the brute squad?"

"No brute squad, especially if it's the evil and twisted monk wanting to nail my ass to a wall." Melissa sat back down and rubbed her hands together as if she was cold.

"Siaak was captured by the military and, god only knows, what will happen to him. He's not human, Beth," she ran her hands over the back of her neck before winding them around her waist.

"Honey, tell me something I don't know. He didn't bat an eyelash when I got on my high horse, which tells me, he ain't any normal man."

Melissa grunted, "You can say that again. I've never met a man who scares me and tempts my self control, all in one go."

"Why I do believe you are smitten." Beth waved her hand like an imaginary fan over her face and winked mischievously over the tops of her fingers.

"Oh stop it Beth. I do think he's sexy."

"What, you two ain't done the bump and nasty yet?"

Melissa glared at her. "If he had his way, he'd have jumped me in a heartbeat and left me wondering what my name was."

"Can I have his number then?" Beth teased as she

inspected Mark's burns. Her face turning serious, "He has a fever Melissa, I think he's in shock. Kiros, I need your help." She called out to the brooding SandWalker as if he was standing nearby.

Melissa caught her breath as Kiros appeared out of nowhere. He held a small round disc in his hand that he promptly placed on Mark's chest right over his heart. "He will live." He bowed low at Beth and vanished from sight.

"He really doesn't like me." Melissa said as she moved closer to see what Kiros had put on her brother's chest.

"Looks like a prop from Stargate," Beth said softly as her eyes focused on the large round glowing stone that hummed.

"Wonder what it does?" Beth reached out and touched her fingertip to it. She immediately jerked her hand back and rubbed it against her other thigh. "Hot!" She looked up at Melissa in amazement as all the burn marks on Mark's body simply faded away.

"Look at the stone, its turned black."

"What's gone black?"

Melissa and Beth watched as Mark shook his head and yawned before sitting up. The stone disc slid off his chest and he caught it with lightening reflexes before it hit the floor. "What's this?" He held it up and gave the women a curious look.

"It healed you," they said in unison.

"Oh," was all he said as he sat it down on the lounge bed. "Where are Siaak and Myaten? I would like to thank them for saving my bacon. And why are you two looking at me as if I've grown a third eyeball?"

Melissa opened her mouth to tell him about Siaak, when she heard a popping sound followed by a low moan. Turning around, they found Myaten laying face down. His clothing, what was left of it, was smoking and smelt of gasoline.

Beth, Mark and Melissa moved to help Myaten off the floor when Kiros flashed between them and Myaten's body.

"Stay back!"

"We only want to help him," Mark said as he carried on walking towards Kiros.

Kiros growled at them, showing his fangs, letting them know he meant business. He reached down and picked Myaten off the floor. "I will see to his needs. I want you all gone when I return, do I make myself clear?" Kiros glared, his fangs growing longer in warning, he sneered at the woman he held responsible.

Myaten raised his arm up and pointed at Melissa. "She is not to leave this place…I promised, Siaak, I would protect her….annnnd….I…" Myaten's dark green eyes filled with pain as he tried to make Kiros understand how important Melissa was to their brother.

Kiros gave her a frosty glare over the top of Myaten's head. His jaw clenched tighter than a vice grip. "Fine! Stay here." Kiros ordered and vanished with Myaten in his arms.

"See, I told you he didn't like me," Melissa turned her back to the searching gazes of her brother and Beth. She felt the burn in her throat as she fought back the tears. Then she stopped. She would go and find Siaak herself. That should prove that she could be trusted with their secret.

"I'll be right back." She didn't offer any excuses as she rushed past the astonished faces of Beth and Mark.

She had been trying to figure out why this room seemed so familiar. She had seen this room before in one of her visions. It wasn't the Pyramid, it was Siaak's temple. They had made love more times in this room than she could count on both hands. She wondered why that room was such a focal point for her visions.

Once she was outside the door, she noticed the familiar hieroglyphics. Siaak had taken her past these rooms when he had escorted her to a bedroom of her own.

As she carried on walking, she noticed the room she slept in. As she turned the corner and entered the doorway, she stopped at the sight of her bags. A soft smile touched her lips at his sentimental side. Running across the room, she jumped up and down.

Taking one of the cases, she threw it on the bed making it bounce. She quickly opened it and pulled out her books and her vest. Taking a seat on the edge of the bed, she hugged the vest to her chest. Her eyes shut as she replayed the events leading up to her capture by Siaak. She sat there listening to her heartbeat as she flipped through each scene until she found something.

Her eyes snapped open. "That's it!" she cried. Her fingers shook as she unzipped the pocket at the bottom of the vest and pulled out a small plastic baggie. Holding it up to the light she smiled a split second before tearing the bag open and dumped the metal object into the palm of her hand.

Raking her fingers through her hair, she dropped to her knees by the edge of the bed and laid the shiny piece of silver metal on the mattress. She had seen one like it before. Tapping her finger against her chin, "now where have I seen it before?" she spoke aloud as she stood up and reached for her other suitcase. Full of anticipation she threw the case up into the air and turned it round. Using her thumbs, she scrolled the three black dials in order to put in her private combination and hoped to god, everything was still as she has left it.

At the loud click, she opened the lid and let it fall back against the bed. Her eyes quickly took in the contents of her case as she scooped all her clothes out and dumped them on top of the bed.

One of the things she failed to show Siaak was another book her father had found in Luxor. On the cover of the giant volume was pressed an image of a pyramid with a cobra intertwined down a staff. Its hood was open, ready to strike. There were dozens of hieroglyphics embedded within the picture itself, as well as down the spine. She had never been able to decode them. Even with the aid of the Rosetta stone, it was still a mystery to her.

She grabbed her vest again and took out a pair of powder free gloves. After she put them, on she carefully opened the book and turned the pages with a special pair of suede tipped tongs.

She scanned the beautiful pages knowing she had seen the piece of jewellery before. All the pictures were hand drawn and dated. She found herself drawn to one picture, in particular, of a man. She reached over, picked up the thin metal piece, and held it up to the book. "YES!" she shouted in triumph. She knew she had seen it before.

CHAPTER SEVEN

Dawson watched as Jonathon's slumped body was dragged into an elevator by a special unit, containing five men and one woman. The entire unit was armed to the teeth and ready to kick ten tons of shit out of him, if he so much as looked at them wrong.

Dawson had radioed a brief message before landing, requesting a holding cell for their good Doctor. If Dawson had his way, he'd throw John to the wolves. He'd like to see how fast his mouth saved his selfish ass then.

In reality, John deserved a bullet to the head and his body tossed into the ocean. The sharks could take care of the left over garbage.

Dawson palmed the ID scanner and caught a glimpse of a knee connecting with Jonathon's face as the doors closed on the elevator.

Dawson had been friends with John for a long time. They had been through some rough times as children. That didn't give John the right to abuse their friendship.

He wouldn't want to be in John's shoes when he woke up. Jefferson and his crew were famous for working out their aggressions on prisoners. Dawson knew it would only be a matter of time before Jefferson got wind of his fallen comrades. Jonathon would wish he were dead.

Rolling his head round on his shoulders as he walked along the corridor, Dawson paused long enough for the jet sprays to hose him down. Closing his eyes, he held his breath as he waited for the wet mist to settle around him.

Turning his nose up at the strong smelling disinfectant, he wondered how anything could penetrate that stink as he paused at another spray point. By the time he got down the end of the hallway, his hair was damp and his tongue felt like an alcohol wipe.

Stepping up to the clean white double doors, he peered through the small window. The SAS officer tapped on the reinforced glass, hoping to gain the attention of a member of staff.

One of the nurses looked up at the knocking and nodded as he mouthed 'Eric'. Dawson put his thumb up when the dark headed nurse pointed at Dr. Silver.

Dawson heard the sound of wheels and stepped back. Siaak was wheeled through on a gurney. The wound on the back of his head had stopped bleeding. He was alive, and to be honest, he was surprised. He would have sworn John had killed him. The blow to his head was fatal.

The flapping of the double doors caught his attention as Eric stepped through after the two paramedics/officers had pushed Siaak into theatre, room twelve.

"What's going on Dawson?" Dr. Eric Silver asked as he swiped his paper hat off along with his blue facemask.

Dawson placed his index finger against his mouth. He ushered his old mate out of sight of the security cameras. "I want you to keep your eye on the man that was just admitted to your theatre. He shows some interesting powers. I think you will be more than amazed by them."

The expression on Eric's face told Dawson he didn't

believe a word he said. So Dawson pulled the good doctor's head closer and whispered. "He teleported into an open field and took out four of my guys."

At Eric's shrug of indifference, Dawson added, "And he blew up a special-op chopper without any weapons." Dawson moved back hoping that put the last piece of the puzzle into place for Eric.

Eric rubbed his tired eyes and nodded. "What tests you want me to run? Baring in mind the higher ups are going to want their pound of flesh, so if you are looking for anything in particular, I have to do it now!"

"I expected that Eric. I want to know what he is and where he came from. Do a full medical on him for me."

"Maybe you should have checked his wallet. As for the teleport thing, lay off the sci-fi programs and get some rest. Your eyes are blood shot," the doctor sniffed and stepped back, "and you stink. Go grab a shower and get some shut eye."

Eric squeezed his arm and shoved the officer back until he was in line with the men's washroom.

"Go, we can talk later."

After washing his hands and shoving on sterile gloves, Eric made his way over to room twelve. He grabbed a blank chart and pen, both wrapped in a plastic film to be incinerated after use. Their government and secret partners were very cautious. Nothing was left with fingerprints or DNA of any kind for fear of detection.

Glancing at his wrist, he jotted the time and date. Dawson's unit would have to submit a report. If he left any blanks on the medical forms, he'd only get it in the neck. Sighing Eric tapped the pen against his bottom lip as he rounded the corner and opened the door.

He peered inside and caught the eye of Kramer and

Freeman, two of Dawson's snipers. Pushing the door open, Eric flashed a quick smile as he dropped the chart on the end of the bed between the patient's feet. "So who wants to fill me in?"

Eric eyeballed the two guards who were armed to the back teeth. Guns didn't bother him in the slightest. The person wearing them set his nerves on end. He waved them away from the bed with an impatient gesture. He donned his favourite no-nonsense look that all doctor seem to be born with. He needed plenty of room to examine the man's wounds.

Eric nodded absent-minded as he ran the pads of his fingers over the back of the male's skull. Raising an eyebrow at the large grapefruit size lump, Eric gentle turned the patient's head sideways and reached overhead for a lighted magnifying glass. Once it was in position, Eric could see a long silver scar that suggested an old wound, strange; it was covered in fresh blood.

Confused Eric shoved the light out of the way, and grabbed his chart and scribbled away. "Does anyone have a name for our new guest?" Eric held the pen posed above the pink form as the guys hummed over his question. "Doesn't matter guys, I can take finger prints and run them."

Eric glanced up over the bridge of his nose. "If you need to be somewhere, please go. I've got it covered here." Eric wanted them out of his way so he could take a few blood samples and put Dawson's mind to rest that the man lying on the bed wasn't some special mutant. Eric beamed a friendly smile as both officers rushed from the room.

Kramer spoke up, "Thanks doc, we both need to grab some food," Kramer stopped at the door and placed his hand on Eric's shoulder. "He shouldn't wake up any time soon doc, John put enough trank in him to put down a herd of elephants."

Kramer laughed, but Eric detected the stress in the man's attempt at humour. "I have it under control men. Take your time; grab a nap if you need it."

Once the guards were gone, Eric took a stool and sat down. He was dog-tired. When the patient spoke to him, he jumped off his seat. "What did you say?"

"Where am I?" Siaak opened his eyelids. Everything seemed to merge into one big splash of color. He saw something move and tried to sit up but his body wouldn't budge. "My sight is blurred, is that a side effect of the drug injected into my body or have you," Siaak ran his tongue over his lips, "given me something else?"

Eric blinked a few times at the man's voice before his questions registered in his brain. "No, I was in the process of examining your injuries. Can you tell me your name? How you got that bump on your head? Why you ended up here?" Eric grabbed a pen light and waved it around the room, testing its strength.

"If you expect me to answer your questions with honesty, then unbind me." Siaak was too weak to defend himself. The drug had pretty much kick his ass.

Eric had heard that one before.

"No, the restraints are there for a reason. It keeps you from attacking me. I don't want to have to call in reinforcements." Eric watched the man close his eyelids and run his tongue over his lips. "Would you like something to drink?"

Siaak opened his eyes and stared straight at the doctor. "Is it pure?"

"Yes, its bottled water– oh, you mean have I spiked it?" Eric shook his head. "No, I don't believe in drugging my patients. If you answer all my questions, I'll give you something for the pain and get you something to eat–"

"It is Siaak. I have no pain and with time, my eyesight will return to normal. That it is all I will tell you."

Eric folded his hands over his chest. "I'm the Doc, do you mind if I check your eyes and see for myself? It is, after all, my job."

Siaak frowned. He knew his luck was up and unless Myaten and Kiros showed up in the next hour or so, the good doctor was about to find out more than he bargained for.

Eric sat down at his desk and punched in his password. He went straight to WORD and opened a new file.

JOURNAL

First Entry: Observation day one 13/4/09

Patient is an adult male. Approximate age is hard to determine, best guess, mid thirties. Height is well over six foot, nothing unusual to note. Hair, eyes and teeth seem normal. Note: Patient shows remarkable healing powers, unlike anything I have ever seen before. I'm hoping to get some tissue samples in order to gain insight into Siaak. Now the male is highly strung. In order to keep him from harming himself and others, I have prescribed a sedative, Valium.

Eric ended his journal and sent it as an attachment to his home computer. Tonight he would stay at work and read up on the records from the archives.

"How are you feeling this morning Siaak?" Eric looked around the large lab room. He had fought to keep Siaak awake and given certain privileges. So far, he had won them all. How long his winning streak would last, depended on Siaak's answers.

Siaak look up at Dr. Silver and snarled. "How would you feel if I stuck needles into your body every hour and treated you like some circus freak?"

Eric knew the bone biopsy and spinal tap wasn't particularly a pleasant experience, but all the normal tests were done now. "I'm sorry about that Siaak. But you'll be happy to know that's the end of the testing."

Siaak graced him with a shrug of his shoulders. "When does the real torture begin?" It was only a matter of time. Siaak knew the humans would dissect him like a frog as soon as they found out he wasn't like them.

"Whatever you may think of me, Siaak, I'm not here to dismember you." Eric bunched his fist up and pressed it under his chin as he walked over to the small eight by ten window. Another 'perk' he had to fight for. No human should be boxed up in a cage. He wished he could set him free.

"I believe you Eric." Siaak knew when a human lied. The doctor was telling the truth and he couldn't fault him for not wanting to risk his life for a stranger.

"Your eyes for instance, why do they shimmer in the light?"

Siaak pursed his lips in deep thought. "That is something I truly cannot explain Eric. It happened the first time I drank blood-" Siaak turned his head away as if embarrassed.

Somehow, Eric doubted this man could ever feel that way.

"Can I assume that is the reason you have fangs?" Eric expected some half-baked story about vampires. Maybe the government had created him from some mutant gene pool they had fashioned from cloning. Nothing surprised him anymore.

Siaak rested his broad shoulders against the headboard. His head barely touched the wall as he stared back.

He could read Eric's mind. The good doctor wanted to know what he was. Perhaps he needed to raise the stakes a little.

"Sometimes, I use them to kill, mostly when I need to protect myself."

Siaak gave him a coy smile before opening his mouth allowing his fangs to grow into long thin points. He shook his head in frenzy and lunged as far as the chains would allow.

Eric leaped backwards. His back hit the wall and he bounced to the floor in a heap. Eric wiped his mouth with the back of his hand. "You didn't have to do that, Siaak."

Siaak dipped his head low and stared over the bridge of his nose allowing his dark glittering eyes to settle on him. "We all have choices Eric. I chose to protect you humans. Look where it got me!"

"Protect us from what Siaak?" Eric straightened his shirt and spoke as he wiped, then tucked his hands in his front pockets.

Siaak didn't like where the line of questioning was leading. He had already said too much. He put it down to the truth serum running through his veins. "An evil creature that threatens to dominate your world, if you keep me here, it is only a matter of time before she is free."

"That must be the woman Dawson told me about." Eric picked up his glasses and slipped them in his white lab coat.

"No! She is merely a human woman who turned left instead of right. Leave her out of this!"

Eric took note of the bark in his tone at the mention of the woman Dawson was sent to retrieve. "Are you lovers?"

Siaak sneered as he rolled off the bed. In a fit of rage, he picked the bed up and shoved it across the room. It hit the wall with a loud bang before it toppled over and crashed onto the tiled floor. Siaak roared as he strained against the chains that held him down.

"I feel that it is of no consequence to you." Siaak's chest

heaved as his adrenaline kicked in. "We are not lovers. Not that it is any of your business."

"Does she know what you are?" Eric didn't move. Sitting on the floor, he took out his Dictaphone and pressed record.

Siaak sneered at his demeaning question. "What exactly 'am I' Dr. Silver?"

"You tell me."

Siaak laughed, as he shook his head no. "I want you to leave. Come back tomorrow. Perhaps by then you will have thought up a few decent questions to ask me."

Second Entry: Observation day seven 20/4/09

Patient has no evidence of scar tissue. Upon further examination, the male has shown rejuvenation on a cellular level. I believe he has the answers we are looking for. I am going to take extra samples of blood and tissue for lab work. If I am right, I could be close to finding something monumental!

I've been requested to 'open up' specimen. Seems my bosses aren't happy with what I've found out so far. I have refused on principle. I will not perform an autopsy on a live human being. I don't care how special he is.

Today we took scans of Siaak. His organs are situated in the same location as a human. The only difference is he seems to have two hearts. Remarkable! I will schedule an MRI and EKG as well.

I'd love to know why he has two hearts. Could it be like having two kidneys? I will ask him during our next meeting.

What is that sound? Hello, can you hear me? Myaten...

Kiros? Where am I? My limbs feel numb and I am unable to see or speak.

Melissa can you hear me? Help me brothers. Find me. Take me home.

"Do we know what he is?" A male voice with a slight Scottish accent spoke near his ear.

Siaak wanted to lash out at them.

"He's not *human* if that's what you want to know sir."

Siaak had heard her voice a great many times in between his moments of consciousness. He didn't like her either and if he got his hands on her, she was dead.

Their conversation faded away as he screamed out in pain. It was like nothing he had ever felt before, tearing through his body. How he found the strength to lift his head he would never know. He opened his eyes to find he was in a cold room with a group of people in blue scrubs, their faces partially hidden behind paper masks keeping their identities from him. Siaak tried to move his arms and legs before he spoke slowly.

"What, are, you doing to me? He managed to say in his own language before his head fell back on the operating table. His eyelids fluttering shut as he lost consciousness.

Eric ground his teeth together before he stepped back from the group of observers. "I expect my patients to stay under throughout an entire operation."

His grey eyes settled on his assistants. "I can't have my patients waking up in the middle of surgery. For one, it's too traumatic for him," Eric's glare settled on Dr. Stockwell. "Regardless of who or what he is. I took an oath! I won't butcher a man for knowledge, of any kind. Dr. Eggleston, sow him up. Alert me when he's awake."

Dr. Eggleston, a tall man in his late forties took Dr. Silver's place and began suturing the cut along Siaak's abdomen.

Eric nodded to his assistant who sat by the patients head stroking his hair from his forehead.

Debbie kept her eyes on the monitors hooked up to their mystery man. Her powder blue eyes drifted up to Eric's before she winked twice and settled back into surveying Dr. Eggleston's surgical seam.

Eric had known Debbie for a long time. Not once had she shown any emotions towards a specimen, before today. It seemed the male was unsettling to the female staff. At this rate, only the men would be allowed to come near him.

Third Entry: 28/4/09

Dr. Angelina Stockwell has begun to interfere with my work. I am well within my rights to have her suspended. Although, with her father being a military man, I also know it wouldn't be beneficial for me to start waving red flags. However, I won't accept them in my theater room and I have left strict instructions that they are barred. Note: Tissue samples have returned after a week. I was right! I have collected extra specimens and emailed results to my home computer, laptops and blackberry.

Eric woke up to the soft chime of his computer. Yawning he stretched up and in doing so he knocked his glasses sideways on his face.

Looking around he noticed he'd slept in his office again. He was doing that more and more here lately since Siaak's arrival.

Ignoring the alert on his computer to new emails, he got up, scratched the back of his head and walked into his private bathroom. An hour later, he was washed, clean-shaven and dressed in fresh clothes.

He sat down to check his emails when he noticed the time. "Shit!" he grabbed his files and dashed towards Siaak's room. When he got there, he found it empty. He was hoping to ask him a few questions before his tests. Siaak was going to be very, very annoyed and angry. He'd told the truth. His boss had lied. He had said there were no more tests, knowing they wanted more info on their new quest.

Tapping his nails against the thick folder, he swiveled around and contemplated waiting for him to return, but he had no idea how long the tests would take. With that in mind, he left the room.

Half way down the corridor, he bumped into Freeman.

"Stay behind. If I were you, I'd be asking myself why the good doctor Stockwell wheeled Siaak into surgery half an hour ago without your permission. Dawson said to warn you and if things get hairy to meet him out front." Freeman slapped his sidearm and took up a position by the elevator. "I'll be here for a few. Get going."

Eric dropped his folder to the floor and ran toward the doors. Panic set in double time, as all kind of crazy ideas entered his head. The door flew open to show him a dark room with Angelina and a sprinkle of staff watching intently through the two-way mirror. Eric stumbled into the room. Almost too afraid to look, when he did he felt the blood drain from his face.

"You can't be serious?" Eric slammed his fists against the two-way mirror in protest. "He's a human being! Oh my fucking god! He's not under!" Eric saw Siaak's arms moving as he tried to break free from his restraints.

"You're insane, Angelina!" Eric's eyes widened as Siaak was cut open from his ribcage down to his navel. More surgeons were hacking away at Siaak's body. Removing bone and organs. One man was holding Siaak's head down as another hovered over him with a dentist's drill.

"NO! STOP! You bastards!" Eric covered his mouth as one doctor reached into his abdomen and Siaak's whole body lurched. Eric witnessed Siaak's mouth open wide as his head flew back; he was in extreme pain and he knew the bitch standing next to him was enjoying every minute of it.

"Doctor, we both know he's far from being human. In your notes, you spoke of his super human ability to heal himself. Today we'll find out how well it works."

Eric's gray eyes turned to steel as he gave Dr. Stockwell his full attention. "Yes," he turned back to the hideous scene," that was minor injuries." He placed his forehead against the glass and cried. "You're killing him!" Eric saw nothing but blood. The teams working inside lab five were butchering him as if he was nothing more than a slab of meat.

This wasn't how it was supposed to be.

"We need to know…"

"WHAT DO YOU NEED TO KNOW?" Eric's voice rose louder with each word. Spittle ran down from his mouth as his eyes bore into hers. He shook his head in denial. "He knew," the good doctor dropped his head in shame, "He knew this was going to happen and…" Eric had never felt so stupid in all his life. He stumbled from the observation room. Guilt eating away at his insides, he knew and I did nothing to stop them. Truth of the matter, even if he'd tried to stop them, he was as good as dead. With that in mind, he made his way to his office.

Forty-five minutes later….

Eric pressed his palm flat against the security plate. It bleeped access denied. "Fuck!" He yanked his sleeve past his fingers, rubbed it against the glass sensor, and tried again. He looked over his shoulder as he waited for the scan to finish a second time. It was only a matter of time before the guards caught up with him. "Come on damn it!"

A long bleep followed by a click and the ten-inch thick steel doors whooshed open. He turned sideways, slid through and swiped his ID card to lock the door behind him.

"Halt Dr. Silver or we will shoot!"

Eric flipped the guard off, turned on his heel and ran for his life. Reaching inside his back pocket, he whipped his blackberry free and thumbed in his password. Scared and running, he knew if luck was on his side, he might just live through this. With a touch of a button, he sent a pre written email to Dawson and a few other people he could trust with his life.

With a quick backward glance, Eric shoved the double doors open and bolted from the building like a racehorse from a starting box. His long, lab coat waving behind him like a white flag as he ran for his life.

"Hey, where's the fire?" Dawson watched his friend running towards him as if the hounds of hell were nipping at his heels. Dawson squared his shoulders and reached behind his back before pulling a gun out to aim at Eric's head.

Eric stumbled to his knees. He couldn't speak as he tried to catch his breath. His arms automatically covered his face. "Don't—don't….shoot!" Eric managed to say in between gasping for air. "I tried to save him Dawson." His voice broke at the image burnt into his retinas. If not for the soundproof room, he would have to live with his screams of agony too for the rest of his life. "They've killed him in their quest for knowledge." Eric spat.

Dawson's lips curled up in what Eric could only described as pure loathing. Eric waved his hands above his head and squeezed his eyes shut. He fell flat on his face at the loud gunfire.

"Play dead!" Dawson murmured from the corner of his mouth.

Eric wanted to ask him what he was playing at, when he heard the static of a two-way radio.

All guards are advised. Dr. Silver has escaped the compound and is armed and dangerous. Shoot to kill.

Dawson fired three shots into the air and let his gun fall to the ground. He dropped to one knee and yanked his black ops pants leg up to unclip his bowie knife.

Eric's head jerked up as he felt Dawson take hold of his hand.

"Gotta be done mate, now hold still!" Dawson blanked everything out. His mind focused on the here and now, regardless of his friend's pain. He placed the edge of the sharp blade against Eric's palm and jerked down.

"Son of a bitch!" Eric's face turned deep red as he felt the sharp cut followed by Dawson's furious pumping at his fist.

"Shut up. Dead bodies don't talk." Dawson took the lab coat and smeared it in Eric's blood before he quickly grabbed his gun and placed it over the lab coat and fired off a few rounds.

Dawson pushed him in the direction of the unmanned gates. "Go, you'll find my jeep parked a few kilometres up the road." He slapped his keys into Eric's good hand. "Go before I really shoot your ass." Dawson took his gun in his left hand, dug the barrel into his right shoulder and pulled the trigger.

Eric flinched as his friend hit the pavement. "You're fucking nuts you know that?"

Dawson rolled over and aimed his gun at the retreating doctor. He squeezed a few rounds off, making sure they only landed close to his feet. The SAS officer dragged his body far enough to make it look good. He took hold of Eric's lab coat and smiled with relief.

THREE MONTHS LATER

The rhythmic bleeping sound went through his skull like a jackhammer. His eyelids trembled as he struggled to open them. The beeping increased. As soon as he opened his eyes, he wished he hadn't. The bright light seared his pupils; he hissed and immediately squeezed them shut while jerking his head away.

His body tensed at the surge of pain that spread through his body. Like a bomb going off in his nervous system, he began to shake. His head connected with something hard, possibly a headboard or a wall. Whatever it was made his head clear from the darkness that had set hard like concrete.

He could remember hearing voices of men and women in the room, but he couldn't move, speak or even open his eyes. They had kept him drugged to the hilt night and day. It meant they were scared of him. That amused him.

Wonder where I am, he thought as he tried to reach out with his powers. That brought on another wave of pain that cut short his first attempt. After he counted to ten, he tried again.

Nothing! He couldn't find Myaten or Kiros in the fog that had settled around his mind.

He swallowed. The coppery taste of blood on his tongue made him feel sick to his stomach. He must have bitten his tongue with his fangs. Running the soft tip of his tongue along the top row of teeth, he paused. Wiggling it round the inside of his mouth, Siaak checked and doubled checked. An audible sigh escaped his lips, he was sure someone had pulled his fangs out. His tongue was numb so that could be the reason, but then again where did the blood come from?

"Oh good, you're awake, about time. I was beginning to think I'd killed you."

Siaak summoned his ghost self which blinked in and out of the room making it hard to see. When it finally settled down, he saw a tall dark haired woman pulling off blood stained gloves as she bent down to look at him.

Even though his vision was murky, he noticed her immaculate black trousers and white blouse beneath a blue lab coat. Her lustrous black hair was pulled up in a tight bun. Her high cheekbones gave a cold stern look to a face partially hidden behind a white mask. When she looked up at a row of monitors, he caught site of her eyes, chips of blue ice, cold and unfeeling.

Her perfume, a light scent of musk settled over him as she reached above his bed to press a few buttons before she examined him. She took out a stethoscope and listened to his two hearts before stepping back from his bed.

Glancing at her feet, she made sure she had returned to the safe zone.

A safe zone or area was the name for the thin green line drawn in a circle on the floor around the bed for visitors and staff, mainly as a warning. If they past the green line, they stood a good chance of being attacked by Siaak, if he managed to break free of his restraints like last time.

She smiled in a condescending way as she gave him her full attention.

"I've been waiting for you to wake up, handsome." She purred as she took a few slow deliberate steps across the room and tossed her used gloves in a bright yellow bin. The word CONTAMINATED stamped across the front of it gave him an idea of where he was, a hospital of some kind.

Without moving his head, he directed his ghost form to move around the room so he could get familiar with his surroundings.

"You don't feel like talking to me? Oops, where are my manners? I'm Doctor Angelina Stockwell and it's been a pleasure knowing you." When he didn't answer, she continued.

"Well, I've heard some stories about you. That you can teleport, is that true, handsome?" She sounded like she was purring as she reached over, pulled up a stool, and sat down.

Tilting her head to one side, she reached up and pulled the white mask from her nose and mouth letting it drop to her chin. She graced him with another smile. "I stopped your medication a few days ago, handsome, so I know you are more alert, even if you can't speak properly." She sighed and crossed her arms over her lap as he ignored her.

"As much as I loved chaining you up and making you bleed, handsome, if you persist in being a naughty boy, there are other ways to make you talk." She paused to run her tongue over her bottom lip as she stared at his naked body. He was a fine specimen. All muscle and not an ounce of fat on him anywhere. She would know. Having had the privilege of touching every inch of that delectable body. Her pulse raced at the memory of swabbing his mouth.

In her line of work, she had seen many things, but she had never seen a male with fangs that extended and retracted. When she tested the tip of one, she found it to be razor sharp.

She got wet at the memory of straddling his waist to take tissue samples for DNA purposes. She would have given anything to make him hard and slide down on top of him. She had tried every trick she knew but nothing made his dick hard. Just thinking about it, turned her on.

She ran an expensive French manicured nail down her left cheek stopping at the seam of her lips. Her pink tongue swirled over her finger in an obvious sexual gesture, but he refused to grace her with an encouraging look.

Of course, the one time he had an erection, she was absent. Security made one of their night cleaners collect a sperm sample. That had pissed her off even more to know that a stupid half-wit cleaner had been allowed to touch him. She was so furious that she'd taken matters into her hands. Smiling at the memory, she knew that the woman's body would never be recovered. She'd tossed her body in the incinerator.

Siaak waited until she scooted the stool closer. He let her continue with her tiresome flirtatious advances, as he tried to break free. His ghost self allowed him to see his body on the bed. His face turned toward the ceiling, but what caught his attention was the thick short chain attached to a metal collar encircling his neck. His arms were held to the side of the bed in leather cuffs. He tested their durability and found he couldn't move his wrists but he could wiggle his fingers.

There was also a thick metal band arched over his mid drift. He noticed a thin slot along the bed frame near his left hip. Maybe that was the way to unlock it. As for his legs, they were free from any restraints.

His upper lip arched showing off his teeth and fangs in protest. He took a deep breath and found her scent all over his body. At the thought of her hands on him, a menacing growl rumbled up from his chest, vibrating as it travelled up his throat and erupted in a loud roar.

Pulling his feet up near his buttocks, he lifted his body up. The metal band moved slightly. Gritting his teeth as he pushed even harder, he could feel the edge of the band digging into his skin. His chest moved up and down with his exertions, but no matter how hard he bucked, it wouldn't budge.

Frustrated tremendously, he lifted his right shoulder off the bed and yanked hard enough to pull his arm out of socket. The right leather cuff ripped and his arm was free, followed by the other arm.

Reaching up to his neck, he wrapped the chain around his knuckles and pulled. He was delighted when it came free of the wall. All that was keeping him on the bed was the wide metal band over his abdomen.

As he reached for it with both hands, a loud beep sounded. It was followed by a soft click. The arm popped up from the bed. He was up in a matter of seconds. Crouched low on the thick mattress, Siaak balanced his weight on his knuckles. His muscular back rippled with power, as he fought with the thick metal collar around his neck. He blinked before he graced her with a feral look.

She jumped off the stool and grabbed a scalpel. "I knew you were strong." She cooed. Her voice filled with excitement as she waved the slim knife back and forth.

"I think my handsome tiger wants to play." She kicked a trolley out of the way, clearing the room for her to manoeuvre around her target as she waved him on.

Siaak roared again. He had felt anger before but nothing like this wild consuming rage that ate at his self-control, he wanted to kill. He wanted her blood on his hands. The only way he would be appeased was by taking her heart. Her death was payback for what she had done to him.

"Where am I?" His hoarse voice sounded strange to his ears. His dark eyes darted wildly around the room before narrowing in on her again.

"Oh, I love your accent and those fangs give you an unworldly look…"

"Where am I?" he repeated louder in case she hadn't heard the first time. He didn't like being ignored. To show his dissatisfaction, he opened his mouth wider allowing his fangs to grow longer.

Her total nonchalance told him how stupid she was. A

SandWalker was not something you toyed with, especially one that was hurt, hungry and needing blood.

The low deep masculine growl made her wet. "You don't know how much that turns me on." She pressed her lips together and made long kissing noises at him.

Siaak sniffed again. Sure enough, he could smell her sex. He scrunched his nose up in a show of disgust.

She ignored his warning growls and taunted him further by coming up close to the foot of the bed, just out of reach of his hands and those dangerous fangs. "I have fantasized about you every night since you were brought in. How it would feel to have you inside me, riding you hard, making me come and, the ultimate turn on for me would be, those sexy fangs in my neck."

The chain rattled behind him as he lunged at her from his spot on the bed. All she saw was his image shift before she could open her mouth to scream. She kicked her legs as she felt her feet lift off the floor and pain as her body connected with something hard.

Siaak held her against the two-way mirrors opposite his bed. He threw his head back making his dark hair brush his shoulders. He felt his jaw pop as he opened his mouth wider allowing his fangs to grow even longer.

"Be careful what you wish for, sometimes it comes back to bite you in the ass or in this case," his words echoed in her mind as he sunk his fangs into her flesh. He ignored the involuntary gagging reflex as blood squirted into his mouth. He pushed the warm red liquid with his tongue from the back of his throat.

Her eyelids fluttered shut as she lived out her darkest fantasy, imagining them together in every position known to man. Wrapping her legs around his waist, she didn't care what he did as long as he didn't stop.

Taken back by her desire to lock her body to his he switched their positions. His back facing the mirror as he tilted her head back, he followed the graceful arch of her body. Hip to hip, chest to chest, his hand at her back holding her close as if he were her dancing partner.

He had to keep telling himself to let the blood fall from his mouth, make it run over his lips. If he swallowed any of it, he would be violently sick. Right now, he needed his strength to get the hell out of here.

Her body thrashed as she tried to push him away, his hold tightened as he clamped his lips against her skin stroking the area with his tongue. Her struggles stopped instantly, replaced by a deep moan. Within a few minutes, she was too weak from the blood loss to defend herself as he reached up to cradle her head between his hands in a gentle manner.

Retracting his fangs, he stared at her for a second before he jerked her head to the right snapping her neck.

"…it kills you." He let her body fall to the floor and stood there staring at his reflection in the mirror. His hair in a wild mess hung into his eyes giving him an evil look with his blood-splattered cheeks, red stained lips and blood dripping off his chin. What tore at him the most were his amber eyes. The wild blood lusts in their depths making them shine. He pounded his fists against the mirror until he saw his chest.

Blood oozed from portions of removed skin that ran in an 'X' that overlaid multiple scars all down his chest.

Running his tongue over his teeth, he looked down at the woman he'd killed. It filled him with revulsion, that he had lost control over the situation. He could have bartered her life for his own.

Shit!

He whirled around at the images from his ghost self,

security guards in riot gear and armed to the teeth where outside the room. He threw his head back and howled, let them come and fight him. He'd show them what a true warrior is. One that had been around since time began.

TEN MINUTES EARLIER

The sound of running heels against concrete and the rustling of fabric with a mixture of bleeping sounds, alerted the guard on duty. He glanced at his watch and quickly stood to attention. He hated his job. Nothing like a regular dose of worthlessness around a colony of big headed know it all's.

When the doctors rounded the corner, he pushed the gum in his mouth to the side of his cheek and waited for them to gather in lines before filing through the highly sensitive scanners. He hated it when he had to work in the compound.

The compound was buried a hundred feet below ground. It housed American and British experiments including the top secret 'ABS' Ancient breed strain, that was first collected a good fifty years ago. He didn't know much, only rumours.

Everyone knew Emilee had been privy to touch the real specimen and was under strict orders, like everyone else, not to mention, they were all 'chipped.'

Their governments didn't play games. The chips allowed the higher ups to know everywhere they went. If information was leaked to the press or any other outside official body, you might as well throw yourself under the nearest bus. Once the chip was activated, it was good night sweetheart!

He leaned over his desk to be nosey. Armed men in riot gear met the mixed group of male and female doctors down the hall. The doctors hesitantly entered the observation room, while the loud growling and heavy banging continued from inside Lab Five.

The security guard hadn't sat down long, before the high pitched whine echoed down the corridor seconds before the lights flickered and died.

"Get those fucking lights back on, NOW, goddamn it!" Dawson leaned his back against the cold steel wall. His dark face shield flipped back on his riot helmet so he could fasten his night vision goggles on. Once in place, he could switch to normal vision if the lights were restored.

He hand signalled instructions to his unit, also equipped with the night vision. His men crouched down in unison on the floor, weapons to the ready. He wasn't taking any chances.

Blue lights swirled around in the darkened hallways. Someone was dead. Dawson tried to figure out which scientists and doctors were working in Lab Five.

Life signatures were monitored at all times in the labs as well as the containment units. He pressed his earpiece, activating the dot microphone by his cheek. "Unit is in place, please advise…"

Dawson cleared the line; he pointed two fingers at his eyes and waved his hand in a cutting motion.

…*Ancient Breed Species Strain: Siaak has escaped, caution advised… do not kill…repeat…do not kill…* filled his ear piece, making him squeeze his eyes shut as he banged his helmet against the wall repeatedly.

Fuck, he swore under his breath. That was all he needed. In the back of his mind, he knew it was Siaak, but he had been hoping it wasn't. That demon had turned his friend into a mindless twit.

Jonathon had been placed in a mental hospital three days after Siaak's capture. He kept babbling on about an apparition. It had started with Jonathon talking to himself.

Dawson put it down to stress at first, but when he became obsessed about some ancient woman with silver eyes and fangs; he knew it was only a matter of time before someone had him committed.

Dawson pushed that thought from his mind. He had work to do, no matter how much he hated to go up against the six-foot plus giant with bad teeth.

Dawson processed the info and like any solider, he began to plan the recapture of the escaped prisoner.

Siaak slammed his body against the two-way mirror. Over and over. Unbreakable, he hadn't even managed to scratch the surface. Without thinking, he picked up the good doctor and threw her body at the window. It hit with a loud wet splat where it stuck to the window for a brief moment. It left a bloody trail as the body slid down and fell to the floor. Siaak stood with his arms out by his sides, his legs braced apart. Not making a sound, just glaring at the mirror from under dark strands of hair, his amber eyes glittering dangerously.

He felt sick to his stomach. His arms crossed his abdomen as he felt his stomach lurch. He knew he was going to vomit the blood he ingested when the female began to struggle in earnest.

As soon as the thought hit him, he was on all fours retching, until his control snapped and he was throwing up the tainted blood. His mind refused to accept that he'd ingested human blood again.

He felt so weak, his vision blurry. Swallowing only made the reflex come back and this time he emptied his stomach completely.

As he managed to pull himself together, he crawled

across the floor on his hands and knees to a water dispenser on the wall near an office desk. Not having the strength to shred tissue paper, he dropped the cup and closed his eyes in frustration. His breathing was shallow.

He flopped down on the floor with his legs tucked under him. Instinctively he reached for his necklace; his fingers brushing naked skin to find it was gone.

Anger tore through his sick hazed mind, giving him a quick boost of energy. Jumping to his feet, he yanked the water dispenser off the wall and swung it at the mirror. It cracked. Before he had time to rain, the contents of the room at the damaged window, the lights blinked out and all hell broke loose.

A Flash Bang rolled across the floor and exploded seconds after the door went crashing to the floor. Siaak threw his body face down on the concrete floor to avoid the blinding light. A loud bang sounded as the room filled with men.

"We have you surrounded. Resistance is futile. We will shoot to kill!" Dawson spoke with self-assured cockiness.

Siaak shifted his hips as he placed his arms out by his sides and pushed all his weight off the floor with an astounding back flip.

Dawson's mouth fell open as he watched the man land on the ceiling. "How in the hell can he do that?"

Siaak's lips moved upwards in a tight sneer, as he smelt fear in the air. It radiated from the men, from their thoughts down to their scents. Nothing insulted his pride more than sniffling hunters who pissed themselves while stalking larger prey.

His deep chuckle mocked them as he showed an obvious sense of humour at their predicament. He was planning to recreate hell inside this room, if they didn't let him go free.

Pulling his lips back, he dropped to the floor and opened his mouth allowing his fangs to shift and grow from the front of his upper incisors. He landed on his feet without making a sound and waved them on, "as you humans say; you ain't seen nothing yet!"

Dawson signalled his men to close in on Siaak while he kept him busy talking. "You speak English?"

Siaak raised a sarcastic eyebrow as he stood to his full height, "do you think yourself more intelligent than I?" Siaak loved to answer a question with a question; it pissed people off.

"I can cut my food up and string a few words together to form a sentence. Is that what you're suggesting, mate?" Dawson retorted as he casually aimed his MP5 submachine gun at his head.

Siaak shook his index finger at Dawson in a patronizing way as he tisked at the men standing around him. He didn't care if he made the situation worse. They had taken him prisoner and tortured him for days on end. He was going to make sure that they never did it again. He may not have the use of all his powers, but he could still pack a punch and tear out their jugulars if the need arose.

Siaak chuckled at the man's sarcastic humour. He liked him. Shame he was going to die. "Well, it seems you have come a long way from being on all fours. Perhaps one day, you humans will learn to accept the things you do not understand, instead of pulling it to pieces to see how it works." Siaak indicated the missing layers of shaved skin over his chest that ended near his navel.

Dawson didn't flinch at the angry red scars all over the man's body. Deep inside he wanted to make them pay for that. No prisoner-of-war should be treated in such a manner. "I didn't know they would do that to you."

"No more talk, human. Diplomacy is for the civilized and right now I feel less than that!"

Siaak moved. Not as quick as he would like.

With a push off the floor, Siaak twisted through the air backwards to land on the shoulders of the armed soldier behind him.

Wrapping his thighs around the man's neck Siaak squeezed with all his strength. Leaning his weight back, he toppled them onto the floor. Siaak dismounted to roll with the strong man across the floor.

Ripping the soldier's face shield off, Siaak slammed the officer's face down into the concrete floor. The sheer speed and force killed him instantly. The splintered bones in his nose shifted and impaled his brain.

Siaak dumped his body on the floor as he moved to his next target.

Dawson hadn't given it a single thought. "Mother Fucker can see in the dark!" He said it loud enough for his unit to hear him and the controller on the other end of his headset.

"I won't allow you to kill more good men!" Dawson threatened through clenched teeth. His rational mind and training set in and automatically he switched gears and blanked out his emotions

Siaak laughed, "What did you expect me to do, 'I come in peace' shit?" He raised his arms out as he stretched his aching muscles and took on a fighting stance with his back against the wall.

"...*tell him we have his woman and if he doesn't comply we will kill her...*"

Damn Saunders, he didn't think for one second his best friend would go behind his back and squeal to his superiors. Tell them what really happened and how they had come across Siaak.

Fucking brown nosier, Dawson didn't agree with Saunders or Jonathon's deceit. As a military man, he had killed men. He had never, under any circumstances, killed women and children. As far as he was concerned, the woman Jonathon was after didn't exist in the real world, only inside his friend's demented mind.

Dawson never liked playing dirty. He was a fair man and if he couldn't take this monster down on his own, he would hang up his guns and retire.

"Men fall back!"

Seven helmets turned in his direction, but no one moved. "I said FALL BACK! MOVE YOUR ASSES DOUBLE TIME NOW!" He waved his arm, indicating the door. He raised his weapon, threatening to shoot them, if they didn't follow orders.

Within seconds, the room was empty, occupied only by him and the ABS.

Siaak had heard the orders given to Dawson and waited for the lies. Instead, Dawson removed his helmet and unclipped his riot gear consisting of bulletproof vest and steel enforced padding around neck, shoulders, ribcage and both kneepads.

"Why did you come after her?" Siaak eyed up his opponent.

Dawson knew it was wrong on so many levels. He wished he hadn't repaid his favour to Jonathon, at least not in that way. "There was never any intention to harm your lady friend or anyone else for that matter. Jonathon led me to believe you had kidnapped his fiancé." Dawson stretched his legs and arms before a quick run in place as he limbered up for what was going to be one kick ass fight.

"Are you ready or would you prefer to get a masseuse in

while I wait, perhaps a hot towel or maybe some yoga?" Siaak crouched low to the floor as the lights began to blink.

Dawson fought back the urge to laugh. He actually found that funny.

The flashing lights made the night vision goggles useless. Tossing them to the floor, Dawson narrowed his eyes against the harsh on-off rhythm of the lights high above their heads. There wasn't enough time for his eyes to adjust to the effects of light and dark. He might as well be blind for all the good his eyes were in this room.

At each three-second interval, Siaak moved around the room making it impossible for Dawson to locate, mark and attack. They weren't playing fair, so he wasn't going to make it easy for the man.

Siaak crawled up behind Dawson as the lights went out and struck fast. Siaak wrapped his left arm around the British special air service officer's neck pushing against his chin forcing Dawson's head back.

Dawson swallowed hard at the realization. He had fucked up.

"How does it feel to know you are going to die?" Siaak pressed his mouth against Dawson's ear.

"You don't scare me, mate. If it's time for me to knock off then so be it!" Dawson had no family so he didn't have to worry about leaving anyone behind.

His job had never given him the luxury of a wife and kids. His parents considered him dead anyway. They were both war activists. They were never behind his chosen career.

If not for him and other men and women like him, his parents and millions of others civilians would have fallen to Terrorists attacks. Even to this day, he swore he'd get the bastards that blew up the Twin Towers in New York. He had hoped to bring them all to justice, his justice, but now that would end, like so many other plans.

Siaak listened to the man's thoughts as he hovered over the carotid artery in his neck. He stopped the growth of his fangs at an inch in length as he tightened his hold on Dawson. "Like you I have spent my entire life protecting you humans. Tell me why I should spare your life, after you gave me to that butcher?"

Dawson saw the body of a woman lying on the floor covered in blood when the lights flickered on. He could just see her head turned at an unnatural angle. If the alien thought, he was shocked by her death he had another think coming. He'd seen worse than that.

"I saw you teleport, you killed my men!" Dawson hissed at the sudden pain then a warm tingling spread through his body before darkness swallowed him up.

Siaak retracted his fangs. He placed his index finger in rapid succession on five major pressure points, three at his ear, one at his temple and forehead. He hit just hard enough to make him unconscious. He wanted him alive.

"Gas him."

"Sir…" Private Clarks yanked off his headset as he turned in his seat to grace General Stockwell with raised eyebrows. "Dawson's still in there sir!"

"I want that thing dead, he killed my daughter Private! Do you hear me?" Stockwell leaned down to stare wide eyed into the computer screen. "Get out! You're a fucking pussy Clarks! The General back handed Clarks, knocking him from his chair.

He would have retribution.

The minute he saw Dawson hit the floor, he hammered his balled fist at the computer terminal. A sick evil smile spread across his features as he pulled the key from under his shirt.

"Get up you snivelling piece of shit!" He needed another officer with a key to activate the nerve gas. Stockwell turned around to grab the private by his hair and cursed to find he had escaped.

Clark scrambled across the floor towards Dawson's twenty-second SAS unit. Fourteen men reduced to seven in a matter of months. He knew they were loyal to one another. If he could get to them in time, they could place Stockwell under arrest.

Jumping to his feet, he ran and dived. He couldn't have timed it better. As he hit the floor, the bullet flew by his head. Clarks knew if Stockwell missed, it was a warning; the next one would take him down. He had no choice. He leapt to his feet and ran for his life.

Siaak whirled around at the echo of gunfire followed by a rather loud explosion. Sounded like Armageddon out there.

Siaak grabbed Dawson under his arms and dragged him across the room. Rolling him on to his side in the recovery position, Siaak looked around the room for suitable clothing. He spied the bed out the corner of his eye.

Storming over to it, he stripped the sheet off the mattress and tore off a large strip, about the size of a towel. Tying it at his waist, he managed to fashion a suitable loincloth. He took hold of the chain used to hold him to the bed and thread it through the bottom by tearing four holes in the fabric. This would anchor the hem of the fabric down when he had to run or walk fast.

He kept trying to use his powers; no different from when he woke up. Telepathy however was a natural ability like sight, hearing and moving. His kind automatically knew how to use them. No matter how weak he was, he could always use it.

As for his magic, he was at a major disadvantage. He couldn't explain why he could manifest his ghost form but not tap into his magic. Maybe it was due to one of the drugs or a combination of drugs that was given to him. He'd never find out by standing there with his finger up his ass. Once he was free, he'd find out what they had done to him.

Walking over to where Dawson had gone down in the middle of the room, Siaak picked up his weapon.

He had never fired a gun in his whole existence. Never needed too, but that didn't mean he couldn't use one. He knew how they worked. It felt foreign to hold one in his hands.

His staff was heavy, but not as bulky and loud as the human weapon. Slinging it over his shoulder, he walked with deliberate steps, keeping his bare feet light as he peered out the doorway. He stepped out into the hallway and froze at the sound of voices.

He felt the cramps return. Lucky for him, he hadn't taken in but a few mouthfuls of blood from the female doctor. In an hour or two, he'd be back to normal.

Unable to send his ghost self out, he kept his body close to the wall and out of any flashing lights. He glanced in the direction of the voices. As he got closer, the voices got louder; he could make out what was being said.

"...you can't do it sir!"

"I am the senior officer here. He is a threat to our allies and us. It is a matter of national security, Clarks. Now be a good lad and hand me the key..."

Dawson's unit was only ten feet ahead of Siaak. He watched them sitting on their knees with their arms crossed behind their heads.

The one-named Clarks was down on his knees with his face on the floor. A man was holding a gun to his head as he yanked at the man's shirt.

"Where's the key boy?"

"I don't have it sir, only another person in similar rank or higher would have the key."

Siaak watched as the young solider visibly relaxed when the gun was removed from his head. His mouth moved forming 'thank you, god' as he quickly crawled over to the other men.

Stockwell tapped the barrel of the gun against his thigh as he paced back and forth. His back stiff as he marched. His dark uniform immaculate, not a single button out of place except for his hair, which stood up on one side as he jerked his fingers through the short white strands.

Everyone could see that he had snapped. Luck was on their side that the only other high-ranking officer wasn't on the compound.

The General turned his attentions on the men lined up on the concrete floor. He observed them in a silent glare. His blue cloudy eyes wandering over each solider, he knew them well enough to try to talk sense into them. If he could convince them, bring them over to his side, he could have revenge on the son of a bitch that killed his child.

"I evacuated the building, all that remains is us lot." He nodded with triumph as he waved the gun over their heads. He squatted down before the front row of men.

He spotted Clarks at the back and spat on the floor. "Get a fucking back bone, Clarks!" Stockwell shouted. He despised any form of weakness and in his opinion, Clarks wasn't army material. No, he was a sniffling, wet behind the ears Mama's boy.

Clarks inched backward on his hands and knees when Stockwell started pacing back and forth again. Tucking his head down he lowered his stomach to the cold floor first followed by his pelvis and long legs before allowing him the time to catch his breath. He hadn't laid there for long when he felt someone was behind him.

Shivering he swallowed hard at the feeling of being watched. Twisting his body, he swallowed again and quickly looked into the dark tunnel behind him. He couldn't see anything other than the tiny blue flashing lights, a reminder to him that someone had died today.

He had never experienced death first hand. Never shot a man and hoped he never would. Sounded stupid, being in the army and not wanting to kill, his pa was right. "I'm nothing but a coward."

Siaak saw the man shifting slowly in his direction until he took a quick glance behind him as if he'd heard something. Siaak couldn't take any chances of being found too early. He reached out and clamped his hands on Clark's ankles. He yanked the young man's body between his feet. "If you speak, I will smash your skull in. Do I make myself perfectly clear?" Siaak flipped the man over onto his back and raised his fist.

Clarks nodded vigorously at the large man looming over him. His eyes seemed to glitter in the darkness and when he talked, Clarks caught a glimpse of his fangs. He'd never seen anyone with real fangs before and was dying to ask him a question, when Siaak's mouth widened to show four long pointed fangs. Clarks immediately clamped his mouth shut and mumbled 'sorry.'

Siaak signalled for Clarks to come with him and to remain silent. He pushed Clarks ahead of him into the observation lab. Once they were inside Siaak took guard at the door. "Who holds the other key?"

"I don't know what you are talking about…"

Siaak scrunched his nose up as he snarled in reply. His head jerked back against the doorjamb as he looked to the right, his eyes began to glitter dangerously. He was beyond pissed. These were the people he had managed to avoid all his life until he had met Melissa.

"If you fuck with me, I vow your death will be an unpleasant event, unequal to the ones I have planned for those that captured me."

"General Davidson has the other key, sir…" Clarks stopped mid sentence as Siaak shoved his hand in the air demanding silence.

The whine of computers and flickering lights was disheartening, as the electricity had been switched back on. Siaak's chances of escaping just lowered.

Siaak grabbed Clarks and dragged him behind. Looking back and forth to check the hallway, Siaak sent a blinking ghost self off in the direction of General Stockwell. "Now tell me how I can get out of here and I will let you go."

"I don't think so."

Siaak turned in time to see General Stockwell fire off a few rounds, all aimed at Clarks. Siaak shoved the Private back thinking he had kept the young man out of harm's way, but a well placed bullet to the head sent him sprawling to the floor.

The General immediately turned the gun on Siaak.

"You killed my daughter you freak! Angelina was a beautiful young woman with ambitions until you were brought here. She became fixated with everything about you; spending entire days with you while forsaking all her duties as a scientist within the compound."

The General moved a few steps closer, his finger coiled around the trigger, his eyes full of madness. He wanted blood for blood.

Siaak didn't take time to think things through, he lunged at the General. Siaak felt each bullet ripping through his body, tearing tissue and muscle. He ignored the excruciating pain as a bullet hit him in one of his hearts, his vision turned red and he attacked. Siaak felt his incisors and canines grow as he flew through the air.

The General stepped back waving his gun around as he hunted for another clip. Too late, Siaak landed on his chest and they both went tumbling to the floor.

Siaak slammed his fist into the General's face, breaking his nose before he spun and rammed his elbow into his throat damaging his oesophagus.

The gun fell from his hand and was knocked around the floor during their scuffle.

Siaak braced his forearm against the General's jaw until he heard the bones crack. Sitting on his knees, Siaak pushed all his weight down on the older man as Siaak placed his teeth against his enemy's neck and with a violent yank, Siaak tore the General's throat out.

Stockwell's body began to twitch as his blood pumped out in long pulsing sprays of red from the carotid artery. It covered Siaak's face, matting his dark hair to his cheeks and neck. Siaak felt numb as he fell back, his hands slapping in warm blood that pooled out around them.

Wiping his face with the back of his hands Siaak hadn't bothered to resist swallowing. He needed blood and as much as it made him sick, he was glad he had killed the officer. The man didn't deserve a merciful killing.

Was this how the BloodSeekers saw it? Was he turning?

Licking his lips, he spat the tainted blood across the room.

He had to get home. He needed to feed soon. Otherwise, he was doomed.

Crouched on the floor, he turned in time to see more soldiers; there was no way he could take them all. His last thoughts were of Melissa and his brethren.

He gave one long loud roar before his body was shot to pieces.

"No, stand down!" Dawson stumbled into the hallway as the man went down on his knees. There was no way he'd survive that many bullet wounds.

Siaak turned to give him a brief meaningful look before he fell back.

Dawson ran towards Siaak. He went sliding through all the blood. God it was everywhere.

What had happened here?

He saw the general laying with his lifeless eyes wide open staring up at the ceiling.

Clarks sprawled across the floor dead with a bullet through the head.

"I want him taken to theatre, NOW!" Dawson shouted making the vein in his forehead stand out. His men jumped to it. They grabbed a gurney and heaved the heavy man onto it. Dawson tapped the mic on his ear, "…I want all doctors to meet me in theatre two!"

Dawson just hoped it wasn't too late.

CHAPTER EIGHT

"So, are you going to teach me how to use this or not?" Melissa demanded as she waved the tiny, silver, obelisk pendant at Myaten.

"No. I'm not. You asked me that five times already, Melissa." He replied, not bothering to look up at her. He was leaned over his desk reading when Melissa entered his office for the third time that morning.

Melissa stood watching him trace the ancient scrolls with his index and pinkie finger. She hated to interrupt, especially when he looked deep in thought, but she couldn't stand wandering around the Casino, doing nothing. She should be out looking for Siaak. After all, it was her fault he was taken.

"Myaten, we need to talk about this," she held the pendant out again as if that would attract his attention. The man had nerves of steel, she'd been pestering him for six hours solid and still he was as cool as a cucumber.

When Myaten finally looked up from the scrolls scattered across his desk, she wanted to dance around the room. Instead, she stood still letting him see how desperate she was to do something, anything to help.

He couldn't blame her for wanting to find Siaak. He wanted to find him too. But he'd do that quicker if she left him alone.

After the second visit, he knew he wasn't going to get rid of her by gambling or shopping, so he offered her to sit in his penthouse suite. Boy was that a bad idea or what?

"How many times do I have to explain that you can't just wave it around like a wizard's wand and poof you find Siaak out of nowhere. It doesn't work that way. As much as I would love for it to be true, Melissa, I can't allow you to even try it. It's too dangerous." And Siaak would have my balls if I let you get hurt.

She opened her mouth to argue, he placed the edge of one finger to his lips. Silencing her with a shush.

"Not even if you had the ability to use it." He hated being that way with her, but he had made a vow and a SandWalker always kept his word.

"I promised Siaak I would protect you and that is what I'm doing. Regardless of how you may think I'm keeping you prisoner in my home," he swept his arms out wide to indicate his penthouse suite, "I'm not." He gave her a wide smile but his eyes stayed firm and sincere. "Now please, no more of this 'riding to the rescue' business, leave the happy endings to Disney." Myaten said as he walked over to his kitchen and poured two tall glasses of fruit juice.

"Here drink this and sit down before you fall down." He ordered as he 'moved' all the boxes of dusty books and scrolls off the cushions with a single thought.

Melissa grumbled a false 'thank you' at him and flopped down on the leather couch. She gripped the glass between her thighs as she stared off into space.

She was exhausted. The visions were coming more and more now. How she managed to keep from going insane, she didn't know.

"Are you sleeping?" Myaten asked softly as he joined her on the couch. He sat facing her, bracing his chin on his arms.

"Not really. The doctor prescribed some pills, but I don't take them Myaten. Because it's the only time I feel him near. It's hard to explain...it's like he's calling out to me. Over and over and I answer, but he doesn't hear me. It makes me so mad," she rubbed her forehead hard enough to make the skin turn white beneath her fingers.

Squinting, she tried to break through the dark cloud that distorted her mind when she thought of Siaak. "I need to find him."

Myaten had felt it too. Even with his immense powers, he was still unable to get a message to or from Siaak for the past four months.

"If you feel like talking, I'm a good listener." Myaten offered as he summoned a large black silk pillow from Siaak's bedroom to hand.

Melissa took a sip of her juice and sat it on the coffee table beside her. She didn't see the pillow until she turned around. Myaten pulled his arm from behind the sofa. "Here. Have a pillow."

Nodding she hugged it to her chest and inhaled. It smelt faintly of Siaak. And that made her feel a little better. "Where did you get this?"

"I'll tell you later, now spill the beans."

"Okay," she flashed a dreamy smile as she held the pillow closer. "The visions have taken a twist from the norm. Like I said before. In the beginning, all of them trailed off leaving me desperate to know what would happen in the next one. Believe you me, it's more intense than any love letter I've ever had." She hugged the pillow tighter as she pulled her knees up and balanced her feet on the edge of the white leather couch.

"Now, all I feel is an agonizing pain. I see blood everywhere and he's covered in it. Every time I offer to help, he snarls and attacks me! It's like he's changed. He's become a wild animal." She looked at Myaten with desperation in her eyes. "What does it mean? I know we're connected in some weird way. Nevertheless, how did it happen? Did he do something to me when he bit me?"

She reached for her glass as it lifted off the table of its own accord. As long as she lived, she would never get used to that.

"Thanks," she acknowledged politely. She sipped her drink all the while watching him for the usual signs.

A shrug of one shoulder, a cocked eyebrow followed through with pursed lips and then a mild scratching session of either his jaw or scalp.

"Melissa, you know I don't have all the answers." At her audible sigh, he decided it was time to tell her the truth.

"Look, I'm going to be honest with you. I've seen you before in a vision that still bugs me to this day."

She opened her mouth to ask how that was possible as he held his hand up.

"I saw you and Siaak together," at her look of 'oh yeah' he nodded vigorously. "Yes, I saw you both together on the floor in your hotel room, you were-"

"I was what? Oh, let me guess. I was naked and being groped by your drooling testosterone of a brother?"

"Yes, you could put it like that." Myaten chewed the inside of his bottom lip. This wasn't working out the way he planned it.

Myaten scratched the bridge of his nose and grunted. "I knew about you before Siaak put us in stasis Melissa. See," Myaten scooted to the edge of the couch and looked her square in the eyes. "Siaak made me promise to never speak of the future to him. He always proclaimed he liked to take one day at a time."

"I don't understand, Myaten." She squeezed the stuffing out of the pillow as she wondered where he was going with all of this.

"One of my special skills is being able to travel back and forth in time. I left five months ago to travel to Egypt on a business trip; you can ask Sarah she will vouch for me. It was an excuse to travel back in time. Don't ask me to explain it, just listen; I wanted to warn Siaak. To tell him about you, but he refused to listen. He was only interested in capturing Osiris and I don't blame him."

"That's the reason you said Siaak would meet his woman in this century."

"Yes, so now you know." Myaten finished off his orange juice and rolled the glass between his hands.

"Can't you go back and warn him again, tell him that people are after him?"

"No I can't Melissa. What is happening now has to happen as it is. If I go back a second time to warn Siaak that he'll be captured, history won't repeat itself." He'll let you go, not really understanding what you meant to him. If I tell him a human is destined to be his mate, he won't believe it without proof; Siaak is one hard nut to crack."

"If you had the proof would you go back and show it to him?"

"No, Melissa, I would be altering the course of the future, our future. You and I wouldn't be here now," he pointed at the couch, "having this conversation right, because Siaak would have tracked you down before it was the right time."

"So how do you know we are destined to be together?" She felt her stomach lurch. Did she really want to know what Myaten knew? Yeah, she did.

"I decided against my better judgement to go back even further in time. To a point before I was born."

"Isn't that dangerous?"

"It is very dangerous Melissa. However, if you had seen Siaak, he was so preoccupied with you night and day. As far as he was concerned, it was essential that he obtain evidence from our ancestors. Anything to confirm the marker was telling him the truth." At her look of disbelief, he carried on.

He moved his hands around as he talked. "See, we were always taught that a matching marker or missing half of it indicated a pair. A match. The other half of our soul. Yin and yang. Humans call it marriage. A bonding of two people. Husband and wife-"

"I get the idea Myaten." She rolled her eyes at him. "So what did you find?"

"Not much really. Just a few scrolls that are very hard to read. It seems that the fathers of our clans restricted us from the other races, forbidding us to feed or breed outside our own."

"Sounds like the typical speech a father gives his dating offspring." She remembered her father telling her something along the same line in her teenage years.

"Well there is more to it than that Melissa. As I was saying. There were seven races, or ancient civilizations for a better word, spread across the earth. I can't tell you the names of the other six, but I'm from one of them, the Egyptians," he pointed to his chest. I did find a reference to a secret place of stored knowledge. Unfortunately, I don't know how long it will take to find it. I can't promise it will explain how you have the mark of our clan, but maybe, just maybe it will shed some light on the subject."

She offered a smile but what she really wanted to do was roll up in a ball, close her eyes and let her mind wander. When she wasn't focusing on anything, she seemed to 'see' Siaak and last night he was in so much pain.

Myaten closed his eyes for a second as her thoughts drifted into his mind; he had to calm his emotions before looking her straight in the face. "What do you want Melissa? Tell me how you feel about all of this? Do you want to be a part of Siaak's life? Nobody is forcing you. I know he would never pressure you into a relationship because of our ancestors' beliefs.'

"I don't know Myaten, to be honest. I don't know how I feel about him yet. If this mark I have is a key to our future, then I won't know until we have found him."

She kneaded the pillow between her fingers and stopped when she caught him staring at her. "I mean it would be nice to get to know him without the ending of my life cropping up in conversation every ten minutes." She bobbed her head side to side, as she threw the pillow down on her lap. "What I'm trying to say, is it would be nice to get to know him without all this hocus pocus."

Myaten summoned a long black box inlayed with silver and diamonds. He held it for a minute before he offered it to her. "Look inside and tell me what you see."

Melissa took the box and rubbed her fingertips across it before removing the lid. "I can see water. But how is that? It's not heavy at all." She tilted the long velvety box sideways, expecting the water to move. It didn't. Instead, she heard voices speaking, but she couldn't make out what they were saying. "I hear whispering, Myaten." Her voice lowered as she leaned over the rectangular box. She gasped as she saw Siaak's face. The sudden urge to dip her fingers in the silver liquid made her hands shake. Lifting her arm up, she reached inside to touch it.

Myaten snapped the box shut. "You can't touch it without Siaak unless you like your flesh crispy fried in silver coating?" He took the box and returned it to his ancestor's temple.

"What were the voices I heard?" she asked.

"I can't tell you. That is something very extraordinary that only Siaak can explain to you. This box is honoured among our people as a symbol of wisdom. The rest I think you should hear from your mate."

"Okay I can go with that but I have to ask you, why did he bite me?"

"It is one of our customs to feed from a nominated blood source." At her look of shock he continued. "Before you start gagging and fainting on me, just listen. It's no different than having a blood transfusion between twins or another blood type that matches yours."

At her raised eyebrows, he decided to elaborate. "So we use our fangs to filter the vitamins and nutrients from the blood we take from a blood source or our mate. In the old days, they were called BloodSlaves. We don't actually drink blood, unless we are in dire need."

"Like dying…" her soft reply made Myaten sigh and nod his head.

"If Siaak needs blood, he would seek out Kiros or me. If you are his mate, then he'll come to you first." Myaten waited for it, he knew she was going to make some comment about vampires any second now.

"So I'm part of the walking dead club? Does this mean I'll sprout fangs and have more moody sessions on top of the ones I already have?"

"No," he snorted. "Melissa, SandWalkers have fangs for two reasons. One, to hunt down the BloodSeekers. Two, to feast on the energy our blood creates to keep us healthy and maintain our bodies."

"Okay, so what about sex? Surely you guys don't go without; I mean that's a long time to be celibate."

"Umm, I never said that, Melissa," he coughed and cleared his throat, "I've had a few lovers in my time, but none of them had my marker. All of us assumed we would be bachelors for life since we are all that is left of our people."

"I'm sorry Myaten."

"Don't be, I know she is around somewhere, now that you have entered our lives." Myaten gave a boyish smile and played with the hem of his black slacks. "Our time will come, just as yours has."

"Thank you Myaten for being honest with me."

"No problem. Now tell me, how is your mark, does it still itch?"

"No it stopped a few weeks ago, now its weeping clear liquid, the doctor thinks it's a skin infection, so he gave me some ointment."

"Why didn't you say something earlier? May I have a look?"

The worried tone in his voice brought her off the couch and immediately she slipped her jeans over her left hip so he could see.

"Oh that does look nasty." He whistled low as he stared at the discoloured marker.

"Thanks a lot." She felt like yanking on his ears.

"Don't mention it. Seriously, it does look infected. It's bleeding. What did you do, scratch yourself with a rusted razor blade?"

"What!" she glanced down and sure enough, there was blood mixed in with the ointment. "That wasn't there this morning."

"Make sure you keep an eye on it. You might need antibiotics, you must have scratched so hard you cut the skin with your nails, it's easily done." He left her to get a dressing for it. They just finished when Sarah entered the room.

"Hey boss," she waved as he settled himself behind his desk again. He wasn't any closer to finding the rest of the coordinates to the secret location of his people's history. Not to mention, he was waiting for a call concerning his brother. His informants had come up with something and he did not intend to tell Melissa. He had brought her to his Casino to keep his eye on her. She would demand to go and he couldn't keep his mind on his mission if he was worrying over her.

As for Kiros, he was still being a dick. He blamed Melissa for what happened to Siaak and Myaten totally understood his reasons for believing that. Kiros could hold a grudge, but seriously, he needed to get over it.

"Boss I need a few…"

Myaten held his hand out as he continued reading about a reference to another temple. He scribbled his signature on all ten invoices and told Sarah to cancel his appointments for the day.

She raised a bemused eyebrow at him, "are you feeling okay Boss? It's not like you to cancel a lunch date."

His eyes shifted from the ancient texts to hers. "I know. Hey, you go in my place, you know how things are done here and I trust you." He reached into his desk and pulled out his wallet. When he offered her his black American express card, she almost fainted.

"Umm, unless you think I'm gonna buy the restaurant or I'm gonna eat them out of business, that isn't necessary. I'll have water and a salad. I need to lose a few pounds here, here and over here." She pointed to places that Myaten swore he'd need a microscope to see.

Melissa laughed and spoke up, "where are you going to eat lunch? Perhaps, I can join you…"

"No, you, stay here where I can keep my eye on you."

Myaten stood up, took Sarah's hand, and placed the card there. "You need to eat more and I don't care what you spend. If I get the bill and you only ordered bread sticks or some low fat yogurt, I'm going to personally make you eat breakfast, lunch and dinner at McDonalds."

Both women gasped in mock horror.

"I didn't know you ate there?" Sarah teased, "I figured you as the yuppie type. You know finger foods with strange names that nobody can pronounce or spell."

Melissa watched the by-play between them. She had wondered if they were an item but as the weeks turned into months, she knew they were friends.

"Just for that, I'm going to buy a Taco Bell and make you the manager." He threatened, she just laughed at him on her way out the door.

Myaten 'watched' as Sarah walked down the hallway and stopped. She smiled mischievously as she turned and backtracked to the door. She tucked the plastic card behind the metal numbers and gently patted the door. With a satisfied gleam in her eyes, she dusted her hands together at a job well done and walked off with a spring in her step.

He continued to watch as he placed the card back in her bag just before the elevator doors shut. If she wondered how it got back in her bag later, he'd say he slipped another card in her bag before she left knowing full well what she was like.

Myaten turned to look Melissa square in the face. "You can't mope around all the time Melissa; it's not good for you. Why don't you come with me this evening and enjoy a meal and a show? I can't promise I will brood like Siaak, but I can make a woman laugh."

"Siaak doesn't brood; he just takes his responsibilities a little too seriously sometimes. I don't blame him either. From the stories you've told me, I hope I never run into Osiris or any other BloodSeeker for that matter."

With that said, Melissa picked up the store credits and left. She needed some time on her own to think. Besides, Myaten really did need some time on his own to look over the scrolls.

"You look beautiful." Myaten offered his arm as Melissa joined him by the front entrance to the Casino.

"Why, thank you," she said as she leaned forward to stare in astonishment at a white stretched limousine that crawled to a stop.

"Your coach awaits, sorry it's not six white steeds but it's the best I could do on such short notice." He teased. "Come on, Melissa, I promised you a nice evening out."

"Yes, I know but I thought you meant a show here," she pointed at the floor.

Closing his eyes as if he were trying to calm his nerves, he smiled generously as he tapped her hand with his. "I never take my dates here. Come on now, be a good girl and I might let you stick your head out the sunroof."

Melissa chuckled and allowed him to pull her toward the luxury car. "It's not stolen, is it?" She batted her eyes lashes at him as she slid in the back seat.

He gave her a 'that's–not–funny' look before he shut the door and walked up to the driver's window. With a tap on the glass, the driver rolled it down and they spoke briefly.

Melissa sat waiting patiently, smoothing out invisible creases in her red evening dress. Myaten had given it to her as a gift along with the shoes, handbag and jewellery.

As she played with the quarter of a million dollar diamond bracelet, she paused and looked up when the car moved.

Myaten smiled sheepishly and blew a kiss as the car drove by.

"Excuse me…driver…where are you taking me?" She repeated as the tinted partition lowered behind the driver's head.

"I was told to take madam to meet with her date for the evening. Is there a problem?" The driver asked as he drove the car down the lane away from the busier side of town.

Melissa huffed and blew a single strand of hair out of her eyes. Myaten was up to something, two could play this game. "No problem, could we find a rest room-,"

The driver locked eyes with her in the rear view mirror before he spoke. "There is one available to you in the car."

"You're joking right?" she asked as she looked all around the limo for signs of a toilet. "I mean who would use it with other people in the car?" That was just so not right as far as she was concerned.

"The car is sound proof and the glass prevents me from seeing into the compartment where you are seated. So please feel free to press the small silver button behind the third seat to your right. It will automatically flush when you are done."

"No thanks, I'll hold it." She gave a tight-lipped smile and wiggled her fingers bye as the partition closed leaving her alone to think.

Myaten watched the limo until it disappeared through the foliage of trees. He knew Melissa would be hot for his head when she saw him later. By the time she returned, he would be long gone.

Looking around, he opened his hand and held his palm flat to stare at the pendant. It was one of a pair created for 'jumping' from place to place. Over the centuries, Siaak had been using his to take him home when the need arose to secure the pyramid from intruders. Now, he hoped that it would lead him straight to Siaak.

Closing his hand around the silver shard of metal, he felt a twinge of guilt. He had lied to Melissa for her own protection. Over the last six weeks, he had noticed many changes in her. He knew when she was around. He could feel her presence.

Who ever took their brother would stop at nothing to take her hostage again. Only this time, Siaak would give his life if he knew Melissa was his mate.

With that in mind, he jumped.

Myaten shivered as he stepped from the hot dry climate he was used too all his life into cold rain, snow and ice before he hit hot weather again. One thing he disliked about teleporting and jumping was the inability to prepare yourself for the eventuality of adverse weather conditions.

Some of the Obelisks he jumped from where covered in ice, moss, mud, thick disgusting grunge to salt water and yes sand. As much as he hated sand, he hated the last one he jumped from; it was covered in mud and mosquitoes. He was sure he had lost two pints of blood after that jump and made a mental note to bring insect repellent next time.

Two of the scrolls on his desk gave him the instructions on how to work his 'key' and the history behind them. The pendant he wore around his neck was an exact copy of Siaak's and one that every SandWeaver wore once they finished their apprenticeship with a Master.

Myaten hadn't known much about them since he was a SandWalker. He was glad he had found them; otherwise, he wouldn't have known how to control the one he had.

He still didn't know how Siaak managed to use one as often as he did. It was taking every ounce of control he had to keep the stone from absorbing his body.

He assumed the closer he got to Siaak, the pendant would tell him. Maybe beep, hum, glow or point him in the right direction. The scrolls didn't specify what the signal would be.

After three hours, he was losing his calm about the whole situation. He felt like he was being lead in circles like a dog chasing its tail.

Myaten felt a pull as he formed an image of Siaak in his mind. In the scrolls, this was the quickest way to find each other out in the desert. It sounded logical to him, especially when there were sandstorms.

When he stepped away from this Obelisk, the pendant lifted off his chest, pointed behind him, and spun. "Great, another jump," he said out loud as he looked around at the drab environment, nothing but miles of barren dry cracked earth in every direction, great.

He kicked the ground with the heel of his boot making dust rise up in small clouds. Stepping backwards Myaten felt the burn of the Obelisk against his skin as it drug him away from space and time and spat him out in another.

Walking out the other side, he heard voices and fell to the ground. His eyes searching the clearing ahead of him as a smile crept across his face when he saw armed guards.

Could this be the place they were keeping Siaak?

Myaten sent a mental shout and waited until he heard nothing. As he crept along the uneven ground, he felt the chain around his neck pulling.

"Damn it!" He was sure this was it. Turning around he headed back to the Obelisk and resisted the urge to slam his fists against it as it swallowed him up

CHAPTER NINE

Dawson sat in the corner of the semi-darkened room with his guard up. Watching and waiting for Siaak to take his last breath and yet at the same time, willing the man to live. Dawson was tired of all the killing. For once, he wanted to be responsible for saving a life instead of taking one.

After four days of surgery, Dawson didn't put a lot of faith in Siaak's survival. The phenomenal amount of blood loss was a sign of Siaak's imminent death. Yet his will and determination to live was outstanding. He surprised all the doctors. They had bet that he wouldn't make it past the first twenty four hours.

Each time Siaak woke, he fought them at every turn. Like a wild wounded animal, he tried to bite anyone that dared come near him. Not one specialist could give a realistic reason to why Siaak's body was rejecting the blood transfusions. They had theories but none Dawson thought could possibly be rational explanations.

Standing up, he winced as he walked over to the bed. The man knew how to fight and Dawson was feeling it as he rubbed at his throbbing jaw in reflection over the few days.

His life had been turned upside down since the day he let Jonathon squeeze his heartstrings. Telling him some bollocks about stolen love and how he would fight until the death to have her back.

Dawson had known Jonathon for a long time. Obviously, not long enough. The man had gone insane, spouting nonsense about a woman with silver eyes and fangs, shouting to doctors that she was after him. That she was trying to lure him to her in order to kill him.

Dawson had no idea what had sent him over the edge. He knew it wasn't the sick fascination with the American woman. It had something to do with the man lying on the bed clinging to the thin threads of life.

Looking down at the man hooked up to so many machines, it was hard to tell where one wire ended and the next began. They were fighting to keep him alive regardless of the costs and work force. His superiors had called in the best doctors in the world. These were ones they had trained and retired until the time came when their country needed them.

Dawson rubbed his eyes. He was so tired. If he got his head down for a few hours, maybe he could fly out to America tonight. His informant had located Miss Ambers. He knew if anyone could give him the answers he needed, she would, especially if he offered her Siaak.

Melissa sat down at the bar tapping her French manicured nails on the counter, compliments of Myaten. Her date had to be the most boring man on earth.

She flashed a smile at the guy working the bar when he made eye contact with her.

"What's your poison honey?" The young man asked as he leaned a narrow hip against the leather-padded counter. He tossed his towel over his right shoulder as he waited for her order.

"I'd love a glass of ice water and a pair of new feet if you

310

have them in size 7 please." She balanced her elbows on the counter with her chin braced in her palms. "I will never dance again in my life. I'll be lucky if I can walk in a straight line."

That brought a chuckle from the bartender, "I take it your date wasn't prince charming?"

Melissa made raspberry sounds as she blew her lips in a show of irritation. "No and if I'd known he was going to break my toes, I would have given my glass slippers to some other poor unsuspecting woman." She grinned as he turned and placed her glass of water down on the long gleaming table that made up the counter top. There wasn't an empty glass or used ashtray anywhere. He kept a tidy ship by the looks of things.

They chatted about different topics, from the weather to politics and like most bar tenders he was open and friendly. He was willing to take the time to offer advice until the bar filled up with a group of college students.

Melissa watched the young men and women turn the dead silence into out breaks of laughter and the clink of glasses as toasts were made. One person caught her eye; he winked and waved her over. She mouthed 'thank you' and nodded 'no' after flashing him a sincere smile.

She glanced at her watch; it was two in the morning. She was trying to stay awake in the hopes that whatever was connecting her to Siaak would re-establish it and maybe she could see something that might help Myaten's search.

"'Ello, can I buy you a drink luv?"

She turned around smiling, ready to give the English speaking man a gentle brush off when she caught his reflection in the mirror.

Her eyes narrowed as they filled with hatred. He was the one that had kidnapped Siaak.

Myaten had shown her a sketch of the officer he'd drawn from memory. It was a perfect rendition. From the crew cut to the square of his jaw, right down to the scar that crossed over his right eyebrow that left a bare patch of white skin.

She pulled her arm back and gritted her teeth as she put all her anger, all her pent up frustration and fear for Siaak into that one punch. Jerk, how dare he come here!

Dawson noticed immediately how the woman went from a graceful elegant stance to fighting she-ninja. As she leaped off her seat, he jumped back out of the way.

"Settle down Miss–" he reached out to take her by the arms. "I need you to come with me, now."

"I'm not going anywhere with you!" She looked around for a weapon of some kind. She kicked off her shoes and bent down to grab the legs of a barstool. She lifted it off the floor and slammed it into Dawson's head knocking him to the floor.

All noise in the bar ceased as everyone watched the woman holding the metal stool in her hands.

The barmen vaulted over the bar and just managed to reach her before she caved the man's skull in.

"Hey! Put that down, lady!" He ordered hoping she didn't use it on him too.

Melissa turned and hissed at him. She opened her mouth and felt her teeth grow along with the sudden need to tear the man's throat open.

"Stand back!" she ordered. She felt her heart hammering against her chest as she felt Siaak. Was this what it was to be a SandWalker? She looked up at the long mirror behind the bar and saw Siaak's reflection. He nodded slowly before his image faded away.

Dawson groaned. Damn, she hit like a man. He managed

to stand up. Shaking his head to clear his vision, he placed his hands to his head. He pressed his fingers against his temple where the throbbing pain made his left eye twitch. He was sure there was a dent in his head, god! That fucking hurt. He dropped his hands when he felt himself being towed backward by something.

His eyes shifted to the right and found Melissa holding him up in the air with one arm and the bar stool in the other. What was she going to do, use him as a fucking cricket ball? "I came to take you to Siaak."

She watched him closely before she opened her hand. He dropped to the floor. Melissa looked at the blood running down Dawson's face from the long gash in his head. Before she could answer, she felt a wave of dizziness as she fell to the floor, the barstool landed with a clatter, the sound echoing through the club.

Melissa woke to darkness and the hum of turbines. She was on a plane! Her heart skipped a beat when she felt movement. Oh wonderful, she thought as the vibrations from the powerful engines made her body shake. She felt like one of those bobbin heads you see in the back of people's cars.

She was actually glad about the wad of cloth in her mouth; it kept her teeth from knocking together. Although she couldn't say the same for the heels of her feet which were tapping against her seat like a woodpecker on speed.

Turning her head left and right she tried to listen for more clues. There was no sure way to tell where she was, due to the blindfold over her eyes. Had she left American soil?

She couldn't tell if the plane was commercial or military. It did sound chunky like a military plane, but that didn't mean anything.

Someone wanted her bad enough to send another agent after her. She bet her last quarter, it wasn't to go sightseeing.

Struggling, she dug her heels into the metal floor and pushed, nothing happened. She couldn't wiggle her fingers, he'd tied her arms down tight.

The officer was obviously afraid she was going to get loose and kick his ass again. He didn't have to cut off her circulation though. So she rocked her body back and forth to test the seat; it didn't budge an inch as she hoped it might.

Panic stricken, she fought the restraints with all her strength. After a few minutes she gave up, it was useless. All she was doing was stressing herself out. That wasn't going to help her any.

Once Myaten found out she was missing, the officer would be in deep shit. She wasn't going to score any brownie points, either. Wait, what was she talking about? She hadn't done anything wrong, why was she worried? Myaten was the one that had left her with the reject from Dancing with the Stars.

Then it hit her. If nobody could locate Siaak, what made her think Myaten would be able to find her?

Dawson sat in the seat opposite Melissa. He held his bowie knife in one hand, tapping the stainless steel blade against the thick rubber sole of his black SAS issued boot.

He stared at her through his aviator sunglasses. She didn't look comfortable, but what did he care. She was the one that knocked him two for six with a fucking barstool. He watched her struggling to get free from the ropes bound around her legs and arms. The overhead lights flickered on and off as the plane taxied down the runway.

Leaning forward, he whipped the glasses off his face and squinted in the semi lighted compartment of the cargo bay. He had seen something when she tried to lift her body out of the seat. The dress she wore had a long rip down the left side exposing her ribcage down to her hip. Looked like a tattoo. He had seen that before.

Then it hit him, god she must have knocked him harder than he thought. Of course he had seen it before, it matched the one Siaak wore. Smiling, he sat back in his seat and slid his glasses back on.

Glancing at his watch, he estimated their arrival at 22:00. He was way behind schedule and that pissed him off. Nothing had gone the way he had planned it. He was supposed to meet Melissa, bring her back with him and take her to Siaak. Drugs and restraints weren't in his game plan, not with women anyway. She looked like a stock pig with that gag in her mouth.

Rubbing his head, he was glad this was the final stretch to their journey. After Melissa's show down in the bar, it had taken him almost an hour plus five thousand American dollars to make the witnesses forget what they had seen.

Flashing his I.D., he gave them the usual fake American/ British bullshit escapee story. He blew off her fangs and strength to nothing more than party gags and drugs. They bought it hook, line and sinker.

With that in mind he closed his eyes and took a nap since he hadn't slept much in the past seven months, he needed a little shut eye.

Myaten slammed the door shut with the back of his heel. He was beyond mad. He was fucking pissed off!

His eyes swept over the open room design of his suite as he walked, weaving past furniture and boxes, straight to the guest room. The door was shut.

He was in half a mind to wake her until he realised the

time. He knew he would have to face the music eventually for his actions, but not at this ungodly hour. If luck was on his side, he might be spared a tongue lashing if she had a good time with her date.

He had planned the evening out with her in mind. Dancing, a terrific meal with a show afterwards, maybe a few drinks and Lenny would drive her back where she'd crawl into bed alone.

He paused at that. Was she alone? Maybe he should check.

His fingers brushed the door handle as he took a step forward and then stopped. What was he thinking? Man this was fucked up! Siaak would kill him if she got drunk and went to bed with another man. He was screwed now for sure! No! He had to mind his own business; Melissa was a grown woman and could make her own choices. He was going to have a shower while she slept in. Then, he'd wake her to tell her the bad news, regardless of who was in the room with her.

Muttering to himself, he went to the bathroom and shut the door behind him. He sat down on the toilet with his face in his hands. Why did he always follow the rules? Dragging in a deep breath, he pushed his hands up to his forehead and stared at the blue marble tiles with the signature silver hourglass.

He could change the outcome. Go back and alter the past. Make the present a whole different stage. That sounded great, until his conscious won over. It wasn't right to suddenly take over and become the director of so many lives! He wasn't God! He had no right to do what he wanted just because his heart was breaking!

Dropping his hands to his thighs, he leaned back against the tiled wall. He let the events of his investigation take control of his mind.

He had been so close. His contacts moved in some

pretty important circles, FBI, CIA and INTERPOL. One of his friends tipped him on recent discretions concerning a SAS unit. It wasn't something the American government could ignore. When the senior officer was found, he could be brought up for disciplinary actions that could lead to court-martial. If he were found guilty, he would be given a Dishonourable Discharge or DD.

Apparently, witnesses saw their activities as suspicious. It had been reported to both bodies of government with interest to national security.

The airport, where the flight had taken off, was the last place Myaten visited after his trek through the Obelisks.

He went back in time long enough to witness Siaak's body being loaded onto a military Boeing 747. The feelings of desperation made him second-guess his own morals.

Leaning forward, he reached down and tugged his muddy boots off before peeling his socks off one at a time. Standing up, he pulled his shirt free of his waistband. Reaching over his head, he pulled the wet musty fabric, gathering it up in both hands and slipped his head and arms free before he tossed it in the laundry hamper.

He walked across the bathroom to stand at the sink, looking in the mirror wishing, he knew how to use them to contact Siaak. He leaned forward, ignoring the cold steel sink biting into his skin, as he probed the raw pain reflected back at him.

Could he have done more?

Dropping his dark head Myaten pressed the palms of his hands against his closed eyelids. When he finished rubbing his wet eyelashes, he caught a glimpse of his blurry reflection as hot tears ran down his cheeks. He turned his back, unable to stomach looking at himself.

Crossing the room, he jerked the waistband of his jeans open and tore the seam down one side of the zipper.

When he reached the shower, he rotated his hips as he shoved the damp muddy black denim to his knees. He didn't bother to look down as he stepped out of them and climbed into the shower.

Not caring about the icy cold stings of the shower, he braced both arms above his head. His hands rested on the glass wall that surrounded him. As the water heated up, steam filled the bathroom making his hand prints fade from view as he shifted his position under the spray of hot water.

His body began shaking harder at the realization that he might have lost his brother forever. Why was he losing it now when Siaak and Melissa needed him the most?

With his head bent low, he let the water wet his hair as it ran down his shoulders and back. With each shake of his mighty shoulders, he sank lower and lower until he lay on the rough tiled floor in a heap.

He knew how long he'd laid there with the icy cold shards stinging his skin. The hot water had run out twice and his body was dry in places where the water couldn't reach.

He cursed as he pulled himself up to his full height and got a face full of cold water as payment for doing nothing for three hours, but lay on the floor of his bathroom shower stall wallowing in self-pity. He shook the wet tendrils of hair from his eyes and grabbed his bottle of Lynx. He quickly washed his body before attacking his hair.

He reached up and with the press of a button, the water stopped. He shook out his hair and wiped the water from his eyes, before he released the lock on the door.

Standing there naked, water dripping off his body Myaten leaned over and palmed the power switch for the Thermal body dryer. It was similar to a hand dryer, instead of being mounted on the wall near the sink for drying your hands; the body dryer was mounted on the ceiling pointing down at him.

As soon as the heated air had dried every part of him, he stepped away from its warmth and the unit automatically shut off.

He left the bathroom and stood glaring at her door again. His damp hair hanging around his shoulders. Ignoring his stomach, he grabbed a box of Capri-Suns. Tucked them under his arm and disappeared into his bedroom.

Half an hour later, he stood in the middle of his living room when his cell phone rang. He reached into his tailored black slacks to retrieve the touch screen phone. Staring out the window, he pressed the phone to his ear. "Hey Lenny, what's up?"

Lenny spoke into the phone and, before the chauffeur finished his apology, the phone slipped from his fingers. As it landed on the floor, Myaten was standing in the doorway, his arms stretched out as his fingers dug into the doorframe. He stared in horror at the empty bed.

"Fuck!" He turned and ran. In one smooth fluid move, he scooped up his phone and took a deep breath. The Obelisk buried inside the wall of his suite swallowed him.

Myaten emerged from the Black Obelisk bellowing for his brother.

"Kiros, we got a problem!"

"What problem might that be?" Kiros appeared half a foot away from him, nibbling a powder-sugar donut.

Watching Kiros eat a donut is a remarkable sight. The

man adores Krispy Kreme and will find any excuse under the sun to buy large quantities of the delicious deserts. The way he holds them with his little pinkie out, well, you just have to see it to believe it.

"Melissa is missing." Myaten proclaimed at the top of his lungs as he marched away from the Obelisk.

"Remind me 'why that's a problem?" Kiros shoved the rest of the donut into his mouth and chewed as Myaten wheeled around to face him.

"I don't find that funny Kiros." Myaten stormed from the grand throne room. He didn't care if Kiros followed him or not. He faded away as he jumped into the Great Library.

Kiros shrugged his shoulders with a reply of 'I wasn't joking' before he attacked the sugar on his thumb and index finger.

Beth was in the middle of texting a friend when Myaten popped in. She squeaked and dropped her phone. After a wild juggling act, she just managed to catch it before it hit the floor. "I really wish you guys would use a damn door once in a while." Beth swore as she turned her phone right side up and began to tap out a message on Facebook about men and manners.

"You're going to wear holes in that thing before too long Beth." Mark glanced up from the book he was reading.

Beth's middle finger slid up the edge of the phone.

Mark tutted at her gesture, "yeah right, in your dreams, honey."

"Both of you act like a married couple. Call a truce before I freeze your butts right where you stand," his eyes drifted over Mark, "and sit."

Myaten wasn't in the mood for their antics. He stormed past them to the scrolls Siaak had been deciphering before he was kidnapped.

"She started it," Mark's childish comment rubbed a raw nerve with Myaten.

Beth opened her mouth to retaliate when she felt a blast of wind across her body, pushing her backwards. Books and paper flew around the room in mini whirlwinds as Myaten vented his anguish like a child being refused a favourite toy.

Mark held his desk as the furniture rocked and his seat danced under him.

"That's enough, Myaten." Kiros touched Myaten's shoulder with a gentle tap. Within a blink of an eye, the wind was gone. The only sound in the room was a few sheets of paper fluttering to the floor.

"She's gone," Myaten's voice was so soft that everyone in the room had to strain to hear him.

"So she ran off, I wouldn't give it a second thought. Siaak doesn't need her—"

"SHUT UP KIROS!" Myaten kicked a pile of books over with his foot and swore in his native tongue. His out swept arms toppled a row of chairs and Beth ducked as a few went sailing over her head.

"Hey! Watch where you're throwing things! You nearly took her head off!" Mark knocked his own chair over in a rush to cover Beth.

"Brother why are you so angry? Siaak doesn't need a human female…"

"That's where you're wrong Kiros! He needs her more than you think. She is his mate. The marker is proof she belongs to him. And he's already claimed her!"

"Oh my god, they slept together! When did this happen?" Beth pushed Mark away making him trip over a pile of books on the floor.

Both SandWalkers graced her with a droll look. "Sex isn't

everything." Kiros voiced before Myaten had a chance to speak.

"Yeah right, and I'm Spock's sister." Beth's voice dripped with sarcasm.

"I can believe that." Mark muttered as he carefully restacked the pile of books that cushioned his fall.

"I expected more of a reaction from you, Mark." Myaten stopped pacing and whirled around with his arms braced across his broad chest. "If she was my sister, I'd be extremely enraged to the point of wanting someone's head." His green eyes searched Mark's face for some kind of response.

"Let me clue you guys in on something." Mark stepped over a pile of papers and turned his chair over. He avoided eye contact with Beth as he concentrated on what he felt needed to be said.

"I love my little sister and don't ever think I'm incapable of showing emotion where she's concerned." Mark let his eyes linger on Myaten's face before he looked at Kiros. "If I had anyone to be upset with, it's you Kiros. Every time her name comes up, you run her down." Mark's voice got louder as he waved his hands in front of his chest. "Do you know she hasn't slept for weeks? She told me, she feels his pain and if she could take that away from him, she'd do it in a heartbeat."

An angry tic beat repeatedly in Kiros's jaw as he took in Mark's little speech. He didn't care, all women were the same.

"Women are liars. Their words are nothing more than another form of deceit." His blue eyes blazing, he clenched his jaw tighter as he looked past Mark, staring off into space. "I hope you find your sister and I'll keep my opinions to myself in the future."

Mark looked away. He hated getting angry, but he'd had

enough of listening to the put downs. "Look, I know there's something going on between Siaak and Melissa. I'm not stupid, but I definitely can't get my head around how you guys can be alive…" he paused as he tried to put his feelings into words.

"I don't blame you Myaten. Melissa told me she was going to try to use the pendant. She'd seen Siaak use it loads of times and she was willing to do anything," Myaten's eyes fell on Beth, "to make things right again."

Beth joined him and wrapped her arms around his chest. Mark didn't even notice as he continued, "But whatever you think of my sister, she doesn't deserve your animosity Kiros." Mark blinked and looked at Beth in confusion. He pulled her arms down and walked off.

"Wait Mark," Beth shouted. She eyeballed the two mighty Egyptians, making sure they knew she wasn't happy. "Kiros," she didn't bother to reach out and touch him, "I know one day you'll meet the woman of your dreams and fall in love."

His eyes turned cold and his cheek muscles twitched under his cowl. "It's a shame you weren't around to warn me a few thousand years earlier." He tipped his head and with a flourish of white robes, he was gone from the room.

Beth turned to Myaten for an explanation and he shook his head no.

"His story isn't for me to tell Beth. All I can say is that if there is a mate out there for him, I can't imagine any woman being able to mend the scars on his heart."

"Are you CRAZY?"

"Keep your voice down Eric. I'm not deaf!" Dawson craned his neck as he searched the curtain pole, ceiling light and behind three wall-mounted paintings in Eric's hotel room.

"It's clean for Christ sake! I do know how to check for bugs, Dawson." Eric chewed on his thumbnail and hissed. A habit he'd recently picked up again, at least it wasn't cigarettes.

Dawson hopped down from the tall stool. "Bad habits are hard to break and…" he paused as he placed the stool back under the breakfast bar in the kitchen. "Sorry, about that. Did it need stitches?"

"Fourteen, I think. I lost count while I was cursing your name."

"It was the hand or your head. I think I chose wisely." Dawson teased.

"Well that's certainly good to know." Eric interrupted his lame apology, to check in on their guest.

Melissa was wide-awake and listening to every word they said.

That wasn't the problem. What bothered him was the fact that Dawson had taken her illegally from one country and deposited her on his lap to baby sit. He was in for one serious court martial.

"Let me remove the gag and get you a glass of water." Eric used his gentle doctor's voice, hoping it would keep her calm.

Her eyes closed as she moaned with sincere relief. Her mouth was so dry, her throat hurt.

"Who taught you to tie knots Dawson? You got her hair caught in it." Eric screwed his face up as he scrutinized his friend's handiwork.

"Let me do it! Anyone would think you're trying to disarm a bomb, Eric." Dawson knocked the doctor's hands away. "Get out of it. Do something useful and get us all a drink."

Melissa closed her eyes. How in the world had she ended up being kidnapped by dumb and dumber?

"I'm going to remove the gag if you promise to sit still and listen this time." At her nod, Dawson slid his knife up under the scarf and cut right through the material as if it was tissue paper.

"Now," Dawson took a seat on the floor and stabbed the carpet with the tip of the blade. "…I want you to help me break Siaak free."

Melissa stopped in the middle of spitting her gag out when Eric entered the room with their drinks. "I'll take that for you." Eric offered and threw the wad of wet material in the trash.

"I don't believe you." Melissa barked back, her voice cracked where her throat was dry.

"I don't believe you, either," Eric chirped in as he handed Dawson a beer and held a glass of water up for Melissa to drink.

"You made a terrible mistake bringing him here and an even bigger one by bringing her, too. You know they are looking for any way possible to make Siaak talk. Once they learn she's here," Eric untied Melissa's arm and gave her the tray to hold, "they won't hesitate to use her as collateral."

"He's dying," Dawson said as he stabbed the carpet with his bowie knife. He embedded the blade into the under lay and the tiles beneath it.

Eric took the tray back and tossed it on the floor. He glanced at the ceiling as he rubbed his face between his hands and walked around in a daze. "You said his injuries had healed…"

"His body had healed from the," his eyes stayed focused on the hilt of his bowie knife, "first lot of wounds."

"What's bloody happened now?" Eric demanded.

"He was taken down by my unit after killing General Stockwell and his daughter."

"What did they do to him?" Melissa felt the sting of tears and looked back and forth between her two captors. Her bottom lip trembled in anger as neither man answered her.

"What did you do to Siaak!" her eyes danced with fury as she repeated her question.

"We—"

"...didn't do anything." Dawson cut off Eric's attempt at fixing the terrible wrong done to the man lying half-dead on a bed surrounded by his enemies. "Eric tried to stop them and now he has a bounty on his head."

"What happened to him? Answer me, god damn it!"

Dawson stood up and stretched his arms. "You're already stressed enough as it is Melissa. You need to be calm and listen. Siaak needs your help. If you promise me you'll take Eric with you, I'll make sure you and Siaak get out of here in one piece."

"But you just said he was dying!" Hysteria crept into her voice as she shouted at Dawson. "What makes you think I can save him?"

"Well, maybe if you are in the room with him... he'll cooperate. If you talk to him, it might calm him down long enough to allow the blood transfusions—."

"I don't know if he can hear her," Eric piped in, "he's in a coma." Eric hated being the one to drop the bomb like that, but she needed to know.

"Oh my god...No...you can't! Siaak can't have blood from us. It's poisonous!" she banged her fist against her right thigh at their stupidity. "Just because he has fangs, doesn't make him a blood sucking vampire!"

In the back of her mind she suddenly realized, that's what he had been trying to tell her all along. Shame, it had taken all this time for her to finally understand.

Dawson crouched down to her knees and cut the plastic tie around her ankles and her left arm. He stood and folded the blade up, "Then we make our move tonight."

"I don't see how we're ever going to find her." Moaned Beth as Mark pushed his sunglasses on top of his head. They had spent two days searching the bars where Lenny had dropped Melissa off.

So far, nobody had seen her.

Myaten slammed the door on his Jag and tapped his hands on the roof. "I'm guessing someone's seen her, but they aren't talking." Myaten shifted his feet as he looked around at the busy sidewalks. "Lenny said he stopped here. She was adamant about having a drink and using a real toilet."

"Come again?" Beth's smile faded when a guy asked her out on a date. Shaking her head 'no', she handed him a flyer with a recent image of Melissa and Myaten's contact details.

"The Limo's for my Casino are equipped with fully working toilets."

"I just can't see why she didn't find that thrilling." Beth's sarcastic remark went unnoticed as Mark joined Myaten by the car.

"Be honest with me, Myaten. Is Melissa right for Siaak? I mean, she's human…," Mark scrunched his face up as he struggled to admit his doubts about the compatibility of a human and a SandWalker.

Myaten took a deep breath before he shrugged his shoulders. "I don't honestly know Mark. I'll tell you the same thing I told Melissa." Myaten locked his car and joined Beth on the sidewalk.

"I can see the future," he put both hands out at Beth and

Mark, "and before you start with the "why didn't you see this coming!" I'll explain. I only see certain things. I know Melissa and Siaak are meant to be. Like I know what my mate looks like, but I don't know her name."

"Damn, whatever happened to dating with you guys?" Beth didn't catch his frown as she went back to handing out more flyers.

"I tried dating. All it does is cause emotional stress. I don't feel comfortable having to explain to a woman why I don't do second dates. Does that answer your question Beth?" Myaten took his wallet out of his back pocket and removed his bankcard.

She nodded as she handed out the last of her flyers.

"Good, wait here, I'll be back in half an hour."

Myaten returned an hour later.

"We thought you'd skipped town." Beth waved a magazine at her face as she glanced at her watch.

"Sorry. It seems in order to withdraw a large amount of cash; you need to sign your name in blood with every manager present and accounted for."

"What's the money for? You expect a ransom call or somethin?" Beth smacked Mark on the shoulder with her rolled up magazine. "Hey you gonna share that ice pop today or what?"

Mark held the melting tropical fruit push-up above his head. "I asked you if you wanted one and you said no, so I'm not giving you mine! Go away! You can have the stick when I'm done." He snickered as he turned his back to her and made 'yummy' sounds as he licked the cold dessert.

Beth pulled her arm back aiming for the back of his head when Myaten took charge and removed her offending weapon.

"What did I tell you earlier?"

Beth twisted her lips up as she glowered at him. And as soon as Myaten wasn't looking she reached up and smacked Mark with her hand.

"Ouch."

"Now I feel better."

Myaten opened the car door and pointed at it. "Get in, Trouble."

"I didn't do anything. He started it and he knows when I say 'no' I mean 'yes.'"

They watched Beth walk off and disappear in the traffic of people.

"She's the reason I don't date." Mark threw his left over push-up in the trash.

"You're in love with her."

Mark wiped his mouth with a tissue and coughed. "Sure am. I've loved Beth for a very long time."

"You should tell her."

"No!"

"What are you afraid of?"

Mark shrugged his shoulders. "You wouldn't understand. Beth is one of those women that need adventure and mystery. She wants to be swept off her feet and rescued," his eyes stayed glued to Myaten's. "She wants someone like you. I can't say I blame her…"

"I'm sorry."

"Don't be. It's life. I stay with her like a faithful pet. Accepting my place in her life as it is." Mark chuckled as he blew off the reality of his relationship with Beth. "I'd rather have her as a friend, than not have her in my life. She's my sunshine, she makes me laugh and, one day, I know in my heart she will find someone to love her even if it's not me."

Myaten saw Beth coming and waved his hand, slowing time down. He touched Mark bringing him out of the time spell. "She's coming. I figured you might need a little time to compose yourself." He pointed at Beth.

Mark blew his cheeks out in relief, his eyes watering. "Thanks buddy."

They talked for an hour until Mark was feeling better. Then Myaten released his control over time. Everything around them jerked like a computer glitch and time resumed.

"Here," she handed the guys a hot fudge sundae. She took a bite and swallowed. "So, what you guys been talkin' about?" she licked the spoon with the tip of her tongue before dipping it back into her ice cream.

"Not much." Mark eyeballed Myaten hoping he wouldn't blow his cover.

Everyone looked at Myaten when music began to play. He smiled, "it's my phone." He handed Beth his sundae and answered his phone.

"I…I'm calling about the missing woman…."

"Can we meet?"

"Look across the street."

Myaten held the phone to his ear as his eyes scanned the opposite side of the street.

"I'm wearing a white tank top with a yellow smiley face. Meet me in Subway in ten minutes."

The line went dead as Myaten tried to see her from his side of the street.

"Who was that?" Beth and Mark asked at the same time.

"I don't know. It's about Melissa."

"Yes that's her."

"I thought you said we'd be on our own?"

"I never leave anything to chance Melissa." He held the gun out waiting for her to take it.

"You should've let me call Myaten. He'd know what to do to."

"I can't risk it. Now are you in or out?" Dawson kept his eyes on hers. He had to know if she was dedicated to the mission. If not, he'd have to do it on his own.

She took the gun and watched Dawson aim a small flashlight with a blue lens at Eric. It blinked on and off repeatedly in Morse code fashion while Eric drove off in the opposite direction. He was heading to the airport for a plane bound for France. He was taking all the evidence of Siaak with him to await further instructions.

Dawson watched until he couldn't see the tail lights any longer, then he placed an arm on Melissa's shoulder. "Stay close and follow my lead."

Melissa gave him a sharp nod and sunk down to his height. They had spent three tedious hours going over and over the grounds of the compound. He refused to take her in blind.

After that, Dawson taught her a few moves using Eric as his partner. Then she had to show him by beating up poor Eric. If not for the seriousness of the mission, she'd have found the whole event comical.

Blinking her eyes against the rain dripping into them, she found it impossible to keep track of him in the dark. The little whistles were hard to hear against the pelting rain. Everywhere she looked was a veil of darkness. Her footsteps unsure, should she go left or right? Damn, she lost him!

Her fingers numb from the wet and ever so often she'd warm them by blowing on them. Dawson crept up on her and spoke into her ear, telling her to stop making unnecessary noises. After that, he stayed right next to her, letting his arm or thigh brush against hers.

Melissa had no clue how far or how long they had been walking. It seemed like hours, but she kept going and stayed quiet.

Dawson stopped and she ploughed into the back of his wet poncho. She stumbled and fell back. Her arms automatically went down to brace her fall. Instead, strong arms pulled her back up.

"Steady on."

"Sorry."

"We're making good time. Stick with me another few yards, and then you can get changed."

They made it to the edge of the woods. Dawson helped Melissa dress in the dark. His hands were impersonal and she ignored the brush of his fingers against her breasts as he buttoned her uniform top. He held the pants open and she just managed to put both feet in the right holes.

Once they were ready, Dawson took the lead again. Melissa's mouth dropped open when he crouched down, drew a gun with a silencer and fired two shots. The sound of bodies hitting the ground made her doubt her sanity. Three more shots! Dawson yanked her into the shadows of the building as he stripped off his poncho.

He took Melissa's hand in his and the next thing she knew, they were running full out towards the entrance of the building. The door slid open and Melissa jumped as a group of men, dressed like Dawson, stood to attention.

"At ease!" At Dawson's command, the men lowered their guns.

Melissa looked over her shoulder as more bodies pressed in to form a tight knit circle around her and Dawson.

"Jefferson, I need your unit to follow me. Kramer, if anyone enters that door, Shoot to kill! No questions asked! Do I make myself clear?"

Kramer saluted and wheeled on his heels to face the door.

Melissa scooted by, trying not to make a sound. When he cocked his submachine gun, it made her jump.

Dawson reached over and took her by the arm, steering her down the hallway. "This is where it gets tricky–"

A door opened suddenly and a man in uniform entered the hallway. When he looked up and saw them, his face turned angry. His arm reached up to press the alarm and went slack as he fell hard onto the floor.

Melissa saw it in slow motion. She was still focused on the dead guy sprawled on the floor with his eyes wide open staring at the ceiling, when she heard gun fire behind them. Why had things gotten so out of control?

"Why are you killing these men, can't you just knock them out?"

Dawson heard a voice to his right. He looked down and saw Melissa's big brown eyes, and then her query hit him. A deep frown creased his forehead.

"It's kill or be killed. Siaak is more important than any one man in this compound. You aren't naïve and I warned you of all the possibilities."

They both looked over their shoulders when someone shouted. Then Dawson was running and dragging her behind him. She had lost count of all the doors and hallways they'd past. The endless amount of stairs leading to more hallways, made her feel like a rat in a maze. She was glad Dawson knew where he was.

"Almost there," Dawson dropped her hand and ran toward the end of the hall.

Melissa gagged as she was sprayed countless times before reaching the large metal door with a scanner. It reminded her of a vault door, all it was missing was a great big wheel-like handle in the centre.

"Glad you could join me." Dawson glared at her before he placed his hand against the scanner. It bleeped and lit up green. As the door opened, Dawson swiped a card and punched in a code.

Melissa heard the fast beeping sound and panicked when Dawson jammed his body between the massive door and its frame to keep it open for her. "Go!"

Melissa climbed over him and he rolled his body out of the way, as the door banged shut.

"What did you do?"

Dawson rubbed his shoulder where the door caught it. "I've locked us in and everyone else out."

"Is that good or bad?"

"For us," he nodded and wiped the sweat from his forehead, "it's good." As he reloaded his weapon, he led her through an office. "This is the control room. All those small TVs show us what's going on inside each lab." He tapped on the fifth one down, "that was Siaak's room."

"Was? What do you mean, it was? What happened?"

"Siaak broke free and killed three people." Dawson pressed a few buttons on the keyboard and a drawer slid open. He took the disc and handed it to Melissa.

"Proof of what they did to him. I suggest you don't watch it."

Melissa looked at the small disc in her hand and instantly she wanted to smash it.

"We need to get a move on." He moved over to the door and held it open for her. When they rounded the corner, she saw a small desk and a scanner. They bypassed the scanner and Melissa's mouth fell open at all the bullet holes. The ceiling, walls and floor looked like Swiss cheese.

"You watch my back." Dawson ordered. So she stood behind him with her gun aimed towards the corridor outside, as Dawson swept the room for any guards. He repeated it on all seven labs, before he opened a concealed door in the last lab.

Melissa slipped inside and immediately her eyes flew to the man on the bed. "Siaak…" Tears filled her eyes as she took in his appearance.

His cheeks were hollow and his skin pale, he looked like death warmed over. The plastic facemask didn't make him look any better; in fact, it made him look even frailer.

Her eyes skimmed down his chest and stopped. Covering her mouth with her hands, she let her eyes wander around his chest; it was riddled with bullet holes. Nothing had prepared her for this.

When Dawson said gunned down, she envisioned a few gunshot wounds, not this. How had he managed to survive this?

A loud buzz drew her eyes to the wide range of monitors above his bed. An erratic beeping sound followed the green bouncing lines on one screen. It told her his heart was having trouble beating.

The sound of oxygen being pumped into his lungs clicked on and off. When she touched his fingers, the heart monitor beeped, setting an alarm off making her draw her hand back to her chest.

"See, he knows you are here. Talk to him, I bet he can hear you." Dawson winked at her as he planted himself by the door. Nothing short of a bomb was going to get past him.

Melissa walked around the bed and stood there looking at him. "I'm so sorry. Siaak if can you hear me…"

"He's in a coma."

Melissa whirled around as a man stepped out of the shadows.

"Hello, princess."

"What are you doing here?" Her gut feeling told her, it wasn't good.

"Is that how you greet your dear old Dad?" Robert held his arms out to his daughter and poked his bottom lip out in a fake display of sadness.

"I want to know why you're here." She repeated.

Robert dropped the loving parent act. The caring look vanished from his face. Immediately, he became the cold dominating man she'd grown up with.

"You want the truth?" He shoved his hands in his trouser pockets and looked at his shoes. He rubbed the toe of his right alligator shoe against the back of his left trouser leg before he looked up. "I think, for once in your life, you're right."

Melissa stepped back until she felt the cold metal railing of to Siaak's bed. She wasn't going to let anyone hurt him again.

"Oh, that's precious." He clapped once before placing his fingertips to the edge of his nose. "I knew you'd fall for him."

Melissa screwed her face up in horror. "You make me sick! You self absorbed, sick, son of a bitch, you honestly expect me to believe you planned all of this?"

"Princess, you don't know the half of it." Robert waved his cupped hands at her. "You made it so easy. When the location of the Black Pyramid was found a year ago by our satellites, we knew from top-secret files what was inside it. We immediately put all our resources into figuring a way to jam the frequency keeping it from view."

"That's why Jonathon asked me to join him on the dig." She drew her hand up and pinched the bridge of her nose. Her stomach curdled at the realization, she'd been played, big time!

His hands parted and did a little twirl at the wrist before he examined his nails. "I knew Jonathon would have you eating out of his hand. Unfortunately, Jonathon found out our plans for you." Robert snickered as he looked up at the ceiling in wonder, before he tucked his hands in the pockets of his expensive Gucci jacket.

"The stupid dick fell in love with you and took matters into his hands. Therefore, I did what needed to be done. I had him committed. He'll need the president's signature, in triplicate, to get released."

"I can't believe you'd do this to me, your own flesh and blood!"

He tilted his head down and tisked. "Well, you see, that's the problem… I am not your real biological father. You were created for this purpose, princess. The male SandWalker and you will create our new race of super warriors."

"I'd rather die than be used by you. I won't let you touch him again!"

"Ha, you can't stop us. I created you and now it's time for you to be a good daughter and give me some grand-children."

"I think you should kill her and allow me to breed with the SandWalker."

Melissa looked from Robert's startled face to the tall woman with glittering silver eyes. She appeared out of nowhere and pushed her father to the side.

"I prefer Kiros, but Siaak will do nicely."

"No!" Melissa felt like gagging at the over whelming smell

of blood. Suddenly she felt dizzy. Her muscles went tight. With a surge of adrenalin, she turned into a blurring line of white and brown.

Melissa heard choking sounds as she held the BloodSeeker by the throat. Flexing her fingers, she squeezed harder and harder. She didn't care if she killed her, but something told her strangulation wasn't the way to kill a BloodSeeker.

She didn't give a shit! The woman threatened Siaak and Melissa hoped her head popped off. Height didn't help the evil leach as Melissa lifted her off the floor. With strength she never knew she had, Melissa flung the BloodSeeker's body around like a rag doll before tossing her across the room.

Melissa let a smile slip over her lips, as she bowled Robert to the floor with the other woman's body. "You won't touch a single hair on his head!" Melissa opened her mouth and Dawson watched in stunned silence as her fangs grew into place joined by a second set and then a third. Melissa went after the BloodSeeker, not holding back a single punch. Dawson yelled at her but she wasn't letting the BloodSeeker get up off the floor.

"I shall eat your liver *newborn* while I fuck your *immortal warrior*." Kirara's red-stained tongue flicked out as she curled her lips back maliciously. Slurping noises filled the room as her eerie silver stare raked Siaak's body with open approval.

"I doubt that!" Melissa reached behind her back and whipped the gun from the waistband of her jeans. "I admit, I don't know how to kill you yet, but I'm willing to bet a bullet to the head stings like hell!" Melissa added a raised eyebrow before Dawson stepped in line with her.

The BloodSeeker bowed her head. Her long dark lashes swept up as a bemused smile tugged at her lips. "We shall meet again *walidah.*" She hissed softly in warning and took hold of Robert. They vanished before Melissa could pull the trigger.

Dawson lowered his gun as he touched her shoulder, "you alright?"

Melissa looked at him oddly. She nodded once before she moved across the room in a single second. Standing next to Siaak, she sat on the bed and took his hand in hers.

MELISSA!

Stop shouting, I can hear you.

I have been trying to communicate with you since you entered the room. Kirara was blocking me.

She's gone now. Listen. I don't know what's happened to me, Count, but you better fix it.

What happened to you? Are you hurt?

No, I'm fine. It seems 'you' turned me into a SandWalker.

Impossible!

Then explain why I grow fangs every time I get upset about you.

You already know the real reason.

Whatever! You need to bite me again.

Why would I bite you? I am not a vampire. How many times do I have to repeat myself?

My father, Robert, seems to think he orchestrated this whole escapade. He said he created me to mate with you. You bit me and suddenly I'm growling like a dog, moving faster than light and have teeth that would give any dentist nightmares!

I wish I could explain why I bit you, urbi, and if it makes you feel any better, you were the first human I have bitten and not killed.

Dawson tapped his gun against the metal table to get her attention. "It's time to go Melissa."

What is urbi? Is it some kind of insult?

It is better than newborn. I called you princess in my language.
Nice, now tell me how to use the pendant.
It is too dangerous. Besides, they took it.

She reached into her front pocket and held the silver necklace up to his face, then realized he couldn't see it.

I have it here with me. Now, tell me how to use it before it's too late, Siaak!

Images poured into her mind. Once she was sure she had the principle down, she looked at the officer standing behind her. "Dawson, gather your men and bring them here, we're outta here."

Kiros jogged towards the Temple. When he reached the long stretch of granite steps leading up to the temple, he cursed Myaten. Resisting the temptation of jumping, in order to get his body in shape, he took Myaten's advice to exercise. Huffing, he blew out his cheeks as he launched himself forward taking three steps at a time. He loved being outside. It was the intense UV rays and the extreme heat from the sun that were the problem. In this era, it drove him indoors after only a few hours.

As he entered the massive doorway, he peeled his sweat stained tank top from his chest. He needed a shower! He was striding towards his room when the first body hit the floor. "Myaten, get your ass down here!" He bellowed as his whip materialized over his left shoulder. Another body in black sailed across the floor and rolled to a stop. Neither of them got up. Kiros was checking one, when Myaten strolled into the old throne room.

"This better be good… hey, Kiros what did I tell you about bringing strangers home with you?" Myaten teased until he noticed how the hieroglyphics began to glow within the Obelisk. "How long has it been doing that?"

"How the fuck should I know. I just got here!"

Four more bodies went flying past, as Kiros and Myaten watched in amazement. There was nothing they could do without knowing 'when' they needed to 'catch'. In order to know that, they had to be in contact with the person controlling the Obelisk.

"*It's raining men…hallelujah…it's raining men*" Beth carried on singing as she leaned against the wall of the main corridor between the old throne room and entrance hall.

Myaten frowned at the sound of her voice. "Stay there," he ordered. That last thing he wanted was for her to get hurt.

"Do I look like I'm moving to you?" Beth glared back. She opened her mouth to ask him what was going on, but he beat her to it.

"Someone's using the Obelisk to get these people here in a hurry." Before he got a chance to finish his theory, another six bodies had piled up on the floor. That was twelve in total!

"This one's awake!" Kiros pointed at one person out of the first batch.

The man was rubbing his head and moaning. He sat up, took one look at Kiros, saw the Obelisk glowing and fell back on the floor again.

"Umm, strike that, I think he fainted." Kiros chuckled as he walked over the bodies, avoiding them as if they had the plaque.

Myaten began inspecting the group of bodies nearest him. They all had weapons. Not good. Myaten held his arms out and two swords materialized into his hands. "Beth, leave now!"

"Are you kidding, this is getting good." She pushed herself

off the dark granite wall intending to march her butt over to Myaten when she felt hot air blowing at her body. "Christ sake!" she lunged backwards as a wall of fire rose fifteen feet in front of her. With a whooshing sound, it spread out blocking her access to the throne room.

"You bully! Haven't you heard of women's rights?"

He ignored her accusations as he stepped around the bodies that littered the granite floor. Thumbing the red leathered hilt of his swords, he opened his mouth to ask 'what the hell was going on' when he went flying through the air. His swords clattered as he threw them away from his body and the metal made contact with the granite floor.

"Damn! Where did she get her license to drive that thing?" Dawson put his hands down and found he was laying on somebody. "Sorry mate," he jumped up and held his hand down to the poor sod that broke his fall. "You wouldn't happen to know a bloke by the name of Myaten?"

"Yeah, you landed on him."

Dawson whistled when he stood up. "Damn, you're a big bloke. Look, Melissa is bringing Siaak here. He's in a coma. She's sending him next and I don't know how long you got…" his voice trailed off when he noticed all his men were sprawled all over the floor.

The moment Myaten heard Siaak's name and the word 'coma', he flashed to the front of the Obelisk, "Kiros get ready to catch!"

No sooner than both SandWalkers planted their bodies a foot away from the stone pillar, Siaak's body hit them full force. He was wrapped in sheets like a mummy and surprisingly, very light.

All heads turned, as Melissa stepped out of the Obelisk. Her facial expression showed her relief when she saw Siaak being carried away. "Good, everyone's safe." She saw Dawson striding towards her and blew the strands of hair out of her face. "I can pass out now?"

Dawson hooked her up into his arms before she hit the ground. He hurried after the three shadows bouncing off the wall.

"How did you learn to use this?" Kiros loomed over her head, shouting and waving the pendant in her face.

"Wha...." She pushed him away and tried to roll on her side. Her head hurt and she felt sick.

"No you don't— look at me!" Kiros took hold of her shoulders and shook her so hard the gurney bounced on its wheels as her confused brown eyes focused on him.

"Tell me why you sold us out!" His head cast a shadow over her as he lowered his ear to her mouth.

"Go away, Kiros, I'm tired." Her eyelids fluttered shut.

"Wake the fuck up!" He moved back and smacked her across the face.

"Get your hands off my sister!" Mark demanded. He couldn't believe he'd seen Kiros strike her, especially after risking her life to save Siaak.

Kiros flung his hand up and Mark found to his horror, he couldn't move. Kiros took the time to glance at him out the corner of his blue eyes. "Your sister sold us out to the humans. She let them capture Siaak and now his life hangs in the balance. She will pay for this one way or another, I swear it!"

"What's all the commotion about?" Beth stopped dead in her tracks. The crazy look in Kiros's eyes was enough to make her want to turn tail and find a place to hide. But the second she saw the angry hand print on Melissa's face, she stepped back and screamed. "MYATEN!"

"My brother stands with me and believes as I do." Kiros cut everyone a smug look.

"You're way off base with this one, Kiros." Myaten blinked into the room behind him. "Melissa saved Siaak. She is his *merit*," he glanced to Beth and Mark, "it means *beloved* and that means we have to treat her with love, not hatred."

Kiros wanted to believe them but a woman could never be trusted. He growled low in his throat. "You will regret this."

"Kiros shut the fuck up! If you don't want to help, then be quiet." His green eyes dropped to Mark and instantly he was free of the spell. He picked Melissa up off the gurney and teleported everyone to Siaak's resting chamber.

"I need you to wake up, Melissa. Siaak is in danger of dying. He needs your blood as well as ours to survive."

Melissa moaned. "I'm awake. I dreamed Kiros turned psycho on me." She licked her lips and rubbed her face. She saw the pissed off look Kiros was wearing and knew it wasn't a dream. Bobbing her head she agreed, "Yeah, I'll help."

"Good girl, but first you need to feed from either myself or Kiros. Right now, Kiros isn't an option, so..." he pressed her face into the side of his neck. "I'm afraid it'll have to be me."

"Oh yuck, no way!" she batted him away with her flying hands. "I'm not sucking anybody's neck." She narrowed her bloodshot eyes at him.

"You might like it," he teased trying to lighten the situation.

"No...no...no and that's my final word on it." She reached up to her neck for Siaak's necklace. "Who took it from me?" She eyeballed Myaten until she remembered Kiros yanking it from her neck earlier.

"Look, I will do whatever it takes to save Siaak's life, but when we are through here, I want out! I don't want to be one of you people. I want my normal life back. I plan on going home!"

"You can't leave him! You are destined for him. *Urbi,* stop and think this over!" Myaten shouted as he glared at Kiros.

She whirled around on shaky legs. "Stop calling me princess!" She cried at Myaten. "I didn't ask for any of this. All I want is to be left alone!"

Then she flew at Kiros, stabbing her index finger in his chest. "You think I'm a traitor, that I let your big secret out," she waved her arms above her head. "Let me tell you, buddy! I never told anyone about any of you. So, if you can get over your fucking gold gilded ego for a second, you'd see that I did the only thing I could do."

"Melissa," The desperation in Myaten's voice caught Melissa's attention.

"Where is Siaak?" She looked past Myaten and gasped when she saw Siaak. He was laid out on a bed. His arms folded on his chest. He looked dead to her. She marched over to the bed and carefully climbed up next to his body. She could feel his body temperature was dropping. When she placed her hand to his cheek, it was stone cold.

Instantly she reached out to him. *Siaak you need to wake up and feed.*

Her eyes searched his face and chest. There was no movement. Her heart raced.

"NO!" she struck his chest with her small fists making his body bounce. "How dare you make me into one of you and then leave me on my own! Speak to me!"

He didn't answer.

Her eyes searched his body. He wasn't moving. "Oh shit, no, don't you go now!"

"We were too late." Myaten bowed his head, tears running down his cheeks.

"NO! I want the doc here, now!" She whirled around and looked at Myaten. "Ask Dawson where he is! Bring him here!" She held her right arm out. "Cut me Kiros."

"Are you nuts, you'll bleed to death?" Mark placed his body between them and the bed with his arms out. "Don't touch her!"

"It'll be okay Mark. Do it Kiros."

"But she'll bleed to death." Mark argued, trying to make them see sense. He didn't want his sister to die and he wasn't going to stand there and let them kill her.

"COME ON!" Melissa waved her arms at them; she couldn't believe they were standing there as if they had all the time in the world. "MARK, GET OUT OF THE WAY!"

"I can't believe you're doing this." Horror filled his eyes as he witnessed Kiros lifting his dagger.

Melissa's body jerked at the flash of pain. Blood flowed from her wrist, squirting a trail over the bed and Siaak's chest as she put it up to his mouth.

"Drink Siaak, for me." she ordered and within ten minutes, she blacked out.

Melissa woke up looking at the ceiling. She smiled until she saw the bandage around her left wrist. "Siaak…" She sat up to be pushed back down.

"It's okay Melissa." Eric's low voice made her relax for a second.

"I need to see him."

Eric kept his eyes down. He couldn't tell her the truth.

"Is he sleeping? I can check on him, right?"

Eric nodded and pulled out a syringe. "This will help you sleep."

"I'm not tired."

"You need your rest, doctor's orders." He pushed the plunger, squirting a watery arch of medication up into the air.

"I want to see Siaak, and then I will come back to bed, okay?"

"Let her go and see him doc, my sister won't take 'no' for an answer."

Melissa heard her brother's voice and sat up again. "She needs to know, then give her the sedative."

Eric capped the needle and placed it on the table near his bag. "I'll be here if you need me."

She jumped down from the bed and raked her fingers through her hair. "I need to know what?" Her voice caught. "What's wrong with Siaak?"

Eric coughed and turned his back to her. He hated being the one to give bad news. He was a doctor. His mission in life was to save people. When he lost a patient, it hit hard.

"Siaak's dead," he turned to face her, "he wasn't in any pain…" He wanted to reassure her, to give her some measure of comfort that in his final moments he hadn't suffered.

Her lips trembled as her heart sped up. "NO…I have his mark…see?" She pulled her jeans down and choked. Shaking her head in denial, she clawed at her skin. The marker had faded to a pinkish outline of its former bold darkness.

"NO! No, he can't be dead. SIAAK!" She needed to be near him and instinctively she found she had jumped from her room to his.

Myaten turned. For the first time, he looked uncertain as to what he should do. "Melissa, I…"

Melissa put her palm up for silence as she stood over Siaak's body. He looked so young. She had heard that in death, a person looked younger and now she knew first hand. Lifting her hand, she gasped in shock at the icy feel of his cheek against her fingers.

"When did he die?"

"A few minutes after you fainted– I located Eric, brought him here and he patched you up. I asked him to give you a sedative so you could sleep. That was four days ago," he added with a low cough as he tried to clear his throat.

She crumbled to her knees, blindly grabbing his hand and crushing it to her cheek.

"You can't go! Not now! I saw us together. I saw our future, this wasn't supposed to happen!"

"Melissa, don't do this to yourself."

"Take me back."

"I can't."

Melissa looked up at his face, her eyes dark, full of anguish and hurt. "Take me back. I have to fix this! He said I was his mate. So take me back!"

"I'm afraid it doesn't work that way. If you go back now you might change the course of events leading up to his rescue."

"Take me back now! I can heal him, that won't change anything serious other than he won't be DEAD!"

"She's right, ya' know. I can give you the time and the day when to do it. I was there with Siaak when he was awake. He only slipped into a coma after I flew to Nevada and kidnapped Melissa." Dawson stepped into the room. "I saw you both on camera. It's why I decided to go after Melissa. I didn't know then what I know now. So you have to go back, otherwise you'll be changing history." He looked at Melissa and licked his lips before he crossed his muscled arms over his chest. "I, um, know now isn't the perfect time for this, but Melissa…thank you for saving my men. We are forever indebted to you."

Melissa gave him a half-hearted attempt at a 'you're welcome' smile, but she didn't feel like smiling. She turned her back to them as her eyes filled with tears. Not caring what they thought, she stretched her body out and cuddled up to Siaak. She stroked his hair and wished she had the power to go back, to have another chance at fixing things.

"Take her back, Myaten."

One by one, everyone turned to see the shadowy figure of Kiros as he hovered in the archway. "Siaak deserves more than this. They both do." He bowed once, graced Myaten with a nod and left without another word.

"You test my strength, Melissa. Do you know how hard it's going to be for me to sit back and do nothing?"

"Yes, but it has to be this way, otherwise we lose him forever."

"Fine, have it your way." Myaten bowed his head and offered a prayer of protection over Siaak's lifeless body. His wet eyelashes brushed his cheeks as he wiped his eyes. "Dawson, the ball is in your court, now come with me."

As soon as Myaten released her, he took a seat, crossed his legs and flipped through the selection of magazines on the table next to him.

"Ah People's magazine, let's see who's top of the food chain this month."

Melissa raised her arms in wonder. "I know you aren't going to sit there and watch."

"Nope, I found a dating quiz to fill in. You go on, ignore me. I'm not here." He pursed his lips as he searched the tabletop for a pencil. Shrugging, he flashed one to hand and started filling in the quiz.

Melissa took a spot by the side of his bed. This room was about the size of a normal hospital room for a single patient. Other than the bed, Melissa could just see the outlines of a wardrobe and dresser. All of it located near the unlit part of the room where Myaten sat doing his quiz.

Pushing her hair behind her ears, she looked up at all the monitors around Siaak's bed. It was state of the art. Touch pad sensors on the arm rail would lift and lower the bed and fold it into any conceivable position.

A single light shone from the strip light above his head, casting an eerie white tinge to his skin. "Siaak, can you hear me?"

His head was turned away from her facing the door. Half of his face was pressed into his pillow and his eyes were closed.

She wanted to see his eyes with their breath-taking sparkle that reminded her of shiny pennies. She reached up and smoothed the hair out of his eyes. He turned his head into her hand and his eyelids fluttered open.

Her gentle loving smile faded as his face contorted with pain.

"Why are you here?" His eyelids slammed shut and his teeth clamped together as he gripped the metal railing with his hands. "GO before they find you Melissa. I....I ... ahhhhhhhh," he cried out in pain.

Melissa put her hands out to help him, her eyes frantically searching his body, wondering where best to comfort him. He was thrashing around so much; she decided it was a good idea not to touch him at all. Her brown eyes misted over as she knuckled her mouth against the pain she desperately wanted to stop.

Wiping her eyes, she reached up, gathered her hair and tied it onto the crown of her head.

Looking at the bed, she noticed two leather cuffs attached to the metal frame. When he settled down, she took the opportunity to carefully tie both of his hands to the side of the bed.

"What…you…..dooooooing?"

"Doing what needs to be done." She crawled up on the edge of the bed near his chest, careful not to jar him. The smell of old blood mixed with bleach made her queasy but she carried on with what she needed to do.

Taking all her weight on her arms, she lowered her chest to her knees placing her neck above his mouth. His hair tickled her skin as he moved his face into his pillow.

"No…go…leave me now. It has been too long since I last fed Melissa."

"I trust you Siaak. Please do this, for me."

"Foolish woman! You have no idea what you are offering." His voice caught as he took in a sharp burst of air through his nose. "I can smell your blood!"

Her eyelids drifted shut as his nose and mouth pressed against her neck. "You were injured recently."

"It's nothing serious." She licked her lips at the feel of his hard teeth and pushed into his mouth. She had to save him this time. Then the heat of his mouth was gone.

"Come on Siaak, you need to eat."

"I have little to no faith left in my reserve where you are concerned, Melissa. If I start, I know in my heart I cannot let you go, until I have drunk my fill."

"So in other words, you refuse to bite me?"

"Yes. I would rather die than hurt you."

"Fine, if you won't take what I offer then I guess we'll do this the hard way, again." She lifted her bandaged wrist and tore at it with her teeth. Shredding the tape, she sat up and quickly unwound her wrist before she lost her balance.

Looking around she couldn't see anything to cut the neat row of stitches.

Holding her wrist up to her mouth, she saw the realization in his beautiful eyes.

"Melissa stop, think about what you are doing." His color was returning but his voice was hoarse.

"If I don't do this, Siaak, you'll die and where does that leave me?" She searched his face. He had aged since his capture and it was all her fault.

Crow's feet marred the corners of his eyes giving him a weathered look.

"Better off, you forget what I am. You know fangs and all."

"Sorry, you don't get off with that excuse."

His smile made her heart soar and she wanted nothing more than to keep it there. He opened his mouth to argue. She took the opportunity offered and kissed him. She knew it was only a matter of time before his hunger would kick in. He'd have no choice, but to feed from her.

"Melissa…"

"Shush." She brushed her lips against his, letting her tongue lightly trace his upper lip.

"I know you are taunting me."

She laughed, her eyes dancing with merriment. "Honey, until you see me pole dance, you ain't seen nothing yet!"

"Hey, I'm in the room, if you don't mind. You two can hump later. Siaak feed so I can return her to the right time."

Siaak looked in the direction of Myaten's voice. "Right time?" He struggled to see into the dark. With a sigh, he turned his head on his pillow and looked her in the eyes, "What have you done?"

"Don't worry about it." Melissa kissed him again, forcing his mouth open as she slipped her tongue inside. His moan told her it was working. She moved to his earlobe and planted soft kisses down his neck, willing him to bite her. When he did, she cried out.

The sharp pain as he broke the skin, stole her breath. When his warm mouth latched onto her and the sucking began, her eyes glazed over as she let go. She was willing to give him whatever he needed in order to live.

The man she called father had abandoned her. All these years he'd proclaimed his love for her. It was all a lie. Her life was a lie.

Siaak had known her for a short time and had given his life in order to protect her. It felt good to return the favour. A life without him wasn't liveable.

Her eyelids closed though she fought to open them. She felt sleepy. "I love you," rushed from her lips before her body went lax.

He was lost in the taste of her. The nutrients from her blood were filtered through his fangs as he sucked harder. He felt his strength returning. He needed more.

"Siaak! You need to stop now before you kill her."

Myaten made a move toward the bed and Siaak made a guttural growl low in his throat.

She belongs to me! Back off!

Myaten's head jerked sideways as the mental shout slammed into him like a well-placed punch.

He wasn't angry. Siaak was enthralled with Melissa's taste and the need to feed enhanced it to sweet nectar. "I know that Siaak, I'm just trying to keep you from hurting her! You don't want that any more than I do. She refused to let you die, so don't let her go so easily."

Siaak pulled back. His fangs retracted and he turned his head to the side.

"Please take her, Myaten."

Myaten reached over the bed and carefully picked her up and cradled her to his chest. "Tonight at seven pm, you will slip into a coma. I suggest meditation. Don't make me have to come back again, just so I can kick your ass!"

Siaak smiled, his eyes glittering as they settled on Melissa. "Keep her safe until I return."

"You mean, until she rescues you." Myaten corrected and nodded yes at the look of genuine surprise on his face. "She's gone through a lot for you, Siaak."

"You brought her back in time. Why did you break your vow?"

Myaten bend his head close to his chest to make sure Melissa was breathing okay before he answered. "You died."

"I am indebted to her."

"We all owe her one. But, Maybe I wouldn't put it quite that way. Not unless you wanna end up sleeping on a sand dune!"

He turned to leave and remembered, 'Oh, by the way, don't forget. Seven pm, you're out for the count."

He saluted and faded away, leaving Siaak to figure out how he was going to get his arms free of the bed.

CHAPTER ELEVEN

Myaten felt time drag around him. It was like moving through molasses. The more steps he took, the longer it seemed to take. Then his ears popped as he entered the right time zone, as he liked to call it.

"Siaak, I need your ass here, pronto!" Myaten held his breath and looked around. Where was he?

SIAAAAAAAAAAAAAAAK!

His mental shout made Melissa flinch in his arms. "Shush, I've got you."

"Give her to me."

Myaten cracked a smile that made his eyes shimmer with tears. "About fucking time you showed up!" He handed Melissa over Siaak and walked with him toward his room. "Where is Eric?"

"He is busy treating the wounded. Seems the government decided the Black Pyramid was a threat after all. They blew it up two hours ago."

Myaten froze. "That means there's the possibility that Osiris is free."

Siaak nodded and carried on walking. "Kiros and Dawson are on it. You are welcome to help them. I have my hands full at the moment."

Myaten clapped his hands together and gave a wolfish smile. "I'm on it, boss." And he disappeared.

Melissa rolled over and caught her body from plunging off the edge of the bed. She pushed herself upright and let her legs dangle off the edge as she rubbed her face.

"I have to ask myself, what makes a person go back in time, risking everything, to save the life of another. Some would say love and others might say devotion. Personally, I think it was done out of stupidity. " He knew the moment she was awake and he made sure to keep his distance. If he so much as looked at her now, he would crumble. And there was a lot that he needed to say to her first.

She slid her face out of her hands. Her eyes watered as she tried to focus them in the dim light. When she could see, it took every ounce of will power she had, not to rush over and search him from head to toe.

Then he openly ridiculed her reasons for saving his life. "It wasn't your time to die." She stared daggers at his back. It was hard to believe he had died. And there he stood, very much alive and being an insensitive dick.

"What gave you that idea?"

His clipped tone irked her even more. Why was he so mad at her? She had saved his life for Pete's sake! Did he have a death wish or something?

She stood up and straightened her clothes in an agitated jerk, before tucking her small hands underneath her armpits. Shaking her hair out, she paced back and forth, as she struggled with the idea of kicking something, hard.

That's when she noticed the table.

It wasn't a bed, at all.

Then it dawned on her. She had been here before, in her vision.

Without thinking, she stopped pacing and reached down to touch the surface. Immediately, she was flooded with a sense of Deja'vu. Pulling her trembling hand back, she placed it against her cheek and smiled dreamily. "I saw us together, here in this room. I saw our future…"

"I see. It was one of your visions." Siaak spoke softly as he took a step back before he looked at her over his broad shoulder. "You had no right to push Myaten. He broke his vow and used his powers to alter events of the past. No one is allowed to change a person's fate Melissa, not even mine." Siaak shifted his weight as he turned completely around to look at her. Gods, she was breath taking. Her chestnut hair hung around her face and those big brown eyes. He could lose himself in them. Part of him wanted to shake sense into her. The heart wrenching need to make her aware that time travel is a dangerous game. It scared him to death to think she could have inadvertently sacrificed herself for him.

"I did what I had to do. I care, you know. Never mind." She fisted her mouth and shook her head angrily. "I won't make excuses. You can talk rules until you're blue in the face! I know in my heart," she slapped her chest with her hand, "I did what was right. Saving you was the right thing to do. And I'd do it again!" She huffed and stormed across the room.

She got as far as the doorway before she felt her body being towed backward. She strained to move her legs and arms. The more she struggled the more pressure was applied. "Let. Go. Of. ME!"

"Not until you answer the question." The second her body came into full contact with his, his arms swung out and locked her in place. "Tell me the truth Melissa." He rubbed his cheek against hers, "I want to hear why you risked your life to save mine. I need to know."

"Because… I felt guilty, I felt responsible for your death and I had to fix it… what else do you want me to say?" She knew exactly what he wanted to hear and she wasn't going to say it a second time.

"I simply want the truth Melissa. No lies between us." He turned her in his arms. He wanted to look into her eyes. To see the truth.

She wanted to tell him the truth. She wanted to scream it to the rooftops. To tell him she loved him more than anything in the world. And the thought of being without him made her heart snap in two. However, she couldn't let Robert use them. She refused to become part of a breeding program for the government. She'd forfeit her life to keep Robert from hurting any of them again. She had to protect him at all costs and if it meant lying, then that's what needed to be done. Even if it hurt him. And broke her heart.

"I don't love you, Siaak. I did what any friend would do. Besides, you only have feelings for me, because of these damn markers!"

He took hold of her chin and jerked her head back. "How dare you imply my feelings for you are false? You have no idea the full meaning of the mark we share. This is only the beginning for us, Melissa. The visions, even in their intensity, will pale in comparison to the yearning, aching, desire you will feel. The longer you fight it, the more you will be consumed by it."

"Let go Siaak, this won't work." She jerked her face free of his grasp.

Anger contorted his face as he took her by the shoulders and shook her hard. "What are you afraid of, Melissa?"

She tried to pull away, but his grip was stronger. "I'm not afraid for me!"

"Then, why are you running from me? Why do you refuse to admit your feelings for me now, when you were so open about it before?"

"I don't know what you're talking about."

"Lies!" At her blank look, he swore, "Damn it woman, say it!"

"No, I can't, Siaak. I won't love you. I can't love you. It's safer for you if we part company now. Let me go, I don't want to hurt anybody, least of all, you."

His grip tightened at her words. "I will never let you go, do you hear me?"

She shook her head in denial. "You have too!"

"You were made for me, as I for you. We were destined to be together, Melissa, like night and day. One exists only for the other." His face lowered, his dark eyes rapidly searching her face for some reaction.

She nodded in agreement, "I know Siaak, and I can feel it. But I have to do this. It's the only way to keep you, Myaten and Kiros safe. Don't you understand?" She shoved with all her might, succeeding in knocking him back a few feet.

His deep rich laugh made her stop and stare at him. "Laugh at me all you want. My Fa-, Robert won't stop till he gets his way. He wants you and he'll get that through me. I won't have him hurting you ever again. If it means I sacrifice my life with you, then so be it."

His features turned sincere, as his eyes filled with understanding and pride for her selfless thoughts. "I accept that."

"What..." she stepped back at the unexplained change in him. The spark of copper red in his eyes made her feel uneasy. "Why are you looking at me like that?" She felt hypnotised, compelled to do his bidding.

Then, unexpectedly, her mark began to burn. Alarmed, she turned away from his beguiling eyes and unfastened her jeans. She scooted her hand under the material and carefully skimmed her fingers across the patch of irritated skin. She grimaced and hissed, as the burning sensation turned to a throb. The urge to dig her nails into the skin made her rub harder. "Damn that hurts!"

He watched in silence while his mark throbbed in time to hers. Every soft, light touch, every stroke and scratch made his body tense up. He was like a tightly coiled spring. If she didn't stop soon, he was going to explode. Rolling his head on his shoulders, he caught his breath at the sight of her bare skin.

She had no idea what she was doing to him. When her head tipped back giving him a tantalizing view of her throat, he licked his lips. His eyes darted to the low cut of her blouse. His jaw muscles twitched with the sway of her breasts. The sight of her shoulder pumping up and down in the midst of scratching snapped his control.

He was at her back. His left arm like a steel bar, curved around her rib cage as he adjusted his height to match hers. With a rough jerk, he held her back to his chest. His cheek touched her soft earlobe. "Scratching only makes it worse, Melissa. Let me ease it for you."

She gulped a mouthful of air as his hand disappeared under the waistband of her jeans. Her eyelids closed slowly as he brushed her hand away. His touch was like warm water, soothing, comforting and instantly she relaxed into him.

The pulsating throb ebbed away, making her sigh with relief, until his warm palm drifted across the flat of her stomach. That started another ache between her legs.

Her slim fingers slipped over his, dragging its warmth to her hip. What she really wanted was his hand between her thighs, to make the painful ache go away.

Siaak grit his teeth together. "That will work for now, but it will flare up again. The only way to stop it permanently is to connect them." He confessed aloud. In his mind, all he could think about was having her.

Melissa nodded and rolled to her knees. He coughed and looked away when she tugged her jeans down the length of her body and crawled towards him. She really had no idea how sexy that was. When he turned his head back, she placed a foot on each side of his waist. Her thighs opened wider as she hovered above his crotch.

"Melissa…"

"Yeah…" her face flamed at the idea of their position and she quickly stood back up.

He growled and sat up on his butt. He'd had enough of this. His hands connected with the backs of her knees, with a swift pull she went down fast. He took all her weight on his arms and let her body down until she was straddling his waist. "Now, we are getting somewhere."

Melissa's hands flew to the floor and immediately she lifted herself up and Siaak tugged her right back down.

"You've got a hard on." She explained as she lifted once more.

"Yes," he pulled her back in place and held her there, "That tends to happen from time to time when I am around you."

"Maybe this wasn't such a good idea after all…" She moved backward and his cock jerked. She froze instantly and dared a peek from under dark lashes; he was biting his bottom lip. She liked that. Her breath caught deep in her throat when he pushed up rubbing himself against her. Before she had a chance to utter a single apology, he rolled their bodies once. His hand cradled her head against the hard floor while the other hand held her hips to his.

"In principle, the idea was fine. Carrying it out was considerably flawed on both our parts. I think we should try again." He crawled a little further up her body, making sure when he stopped, his mark was in alignment with hers; "Only this time, I get the pleasure of being on top."

Melissa couldn't move a muscle as he took control and pressed her down on the floor. In truth, she loved the feel of his hard body against hers and resisted the urge to pull his shirt off. "I can see that. Well, you'd know how all this works, it's probably better this way."

His impish smile and gentleness made her throat close up. Rolling her head off his hand, she pressed her cheek against the cold floor and waited for him to get this over with. She had no idea what was going to happen. She just hoped it worked and the terrible, aching, throb would go away forever. If it went on much longer, she would burst into tears.

He watched her closely. The merging was going to be hard for both of them. He had told her the truth. Sex wasn't part of the ritual, but before the merge was complete, she'd be begging him to make love to her. If he were any kind of gentleman, he'd fight her every step of the way.

When he pressed his mark to hers, a rush of heat blasted them both. He felt her body tense up. Without thinking, he placed a tender kiss to her neck. "Shush, it will be over soon."

Her head flew back hard enough to snap her neck as she cried out, "Burning, hot, can't breathe," Melissa, croaked as she fanned her face. "Hot–so, hot, too, hot." She repeated as she tore at her shirt. "Need it off," her head rolled back and forth, as she tried to wet her lips with her dry tongue.

He knew exactly how she felt. His body was drenched in sweat already. His shirt and slacks were stuck to him. With a single thought, he removed their clothes.

The extreme sensation of heat they were experiencing was symbolic of the fire between them. It was only going to get worse, until their marks merged completely.

She hissed and clawed at her skin. "I'm on fire Siaak. Make it stop!"

"It will be over soon, I promise." He repeated for her

and the small wounds closed up as he nipped, sucked and licked his way down her body.

"Siaak…?" He heard her sweet voice. His head tilted to one side. It had come from across the room. He jerked his head away from Melissa's delicious body, his wet hair smacking against his face and neck as he searched left and right.

And then he saw her.

She was standing in the shadows; her chest heaving, her face flushed. She was clearly affected by the events in the room.

"Do you like what you see my little zahur, my little sweet flower?" He opened his mouth making sure the Melissa in the past knew he was going to pleasure her. Then suddenly, she was gone.

She couldn't believe how good he felt. And even thought she was dead against hurting him, she could hear his thoughts. She could feel what he was feeling and it made her love him even more. His fierce need to protect her from him. Trying to be gentle when all he wanted was to be inside her. That made a smile flash to her lips up until the point where his tongue did the most devilish things to her.

He smiled with triumph as his Melissa squirmed, begging him to end it. He answered by flicking his thumb over her clit, rotating it back and forth. He had to have all of her; he was addicted to her taste and needed more. His nose pressed deep, as he took her into his hot mouth. His thumbs and fingers massaged her quivering muscles as he satisfied his palette with her flavour. Her desperate, breathless pleas were ignored as he slid a finger inside. She was so wet for him.

"Siaak, please, no more."

Her pleas caused his breath to catch in his throat as he rocketed up her body. His hands gripped the edge of the table. With one thrust, he was inside her. "Forgive me," his face loomed above hers, his jet-black hair, sleek with sweat fell around her face as he strained to collect himself. He pulled out and hovered above her. His cock jumped as he ran the bell-end against her own short wet curls. "Do you accept me as your mate?"

The second she said yes, he crushed her mouth under his. His breath uneven as he kissed harder then drew back suddenly to run his tongue over his lips, to savour her taste. Wrapping his arms around her waist, he turned her on her side. One leg between his, the other he stretched up over his shoulder.

She moaned as he entered her body with a jerk of his hips. And cried out as his warm tongue traced little wet circles down her leg before he released it and concentrated on loving her. Her panting spurred him into a faster pace. He kept his eyes on her body, as he enjoyed the feeling of being inside her.

Her moans of pleasure made him high, until he saw the red bruises on her back from the hard table. She should be on a soft bed and instantly he moved them across the room.

She paused at the soft mattress and opened her mouth to ask how until he took one of her breasts in his mouth.

"Need more," he growled and Melissa felt the room blur. The bed blinked in and out of sight as his powers surged. His fingers intertwined with hers as they shared a long kiss.

She couldn't breathe as her body lit up. Each sexy slide of their wet bodies made her yearn for the next jaw-jarring thrust. Drops of sweat fell from his body, coating her in his scent. She craved more. She wanted all of him.

The marks on their bodies shimmer and flared. Her vision turned hazy as her fingers dug into his back. Both of them desperate for more, needing, reeling from the energized wanting, feeding, loving, and taking everything the other had to give. One last thrust and they came together. Her body quivering as she held him to her chest.

Cradling his head against her breasts, he rotated his hips, making her hiss with renewed fire. Their marks flared bright, locking them in place. He rocked his body against hers as she pulsated around him, drawing every last drop of semen from him, as he resisted the urge to start again.

"I love you, my *azizi*, my precious one." He confessed into her hair. "I will never allow anyone to take you from me again." His dark eyes locked with hers. "But I want you to know that it will break my heart to let you go." He trailed his fingertips down her sides as their marks kept them locked tightly together. "Perhaps in time you will confess your love to me again, but until that time, we can, dare I say it, date."

She chuckled softly as she pressed her index finger against his tender lips. "I love you Siaak." She wound her arms around his neck and pulled him down for a series of short kisses.

"I am serious, Melissa. I want to get to know you better." He shifted his weight and she pulled a face as their marks unlocked. "Ouch," she imagined peeling him off her like a band-aid as their skin pulled when he rolled to her side. His legs slid between hers. She noted with joy how he curled his arm over her in a possessive way, after he rubbed the sting from her mark.

"So, tell me what you wanna do with me." Her lips spread away from her teeth when his hand reached between her legs to fondle and caress her. "I didn't mean that," his hand went still, "but don't let me stop you." She added quickly.

"I was thinking, perhaps, I could teach you how to read and write my language." He waited for it.

"Are you kidding?"

"No."

"I'd love to, oh Siaak, thank you." She leaned into his body and kissed him.

"There is another matter we need to discuss."

"Yes," she said in between raining kisses over his eyelids. When he didn't say anything she pulled back. "What's the matter?"

"You must trust me to be able to protect you. I refuse to apologize for my outspokenness earlier. The thought of loosing you fills me with dread. I lashed out in anger for fear of what could have been."

"I understand but I warn you now. I won't let you hide me away trying to keep me safe from the BloodSeekers." She ran her fingers down his chest tugging at his dark hair.

"I will teach you how to use your powers and hone your 'throwing'. I was told you broke a few bones when you rescued Dawson's men."

"I didn't mean too. I was kind of in a hurry. Working under stressful conditions, I had to get you back here."

"I know. I am teasing you." He took hold of her earlobe and tugged it with his teeth. "There is another ritual for marked mates such as us. It lessens the sexual urges our markers produce."

"Why would anyone in their right mind want that?" She turned her nose up and placed her hand over her mark. "Don't even think about it, buddy!"

Melissa eyeballed the silver box inlaid with diamonds that appeared in the tiny gap between their bodies. "You can remove the cap when you want too. There are going to be times when you need to be away from me. If you want a repeat performance of the shower, than we can skip this ritual."

That was definitely *not* a good idea. "Okay, so what now?"

"Lace your fingers with mine and we put our hands inside the box."

Within seconds, they both had their hands in the box.

Lovers for eternity, your souls belong to one another and shall never part. We bless this mating and will watch over our son and daughter. Call on us in time of strife; we will always be here for you.

An image of a naked woman in glittering silver filled her vision. She pulled her hand out with Siaak.

"What in the world?" Melissa rubbed her fingers together at the slippery warm feel of liquid silver against her fingertips.

"It is pure silver; it will cap our markers, giving us breathing room as you humans say."

Melissa watched as the silver drained from her fingers, travelling from her hand up to her elbow. It tickled as it went over her shoulder. Holding her breath, she tried to ignore the silver patch as it slid down the curve of her side. It made her feel like something was crawling on her.

Siaak took her hands in his, keeping her from touching it. And before she could blink, it slipped over the outstretched falcon. "So how do we get it off?"

She paused as a soft voice entered her mind.

Fashion it into a piece of jewellery and it can be worn by you until which time you need it to cap off the marker.

Melissa cut Siaak a look. "Um, do you wanna tell me who's talking in my head?"

Siaak narrowed his eyes and nodded, "Male or female?"

Melissa rolled her eyes, "it's a woman's voice. Did we download some kind of tutorial or something, when we dipped our hands in that box of yours?"

He laughed, "No, but if you hear a woman's voice, then in all probability, it is *Djeserit*, the holy woman, the voice that speaks to virgins on their wedding night."

"I'm not a virgin."

"No you are not, but you know nothing of our ways, so

she must feel the need to help you. It could come in handy, so be nice and respectful."

Melissa frowned at him. She thanked the holy woman and, at once, the cap on her tat shimmer and disappeared.

"I must say, silver suits your complexion Melissa." He brushed his fingers against her cheek as the liquid silver formed a complex circlet that sat over her forehead. When his appeared, she gasped in disbelief.

"I can't wear that!" she sputtered, "Are you some kind of prince?" she eyeballed him, not sure if all this was real.

He nodded slowly, "does it bother you to know that I am of royal blood?"

"No, it doesn't bother me, but I can't go around wearing a circlet, people will stare."

"Then, tell it what you want it to be."

Within a blink of an eye, it reappeared around her neck in the form of a delicate silver chain with a silver ankh pendant that hung between her breasts. "That's nice, what are you having?" she asked Siaak.

When she looked up, she smiled at his matching necklace. "Nice one."

"I thought you might approve somehow; now let us discuss this dating–"

Melissa reached up and kissed him on the mouth. "Yeah, we can talk about it, later."

"As you wish my princess."

CHAPTER TWELVE

Six days later

Myaten flopped down in the nearest available space, which happened to be the cold damp marble floor. He was so tired; he didn't care if it was a bed of nails. It was just nice to take the weight off his aching feet and battle worn body. After five days of chasing Osiris and her new lackeys, he just wanted to lie down and sleep for a week.

With a single thought, his heavy armour vanished from his bone-tired body. He sighed as he imagined having a nice long hot shower. Then, maybe raid Melissa's fridge before he took forty winks.

"Myaten, get off my clean floor!"

Myaten groaned as he rolled to his knees. He was even too tired to 'jump', much less walk, so he crawled on all fours along the floor. The hard marble bit into his kneecaps with each slow deliberate drag of his thighs. He paused at the sharp tingle down his spine, as Melissa grabbed him and deposited him on her couch.

He breathed a sigh of relief. "You don't know how much I appreciate that…"

Melissa's stern look turned soft at his light snore as his head turned into the cushion she'd put on the arm rest for him. She repressed an oath of stupidity on all males, when she saw his long legs hanging off her white sofa. Reaching down, she tugged his boots off and managed to pivot him on his backside. She slid him around without pulling him off the short lounge couch.

"You could have called me and I would have seen to him."

Melissa knuckled her hands in her kitchen towel, before looking up at her lover. "He's lucky I didn't kick him in the ass for plonking his dirty body all over my floor." She crossed her arms over his as he settled his body behind her, hugging her tightly against his chest. "But seriously Siaak, he's killing himself, he needs to stop hunting Osiris." She shook her head in disapproval at his pale face. "You need to feed him first, then, have a long chat."

"I will my azizi, but first we need to have a long chat. Can you tell me anything more about the conversation you had with Robert?" Siaak rubbed his cheek against her soft hair as he waited for her to think back.

"No, why?"

"Eric showed me some video files he managed to acquire before changing sides. Let me just say, you are not alone Melissa."

She turned in his arms to stare him straight in the face. "I hope this means we're going to rescue them?"

Siaak cleared his throat and kept his anger under control. The last thing he wanted to do was hurt her. "Yes and no. We have a list of names that Eric managed to pull before he was shut down." He took a deep breath and continued. "Your brother's name was on it."

Before Melissa could reply, Kiros and Dawson's unit appeared in the room. He opened his mouth to warn them and closed it. He covered his eyes as Melissa marched over to them waving her red towel at them like some crazed female matador.

We will talk about this later Siaak.

"All of you OUT! I want clean bodies in Siaak's house." She twirled the towel up and slapped Kramer's behind on her way past into the kitchen.

A murmur of apologizes in various accents filled the room, as the boys dispersed, heading off to get cleaned up for dinner. Kiros stayed behind long enough to give Siaak his report, and then he too faded from the room to grab a quick shower.

Melissa set the large oval marble banquet table to feed twenty. The silver ware sparkled in the candle light, after Siaak took a second to light them, all at once.

When everyone was seated, Melissa practiced using her telekinesis by grabbing the food from the kitchen.

"I'd stand back in case I spill anything," she warned as six bowls of steamed vegetables landed with a slight ping as they touched down on the table. Quickly followed by three large bowls of mashed potato, ten platters of grilled chicken and four baskets of buttered rolls. She was very pleased with herself. No mess this time.

"This looks delicious, Melissa." Dawson piled his plate full of green beans as he spied the chicken.

"Yeah, I half expected KFC again. Siaak isn't known for his cooking skills." Kiros stabbed his fork into the pile of chicken and took three breasts while nodding, "It's true, why do you think I'm so damn skinny? I'd rather chew on my Enforcer Bates Steel toe boots than eat his 'umm' mystery meat."

"As I recall, you never complained about eating snake when you were half starved." Siaak took a bite of his mashed potatoes and groaned at the fluffy texture before biting into a succulent juicy chicken breast.

"But I have to admit, this is much better than any snake, rat or vulture. Now scorpions are good roasted, kind of like eating beef jerky, so I understand." His jaw moved as he chewed until he looked up and saw all the women making faces at him.

"What...what did I say?"

Melissa choked on her food and grabbed her water glass. "Siaak– we humans, the normal ones, like to eat without revisiting episodes of Fear Factor."

"In his defence..."

Everyone looked up at Myaten leaning his jean-clad hip against the archway. He'd showered and changed, and by the looks of things, was feeling massively better.

"Siaak hasn't needed to cook for anyone before, so cut him some slack. We ate what we had to survive. Soldiers do it all the time," he took an empty seat near Dawson and rubbed his hands together. "Would you pass me the rolls, Melissa?"

Melissa stooped over Siaak in order to reach the breadbasket with her left hand. Myaten stopped her forward movement with an accusing glare in his green eyes.

"Your wrist, it's healed. When did that happen?"

Melissa looked at her wrist like she didn't know what he was talking about. Then it hit her, "Oh, I'd completely forgotten about it." Shaking her head, she sat down and held her hand in her lap as if it suddenly made her feel uncomfortable.

"I noticed it was better yesterday. Eric doesn't have a clue why it healed so fast. He puts it down to mating with Siaak." She smiled at her mate and picked up her fork to start eating again.

Myaten's eyes lit up. "Congratulations, guys..." He jumped out of his seat and disappeared into thin air. He reappeared before Melissa could question Siaak about his bizarre behaviour.

He wore a satisfied smile as he stood still with his arms behind his back. "Everyone knows I love being right and I knew you two were right for each other."

Melissa was awed when Myaten held out a long thin black velvet box to her and then an envelope to Siaak.

Siaak gingerly took the white envelope and masked his surprise at the old custom of giving gifts to celebrate their union. He hadn't expected Myaten to remember. "Thank you Myaten–"

Myaten coughed, "Siaak you have to open it."

"Oh," slipped out of his mouth as he immediately tore it open and took out the folded wad of pale blue paper inside. Siaak's confused looks made Myaten swear, as he jerked the documents out of his hands and unfolded it with a flick of his wrist, before he began to read aloud.

"Deed of Ownership," Myaten flipped the paper around and held it up by his fingertips. "You are now the proud owner of a modern, up-to-date I might add, house." He winked slyly at Melissa. He knew she didn't like going without electricity, even though Siaak was willing to waste his energy charging everything she used, which was mostly her cell phone and laptop.

Siaak was speechless. He watched as his mate threw herself at Myaten. She wrapped her arms around him in a bear hug.

"Myaten, I can't say 'thank you' enough–"

"Hey, it was the least I could do. Now open yours and I don't want any of those womanly speeches." He drew in a deep breath and waited for the female gasp of air, followed by the head shaking, as she took in the special meaning of the gift. If she told him 'no' on such a small gift, wait until she got the other thirty-nine.

"Myaten, its lovely..." she ran the tip of her index finger over the silver diamond inlaid watch. Like a child at Christmas, Melissa flipped the box upside down. The cold metal of the timepiece landed in her cupped hand. "Would you do the honours?" she held her slim wrist up as Myaten slipped the thin delicate band around her wrist and clipped it in place.

Siaak winked at Myaten over Melissa's head as she held her arm up at an angle, letting the light reflect off the double row of diamonds as she admired its beauty.

A cough from Kiros caught their attention. "I have a gift for you Melissa." Kiros held his arms out straight like a zombie and a long roll of emerald green fabric appeared. You could tell it was old and used by the threadbare patches in the velvet.

Melissa was taken aback by his gift. She had a feeling it wasn't something he did very often, when his brothers stared at him in dumbfounded confusion.

"Thank you, Kiros," she reached up to touch it. With a slow deliberate slide of her palm, she took in the soft texture of the fabric against her skin.

Kiros watched her quietly. She didn't have a single clue what she was touching. That made him wonder why he had chosen such a magnificent, honourable gift for the mate of his brother. How could she appreciate a weapon of power, just by touching the sheath that covered it?

"Melissa..." Kiros spoke her name in a loud, sharp tone that caused her to jerk her hand flat against her chest and stare angrily at him.

What had she done to piss him off this time? Probably breathing or perhaps she had stood the wrong way. Who knew, but she was getting fed up with tap dancing around the man. She always felt like she needed to say she was sorry. It was on the tip of her tongue, when he dropped to one knee and began unwrapping the velvet in such a gentle manner, it made her blink in bewilderment. Next thing she knew, she was on all fours, holding her breath to see what was inside.

"The gift is inside the sheath," Kiros felt his cheeks lift as a smile played on his lips.

"Wow! That's beautiful Kiros…" her voice drifted off as the velvet pooled around Kiros's knee. With one nod, he encouraged her to take the weapon.

"This was Cleopatra's sword." At Melissa's astounded look, he continued. "She was a fabulous swordswoman and knew how to take down any adversary. It is with great joy, that I bequeath her sword to you. May it protect you and keep you safe from harm." Kiros waited for Melissa to take it before he stood up and carefully held the green sheath in his hands before passing it to Siaak.

As soon as Melissa picked up the weapon, she heard a soft voice inside her head.

I have waited long for one such as you.

Melissa almost dropped the heavy sword as the disembodied female's throaty laugh erupted inside her head.

Please forgive my rudeness. My aim is not to frighten you child. It has been so long since I have had another female with which to converse. It pleases me to hear you speak aloud.

Melissa glanced up as she swept the hair out of her face. "Um, Kiros, did you forget to tell me this thing's possessed?"

Kiros did a double take, as did Siaak. The other men sitting around the table had no clue what was going on, but figured it best to stay quiet and listen in.

Dawson knew that Melissa was a hard nut to crack. If she needed help, her man was right there. But just to be on the safe side, he unclipped his holster and placed his hand on his lap.

"What do you mean?" Kiros's voice full of suspicion.

"Okay, I know what this is." Melissa placed the sword on the table and sat down. "It's some kind of initiation rite to allow me into your secret society…right?"

Unlike everyone else in the room, Eric spoke up. "What happened?" He forked a heap of squash into his mouth and chewed as he waited for an answer.

The silence unnerved her. "It spoke to me. So come on guys, where's the batteries.

I beg your pardon! I, the sword, was created of high quality forging—I do NOT take batteries. As I understand, they are merely for toys.

Siaak leaned near and took her hand in his. He wasn't sure what was going on, either. "Melissa, explain."

She squeezed his hand back and rested her chin on her cupped hand. Elbow resting on the table, she eyeballed the silver sword. The hilt looked frosted over with ice crystals or coated with diamonds. It was very stunning to say the least. When she caught site of a series of engraved symbols down the blade's length, she wondered what it meant as she spoke softly. "Siaak, it talks."

Her breathless manner and shaking voice, told him she wasn't joking. His eyes connected with Myaten who held his arms up.

Kiros frowned as he moved to touch the sword. It spun around on its own and began to vibrate against the marble table, making some kind of strange noise.

Everyone clapped their ears with their hands as the sound grew into an ear-splitting foghorn. Melissa placed her right hand inside the curved metal casing that went up to her elbow and let her fingers grasp the hilt.

The sound stopped.

How dare he! If he tries that again, I shall cut his fingers off one digit at a time!

Melissa giggled and felt her eyes watering. The sword had a sense of humour. "It would seem it doesn't like you, Kiros."

Kiros's back stiffened as he crossed his arms over his broad chest. His eyes wavered between her and the sword on her right arm. "You sure it's the sword talking?"

"Kiros!"

Siaak tilted his head in a threatening manner until Melissa squeezed his hand.

"It's okay; he has a right to think that. No Kiros, it's the sword, she's not happy about being touched by men, so you can chill."

I don't recall saying that. I kind of like the male over there with the silver eyes. By the way, none of those Neanderthals know of my origin and I plan to keep it that way, mistress. If you have no use of me, can you refrain from sticking me back in that awful smelly, dank, drab excuse for a pillowcase and enjoy your meal while I have a nap.

Melissa heard a sigh of pure bliss, as the female sword muttered something about men and their noise.

"So Kiros, what made you decide to give me that sword?"

Kiros wasn't really sure. He had found it in Alexandria with Myaten, on one of his time bandit moments, and thought it would suit her. "I honestly can't say, but if it talks, I'm betting anything, it's gonna talk your ears off." He gave her a shit-eating grin as he sat down and waved his hand over his food, reheating it with his powers.

Dawson's men had finished their meal and offered their thanks, before being excused from the table.

Dawson noted the atmosphere had shifted into the usual

sarcastic byplay between the male SandWalker and Melissa. He took in the amused look on Eric and Myaten's face, but what caught his attention was Siaak's smoking glare from under dark brows.

"Melissa, may I have a look at your weapon?" Dawson rose from his chair and came to a dead stop at her furious nod.

"She's not in the mood to be man-handled, hold on, she's talking. I can't believe you said that. There has to be a name I can use, instead of 'sword'?" Melissa looked at Dawson and rolled her eyes.

"I'd name her 'Ginsu'." Kiros offered while he chewed his hot chicken.

Melissa waved her hand in front of her face, as she was hit with another wave of the giggles. If she didn't know any better, she'd have thought someone had spiked her water. "Ginsu, I like that. Thanks Kiros."

He waved his fork at her in acknowledgment. Everyone went back to eating and chatting about their day.

"Kiros said he had no clue that the sword was cursed." Siaak offered as he took a plate and dried it for her. He stacked them on the side as he waited for her to say something. When she didn't, he began to make apologies for his brother. "He will understand if you refuse the gift. Perhaps, you will like another?" He held his dishtowel up and took another wet plate from the pile next to the sink.

"I'm sorry Siaak, I'm not ignoring you. It's Ginsu; she's doing exactly what Kiros said she'd do. She's telling me how Kiros kept her awake for three days solid watching Star Trek movies."

Siaak pursed his lips as he leaned his hip against the row

nothing to them. Then, one man rose above them all and conquered the lands. He called himself 'Pharaoh'…" Siaak shook his head at the memories, his head spinning. "There was so much death and destruction, Melissa. The Nile became tainted with blood as Osiris began her war again, this time, it was against the humans."

He coughed and inhaled her scent of fresh lemongrass. Instantly, he relaxed, knowing that time was over.

"You don't have to say anymore."

Shaking his head no, he flashed a brief, reassuring smile that turned into a thin line across his handsome face. "She killed millions of people all over the globe. She plagued the world with her disease and there was nothing we could do. Nothing, I could do. We watched helplessly as the Ancient Breeds began to fall, one after another. Then, before we knew it, the humans began to revolt against the Blood Princess, making it hard for her to find BloodSlaves to feed from. That is when Myaten and Kiros, with the last SandWeaver Sehkem took up arms with me. They helped me capture Osiris and place her in the Black Pyramid…"

"Why didn't you kill her instead of sealing her inside a prison?"

His body went tense at her question; he opened his mouth to tell her the truth. Nothing came out. His hearts raced in double time. *If you tell her, she'll leave you.*

"She was my si—" he choked on the word as he sucked air in through his nose. The room suddenly felt too hot, it was more than he could bear.

Melissa looked up at his wide-eyed stare, full of horror and laced with pain. He looked ready to bolt, until she reached up and stroked the sides of his face with her fingers. "Shush…it's okay honey. It doesn't matter. I'm just happy I found you. Everything else is inconsequential." Rising up on her tiptoes, she placed her mouth against his in a soft kiss. Demanding nothing of him, it was meant to comfort.

"She is my sister. Omorosa *was* my sister before she turned into Osiris."

Melissa watched as tears formed in pools around his amber eyes. Now she understood why he'd locked her up inside the pyramid.

"I want her back, Melissa. I want the sweet young innocent girl who sat with me as a young boy, playing and laughing…" His cheeks glistened with wet trails as he blew out a gust of hot air, trying to calm himself against the torrent of memories.

"I live with the knowledge that some kind of evil reins her body and mind," his hands fisted, as anger flushed his skin turning his eyes into burning coals. "And, by my hand, I shall bring down Osiris and free Omorosa, once and for all!"

It was at that moment; Melissa knew she had to be with him, no matter the consequences. "I will stand by your side, Siaak, if you think you'll be able to put up with me?"

Siaak bowed his head and dropped his fists to his sides, letting the anger drain from his body at Melissa's words.

"I love you Melissa." He touched his double heart and hers. "No matter how long it takes for you to decide if you truly love me-"

"I do love you…" Melissa's hands flew to her mouth as his eyelids opened fully. His eye color shifted from amber to pure amethyst and back again. Before she could utter a single word, Siaak captured her mouth with his and showed her how much he wanted her to stay with him. For always.

EPILOGUE

Four minutes earlier

Osiris concentrated all her senses as she came awake to the scent of blood all around her. One eyelid peeled open followed by the other. Purple eyes, like twin amethysts under dark lashes, focused as she shivered with a sexual throb between her legs.

She was in a room full of humans and she was famished. Her stomach cramped with hunger pains. It had been a very long time since she'd had a good feast. Then she saw him.

Robert stood in her line of sight. Crouched down, he didn't see the tiny surges within her eyes. He was ignorant of what the Blood Princess envisioned doing to him.

She licked her lips with her soft tongue and growled low in her throat like some crazed animal. Her long straight hair hung over her breasts as she rocked her shoulders back and forth. Trying to pull free of the thick chains holding her against an eight foot, steel enforced beam hotwired with electricity.

Robert tilted his head up to look at her body. A slow menacing smile spread across his face as he imagined throwing the switch and watching her convulse on the 'pole.' That made his dick hard and he wanted her, right now, up against the pole.

Glancing up, he caught a flash of fangs and then a soft hum filled the room. His head buzzed and all rational thought was gone. Like a cloud of smoke, it dispersed inside the room leaving no trail.

What was he doing? It didn't matter.

His green alligator shoes took one step followed by another and, before his brain acknowledged his actions, he was standing toe to toe, eyes level with hers. He swallowed knowing this wasn't right. Part of him wanted to scream as her head turned with a slow elegant grace that only one born of royalty could pull off.

When she pinned him down with those soulful eyes and spoke, Robert's mouth fell open. His eyes rolled back into his skull showing the whites of his eyes as his back arched, his muscles seized up and his last human thought was pleasing her.

Osiris was too weak to laugh at his fumbling shaking hands against her restraints. She eyed him with hunger. Once the band around her left arm was removed, she took hold of him and shook him like a rag doll. She heard his teeth rattle together, before she lowered her head to feast upon his life.

Osiris paused as a soft voice entered her head. A voice she had thought buried long ago. A woman that was long dead to her.

No! Stop!

Like so many times before, she pushed the annoying pitiful creature's voice to the side and flicked her pink tongue out. Osiris licked the man's neck, up to his ear then back down again. Swallowing a deep lungful of air, she craned her head back like a catapult and struck like a cobra. Her feeding fangs buried deep in his vein, her basic instinct to eat took over. As his body shook in response, her eyes flared bright silver, almost glowing with the power of his blood in her body. Yes, this is what true power was, pity it wasn't a SandWalker.

Thinking of a time long ago, she finished off the man and dumped his body on the floor by her feet. The hum got louder and louder, until it turned into a sexy purr. Thanks to his blood, and his memories, she knew all about this new world she had awaken in.

Looking up to her right arm, she pulled with a little jerk of her arm and the chain broke, releasing her from the steel beam. Licking the blood from her fangs and mouth, she stepped down. She decided now wasn't the most opportune time to strike. She would wait to see what her enemies' next move would be.

Two weeks later

Traffic was particular slow this time of morning. Seven am was too early as far as Myaten was concerned. He was a night junkie. He loved the nightlife, wild music, fast cars and sexy women.

Reaching up, he glanced into the rear view mirror as his nimble fingers unravelled the black bow tie Sarah had convinced him to wear. He didn't mind the tux. But after twelve hours, he was craving his comfy ripped jeans and tank top.

Leaning his dark head against the leather head rest, he heard the wail of sirens. Pinching the bridge of his nose, he focused his hearing. Ten minutes later, he glanced to the left lane opposite his car as four ambulances flew by in a blur of red and white streaks.

Right on cue, the lights changed and they were moving again. He tried to fight it, but the sight of four emergency vehicles set off warning bells.

Kiros had actually stopped travelling with him, because

they couldn't get from point A to B without Myaten stopping to help someone.

"You're giving Red Cross a complex, so stop with the fucking hero shit!" Kiros slammed the car door and teleported home. That was six months ago. He missed his pal riding shotgun.

Myaten couldn't help it. He was an honest to god do-gooder. Being a SandWalker meant he had special abilities that normal humans would envy. It also meant, keeping secrets from the few humans he'd allowed in his life.

When his green eyes caught sight of the flashing lights, all forward movement came to a standstill. Turning the wheel, he pulled to the side of the road.

"Hey, get back in your car, dick head!"

Myaten could ignore rude people. Kiros, on the other hand, would have turned the guy's car upside down and wished him a 'happy fucking day.'

Shaking his head in wonder at his buddy, Myaten swung his long legs over the barrier and jogged towards the accident. He knew the police would refuse him access to the scene of the wreck. So he entered slow mow. Everything around him slowed down as he ran at his normal speed. He loved being able to do that!

The six-car pileup was a massive wreckage of twisted metal. Shattered glass littered the ground and the strong smell of gasoline made, even him, worry. If one car blew, the rest would follow in a matter of minutes. A domino effect that would cause utter devastation. Even Kiros would have agreed with him on this one. The death toll would be in the hundreds!

Looking around, he noticed straight away, there weren't any fire-fighters around. Then he picked up on the long honks and drawn out sirens. In slow mow, sound was almost nonexistent; he had to strain to hear. That's when he heard the sound of a woman shouting.

He ran to the sports car that lay on its side sandwiched between a bread truck and the wall of the bridge above them. The driver of the truck hung limp over the steering wheel. Myaten knew there was nothing he could do for him. Sad but true.

Focusing on the woman, he walked up to the rear of the red mustang. The first thing he noticed was how badly the roof was caved in from the weight of the truck. He removed his tuxedo jacket and threw it behind him. He rolled up his sleeves and placed his palms flat against the pane of glass.

Concentrating, he intended to melt the glass and make a hole so he could climb in and pull her from the wreckage. When he fell through the pane of glass, he landed face down on the back seat.

"That was different." He leaned over and looked up at the back window. Not a crack or break anywhere. Okay, even for him, that was strange. Dismissing it, he managed to wedge his arm around the seat and unclip the seat belt. Once he released it, the safety belt was instantly caught in the time spell. While he waited, he checked out the chair. If he reclined it all the way back, he could pull her from the car. Good idea, only the controls for the seat were located at the front, not behind it where he was.

He was going to have to 'jump' with her by the looks of things. He remembered Melissa's reaction to teleporting. He suspected this woman's reaction would be about the same, if not worse, considering the circumstances she was in!

Once the belt was out of the way, he reclined the chair flat. Placing both of his hands under her arms, he pulled gently. He wasn't sure how badly hurt she was. The last thing he wanted was to add to her injuries. The second her feet cleared the seat and her body was cradled in his arms, he 'jumped'.

Standing a couple of feet from the wreckage, Myaten broke the glass on the back windscreen with a single thought. The sound of breaking glass went unnoticed due to the time spell. He had to make sure it looked like she'd gotten free of the car on her own.

Holding the woman as he looked around for a paramedic, he wondered if he should leave her. His normal plan of action was to place the person out of harm's way and direct someone to their aid. Instead, he found he was carrying her over to the nearest ambulance. He released the time spell and immediately they were surrounded by the chaotic, but, 'well practiced' motions of a 'rescue in progress'.

"Excuse me! I found this woman climbing out of her car." Myaten explained at the look of suspicion on the paramedic's face. "Can I put her down somewhere; I think I need to sit down. I feel kind of shaky." Myaten lied. It worked like a charm.

The female paramedic flashed him a reassuring smile and guided him into the back of the ambulance.

"If you can put her down on the bed, I can check her over." The paramedic stood to the side giving him room to move in the cramped space.

As he bent down to place her on the bed, the woman's eyelids fluttered open. "Thank you, Myaten…." Her groggy voice, drifted off mid-sentence. He was thrown for a loop. How the hell did she know his name?

Sands of Time

PROLOGUE
EGYPT 5147 BC

"ATTACK!"

Myaten shoved his staff into the air and shouted a curse in answer to the enemies challenge. His face full of rage as his mounted army galloped headlong into a battle that would only result in more, senseless deaths.

The BloodSeekers- a ruthless vampire race hell bent on ruling the world, after dinning on every human, ate up the distance between them, throwing dust clouds in their wake. The sound of thundering hooves made his blood roar. This was his life. As a SandWalker, he protected the two kingdoms within his Lor'ship's empire.

Turning in his saddle, which he had fashioned together from one he had brought back from the future. Myaten waved at the approaching SandWeavers. Letting a smug smile cross his face, he felt a hundred times better now that they were here. The rulers of the sands, they could control it; shape it to any form they desired. Roris, their Leader, was his *iz'isha*. As Myaten's *Master*, Myaten would give his life to protect Roris.

The ground shook and thundered beneath him. Myaten knew Roris's signature anywhere. Laughing he pulled back on his mount. His legs controlling his powerful steed, its flanks shinning in the sunlight as it bucked and thrashed beneath him before racing headlong to meet the one they called Lor'ship.

Roris sat straight on his mount, the mighty Sphinx. Its body shimmering in the sunlight as it reared upon its hind legs. Wings thrown back showing off beautiful colored feathers along with a coat of short white fur now bristled with agitation. Its giant head swivelled, tilted at an angle to take in the approaching enemy. Eyes of liquid green shined full of intelligence, sized up the army before it let loose a loud roar that made the ground shake and whipped sand up into the sky with the beating of its mighty wings.

Roris laughed with amusement at Sphinx's unique way of upsetting its adversaries. He watched as the approaching enemy halted at a neck-breaking stop. Countless riders flew off their mounts and were crushed to death beneath the hooves of their own horses.

Myaten jumped from his horse and flashed onto the back of Sphinx. "Well done my Lor'ship but I am afraid it won't take them long to gather up their balls and start again." He chuckled with merriment as he reached down to stroke Sphinx's fur.

Roris nodded in silent agreement as Sphinx joined in with a loud screech that made them quickly cover their ears.

"I know I'm old but I don't want to be deaf, we don't have earring aids yet!" He shouted as he thumped Roris on the back in a playful mood.

Roris clicked his tongue before answering, "Hey?"

Myaten snorted and resisted the urge to flip him off, not that he'd know what it meant. "What do you want to do now? I have never seen so many BloodSeekers together before. Isn't it against their nature?"

"Yes it is but that is another story for another day Myaten. I think Sphinx and I will gather the SandWeavers together and attack from the rear. You take your men divide them into groups, we'll surround them from all sides."

"That's not exactly original Roris." Myaten wasn't in for battle tactics; he was more the kind of person that jumped in with both feet swinging his sword like a raving madman.

"Trust me Myaten; I know what I'm doing. Take your men and get into position. Let me know when you are set, I will direct the sand to cover you, when the BloodSeekers charge they won't expect it."

"I still think my idea of a Trojan horse was better." Myaten poked him in the shoulder before he flashed back to his horse.

'....what is a Trojan horse...'

Myaten twisted his mouth up in a lopsided grin as he grabbed the reins in his hands and shifted his weight forward.

'...it's a long story for another day...'

Roris waved to Myaten during takeoff. Sphinx was air borne before he could open his mouth in farewell. He enjoyed the freedom Sphinx gave him with flight but sometimes he wondered who controlled whom.

They circled high above Osiris's troops. Roris noted her La'ship tucked away safe behind her legion of BloodSlaves. A fitting title for the men Osiris controlled with an iron fist. Human males unlike SandWalkers and SandWeavers, with no defence again her beauty and venom. One tantalizing bite anywhere on the body resulted in an unending mindless servitude to the leader of the BloodSeekers.

Roris knew all too well her bite, he shivered at the memory of her sharp teeth and nails ripping his skin open on his chest and shoulders to feast on the energy contained within his blood. Her beauty combined with her sinful voice had lured him close as a young man and even now, decades later he had to force control over his mind on the here and now.

Sphinx turned its head to face the leader of the SandWeavers sensing his distress its large emerald eyes softened as it hummed a soothing tune to calm Roris. It knew the pain Roris felt and as a creature born of extreme heighten senses of sight, sound and touch it keened at the memories within the man.

Roris relaxed at the soft humming he could hear between the loud flapping of her wings. He shook his head pulling himself out of the nightmare and looked around. Sphinx was hovering in mid air. Its neck arched so it could look back at him. His eyes misted over as he patted the kind-hearted beast in a reassurance.

Sphinx cooed loudly before licking him across the face. Roris scrunched his face up. He really hated it when Sphinx did that, but it was nice that someone cared about him. He gave Sphinx a visual of his plans. Sphinx lowered its head and dived allowing its long body to fall through the air over the enemy. Roris tallied up a force of six hundred at least.

'Damn!' Even with their combined forces, there were not a third of his people left to defend the population. Even thought he had the aid of one Sphinx that still was not enough to fight them all!

His face screwed up in pain as his chest tightened while his lungs burned as if on fire. All visions started this way for him. He made his body relax and allowed the misty vision to clear so he could see it. No sooner than his hearts slowed to a steady rhythm, they soon started hammering away in unison to his erratic emotions.

'NO!' He cried out. He would not allow Osiris to win, if it meant sacrificing himself, he would put an end to this here and now.

He lifted his arms up wide as Sphinx got in position. Roris clenched his fists and summoned the sand, commanding it to hide his people. With a loud rumbling, the ground shook as sand spewed up in a geyser a mile high.

Myaten settled down with his men not knowing his friend and mentor was about to give up his life to save them all. Darkness surrounded him as he waited for the signal to attack.

Roris patted Sphinx once before they rocketed across the skies heading straight for Osiris.

Roris touched his chest once to pay tribute to his Colony as he summoned all his energy together into forming two small spheres. A sphere in each fist he opened his mouth and ordered the sand to part as he broke the sphere in his right hand and sprinkled it over the army below him. The moment he heard the outraged screams from Osiris he smiled and burst the second sphere.

Myaten clawed at the darkness. Something was not right. He couldn't see the future. No! His mind shouted in denial as both arms sprang up. When he felt the barrier of the blanket covered in sand he gritted his teeth together and pushed as hard as he could. It wouldn't budge. Furious he kicked and lashed out as he managed to rip the cover off him. He couldn't breathe; he had been buried alive!

CHAPTER 1

'YOU BASTARD… NO!'

Myaten woke up gasping for breath. His hearts pounding in double time, mimicking an intense drum beat. He sat up on his elbows while looking around the room. Swearing he closed his eyes and fell back on his bed making the mattress move and the headboard thud against the wall.

How many times was he going to dream about Roris? Surely, he could have some peace now. Thousands of life times had past and still he was forever imprinted with the memory of his friend's death.

Laying there, his chest heaving, his head tipped back as he looked around the ceiling for some clue. Instead, he found empty cobwebs and dust bunnies from hell. Lifting a shaking hand, he ran his fingers through his wet hair. Nothing new there either. Every morning he woke up to seeing his friend's death. It played repeatedly in his mind after he clawed his way to the surface spitting sand from his mouth and wiping tears from his wet stained cheeks.

"Why Roris, why did you do it?" He had asked that question too many times and still he knew deep down that he needed to let it go, but he couldn't. It wasn't fair. Osiris was free to roam around the world and his best friend was gone.

Angry beyond belief he tossed the black silk sheet off his

damp body and sat on the edge of the bed. Gripping the mattress, he growled and yanked his arms up. Bits of fabric and foam filtered through the air. He had to stop doing that. Opening his hands he let the remnants of his mattress fall to the floor as he stood up and left his bedroom.

'Boss get your lazy ass out of bed!'

The voice of his secretary entered the room via his mind. He could hear her thoughts as she sat by her computer; they weren't truly directed at him so much as she was talking to herself again.

Myaten cocked his head to the side as he strode bare ass across the black ash hard wood floor. Standing there stark naked he immediately realized the time. It hit him like a forgotten task, suddenly recalled too late to complete. "Shit," he replied. He was supposed to meet with Sarah this morning. She had refused his proposal. Why, he had no idea. It was just money. She needed it and he had plenty of it. So why the woman had to be stubborn other than the normal female reasons he didn't know. And he didn't wish to go into the complexities of the working human female mind at nine twenty seven in the morning.

He stopped and swept one leg up so he could have a good scratch and rolled his head back on his shoulders as he dug his nails into his mark. For some reason it had begun to itch more and more here lately. Dropping his sinewy clad leg to the floor, he yawned and padded across his penthouse suite not worrying one bit if anyone could see him on the security cameras. Served them right for having them on in the first place, his staff knew when he was visiting.

He grabbed an orange on his way past his wet bar which was cluttered with all kinds of weapons. He needed a maid. His mouth lifted at the corner. He owned the place, he had cleaners aplenty but he liked his privacy, besides the last thing he wanted or needed was a young female around him right now.

He palmed the citrus fruit, juggling it up in the air before blasting the thick peel leaving behind the succulent flesh. He ate them like an apple, gods he loved oranges to the point of being an addiction, laughing at himself he licked his lips in anticipation. His fangs ejected tearing into the orange first, making the juice run down his chin, and dripping onto his chest. He would definitely need a shower now.

Grabbing a towel, he wet it and wiped away the sticky juice while hissing as he pulled chest hair. "That'll teach me to eat fruit naked." He tossed the towel in the trash and stretched up making the muscles ripple down his back and across his shoulders as he reached for a clean glass. He moved around his kitchen with ease, his stomach rumbling in loud protest as he opened the fridge and glanced around the large white empty space.

Frowning, he imagined the kitchens downstairs and took six cartons of Tropicana. He placed them on the counter next to his glass. Then he ran through a checklist of food items as he *grabbed* from the well-stocked kitchens that fed over four thousand guests a night. Standing there holding the fridge door open he shivered from the cool air blowing from the large silver appliance.

The soft popping sound met his ears as an array of foods blinked into various compartments combined with the ping of glass jars as they knocked together. His green eyes flickered from top to bottom as he placed enough food inside to feed an army.

Closing the door, he grabbed a clean stripy apron and placed it around his mid drift. The black striped cotton apron reached just past his thighs as he pulled the protective cloth around his waist and tied it securely at the base of his bare back. The ties dangled down brushing past the cheeks of his ass as he moved around his kitchen preparing his breakfast for one.

Half an hour later, he sat at the dining table looking out the window, silently enjoying his scrambled eggs with cheese and three slices of buttered toast.

"Myaten I let myself in," she walked into the room and stopped dead in her tracks as her mouth fell open. "...oh my god, you're naked!" Sarah covered her eyes with the black leather folder she had brought up to show him before she jerked her head round fast enough to give herself whiplash.

Myaten rolled his eyes and finished the slice of toast he was eating as he stood up from the table. "I've got an apron on Sarah. Besides you can't tell me you've never seen a naked man before?" He pried the folder from her death grip before sauntering past to bend over and place it on the coffee table in front of her. A mischievous smile appeared at the sound of her sharp intake of breath as he mooned her.

Shaking her head, she frowned at her boss. "I've seen plenty of naked men Myaten but on a professional level as your secretary I don't think, no I know it's not ethical for me to see you like that!" she pointed her finger waving it at his nude bottom and covered her eyes. "Can you put some clothes on before you ruin my day?"

"Sarah you are a strange woman indeed."

"I might be strange but I'm not dead, you could make a woman blow a gasket walking around like that. Never mind the fact that I've not had sex in weeks." She fanned herself as she made herself busy pouring a glass of OJ.

"I apologize for my lack of attire. But this is my home and

403

I don't expect my secretary to come in unannounced with keys to the front door." He held his hand up and caught the set of keys as she tossed them at him, avoiding eye contact as she finished her juice and washed her glass out.

"Wanna talk about it Sarah?" He asked as he left the room to put on a thick black robe. He didn't want Sarah to see his mark and start asking questions. Besides, she was right; he should be dressed with her in the room. It wasn't right. If Siaak or Roris had been there, they'd bludgeon his skull in at being disrespectful in a woman's presence.

"You say I'm weird Myaten but no normal man wants to hear my problems," She pushed the images of Tom out of her mind. She could never tell her boss that Tom wanted her to steal from the company. She wouldn't do it either. Myaten had been the most amazing man she had ever met. And she tried not to let herself dwell on the things he'd done in the past for her or she would start crying again. How could Tom do it? He was supposed to love her; in fact, he said he did. She knew different. Part of her had hoped Myaten was attracted to her as a woman. Funny enough after seeing him naked she hadn't felt the moist desire she often felt when she woke from one of her night time fantasies about him.

She could quit. No, that would mean explaining to Myaten the whys and ifs behind her leaving his employment. Her cheeks flamed with embarrassment, she was too ashamed, "…especially when it's to do within the bedroom." She added quickly before he started asking too many questions. She figured that would put him off. No man could deal with intimacy; it just wasn't in their nature. Women could talk and talk about it until they were blue in the face but men on the other hand would rather swill down a few bottles of beer than tell a woman how they felt.

He had to pause at that. She was right again. Most men didn't want to know, but he wasn't a human male. He was a SandWalker, a race of immortal, sand bred, warrior-sorcerers. He and his brothers kept the humans safe from the BloodSlaves and BloodSeekers that roamed the world. But most importantly he was her friend and he could tell she was upset. He caught images of her and Tom in bed and he had to clench his jaw shut as his fangs burst into his mouth in anger.

"Did he force himself on you Sarah?" he asked as he walked slowly into the living room.

The concern in his soft voice combined with the need to tell someone crumbled the iron mask she wore."It's my fault…" Her bottom lip trembled as she turned away.

"Sarah, we don't live in the dark ages. You have the right to say no. If he forced you to do anything you didn't want to do, I'll kill him." His voice low and deadly made her shiver. Not out of fear, it was his mannerism. She knew deep down that he cared enough to carry out the act. In an odd way, it made her feel special. It was all she ever wanted from Tom.

That was just one reason why she shouldn't have said anything to her boss. What she should have done, was call in sick but then he would have come by her house with a sack full of home remedies. She was so thrilled to see his car parked outside when she arrived early to work this morning. He'd been away on a business trip in Egypt. He visited quite frequently and sometimes on very short notice. She never asked, feeling that if he wanted her to know, he'd tell her. It had taken her two hours to work up the gall to come upstairs to see him. All her good intentions went right out the window when she saw him standing there naked. She really needed a hug but the last thing she wanted to show was weakness.

"Stop crying Sarah." He hated seeing a woman cry. It tore his insides up standing there watching and listening to her fighting back the urge to seek comfort in his arms. If Kiros had been there, he'd have bought donuts. For some reason Kiros thought Krispy Kreme solved everyone's problems. Personally, Myaten thought it was a way for Kiros to eat an unlimited amount of the delicious round cakes without having to confess his obsession.

"He didn't force himself on me. He just, he doesn't find me attractive anymore and wants to leave me. I'll sort it out and I won't allow it to affect my performance…I promise…" she grabbed a towel and dotted at her eyes, trying desperately to avoid smearing her eyeliner.

Myaten moved without thinking and took the towel from her hands. "I meant that you need to stop crying and beating yourself up." He pulled her close and the moment they embraced, he felt the itching again.

"Ouch!" she yanked her arm away and scratched at the skin. "Have you got fleas?" she dug harder at the tender flesh turning it red. "Oh my god it's a rash!"

Myaten grabbed her arm and pulled her wrist up to examine it more closely. "It's not a rash Sarah and I don't have fleas." His voice filled with amused annoyance as his green eyes stared at her in curious wonder. How could she be one of them? Part of him liked the idea, probably more than he should, but he knew from his visions long ago she wasn't his. This meant he would have to look after her until he found her mate.

When Siaak imprisoned Osiris in the Black Pyramid, he and Kiros volunteered to guard her. If her prophecy came to pass Siaak would bring them back to aid him in the upcoming battle. Only Siaak didn't count on science breaking the spell over his prison. The magic charm was meant to conceal it from human eyes. It wasn't strong enough to combat the ones from outer space. Orbital satellites caught images of the giant from space. It had taken thirty years for the humans to find a way to penetrate the camouflage shield and when they did, they swarmed like locus on a wheat field. Before too long, Siaak and Melissa, a human archaeologist, were caught up in a series of plots against their lives. To save his mate, Siaak confronted the enemy and found himself a prisoner. Deep within the bowels of a secret organization and if not for Melissa, they would have lost him forever.

"Why are you looking at me like that?" she asked.

"Sorry…it's nothing, but you and I need have to have a little chat later." He committed the shape and size to memory as he let go of her wrist. News had come in from Eric, another human. A male doctor who believed that more of his people were kept on ice underground in Labs for experimentation. If she was lucky, there might be a few males available if she wanted one. Their laws prohibited caveman traits on either side of the relationship. Sarah's chance of finding a mate now wasn't an easy feat. Not like it was for him back a few thousand years ago. "Take a few days off Sarah, treat yourself to something nice."

"I couldn't do that Myaten I don't have the money besides you are back and you need to see Mike about security, seems like we've got another streakier and he's becoming a nuisance to the dancers and our female customers."

Myaten knew she was hoping that work would. Trying to make him forget what they were originally discussing. She really would have to try harder. "Sarah it's an order. Now get going and take this with you." He held out a black American Express card between two fingers.

"I can't take that," she blinked fresh tears from her eyes and coughed softly before blowing her cheeks out.

Myaten gathered her up in the crook of his arm and guided her to the door. He shoved the card into her hands and kissed her forehead. "I'm the boss and I said take it. Now off with you unless you plan to watch me shower?"

"Umm, no thanks," She was out the door before he could blink. His ego deflated, he burst into laughter at her thoughts of him growing horns and a tail. He locked the door and shed his housecoat as he entered the bathroom to have a quick shower, all the while wondering how he was going to welcome Sarah into his world.

The black chrome elevator doors slid open with a loud chime. Women stopped and stared, forgetting everything else but the desire to watch, soon followed by the undeniable desire to touch. Myaten graced the opposite sex with slight nods, a few winks followed by a sly sexy smile here and there, as he drifted through the crowds of his casino.

The Hour Glass Casino was his creation. It had taken years to get his little business off the ground. In addition, it just so happens to be one of only a few things that actually made him happy. He used a large chunk of the revenue to fund private charities. By rights he should be flat broke but thanks to his ability to go back and forth in time he could borrow things from the past, sell it, steal it and just return it afterward. Yes, it was wrong but hey, that is what insurance companies were for.

He was making his way to security when he felt time shift and suddenly he found himself standing in the rain. Feeling slightly off balance, Myaten looked around and noticed he was standing in a cemetery. Something red caught his attention. Looking down, he held two long stem roses in his right hand. Bending down he ignored the cold rain plastering his clothes to his skin and the water running down his face. His green eyes took in the name on the stone. Dark black letters chiselled across the face of white marble told him who was buried here. Shock and disbelief turned his body ridged. Pain flooded his senses as his knees buckled hitting the ground, making squishing sounds in the mud. His mind cried out as he pounded the earth with his fists. Something wasn't right. He stayed like that for a long time. Listening to his logic and the rain as it pelted down. How could Sarah be dead?

Sarah obviously hadn't told him everything, unless it was an accident that killed her. As her friend, he demanded to know and he was going to find out today! Rubbing the dark strands of wet hair from his eyes, he took in the date on the stone. Swallowing a lungful of air, he took control of his vision and appeared back in the Casino soaking wet and muddy.

When Sarah left the building in her little red and white sports mini he followed but not in his car, he teleported to her passenger's seat and stayed invisible.

She was tapping his credit card against the steering wheel in an agitated way. "Why do I always end up with jerks?"

Myaten didn't bat an eyelash at her sudden outburst against men. Sarah had a habit of talking to herself, especially when she was pissed off.

"Myaten is going to be so disappointed in me." Her voice broke as she wiped at her eyes almost poking her left eye out with the corner of the card. As they came to a stop at a traffic light, she leaned toward the passenger seat and threw the card in the glove box. He watched her rub her nose and eyes trying hard to stop the tears. "And I'm not using his card either. I don't care if he fires me."

Part of him wanted to delve deeper even thought he promised he'd never scan a friend's mind. However, things were different now. She was going to die if he didn't find out what the hell was going on.

Reaching out with his mind, he peeked inside hers. She was worried. The image of babies flashed before his eyes and he smiled tenderly at her. Could she be pregnant? He knew women were very emotional during that period of their life. If he had the powers of a healer, he could scan her body and know if she had conceived a child. No, it couldn't be that. If she were pregnant, she'd tell him, right? At least he hoped she would. Maybe the marker appearing on her hand was the cause to her roller coaster hormones. Just to be on the safe side, he was still going to punch Tom's lights out. Yes, it was childish, but hey, he was so old that he was permanently stuck in his second childhood, so as far as he was concerned, it was justified.

I am not mad at you Sarah.

She couldn't hear a word he said, which was probably a good thing as she thought she was alone in the car. He ignored her babbling about being fired. That would never happen in her lifetime. He needed her, she was his friend and without her who would keep his head on straight?

He was glad for the lack of his physical body because her car was too small. At the thought of hugging her, he envisioned himself jammed between the gear stick and dashboard. Why would anyone in their right mind make a car this compact? It was like a box on wheels. When he got back to the Casino he was giving her a company car, this mini was a death trap waiting to happen.

"You should have told him the truth." She looked in the rear view mirror. "I know… but I'm going to end it with Tom anyway… and… and I'm never dating again." She vowed as she stared herself in the face. Her blue gray eyes rimmed in red from all the constant tears were puffy and sore looking. She poked her tongue out and slammed her foot down as the light turned green.

Myaten counted time; he knew she was going to hit a car or a pedestrian. Instead, she zoomed through the morning traffic, weaving back and forth, as she shifted gears. He was impressed. Maybe the mini had its good points after all.

Sarah put the radio on and began to sing to one of her favourite bands, Maroon 5. Myaten had heard them before and wanted to hire them for the Casino. They were booked so far in advance, he'd be lucky to get them on stage before they were so old they forgot what they were singing. He tisked as that reminded him he had work to do when he got back.

Fifteen minutes later they pulled up into the circular drive that lead to Sarah's three-bedroom house. She parked the car and jumped out, "shoot, forgot my purse." As she turned, Myaten flashed her purse to the car from her office desk. She poked her arm behind the drivers' seat. Her long fingers latched onto the strap and she yanked. When she slammed the door, Myaten followed. She really wasn't with it. Myaten knew that on a normal day, she would never leave her purse behind.

Sarah took her keys out of her bag and separated the house key from the rest of the bunch with a shake of her wrist. She inserted the key gave it a good twist and opened the door. When she closed it with her foot, Myaten heard something click and the house exploded.

Myaten managed to shield himself from the explosion before he ordered time to stop and reverse. He hated the feeling of going backward but he had to in order to alter the

411

outcome. Now he knew when Sarah died and how. Now he'd have to find out why someone wanted her dead.

Sarah took the keys out of her bag and separated the house key from the rest of the bunch with a shake of her wrist.

"Don't open the door Sarah." Myaten appeared beside her. This wasn't going to be fun; he might as well get it over with. She would have to learn eventually.

Sarah dropped the keys and held her chest. "How did you...I mean where...what the hell is going on?"

"It's a long story but to make it short and simple, your house blew up about two minutes ago and you died. Lucky for you I followed you and oh by the way, you drive like a maniac," he nodded his head as he continued, "but that's beside the point."

Sarah was still on the part about her house blowing to smithereens and her death. "I died? Who would blow my house up," she asked in a dazed voice then paused and rubbed her forehead, "I died?" She repeated the question. Before he could answer, she stepped back and cupped her eyes as she surveyed her home. It looked the same as it did when she left it this morning.

"Sarah believe me..." he reached down and picked her keys up off the bright orange door mat and caught her pointing at the car, the house, him and shook her head. "No I couldn't have died Myaten." She squatted down, slapped her thighs with her hands, and laughed. "No—no—no, see I'm here with you and you weren't here earlier—I'm having a nervous breakdown, yes that's it." She covered her eyes with her hands and took a deep breath as she stood up. "You want to explain how you followed me?" she looked down the drive and threw her hands out. "See, one car, not *two* cars, one, singular Myaten!"

"Sarah, I didn't drive my car. I made myself invisible…"

"Why," she asked.

"Because you came to me this morning crying your heart out and because I have to watch over you. It's part of what I do." And because I knew you were going to die, he thought. He tried to grab her hand but she avoided him.

"No, I mean why would you make yourself invisible? And here I thought I knew everything about you. Okay Merlin, give me the keys to my house." She put her hand out wiggling her fingers impatiently.

He stepped back and clamped his hand into a fist. "No Sarah." His abrupt tone made her angry.

"Hand me my keys Myaten, now!"

"Come and get them." He waved her on. He would do what it took to get her away from the house. Someone was after her in a big way to set explosives in her home.

"You are kidding right?"

"If you want them so damn bad and if you want to die then you have to fight me. And you better make sure you hit me where it counts because I'll knock your ass out to keep you from going back into that fucking house!"

Sarah glanced back at the house then him. "You know I can't swat a fly Myaten."

Myaten held her keys out, jingling them by the key ring, taunting her to come and get them. "Then I get to keep your keys and you have to bunk at my house."

"So does that mean I can't go inside to pack a bag?"

"What part of 'blow up and die' did you not understand Sarah?" He turned her to face the driveway and pushed the small of her back with his palm.

"Well I'm sorry if I don't believe you Merlin." She marched down the gravelled drive kicking stones as she dragged her feet like a child having a temper tantrum.

"Fuck it!" Myaten swore as he glared at her from under long lashes. Thank the heavens she wasn't his mate. He'd have gray hair before he hit his next birthday.

"You want proof? Fine! I'll give you proof!" He waved his hand and froze her in place as he stormed back up to the house. Placing his body at an angle so she could see, he put the key in the lock and opened the door.

Sarah watched with her arms over her chest. He had lost his marbles for sure now. Claiming some kind of god like powers, he had to lay off the glue sniffing.

When the door shut, she tapped her foot. Nothing happened. Throwing her arms down she waved them at the house. "See, I told you..." Her voice drifted off as a loud ground-shaking explosion blew her house to kingdom come.

"He's such a show off."

Sarah whipped round to find Kiros standing next to her eating donuts of all things. Her head was beginning to hurt. Was she dreaming? Deciding she must have hit her head on the sink this morning, she glanced over her shoulder, Myaten was spinning her key ring around on his index finger as her house rebuilt itself in the background.

"You keep eating those things and you'll get fat Kiros." Myaten walked up to them and dissolved the spell. His eyes narrowed in on Sarah as he spoke in a condescending tone."Now do you believe me? I think so."

She had a million questions to ask, but all that came out was a un-lady like grunt before she fainted in an unladylike heap on the ground.

Myaten icy green stare landed on Kiros. "Kiros, you could have caught her!" He was rewarded with a snarl as Kiros stepped back from Sarah's hand.

"Hey, nothing comes before my donuts. She's your friend, you catch, umm pick her up off the ground." Kiros shoved a white powdered donut into his mouth and chewed.

"You know, if I didn't know about your past, I'd swear you were gay." Myaten barked at his old pal as he reached down to pick Sarah up. She was so light. The next time she said *diet*, he was going to make her eat a truck load of cheeseburgers.

"I called you here for a reason. She has the mark of our people." Myaten watched as Kiros spat his coffee out.

"Please tell me it's not mine." Kiros wiped his hands on his jeans as he tried to inspect her body for his asp and cobra mark that ran up the left side of his neck and face.

"You're safe, this time." He added as he walked over to Sarah's car. "You know I can't wait to see the woman that tames your hairy ass." Myaten choked back his amusement at the look of pure horror in Kiros's dark blue eyes.

"Can you give me a warning so I can leave the country?" Kiros asked in earnest. And watched with irritation as Myaten laughed at him. "I'm not joking. Do I look like I'm joking?" Kiros drew a line across his face with his middle finger for emphasis.

Myaten rolled his eyes and stepped aside as the car door opened on its own. He didn't bother thanking Kiros for *not* helping. How could a man of his abilities be afraid of bonding to a female? One would ask themselves that question with an expression of exaggerated fear on their face. Especially when that person is Kiros, a sorcerer with unique powers who was standing there balking at the slim woman Myaten placed carefully in the passenger's seat.

Kiros heard every insulting word Myaten thought. He wasn't afraid of Sarah, she just annoyed the shit out of him. She was as bad as Melissa. Always wanting to do acts of good for other people and that shit had worn off on Myaten. Fuck that! He would never allow another woman near him again as long as he lived. "And don't get any ideas of using my ranch as a nursery. I *don't* babysit humans, especially half-breeds going through the change. Take her to Siaak, he knows how to deal with them, seeing as he has his own."

Myaten opened his mouth to defend Sarah but it was too late. Kiros popped out of view. All that was left of him having been there was an empty coffee cup tumbling across the driveway.

Perhaps he was right, Melissa had become good friends with Sarah and would gladly keep watch over her while he tried to find out who was out to kill her.

AUTHOR'S NOTE

Anita was born and raised in NC and currently resides in England with her husband and three children. When not writing, you can find her knee deep in housework or chatting online with all her friends and family.

If anyone would like to contact me, please go to: www.ancientbreeds.co.uk

To My dear friend Esther,

I dedicate this book to you, in thanks. You've been a wonderful and caring friend down through the years! Thank you from the bottom of my heart.

With love,

Anita Stuart

August 12, 2010

Lightning Source UK Ltd.
Milton Keynes UK
11 July 2010

156828UK00001B/54/P